"Two?" she excl[...]Per-
ryn, for a *man of y[...]*

"I can hardly be [...] protective and quite prudish mamas about."

"Fourteen." She waved her own ribbon beneath his nose,
then set to rolling it in a strip of paper with great care.

"Insufferable," he said, but she saw his smile.

"I have every confidence you will do better at Bridgwater. Besides, according to the itinerary there are at least
two, possibly three, hamlets betwixt. Your fortunes could
turn at any of these."

At the hamlet of Huntspill, Fenella emerged from the
smithy's, where she had been able to gather kisses from
not only the stalwart owner of the forge but his four sons
as well. She hurried in the direction of the waiting coach,
preparing in some delight to gloat over her success, when
she noticed Perryn seated beneath a tree, surrounded by
schoolgirls of a broad range of ages. The youngest, perhaps
four, sat on his lap under the auspices of a plump older
woman who appeared to be in charge of the children. She
was beaming and encouraging the girl, who was permitting
Perryn to put rouge on her lips.

Fenella moved slowly in his direction, her desire to express her triumph dissipating entirely as she watched the
confirmed rogue use his considerable charms to engage
the girls and make them comfortable. When the child
kissed the pretty lavender ribbon and saw the imprint of
her lips, she squealed in delight as the rest of the girls
clapped their approval.

Fenella felt as though her heart might burst at the sight of so
much tenderness. Sudden tears started to her eyes. Was this the
man who flirted so brazenly with her, who had teased her in
Mrs. Almington's garden until she had kissed him, who seemed
to have but a handful of redeeming qualities?

BOOK YOUR PLACE ON OUR WEBSITE AND MAKE THE READING CONNECTION!

We've created a customized website just for our very special readers, where you can get the inside scoop on everything that's going on with Zebra, Pinnacle and Kensington books.

When you come online, you'll have the exciting opportunity to:

- View covers of upcoming books
- Read sample chapters
- Learn about our future publishing schedule (listed by publication month *and author*)
- Find out when your favorite authors will be visiting a city near you
- Search for and order backlist books from our online catalog
- Check out author bios and background information
- Send e-mail to your favorite authors
- Meet the Kensington staff online
- Join us in weekly chats with authors, readers and other guests
- Get writing guidelines
- AND MUCH MORE!

Visit our website at
http://www.kensingtonbooks.com

A ROGUE'S EMBRACE

Valerie King

ZEBRA BOOKS
Kensington Publishing Corp.
http://www.kensingtonbooks.com

ZEBRA BOOKS are published by

Kensington Publishing Corp.
850 Third Avenue
New York, NY 10022

All Kensington titles, imprints, and distributed lines are available at special quantity discounts for bulk purchases for sales promotion, premiums, fund-raising, educational, or institutional use.

Special book excerpts or customized printings can also be created to fit specific needs. For details, write or phone the office of the Kensington Special Sales Manager: Kensington Publishing Corp., 850 Third Avenue, New York, NY 10022. Attn. Special Sales Department. Phone: 1-800-221-2647.

First Printing: September 2002
10 9 8 7 6 5 4 3 2 1

Printed in the United States of America

*To my dear friend, Dorothy Beer,
whose heart is as large as the ocean.
Many blessings, many thanks.*

Author's Note

All of the hamlets, villages, and towns mentioned in this story do exist. However, the manor houses described, and their sometimes noble residents, are merely the work of my imagination.

V. K.

One

County of Somerset, 1817

"I beg you will desist, my lord!" Fenella Trentham pleaded, her voice but a whisper. "You are half foxed . . . again. You cannot know what you are doing!"

She stepped backward and bumped against the garden gate. She was certain that somewhere in her maneuvers to escape Lord Perryn she had trod upon several poor unsuspecting border flowers, but there was no help for it. His lordship, that rogue of rogues, the Marquess of Perryn, had caught her unexpectedly just as she had ambled into Mrs. Almington's rose garden in hopes of enjoying a solitary stroll beneath an extraordinary August moon.

Lord Perryn, his inordinately handsome face sketched eerily before her by the glowing moonlight, smiled wickedly. "Is it my fault you ventured out-of-doors past midnight instead of the lady I was expecting?"

"Oh," Fenella murmured, drawing in a sharp breath. An assignation! She recalled how, just a few moments earlier, Mrs. Sugnell had appeared so flustered when she had fairly collided with her in the hallway before descending the stairs. Mrs. Sugnell had been wearing but a cloak over her nightdress and had stammered some confusing explanation of having forgotten her best gloves amongst the roses earlier that afternoon. The lady's lashes had fluttered nervous-

ly as she turned about swiftly, saying she could just as well
fetch them tomorrow as tonight.

Fenella glared at the marquess. "She is married but these
three months!"

Lord Perryn laughed. "I will not believe you are such
an innocent!"

"I saw her just a few moments ago. She was wearing
only her nightdress!"

At that, Perryn surprised her by seeming a little stunned
himself. "Indeed?" he queried. Then added quickly, "Better and better!"

"You are such a beast!" she growled.

" 'Tis not my fault her husband went shooting in Lin-
colnshire instead of following his bride to Bath. Was there
ever born a greater nodcock?"

At that, some of her own consternation at having met
such a terrible rogue in quite a compromising time and
place left her. "I vow in the five—that is, *four* years I have
known you, you have not altered one whit!"

"To what purpose, *Fennel,* would I desire to change when
there will always be a Mrs. Sugnell prepared to flirt with me?"

"Her conduct does not in any manner justify yours—and
I wish you would not employ that horrid nickname, for you
know how very much I detest it."

"I think it endearing." He chuckled softly, advancing on
her until he was standing but a breath away.

"Please stop," she whispered.

He placed a hand against the gate just over her right
shoulder and caught her chin with his free hand. "But that
would not be fair to me when you have ruined my expectations of a most happy dalliance. I daresay Mrs. Sugnell
will not now have the courage to come to me."

Fenella tried to breathe, but she could not seem to draw
deeply enough. Her heart beat erratically and a certain weak-
ness assailed her knees in the oddest yet most familiar manner.

Memories tore at her of another similar encounter with

his lordship some five years past, when she had first met him. In the garden of his own estate, Morchards, he had kissed her quite thoroughly and, for reasons she doubted she would ever comprehend, her heart, the very center of her being, had been given to him. She despised herself for having become enslaved to so ridiculous and vexatious a *tendre,* but there it was. He had from that hour held the key to her heart, which had caused her to reject no less than seven exceedingly respectable offers of marriage in the intervening years. Even this past Season she had spurned the advances of a most promising suitor, a Mr. Clavering, with whom she had believed herself in love until Perryn disrupted her attachment to him.

Mrs. Almington's invitation for the month of August to her home near Bath, Whitmore Manor, had come as a welcome surprise, since she had been given to understand that Perryn would be visiting there as well. Her intention, contrary to the events of the moment, had been to free herself of his odious hold on her by being more in his company, familiarity hopefully breeding a most desired contempt. She rather thought it a sad beginning, therefore, that upon her first night at Whitmore she must be trapped in this manner by his lordship—without the smallest hope of escaping with her heart any less attached to the man now smiling so wickedly upon her.

She wondered if he recalled their first encounter at Morchards. She doubted it quite strongly, since he had been in his cups at the time. She had frequently thought that had he remembered even a portion of what transpired between them in the center of his yew maze, of their extraordinary conversation, of the kisses they had shared, he would not have been so cavalier in his attentions to her over the ensuing years.

She settled a hand on his chest in hopes of fending him off. "Pray, Perryn, do not be such a sapskull. No good can come of this."

"When have I looked for good to come of anything?" he teased.

She could only smile. He was utterly hopeless.

He drew back slightly and looked at her. "Can it be? Is it possible? Is my dear Fennel actually smiling?"

"No" she answered abruptly, bringing her features to order.

"What a whisker!" he cried. He caught her hand in his and kissed her fingers, which caused her to lose her breath anew.

"I could love you so perfectly," he added in true rakish fashion.

Just when she thought she had come to comprehend fully the limits of his depravity, he shocked her. "What a dreadful thing to say! How can you speak so to me? Besides, I know very well you never trespass upon maidens and that you are not beyond all redemption."

"In your case, I would be willing to make an exception."

She shook her head. "You would not do so. For all your scandalous declarations, I know you are not so bad as that. I have been enough in your company to have comprehended at least that much."

"What of you?" he countered. "Have you never wondered what it would be like to be kissed by a *confirmed rakehell?*"

"As it happens," she responded boldly, "I already know. Several years ago, just such a man as yourself, with precisely the same black hair and fiercely gray eyes, and of course a hopelessly dashing mien, did kiss me."

"What? How is this possible? And I not to know of it? And—worse!—I not to be the one who assaulted these fair lips?" He was smiling now, that wretched, boyish smile that had won so many hearts and destroyed an equal number. "Tell me the name of this scoundrel and I will call him out, for you are mine to persecute and mine alone. As a self-respecting rogue, I could not possibly permit another man to encroach upon my domain."

"I fear I shall never be able to tell you, my lord, since I am convinced it would be the death of you. He is quite skilled with both sword and pistol. I believe he even fancies himself, how do you say, *handy with his fives?"*

He kissed her fingers again. "How very sweet, for I can see you mean to protect me. However, I begin to think you are telling your whiskers again. Surely you did not give of your kisses freely?"

She could not help but smile at the remembrance. "Too much so, I fear, though I promise not a day goes by in which I have regretted having done so."

"He took sore advantage of you, no doubt. But come, tell me his name, Fair Fennel."

"I promise you I never shall"

He narrowed his eyes. "Let me see. I am searching my mind for every libertine of my acquaintance and can recall only one with black hair—Mr. Darwick, but he is since escaped to the Continent for gaming debts."

Fenella shrugged. "Perhaps it was Mr. Darwick," she offered. She had, of course, heard of this gentleman, for he was known to have belonged to Byron's set, but in truth, she had never once met him. Perryn, however, would not know as much.

"Another whisker!" he cried.

"Indeed? How would you know?"

He leaned a little closer. "Because you blush so prettily when you choose to prevaricate."

She rolled her eyes. "And you can determine that I am blushing when it is so dark?"

"Of course. I do not refer to changes in your complexion, but rather your expression. You appear rather arch when you speak fustian."

Fenella could not help but chuckle. She wished he were not quite so amusing; this particular sort of banter pleased her immensely. "Regardless of your powers of observation and perception, I was very much kissed by a rogue."

He frowned. "I begin to believe you are speaking the truth—only you must give me his name. He shall answer to me, by God, see if he won't!"

"Never!" she cried in response.

"Dash it all, Miss Trentham, why must you torment me?" he cried, exasperated. "Give me his name."

Fenella shook her head. "I will not, but I must confess it gives me some joy to see you even a little confounded."

"I see you are not to be moved." His gaze fell to her lips. "Though I am not surprised another man has assaulted this lovely mouth. I have often wondered myself just what it would be like to kiss you, if but once."

"Well," she drawled, "I fear tonight you are doomed to disappointment, for I shall not permit it." She lifted her chin.

"You only tempt me with your refusals and protests, you know. I vow, someone should melt the frost on your heart."

She laughed outright. "My lord, do tell me, are we actually speaking of my *heart?*"

A new smile, this one crooked. "You should not be so deuced perspicacious."

"I should thank you for the compliment, if I thought it one." She feigned a yawn. "I grow fatigued, Perryn. I think I will bid you good night."

She tried to pull away, but it was clear he had no intention of letting her go. Instead, his arm snaked about her waist. In a brisk movement, he drew her away from the gate and into his arms quite roughly.

She caught her breath. "No, Perryn." The experience was all too familiar, too exhilarating by half! If she did not act quickly, she feared she would relinquish a kiss to him after all. Planting her hands fully against his chest, she eyed him firmly. "Again, I say no. You must let me go."

"Why?" he queried hoarsely. "Unless you truly feel yourself in some danger."

She could not think. She could only remember. Summer, five years past. Five long, agonizing years ago, when he had first held her and kissed her—only he had been so deeply in his cups that he had never remembered his odious conduct. Odious and sweet and wonderful. Odious and exasperating, for were it not for him she would have been married by now, with babes of her own. She was seven and twenty, and his presence in her life had made her a spinster!

Worse yet, however, was that he would never remember that night—how he had embraced her so wondrously and kissed her and made her laugh and in the end completely stolen her heart. From that day she had felt as though he possessed her, body and soul, and she could not for the life of her—though she had tried countless times!—break this stupid spell he held over her. She knew what he was, a terrible, accomplished rogue, with no more respect for womankind than for the stubble he shaved off every morning before his looking glass. She could only suppose his thoughts even now went further than stealing a kiss from her.

For his part, the Marquess of Perryn looked into the face of the most beautiful lady he had ever known. The moonlight might have cast her lovely dark brown hair into an indiscriminate black, and certainly the wonderful color of her green eyes and the sparkle of merriment they usually held was lost to the night, but still he knew how delightful she was to gaze upon. Her face was a soft oval, every feature perfectly proportioned, as though she had been created strictly for the portraitist. Who could blame him for the pleasure he took in tormenting her?

As he looked down at her, she met his gaze fully and fearlessly, challenging his very existence, as she always did, by the mere set of her countenance. He wanted her kiss badly—only, would she surrender to his flirtations?

Who was this lady, he wondered not for the first time, and why had she bewitched him? He could not explain his conduct toward her otherwise. He had never taken such sore advantage of a maiden before as he was of his bold, impertinent Fennel, but there was something so beckoning in her air that he could not seem to help himself.

He had an even greater reason, however, to continue pestering her as he did, for it would seem Fenella Trentham held him in the lowest esteem. Why her opinion of him was so poor, he could not imagine—particularly since he had conversed with her but a half dozen times. However, from the outset of his acquaintance with her, which began during a London Season some four years past, she had made her disapprobation abundantly clear to him, and she but a mere Miss Trentham of Wiltshire!

Therein lay the rub, he thought ruefully. He was quite used to being fawned over and petted at every turn, but Miss Trentham had refused to bow before him. No simpering smiles, no flattery, no nervous, fluttery excitement when he but drew near. Instead, she met his gaze and frowned him down, wretched girl! Worse still, she had made him begin to doubt himself. Was he so puffed up in his own conceit that unless a lady was eager to seek his good opinion, he felt himself injured?

There had only been one woman in the course of his life who had dared to set herself against him, and he had tumbled violently in love with her. The Duchess of Cannock, married to a vile man, was the lady. She had been the true love of his life. He had become her protector, even against her husband, and when she died he believed his heart had perished with her. He still believed as much, for never once since her untimely death had he known even the smallest *tendre* for another lady.

Except . . . for the past several years he had been dogged by sporadic recollections of having been kissed by the most angelic of women, the memory of which was lost to him except in odd bits that would come to him on occasion in brief flashes. He could never seem to hold these images long enough in his mind to form an accurate picture of the lady.

However, the sensation of having embraced, kissed, and even conversed with her was so powerful that he did not enter a drawing room or assembly room without first surveying the party in hopes of finding her. Who she was, or where he had encountered her, were beyond his ability to recall.

At times, he believed her to be merely a fragmented dream that would come to life to haunt him. At other times, he knew she was real—only where the devil ought he to look for her? In a garden at midnight in a manor near Bath?

He was drawn back from his reveries to the exquisite creature he was holding in a scandalously tight embrace. He smiled suddenly, thinking how utterly unlikely it was that Miss Trentham could be his angel. At this moment, however, she was better than his faulty memories since she was here, her lips parted nervously, watching him in a speculative, severe manner, and waiting. But for what?

Did she feel herself in danger? He had thrown the accusation at her merely to see if she would rise to the fly. However, she had remained silent, yet he felt something emanating from her that took him quite suddenly by surprise. Instinctively, he slid a hand down her arm and took a firm hold of her wrist. The movement appeared to stun her, but she did not flinch. He felt her pulse. He had been right. Her heart was beating wildly.

Something within him became deadly serious in that moment. Fenella Trentham, for all her appearance of indifference, was not so very disinterested after all. Yet he could scarcely believe she was in any manner attached to him.

Regardless, she had been right about one thing: he never trifled with maidens. He never gave opportunity for the avaricious young ladies of his acquaintance to have cause to demand a proposal of marriage merely because he had engaged in a dubious flirtation.

Her lips parted. "Perryn," she whispered. Moonlight sparkled on tears swimming in her eyes. Another surprise, for he had always thought her impervious to the more melancholy sentiments. He felt pushed, tugged, and pulled. He should let her go, but he did not want to. She made him mad as fire, and yet he took so much delight in tormenting her.

She should not be so beautiful, he thought as he cast his gaze over her features again. He released her wrist and smoothed his thumb over the velvety contours of her cheek, wanting nothing so much in his life as to settle his lips on hers. He must not do so, however. He might be a rogue, but he was not entirely bereft of honor, just as she had said.

With all the self-control he could summon, he began to disengage her when suddenly she wrapped her arm about his neck and kissed him, not the timid kiss of an inexperienced miss, but the warm, full kiss of a woman.

He paused, if but for a moment, trying to will himself anew to thwart her unexpected advance, but he was too stunned by her lips pressed against his to do so. Passion, quite primitive in nature, snagged him. He was pulled, as by the force of a swollen river, into the strength of her sudden desire.

He drew her roughly against him once more, enfolding her fully in his arms. She did not protest, nor did she attempt to squirm from his embrace. For the barest moment, he had a sense he had kissed her before. But that was impossible. In unholier moments he had imagined doing so, but the thought of Miss Trentham ever having relented before this very moment was ridiculous in the extreme.

Yet she had relented. He teased her lips with the tip of his tongue. To his surprise, her lips parted. He felt her knees give way at the same moment. He held her firmly, supporting her as he drove his tongue into the depths of her tender, waiting mouth.

He heard a delicate moan rippling in her throat. Desire tightened in him. What a dreadful mistake this was, dreadful and delightful and beyond pleasurable. Who would have thought she would have been so wonderful in his arms and so exceedingly delectable to kiss?

He felt as though he had passed into Paradise—but how on earth had this happened? Was this truly his wretched, brangling Fennel? He simply could not credit that she had authored this kiss, nor could he possibly conceive what her present thoughts might be. She had always been a complete mystery to him.

Fenella took from Perryn that which she knew she should not. His lips were like fire against hers, a doorway into a world she had glimpsed but briefly so many years ago. Only in this moment did she realize how much she had longed to be held and kissed by him again. Every second which passed, as he held her pinned so fiercely against him, as he supported her failing knees, as his kiss, so wicked in every respect, put her so forcibly in mind of the marriage bed, was utterly and completely forbidden. She was trespassing where she had promised herself never to trespass again—only it had been five years, and he held her heart in the grip of their shared memories.

What madness this was, particularly since she knew he had been about to release her! Why, then, upon having won her freedom, had she succumbed to his teasing seductions? There was not a single rational reason for having done so except—and this was far worse—she wanted him to know just why she had grown into an ape-leader. Perhaps, just perhaps, he in turn would suffer as she had suffered for five interminable years. She must pull from his arms and leave him. She must. Oh, but let him kiss her a moment longer. Perhaps in doing so she might be sustained for another five years!

This thought was so ridiculous that the spell finally broke. She drew back, relinquishing her hold on him at last, and saw he was frowning.

"Fennel . . ."

"Pray, do not speak," she whispered, a tear trickling down her cheek. "And please, *please,* forget this wickedness. I promise you by morning I shall have done so."

She pulled away from him and he let her go, although his hands trailed over her arms all the way to her fingertips until at last he released her completely. He did not try to stop her.

Two

On the following day, Lord Perryn slapped his riding crop against his buckskin breeches.

Damme, if only she had not kissed me last night.

His thoughts from the time of his leaving his bed that morning had been much taken up with Miss Trentham: her beauty, her passionate nature, and her rather tormenting presence in his life. She had cut up his peace from the time of his first having become acquainted with her four years ago. She was impertinent, showed no deference to his rank, was willing to criticize him whenever it pleased her, and challenged his every opinion. Had she not been so deuced lovely to behold, he would have given her a set down some time ago and have had done with it!

As it was, he could only laugh at himself, since no amount of rational, decisive intent on his part had been able to separate him from her. He found himself drawn to her again and again even though he wished it otherwise, not less so this morning. Why this was so, he could not say. She was, after all, a mere Miss Trentham, a member of the legion of young ladies in whom he had little interest.

The larger difficulty seemed to be that the moment he felt he knew her, she would surprise him—as she had scarcely nine hours in the past in the rose garden. He still could not credit she had been so bold as to have actually kissed him. He had long suspected she would be pleasant to embrace, but he never would have thought her capable of such wondrous wickedness. She had therefore taken up residence in his mind this morning, and he could not seem to rid his head of thoughts of her.

On the other hand, whatever he might have thought of the kiss last night, he doubted very much she would in any manner be content with her conduct. Indeed, even more than himself, he was persuaded Miss Trentham was very likely suffering rather acutely. She had long since informed him that ladies who behaved so scandalously were not fit for polite society. At this, he could not help but smile. He could only suppose he would have no end of enjoyment in teasing her today, and any number of ensuing days, because of her hypocrisy.

With these happy thoughts, so frivolous in nature, he entered the house. How fortunate, therefore, that he had chosen a door which held a view, down a rather long hall, of the foyer. The first sight that greeted him was that of Miss Trentham. She was some distance away and was turned slightly in the opposite direction, as though peering into an adjacent antechamber.

His smile broadened. Damme, but she was delicious to behold in a gown of yellow silk with her dark hair caught up in a knot of curls atop her head. She was frowning as though her mind was weighted, perhaps as it ought to be after the rather abandoned kiss she had given him.

He might have headed in her direction to begin a series of well-deserved torments, but at that moment Beau Silverdale came up behind her and tweaked her arm. She turned toward the most faithful of her three swains and smiled up into his face. He knew that smile—warm, welcoming, endearing. He pressed a hand to his chest. What was it in her smile that made him feel as though she was gripping his heart and squeezing very hard? What was this hold she had on him, this inexplicable, maddening, incomprehensible tug he always felt when she but appeared in a doorway?

He was struck yet again by her loveliness. Among their mutual acquaintance there was a lady, a Miss Madeley—all blond ringlets and large blue eyes—who was the reputed reigning beauty of Bath, but for himself he had always preferred the simplicity and elegance of Miss Trentham's visage and countenance.

He felt in supreme danger of becoming a moonling, pining for something that did not exist—could never exist, given the nature of womankind in general. What was Fenella Trentham anyway but another female with the flaws so rampant in her sex? Better to leave her to Mr. Silverdale.

He rather thought it would be wise were he to seek out his own favorites and forget, if he could, just how delightfully Miss Trentham had felt in his arms last night.

Fenella took Beau Silverdale's arm and at the same time released a silent sigh. His appearance in the entrance hall had afforded her some comfort, for he had been her particular friend for nigh on three years, along with Sir John Forton and Mr. Charles Aston. He was tall, quite a dandy, lean of figure and calm of temper. He swept a stray curl from his forehead.

"You are distressed," he murmured, as he guided her through one of several antechambers in the sprawling mansion.

"Only a very little," she returned quietly. "What a pretty room, all red and gold. Quite lovely."

"Indeed, Mrs. Almington's taste is unequalled."

"This from you?" she cried. "I will have to tell our hostess as much. She will be delighted to know your opinion."

"I already informed her of it myself, but the response was not what I would have hoped. Although she thanked me for the compliment, she had the audacity to remark that my shirt points were far too high, and however did I manage to turn my head when addressed?"

"Shocking!" Fenella returned, laughing. She glanced up at her friend and could see he had not been in the least offended, though he was a considerable Pink of the Ton. "You were not outraged?"

"How could I be?" he inquired, smiling. "For if you must know, she laughed in that charming manner of hers and patted my cheek. Were she not twelve years my senior and married, I think she would be the very woman to charm my heart."

"She charms us all," Fenella responded. "A better hostess or friend one could not find anywhere."

"I could not agree more, but we have wandered sorely from the point." The red and gold chamber was left behind and a hall engaged, down which he led her in the direction of the morning room, where breakfast was being served. "Only tell me, what has taken the bloom from your cheeks? The day is very fine, so I cannot suppose it to be the weather."

"No, it is not the weather," she returned, barely repressing yet another sigh.

"Perryn, again, I suppose?"

Fenella was astonished. "Whyever would you bring his name forward?"

Mr. Silverdale chuckled softly. "I am not a complete sapskull, Miss Trentham, nor have I failed to observe that there seems to be but one circumstance which takes the light from your eye or the rose from your complexion—a quarrel with Perryn!"

"How very lowering," she countered. "To be seen through so readily cannot be any great compliment to me."

"I would like to think that rather than reflecting anything unhappy in your abilities, the insight rather proves the perceptive qualities of mine."

She could not help but laugh.

"Much better," he said, glancing down at her. "You do better to laugh than to frown. As for Perryn, I only wonder that you are able to keep your temper in his company. I have never seen a gentleman so determined to provoke a lady. Were I of the least athletic turn, I vow I should call him out on your behalf."

Since at that moment he tugged on the slight show of lace at his cuff, Fenella smiled anew. She could think of fewer men less qualified to take to the dueling field than Mr. Silverdale.

"If I appear troubled this morning," she said, "it is because I know that I must speak with Perryn in order to settle a particular difficulty with him."

"And may I inquire as to the nature of this difficulty?"

She lowered her voice. "It is a matter of some delicacy."

"Good God," he said, stopping her before they entered the morning room. "Do not tell me he has importuned you?"

Fenella thought back to her own audacious conduct in having kissed Lord Perryn last night at the precise moment he had been perfectly ready to release her and felt her cheeks grow quite warm. "He did not."

"But you are blushing!" he cried. "Now I am convinced I must demand that he name his seconds!"

Fenella laughed heartily. "When was the last time you fired a pistol or practiced your fencing?"

He appeared to search his mind. "I have not the smallest recollection."

"Come, let us enjoy a little breakfast and no more talk of duels. Lord Perryn did not importune me, I promise you. In fact, though I am loath to admit it, he behaved the gentleman, very much to my surprise."

Arriving at the threshold of the morning room, where most of Mrs. Almington's guests were assembled, Fenella

glanced around in search of Perryn. "He is not here," she
said. "Have you perchance seen him this morning?"

He shook his head. "No, but I daresay if you catch a
glimpse of Mrs. Sugnell you will not find the good marquess far behind."

"You are right. He is excessively devoted to that lady—
and I see she is not present, either." The mere mention of
Mrs. Sugnell put Fenella forcibly in mind of having nearly
collided with her last night. She wondered just how far the
flirtation had truly progressed prior to that moment and
recalled that even Perryn had seemed shocked when she
had spoken of Mrs. Sugnell as having been clad so scantily.

"He certainly enjoys the attention of the ladies," Mr.
Silverdale remarked.

"Indeed, he does." She could only wonder just what Mr.
Silverdale would think were he to be acquainted with her
own reckless conduct in the garden last night. She shud-
dered inwardly at the very idea of anyone knowing, beyond
either herself or Perryn, how badly she had behaved.

From the moment her eyes had fluttered open at nearly
the break of dawn, she had been fretting about just what
she was to say to him this morning. Should she speak to
him and pretend nothing untoward had happened last
night? Should she apologize for her incomprehensible and
quite wicked conduct? Perhaps she should ignore him entirely and hope he would return the compliment. She simply did not know. Unfortunately, she felt certain she knew
precisely what to expect of him—he would triumph over
her and enjoy any discomfiture on the subject she might
exhibit! Wretched, wretched man!

Yet he was hardly to blame. She had kissed *him!* What
a fool she had been. Yet for the life of her, she could not
comprehend precisely what had possessed her to have actually slid her arm about a rogue's neck and settled her lips
so wantonly against his! What manner of ninnyhammer
had she become that she would have done such a reckless

thing? Surely in having kissed him, she had fixed in Perryn's mind the notion that she actually welcomed his embraces. Foolish, foolish girl!

The tall, elegant chamber hummed with the happy clamor of a dozen conversations at once as well as the clink of cutlery and china. Mrs. Almington was known for her unusual summer parties, which often comprised two or three weeks of the months of August. Rumors were rife that she had concocted a unique event this year which would keep her guests much occupied. Beyond the cleverness of her gatherings, she was particularly adept at bringing an interesting blend of personages together. Fenella was especially grateful that her three dearest friends, each a confirmed bachelor, were present.

Mrs. Almington, who had been speaking with Miss Madeley and Miss Aston, glanced up and signaled to her.

"Our hostess seems most anxious to speak with you," Mr. Silverdale murmured. "Perhaps she will know where Perryn is to be found. Ah, she is coming toward us now. I shall leave you, then, for I mean to discover whether there are potatoes on the sideboard this morning."

"Are you still following Byron's lead and confining your dishes to potatoes and vinegar?"

"Your obvious disapproval, my beautiful one, makes me entirely disinclined to give you an answer." He then bowed with a great flourish and sauntered in the direction of the buffet.

Fenella laughed at his antics, then turned to greet her hostess. "Good morning, Mrs. Almington. You look very pretty in lavender silk."

"Thank you," that good lady responded cheerfully. There were few ladies so elegant, so charming, and so genuinely warmhearted as her hostess. She was a tall creature with a broad smile, a rather round face, and blue eyes that sparkled with perpetual goodwill. "You are the last to arrive for breakfast, save your brother. Is Mr. Trentham with you?" She glanced into the hallway beyond.

"No, I have not yet seen him this morning."

"We are to begin our festivities shortly," she added, a frown puckering her brow. "I do hope . . . that is, will he be leaving his chambers quite soon, do you think?"

Fenella had no way of knowing. Aubrey might be her brother, but because he was a young man of five and twenty, she had no certain knowledge of his comings and goings. She rather thought it likely he was still heavily in his slumbers. He rarely rose before noon, tending to spend the early hours of the morning at whist, hazard, or vingt-un. "I fear I do not know. Aubrey, as you may well imagine, does not confide in me. Might I suggest you send one of your servants to his door?"

Mrs. Almington laughed outright. "I cannot imagine what I was thinking in having pressed you," she responded, "being in possession of three brothers myself. I shall do as you have suggested. You will excuse me?"

"Of course, but first I was wondering if perhaps you might know where Perryn is to be found. I . . . I have some business to conduct with him and hoped to do so before your festivities have commenced."

"Ah" she murmured, her lips twitching. "Business with Perryn. I vow, Miss Trentham, your curious relationship with my good friend intrigues me entirely."

Fenella felt a blush rise on her cheeks. "I do not take your meaning. I hope you are not suggesting or in any manner inferring that—"

Mrs. Almington chuckled and patted Fenella's shoulder. "You need explain nothing to me." She lowered her voice. "The pair of you have been smelling of April and May for some time, and I am resolved to support Cupid, have no fear!"

"Have no fear?" Fenella cried. "Ma'am, you have now

alarmed me completely! There is nothing of that nature between us, I promise you."

"Of course not," Mrs. Almington returned, winking. "And you were very right to upbraid me, for I would not give the gabblemongers even the smallest morsel of gossip upon which to feast. You may rely upon me to remain silent on the subject."

"Indeed, ma'am, you need not remain silent, merely accurate."

"How very discreet of you, to be sure," Mrs. Almington responded politely. However, the laughing light in her blue eyes and the smile on her lips bespoke the true nature of her thoughts.

"Oh, dear." Fenella could only suppose Mrs. Almington actually believed her to be in love with Perryn and he with her! She felt the worst prescience descend on her that her hostess had intentions of scheming to bring about their union. What else could she have meant by saying she was resolved to support Cupid?

Mrs. Almington lowered her voice. "You need not appear so aggrieved, my dear. All will be well, you may trust me in this. As for Perryn, I chanced to espy him on the terrace but a few moments ago. I daresay he is still there."

Fenella nodded. "Thank you. I would suppose, then, that he was just returning from his ride." She was sufficiently conversant with his habits to know he enjoyed riding out each morning.

"I believe he was—and now I must fetch your brother." She whisked by Fenella with her long, confident stride.

For herself, Fenella made her way quickly to the door leading to the long gallery and began the considerable progress to the terrace.

Whitmore Hall, home to the Almingtons for several generations, was a fine Elizabethan house of grand proportion and comprised of a great number of halls, antechambers, and receiving rooms. The walk, therefore, from the morning room to the long gallery was significant but had the happy effect of calming Fenella's nerves—at least as much as they could be quieted under such a circumstance.

When she at last reached the long gallery, she slowed her steps and through the windows had a first glimpse of the marquess. He stood not far from the door and appeared to be conversing with someone who was seated but whom she could not see. He smiled and nodded and gave all the appearance of being delighted with his companion. Though she supposed he was once more engaged in his flirtation with Mrs. Sugnell, of the moment her thoughts did not rest upon that lady, or her cloak of the night before which had barely concealed her nightdress, but rather upon the visage turned slightly away from her.

How her heart seemed to pause in its beating as she regarded the man who had kissed her five years ago and whom she had so wantonly kissed but a few hours past. Her chest expanded with a sensation of lightness and wonder.

In truth, she could never see him without feeling as though the world in that moment had been made anew. He was perhaps the handsomest man she had ever seen.

His eyes were an unusual sharp gray in color and held a perpetually alert expression, while his black hair was cropped *a la Brutus,* which she believed suited his strength of will. Both his cheek and jawlines were angled powerfully, and more than once she had thought it likely that had he not inherited a title and a very fine estate, he would have made a most excellent soldier. Something in his bearing always put her in mind of a battlefield. For one thing, he could scowl his opinions most forcefully. For another, his shoulders were unusually broad, tapering to a narrow waist and strong athletic thighs.

He had a manner of piercing with his gaze anyone with whom he was engaged in discourse, which more than once had set an unwary lady or gentleman to stammering out an apology for a contrary opinion. Fenella, however, had never once been intimidated by his mode of pressing his will, but rather took frequent delight in countering him whenever it pleased her to do so.

Her gaze drifted to his bottle green coat and buckskin breeches. She had been right. He had gone riding while everyone else was yet abed and certainly while she had been fretting about just how she was to approach him this morning.

The time had come, however. She must speak with him, or she was certain she would never be at ease again!

She took several steps, summoning her courage, when his companion, or rather all three of the most faithful members of his retinue, came into view. He was conversing not only with Mrs. Sugnell, but his two other favorites, Lady Elizabeth Leycott and Mrs. Fanny Millmeece. These three *married* ladies had been his constant companions since the day of his arrival in Bath a full month past. They were each quite different one from another. Mrs. Sugnell had lovely black curls, Lady Elizabeth was an auburn beauty, and Mrs. Millmeece was a petite creature with light brown hair and large hazel eyes. How utterly vexing to find them all engaged at present in flirting with Perryn!

Worse followed when suddenly the ladies arose, each presenting a hand to Perryn. Fenella watched as the rogue made his progression along the line of fingers, taking care to linger over each hand in a terribly rakish fashion. The ladies were delighted with his attentions, giggling like schoolgirls. Lady Elizabeth even added a rosy blush for good measure.

Fenella was astonished by his audacity. Was this the man she had kissed last night and who in turn had kissed her so wantonly? She realized with a truly despairing start that she had somehow believed, if quite secretly, that the kiss she had shared with him had held some significance. How could she have thought anything so utterly ridiculous?

The ladies trilled their laughter, smiled, and fluttered their lashes a little more. Perryn's response was no less obliging as he met each gaze ardently, his own lips smiling in what she felt was a completely enticing manner. She could watch no more, nor could she force herself to intrude upon so ridiculous a flirtation. She felt nothing but contempt for herself for having kissed such a hopeless man— and even more contempt for him that he would have held her in his arms so wonderfully at midnight and yet not hesitate to flirt so outrageously with three married ladies this morning. Vile, vile man! He had in this moment proven his character to her *yet again!*

As she moved away from the windows overlooking the terrace, she promised herself, not for the first time, never to underestimate a rogue's disinterest in what might have proven an amusing dalliance just a few hours previously.

As she returned to the antechamber, which intersected the hall leading to the morning room, she espied her half brother, Aubrey, and quickly hurried to his side. "Did Mrs. Almington find you?"

"Oh, good morning, Fenella. Yes, on the stairs, as it happens. She was greatly relieved to see me. I do not suppose you know what entertainment she has in mind for the next fortnight?" He seemed impatient and bored all at once as he cast his gaze from doorway to doorway as though in search of someone. Shadows lingered below his otherwise handsome brown eyes. "I must have some coffee before the day's trials commence. Will you accompany me to the morning room?"

"Of course. I was just returning there myself."

Aubrey Trentham was just two years her junior and though they were but half siblings, between them there was a Trentham resemblance—if not in temper, in feature. They shared the same nose and chin and general shape of the eye as well as lustrous dark hair. Aubrey's eyes, however, were a very dark brown while hers were green. His complexion was quite pale this morning, and she felt certain his night's sleep could not have been long in duration.

"I have not the faintest notion what our hostess intends for us," she responded, grateful that Aubrey's presence was diverting her from unhappier thoughts. "Her secrecy has raised the greatest suspense among the party, and the only hint I have received as to the nature of the delights she has readied for us is that yesterday afternoon I overheard Miss Almington tell Miss Keele that her father had sent his entire stable, some twenty horses, ahead to The Mendips."

"Do not tell me we are to travel," he groaned as they arrived at the morning room. "I vow I should despise nothing more. I suppose I should have refused her invitation in the first place, which I daresay she only proffered because you are my sister. Good God, Fenella, she fairly dotes upon you. A real mother could not be more indulgent. What do you suppose she means by it?"

Fenella recalled her earlier conversation with Mrs. Almington and rather thought she understood her present purposes. These, however, she had no intention of sharing with her brother. "I cannot say, but I do enjoy her society a great deal. She is a most attentive hostess."

When her brother remained silent, she glanced up at him and saw his attention was caught by one of the young ladies across the room. Fenella followed the line of his gaze and saw that he was regarding Miss Adbaston in a wholly speculative light.

"I say," he ventured at last. "Miss Adbaston has done her hair in the prettiest manner possible. I feel I must tell her so. You will excuse me, sister?" Without so much as a bow, he quit her side and hurried across the room.

Fenella watched him go but she could not keep from sighing. Miss Adbaston was a very plain young lady with a retrousse nose and shockingly red hair who could scarcely speak without blushing. Fenella would have been gratified by her brother's attentions to her had Miss Adbaston not been in possession of some ten thousand pounds. For all of Aubrey's excellent good looks, his charm of expression, and his polite manners in a drawing room, he was a confirmed gamester.

Fenella searched out her own favorites and found Mr. Silverdale seated with dear, portly Sir John Forton and a very sad-looking Mr. Aston. The latter winced frequently as someone nearby laughed a little too loudly, spoke enthusiastically on any subject, or chanced to clatter a fork onto a plate. She was greeted quite warmly by Sir John and in a hoarse whisper by Mr. Aston as she took up a seat beside Mr. Silverdale. A servant immediately offered her a cup of coffee, which she accepted gratefully.

"What make you of Mrs. Almington's plans?" Sir John asked, eyeing fondly a large chunk of a fresh-baked bread.

"I must confess I know very little of them," she said. "Do I apprehend you have learned something of no small import?" She sipped her coffee and eyed Sir John in some interest, wondering what he knew of their forthcoming entertainment.

She would have to wait, however, for Sir John eased the bread into his mouth and chewed with so contented an expression that Fenella was put in mind of cows grazing in a lush field. She rather thought he might have been a handsome man had he not tended to fat as he did. His hair was the color of wheat and his eyes an interesting light blue, but his complexion had grown quite puffy and reddish in hue in his enjoyment of whatever plate was put before him.

After a long moment, he answered her. "Only that the entire assemblage is to be divided into pairs," he responded. Forking a hefty chunk of ham, he added, "I vow Mrs. Almington has the best cook in the kingdom."

Mr. Silverdale snorted. "You said that about the last five houses you visited."

"Pairs?" Fenella intervened hastily. "Sir John, pray do

ignore Mr. Silverdale. Only tell me, in what manner are we to be paired? Whatever do you mean?" Her throat had constricted with apprehension.

Mr. Aston dropped his head into his hands. "My friends," he said, each word an obvious agony as it left his lips, "so much noise is not to be borne. I beg all of you not to speak so loudly. You cannot know the pain you inflict."

Fenella chuckled softly and lowered her voice. "We shall try to do better—only why do you torment yourself with so much wine?"

He lifted drooping eyes to her. "Have you tasted Mr. Almington's brandy? Sir John may offer compliments to Mrs. Almington's cook, but I promise you there is not a finer wine cellar in all of England than here at Whitmore."

"Poor Mr. Aston," she responded. "As it happens, I did not have the pleasure of a glass of brandy, but the wine has been excellent, particularly the Madeiras."

"Oh lord, yes!" he cried, then winced at the pain his enthusiasm had cost him.

She chuckled once more, then returned her attention to Sir John. "So we are to be paired," she said, her voice as soft as she could manage while still being heard. "I hope you mean to tell me all you know, for I find myself intrigued." More accurately she felt suspicious, particularly since Mrs. Almington had just told her she meant to help Cupid if she could.

"Not a great deal," Sir John returned, fairly whispering, "except that our hostess has some absurd—I beg your pardon, but would you pass that delicious apricot jam? Ah, yes, thank you. Now where was I? Oh, yes, it would seem she has some absurd scheme afoot that we are all to be matched with someone of the opposite gender in order to accomplish some ridiculous feat or other." He fairly ladled the jam onto his bread.

"A feat? What sort of feat?" She was now alarmed and settled her cup on its saucer. She found she had suddenly lost her appetite. When a servant drew near offering her a choice of toast, muffin, or bread, she realized she was far too overset to partake of even a particle of breakfast.

Sir John spread the remainder of his bread a half inch thick with jam and shrugged. "I do not know. Damme! The best bread I have had in a twelvemonth!"

Fenella huffed her impatience. "Sir John, I beg you will attend me." Mr. Aston winced and she again lowered her voice. "Have you no information at all?"

He could not answer her. His blue eyes held a glazed expression as he chewed. He was in another world made up of his adoration of every manner of food.

"You promised me no more noise," Mr. Aston groaned.

"I am trying," Fenella said. She glanced at Mr. Silverdale, who smiled ruefully and offered her a shrug of his shoulders. She realized there was nothing more she could learn from her beaus. "I shan't say another word." She slid her gaze over the chamber in search of Mrs. Almington, but it was evident she had not returned to the morning room.

Why would her hostess have determined to pair her guests for what appeared to be a forthcoming journey? Her suspicions now took a terrifying hold of her. The thought that Mrs. Almington somehow meant to match her with Lord Perryn struck her quite violently. She felt desperate of a sudden.

If this was indeed her hostess's intention, then she must speak with her at once. Just as she was about to rise to her feet to go in search of her, Mrs. Almington's butler appeared in the doorway and announced that the entire party was to meet forthwith in the grand salon.

As one, the assemblage rose to obey the summons, although Sir John protested he had not quite finished his meal. As he moved slowly away from the table, he stared longingly at the remainder of a thick slice of ham yet on his plate. His resulting sigh was audible to nearly the entire room.

Fenella excused herself from the attentions of her swains and began moving hastily through the guests in an effort to reach the grand salon as quickly as possible in hopes of speaking with Mrs. Almington. However, upon arriving, she found that good lady already surrounded by several other guests and at least two servants waiting to do her bidding. She moved as near as she was able and attempted to engage her hostess, but Mrs. Almington was clearly distracted with her present concerns. For Fenella to have pressed her in any manner would have been rude beyond permission.

She settled for catching her eye and expressing her distress with a desperate gesture of her hands. Much to her dismay, Mrs. Almington merely laughed and turned back to her servants.

Fenella's gaze was drawn to the serving maid to the left of her hostess. In her hands were two bowls, each containing slips of paper onto which Fenella could see names of the guests inscribed. Clearly Sir John had the right of it, for the names she noted in the left bowl belonged to the gentlemen of the party and those in the right bowl to the ladies. By all appearances, Sir John was not mistaken in what he had heard thus far of Mrs. Almington's purposes.

Once everyone was assembled, some seated on the elegant furniture in varying tones of beige, green, and white silk, some standing about in small clusters, Mrs. Almington stunned the assemblage with the scope of her scheme. The whole of the project involved a caravan of sorts in which the present party was to travel in pairs through Somerset and collect any item of their choosing for the purpose of auctioning the collections at the end of the fortnight. The funds raised during the auction would be used for the relief of the poor of Bath. The journey would take the party into a deep loop through Somerset beginning this morning from

Whitmore Manor and ending in approximately twelve days, again at Whitmore, at which time the collections would be prepared for the auction.

"At the end of the fortnight," Mrs. Almington continued, "when we have grown weary of one another's company and our prolonged effort, I promise you a ball in your honor to which I have already sent out two hundred invitations."

This was an unlooked for prospective delight, and a rousing cheer went up from all the guests. Even Fenella, in all her agony about who her partner might be, could not help but be pleased with the notion of such a fete.

The maidservant who held the bowls in her hands moved forward. Mrs. Almington appeared very sly. "In but a moment, you shall discover who your partners will be. I have the gentlemen's names in the left bowl and the ladies' in the right. First, however, I would like to add that I shall be giving a prize to the very best collection." She paused for effect, then said, "Prinny has most graciously extended an invitation to the Pavilion for a sennight's visit in his magnificent home as an incentive to you all."

This surprising announcement resulted in an astonished whispering, for there were few places so delightful as Brighton in the summer. The Prince Regent was known to be a most excellent host and the Pavilion an intriguing house built and decorated in a fascinating Oriental theme.

Fenella, who had met the prince for the first time at Carlton House during the past London Season, was impressed with his kind manners. The very thought of being in such exalted company sparked a certain competitiveness in her which had always been part of her particular temper. She would have to acquire a new wardrobe at the very least in order to enjoy society on the Steyne, and she should dearly love to do a little sea bathing. Oh, yes, winning the Brighton prize would please her enormously!

Her thoughts were so happily diverted that until Mrs.

Almington actually reached into the ladies' bowl for the
first time, she had forgotten the possibility that her hostess
meant to do some terrible meddling. If only she had known
beforehand what Mrs. Almington intended, she might have
had an opportunity to discourage what she felt certain she
was about to do.

At this eleventh hour, however, there was little she could
do but let events unfold before her—except to wink, scowl,
and grimace at her hostess whenever her gaze passed in
her direction. Mrs. Almington, however, remained entirely
unmoved.

The slips of paper began to be withdrawn, and two by
two the partners were paired. The fifth set distressed her
for it would seem her brother was to enjoy the next fortnight in the company of Miss Adbaston. The latter had
already shown a very strong inclination toward Aubrey,
which did not bode well for her future happiness. Aubrey
himself was beaming in delight at his new partner.

She glanced about the remaining guests and for an instant caught Perryn's eye. He stood but a few feet away
and inclined his head to her. His gaze was somewhat speculative, and then a slow, rather rakish smile overtook his
lips. She rolled her eyes and looked away from him. God
help her if she was indeed to be paired with such a beast!

The sixth and seventh pairs were chosen, leaving herself,
Miss Madeley, Colonel Bedrell, the Marquess of Perryn,
Mr. Rupert Leycott and Mrs. Almington yet to be paired.
Fenella watched Miss Madeley drift to Perryn's side.

"Is not this terribly exciting?" she asked in a voice reminiscent of soft church bells. She was quite a beautiful
young woman, of an age with Aubrey. Her hair was of a
delicate nature and blond in hue, which frequently gave
her the aspect of an angel—as now, with her hair drawn
up into a knot of curls atop her head.

Perryn turned to her and dazzled her with his handsome
smile. "I only hope you may be my partner." Miss

Madeley's smile was equally brilliant in return, which gave Fenella the strong impression that the young woman had an interest in the marquess. She had long suspected that Miss Madeley, having rejected an astounding fifteen quite eligible proposals of marriage thus far in her career, meant to attract not just a peer, but the highest rank she could command. In such a setting as Mrs. Almington's drawing room, with no duke in sight, Perryn was therefore the man to be pursued. She rather thought, given their respective natures, they were worthy of one another and ought to be paired for the forthcoming journey. She could only hope she was wrong in her hostess's thoughts on the subject.

Miss Madeley's name was drawn from the right bowl. Fenella's heart beat quickly. She stared at Mrs. Almington's fingers as they dipped into the left bowl containing the names of but three gentlemen now. A slip of paper appeared. Mrs. Almington slowly unfolded it and called out Colonel Bedrell's name. Miss Madeley pouted prettily at Perryn before graciously taking Colonel Bedrell's arm.

Fenella had but one chance now. Her name alone remained in the right bowl, for Mrs. Almington had no need to place hers within the bowl.

"And to partner Miss Fenella Trentham . . ." In the left bowl two names remained, Mr. Leycott's and Lord Perryn's. Mrs. Almington met her gaze and a wink followed. Fenella shook her head in return, scowled a little more, and grimaced with all her might, but she was steadfastly ignored. She knew which name would be called out before ever she saw the slip of paper emerge. "Perryn," Mrs. Almington stated cheerfully.

Fenella's heart sank. So it was true. Mrs. Almington was playing matchmaker, and she was to be paired with the most notorious rogue in London—whom she had most wretchedly kissed last night. She felt as though she might swoon.

"So it would seem, Mr. Leycott," Mrs. Almington said, "that you and I are to be partners. I could not be happier."

"Nor I," Mr. Leycott responded generously.

Mrs. Almington then announced that the coaches had already been ordered to be brought round and that the entire party would be leaving within the hour.

With all the pairs established, the chamber became a hum of conversation as each set of partners began to explore ideas for their collections. Fenella turned in the direction of Lord Perryn and saw he was eyeing her with a wicked smile on his lips. This was so very much like him, to tease her before they had even begun, that she grew impatient suddenly. She could not help but try to frown him down as he approached her.

"Mad as fire, I see," he murmured. "I hope you do not think I was the author of this?"

"On no account. It would seem our hostess has come to believe she is aiding Cupid in arranging our partnership."

"She was always a great matchmaker."

"We are no match."

Perryn drew very close and whispered just over her shoulder, "We were last night."

She drew back and met his gaze fiercely. "I cannot believe you would say such a thing to me!"

"You disappoint me. I have so much more I would say to you, but I can see you will not take it kindly."

"Not by half!" Fenella cried.

Perryn took her firmly by the arm and turned her away from young Miss Aston, who had been partnered with Mr. Silverdale. Both were watching their encounter with great interest. "Come, Fennel, let us not quarrel," he whispered, leading her into the hall. "At least not in front of our party. I have not become your partner by design, and I can see you had no hand in it. We were on our way to establishing something of a friendship before the ridiculous events in the rose garden overset things. And surely you do not want to set the tabbies to gossiping by brangling with me?"

"Of course not," she murmured, her temper gentling. She

allowed him to pilot her further still in the direction of the entrance hall. When she knew they had progressed sufficiently far from the grand salon not to be overheard, she finally addressed the difficult matter of the previous night's kiss. "Perryn, I had hoped for an opportunity to speak with you. Indeed, I had intended to do so earlier, but you were much engaged in kissing the fingers of your favorites."

"Jealous?" he queried teasingly.

"Hardly. Disgusted, more like. How can you bear to flirt at nine o'clock in the morning?"

He laughed heartily at that. "I have never found an hour that did not suit such a pleasant activity."

"You bemuse me entirely. But this is hardly to the point. What I had meant to say was that I am exceedingly sorry for having kissed you last night. It was very wrong of me. I cannot possibly explain my conduct, except to say that I believe you are far too handsome for your own good. Regardless, I am deeply ashamed and beg you will forgive me."

He was silent, then finally said, "Miss Trentham, I will offer a piece of advice, if you will allow it."

She glanced at him suspiciously, but nodded her acquiescence.

"Never apologize to a rogue for kissing him."

At that, Fenella smiled, if unwillingly. "I should have expected you to say something outrageous. Well, you may be as flippant as you like, but I wish you to understand there will be no more such indiscretions, particularly since we are to be cloistered together in a carriage for the better part of the next two weeks."

"Now you have ruined all my expectations."

"Do be serious."

"No," he responded flatly. "The subject does not occasion seriousness. The very thought of kissing you can only serve to bring a smile to my lips, even if you have brought the subject forward for the purpose of offering an apology!"

She stared at him, her mouth agape. There was no hope

for it. She could not bring him to discuss their wretched encounter of the night before with any degree of rationality. She decided therefore to open a new, more immediate subject with him. "Since you refuse to discuss the matter sensibly, then may I inquire as to what you think we should set about collecting on this odd little caravan of ours?"

The light in his eye dimmed. "I fear you will not find me in any degree enthusiastic about Mrs. Almington's latest notion of entertainment. For one thing, I cannot believe she would consign so many gentlemen to a fate that can please only a lady's interests."

"You forget that her intentions are quite large-minded. You forget the beggars of Bath."

"One can never forget them. They are everywhere."

She rolled her eyes. "Do you study to be difficult?" By now they had reached the entrance hall, where she paused at the bottom of the stairs.

At that, he smiled. "I perceive I am being ungracious. Very well, what do you think our collection should entail? Although I hope we can contrive something that will not put me to sleep for the length of the journey."

Fenella chuckled. "I have little doubt that, given your disposition, unless the collection were to somehow involve the seduction of womankind you would find it a dead bore."

"You have given me the very answer we have been seeking. On this journey, I know precisely what we should collect."

Fenella was hopeful at last. "Indeed?" she returned, a certain excitement flooding her. If they were able to work well together, they might succeed in winning Prinny's invitation. Besides, nothing would please her more than that their collection should be determined best of the lot.

"Yes," he responded, lowering his voice. "What do you think of collecting your kisses?"

"What?" Fenella responded, thinking she could not have heard him correctly.

"We could collect your kisses, dozens of them. I could keep a log—when they occur, how delightful I find them, and to what degree of passion they raise my blood."

Fenella gasped and took a step away from him. "I cannot imagine what Mrs. Almington was thinking! Does she have any notion how abominable you can be? I tell you now, she will have a great deal to answer for in consigning me so to a fortnight, especially in your company!"

She whirled away from him, marching quickly up the stairs. She could not be rid of him so easily, however, for he followed closely on her heels, bounding behind her two steps at a time. "Where are you going and at such a brisk pace? We have not yet determined the frequency of the kisses or precisely how I am to judge each one."

"I am going to begin packing for the journey—or have you forgotten already that Mrs. Almington said we were to be going in but an hour?" Having reached the landing at the second floor, she hurried in the direction of her bedchamber.

Perryn let her go, but his laughter followed after her. He shook his head. For a moment he debated going directly to his friend and hostess and demanding to know just what the devil she meant by interfering in so high-handed a fashion. However, he decided against it entirely when Fenella paused in her steps, whirled around and called out, "And pray do not dither, my lord, for I intend for our collection to be the very best!"

He smiled broadly. "As it will be, since my skills have been rated so highly by so many."

She gasped anew. "I do not hesitate to say that you, my lord, are a complete coxcomb!" With that, she flounced into the adjacent hall and disappeared from view.

Three

"Is anything amiss?"

Fenella turned from the window overlooking the northern garden of the Almington estate. Betsy, her abigail for more years than she could remember, was watching her with a concerned expression as she rolled a pair of fine silk stockings into a careful ball.

Her thoughts wended backward and round and round. Recollections of last night's kiss mingled with Perryn's absurd banter but a few moments ago. She had been completely out of patience with him in that moment and yet charmed all the while.

A fortnight in his company.

"Miss?"

Fenella blinked and met her maid's gaze anew, yet she did not see her. What a ridiculous man Perryn was. She had called him a coxcomb, yet she knew he was nothing of the sort. He had been tormenting her merely to see how quickly or how strongly she would rise to the fly. The worst of it was she always did as soon as he but cast his line!

"Miss?"

"Oh, Betsy, I do beg your pardon. I am in the worst fix, yet there is nothing you nor anyone can do about it. You will have to forgive me if I seem inattentive or distressed. I am certain all will be well as soon as this caravan is drawn to a close in twelve wretched days."

"You do not look forward to Mrs. Almington's amusement?"

"Not in the least, I am afraid."

She turned her gaze back to the window. Below, Perryn came into view, sauntering along the path beside the neatly trimmed yew hedges as though he had been designed to vex her at every turn. Betsy joined her by the window.

"I see Lord Perryn is marching about. He'll not like being imprisoned in a coach for these many days together. La, but he is that handsome. All of Mrs. Almington's maidservants beg to do the dusting in his bedchamber if but for a glimpse of him."

"He would do better, in my opinion," Fenella responded, "were his shoulders not so very broad and his coats not tailored half so well. Then we might not suffer as we do."

"I suppose you wish he were as broad about the stomach as Sir John."

"Poor Sir John." Fenella giggled. "No, I do not wish that at all."

"What is troubling you, miss? It is a rare day, indeed, when I see you in the mopes, and rarer still when you say you do not find a lengthy excursion to your liking."

Fenella glanced at Betsy, the tall, thin woman of some five and fifty years who had served her so very well. The intimacy shared between mistress and abigail was an unusual one, perhaps best explained by the fact that Fenella had been without a mother for twenty-six of her seven and twenty years. There was very little she could not say to dear Betsy.

She watched Perryn for a moment longer as he swung his cane rather absently, flicking the shrubs as he passed by. With a sigh, she turned away and sank into a nearby chair.

A fortnight.

How was she ever to endure being in his sole company, day upon day, for an entire fortnight? She would go mad.

Her dreams were already quite full of him. She could not imagine what being in his presence several hours each day would do to her already overwrought sensibilities.

She looked up at her maid. "I have been partnered with Lord Perryn," she said sadly. "It would appear Mrs. Almington believes we should be matched."

"I see," Betsy murmured, a frown between her brows. She was well acquainted with Fenella's *tendre* for the marquess. "And you could not prevail upon her to change her mind?"

"I did not have the opportunity to speak with her, for she was much engaged in preparing for the drawing—which, by the way, was a complete sham."

"I can well believe it," Betsy responded, chuckling as she arranged a freshly laundered shift into one of the trunks scattered about the floor. "Well, she does pride herself on her matchmaking."

"That she does. Only how will I bear being in company with Perryn every day?"

"Oh, miss, I am that sorry, truly I am." She was silent. Then, with a twinkle in her eye, she continued, "Although I do have something I think can be of use to you in so troubling a situation." She rummaged in a nearby cloth bag and brought an article to Fenella, her smile rather pitying, even if there was laughter in her eyes. "Just in case you swoon."

Fenella chuckled, in no small degree of frustration, as she took the small, well-used vinaigrette from her maid. "I suppose this will have to do."

Betsy resumed packing while Fenella sat staring absently at the silver box, all the while clicking and unclicking the lid. Occasionally, the pungent smell of the small sponge within drifted to her nose. She had no confidence whatsoever that any means, however clever, would serve to protect her from either Perryn's wickedly handsome countenance or his most determined flirtations.

An hour and a half later, she moved onto the gravel drive where Perryn awaited her. Theirs was the last coach to depart, the fault entirely hers. She had been in no hurry whatsoever to take up her seat in a rogue's coach. One thing she had determined, however, was that he would sit opposite her rather than beside her. She could imagine few things more dangerous than having to sit in such close proximity to him, with her elbows, shoulders, and knees occasionally jostling his.

When she suggested the arrangement to him, he nodded politely. "As you wish."

She had expected him to continue in his previously tormenting manner, but there was nothing in his countenance to suggest he intended to resume his flirtatious taunts. She found herself relieved, at least for the present. Perhaps she would not need her vinaigrette at all today!

As he handed her up, she noted with some pleasure how well-appointed and nicely sprung his coach was. Whatever the difficulties she might be forced to endure in his company, at least she would be comfortable in his coach.

"And what is our destination today?" Perryn asked, crossing his arms over his chest.

Fenella withdrew the itinerary from her reticule, unfolding it carefully. "We are to pass through Stanton Drew, Cameley, and finally Compton Martin, though I believe there may be several villages or hamlets betwixt. Apparently, we are to rest the night at the home of Sir Edgar and Lady Burnhill, which is located, I believe, near Compton Martin. Yes, Mr. Almington has marked it on the attending map. If I understand the purpose of this rather meandering route, it has been designed to allow us abundant opportunity for adding to our collection along the way."

Fenella lifted her gaze from the itinerary and watched as Perryn stifled a yawn. No man could be less suited to such a task than the veritable Corinthian seated opposite her. She knew him to be an athletic man who took great

pleasure in boxing, fencing, and hunting. He was even a
member of the Four-in-Hand Club, whose principal object
was the perfecting of driving skill, in particular of the
larger coaches employing two and sometimes three teams.
What interest could such a gentleman have in gathering a
collection of anything? The task Mrs. Almington had given
them did indeed seem more suited to schoolgirls than
grown men.

Regardless, she was not one to complain and quickly set
her mind to concocting some manner of collection which
might appeal to a man of Perryn's stamp. She understood
now that she had spoken more truly than she had at first
thought when she had said that unless the collection involved the seduction of womankind she doubted he would
be much interested in the object of the caravan.

However, her own nature was of a different mold. She
was already imagining standing before the entire party at
the end of the fortnight and receiving the prize for the best
collection. Only how on earth was she to bring Perryn to
the task with sufficient enthusiasm to win the day? What
manner of collection would intrigue a rogue even in the
slightest?

As she watched him stifle yet another yawn, she could
not conceive of just how she was to cross this first bridge.
Surely in the course of the morning some idea for a collection would present itself of sufficient interest to please
Perryn. But as the miles eased one upon another, and the
lovely hilly countryside surrounding Bath brought them to
enjoy a cup of tea at Stanton Drew, she was no nearer to
solving the dilemma than when they had set forth from
Whitmore. Though a score of mundane ideas had presented
themselves, such as the collecting of leaves or birds' nests
or the like, nothing of sufficient merit surfaced for which
she felt Perryn would be in the least enthused.

"I have no interest in collecting mushrooms," he said,

setting his cup with a clink on its saucer, "in case you were thinking along the lines of fungus."

Fenella laughed.

Perryn did not.

Oh, dear. She was not mistaken, then. He was about as disinterested in the notion of creating a collection as he could possibly be.

Boarding the coach again, Fenella noticed, in a field just east of the village, three circles of massive upright stones, obviously ancient in origin. "What about stones?" she suggested, gesturing out the window. "What do you think of collecting these?"

This brought a reluctant smile to his face. "You may have hit upon something, Miss Trentham. In fact, what about just one stone? We could choose the largest of these and hire several hundred laborers to drag it back to Whitmore. Surely Mrs. Almington would be satisfied with such an effort, the enormous size of the stone giving way to actual number."

"How could she fail to approve?" she queried. "Although I daresay our hostess would want to keep the stone for herself as a sort of obelisk for the rose garden."

"A rather tall one."

"Yes, but quite grand."

He peered at the stones. "Do you know, I think one of those stones would actually take up her entire rose garden."

"She could easily transplant all the shrubs. Yes, I believe we may have conceived of exactly the right idea!"

Perryn chuckled as the coach rumbled past the mysterious stones.

A few miles more and the farms and outbuildings of Cameley came into view. "Some of these buildings are roofed in a very fine red tile," Perryn observed. "I suppose we could collect roof tiles."

"How would we get at them?" Fenella inquired, looking up at the roofs.

"I could climb an accommodating trellis and dislodge as many tiles as I was able. I believe they weigh but forty or fifty pounds each. You look sturdy enough to catch them. I could toss them to you, two or three at a time, and should the lady of the house appear unexpectedly, you could hide them in your shawl."

Fenella laughed. "Your plan is a good one but I believe the risk might be too great. Were I the lady of the house I should call my husband to bring his favorite bird gun and direct him to immediately empty it of shot."

"Vicious woman!" he cried.

She sighed. "No fungus, no ancient stones of gigantic proportions, no stolen roof tiles. I vow, Perryn, we are quickly running out of ideas. I begin to think Mrs. Almington was a suit short when she concocted this caravan."

A bird flew from shrub to shrub along the hedgerows. "Feathers?" he suggested. "Were we to capture one or two birds, we could pluck the poor creatures clean with the happy effect that we could complete the entire collection in but an hour or two. Then we might simply return to Bath and await the remainder of the party to return in a fortnight."

"And to think I had begun to suppose you were entirely indifferent to our project—and yet you have all these astonishing and quite sensible ideas!"

"It is just as I always supposed—you underestimate me entirely."

The entire facetious exchange was so much to her liking that she began to be at ease. "Frogs?" she suggested.

He nodded. "An excellent notion. Hundreds of them. And at the auction we could let them loose. I do so love to see ladies race about in circles screaming hysterically."

"In which case I believe mice would serve your purpose much better—though we ought to return to Cameley, for there were at least a dozen outbuildings which would be overrun with the small creatures."

"Well, if we are to poke around in damp farmhouses, we perhaps should attempt to gather something easier to transport than mice but equally as effective in oversetting a drawing room full of ladies."

"I hope you do not mean spiders," she countered, grimacing.

"Whyever not? Do not tell me you are afraid of our little friends?"

"Not a bit, save when they are within a hundred yards of me."

He chuckled.

"Well, I must confess this is very pleasant," she said. "I thought for a moment, or at least for the past fifteen miles, that you were above being pleased. I can see now nearly any collection has the potential of charming you."

He met her gaze at that. "I did not mean for my boredom to be so obvious," he responded seriously.

"Your suppression of at least a dozen yawns in the first hour of our traveling allowed me to understand quite to perfection your disposition toward the project."

He sighed. "I confess I was a trifle disheartened by the prospect of spending so many days together in the collecting of anything. Despite that, I shall endeavor to summon at least a modicum of enthusiasm."

"Oh, dear. I believe this is far worse. I would rather you yawned than promised to do better."

"You will tease me when I am being perfectly serious?" He smiled ruefully.

"Oh, Perryn, despite Mrs. Almington's truly ridiculous scheme of attempting to engage a great number of gentlemen in so tedious a journey, I do so want our collection to be the very best."

"Indeed? But why? It seems a complete mystery to me that you would care a jot for anything so trifling."

"I must say I do not know precisely how it is that I do. However, the moment Mrs. Almington mentioned that there would be a prize for the best collection, I was captivated by the notion of ours deserving such an accolade. I cannot explain it except to say it is my nature. I am a little competitive, as it happens."

His expression grew pinched. "You were coupled with the wrong partner, I fear. I enjoy a good competition myself if it involves a horse or the use of my swords or even a bow and arrow, and that between excellent opponents, but I cannot summon even the smallest interest in the sort of collection Mrs. Almington has in mind. Butterflies, leaves, toads? I vow I had much rather put a pistol to my head and be done with it."

Fenella laughed heartily. "I have no doubt you are but one of twelve gentlemen enjoying the same truly unfortunate thought at this very moment. I greatly fear that in a fortnight, Mrs. Almington will have several apologies to make for having consigned so many good friends to such a caravan as this."

"I could not agree more, though I am loath to say it out of respect for our hostess."

The last few miles of the day's journey passed in silence. Fenella felt they had worn out their ideas. Regardless of how much time was being lost which could be used for the act of collecting, it was no use to begin until an item had been settled upon. For the present, Fenella contented herself with enjoying the northernmost view of the Mendips.

At last, the coach drew into the courtyard of Burnhill Manor, where the party would be passing the night.

Fenella entered the ancient dwelling, wondering if the house would suit the size of Mrs. Almington's party. Her doubts were soon settled as a footman led her on a labyrinthine journey through the much altered house to her bedchamber. Within, she found Betsy already established and arranging a vase of deep red roses, the fragrance of which proved heavenly. "How grateful I am to find you here," she murmured, smiling.

"Was your journey tolerable?" Betsy inquired, eyeing her carefully.

Fenella removed her bonnet and handed it to her maid. "Quite, and far more congenial than I could have anticipated. Perryn . . . was kind, I think. Fortunately, he was experiencing so great a degree of ennui that I found I could be at ease. He is not at all content with the nature of our expedition, you see. But after a time, we were even able to laugh together."

"And what did you decide to collect, if I might ask?"

Fenella removed her spencer. "We are as yet undecided. I was unwilling to settle on anything unless assured it would hold his interest for longer than two minutes together. I am greatly perplexed as to just what would charm a gentleman's attention. Well, this is a lovely chamber and the roses are perfection."

"Aye, miss." She settled the bonnet on the top shelf of the wardrobe. "I am to inform you that dinner will be served at six o'clock. Since it is just past three, were you wishful of a bath?"

She shook her head. "Only to rest for a time. Will you come to me at half past four?"

"As you wish."

When Betsy withdrew, Fenella stretched out on the bed, staring up at the white ceiling overhead. She could not help but smile a little. The journey had been a great deal more pleasant than she had expected, and she had been able to keep her tendency to feel rather dizzy in Perryn's company quite at bay. The difficult task of trying to determine an appropriate collection had served her in that regard. With such a dilemma to occupy her mind, she had not found it at all necessary to steel her heart against Perryn.

At the same time, she realized with something of a start,

he had been a complete gentleman throughout the morning's drive.

Still, he had yawned a great deal. Though his own contentment was certainly his responsibility, she could not help but feel that the equanimity of the journey rested upon her ability to engage him in an appropriate collection. That was the rub! Had her partner been anyone other than Lord Perryn, she easily could have devised a collection that would have satisfied.

Mr. Aston, for instance, would have been content moving from hamlet to village to town and wresting from each place a tankard—properly drained, of course, and that more than once—unique to the area. Beau Silverdale would have been far easier to please than even Mr. Aston. Buttons would have suited him as well as anything, while Sir John would have been satisfied by collecting biscuit recipes—and samples, naturally!—from whatever inn they chanced by.

Lord Perryn was not such as these and certainly not half so easy to accommodate. How did one entertain a rogue short of collecting the prettiest maid from each village, dozens in all, and bringing them all back to Whitmore? She could only laugh at the absurdity of doing so, yet she knew there was a grain of truth in it. Even Perryn had suggested he collect her kisses, one by one.

Later, without having been able to conceive of an idea for the collection, she was descending the stairs for dinner when her brother called from the landing above. She turned to wait for him as he moved quickly to join her.

"So, tell me Fenella," he called out happily, "how are you faring with his lordship? Is he conducting himself as a gentleman, or shall I be required to call him out by journey's end?"

There was so much unusual good humor in his expression that Fenella found herself torn between adjuring him not to joke her about something so indelicate and asking him what had put such a twinkle in his eye. She chose the latter.

"Cannot you guess?" he inquired as they reached the bottom of the stairs.

"I must suppose your partner?"

"Of course. I vow Miss Adbaston is an angel and a perfectly amiable partner." He then took up her arm. "Fenella, you have always been a good sister to me. If there is anything I might do for you, you know you have but to ask."

She stared up at him in some wonder. When he was content, he was the very best of men. "Actually, I do need a bit of advice," she responded. "I cannot seem to devise the right collection for myself and Lord Perryn. Have you any suggestions? What, for instance, are you and Miss Adbaston collecting?"

"That is supposed to be a great secret, you know," he countered, smiling. "However, Miss Adbaston already told Miss Almington, her dear friend Miss Keele, Miss Madeley, of course, and Miss Aston, so I suppose there will be no harm in my telling you."

"I am all curiosity."

Aubrey shook his head. "Old glass bottles, anything of an interesting shape."

"How charming—and if I may say so, a great deal more fun than searching for spiders or the like."

"Is that what you were meaning to foist on Perryn?" he asked, laughing.

"Not in the least. He teased me with the notion himself."

"I daresay you turned the color of a dove and swooned."

"Very nearly," she said, laughing. "Ah, here is Miss Adbaston."

"Indeed," he murmured. "You will excuse me?"

"Of course." Fenella watched him move forward quickly and offer his arm to the young woman. For the briefest moment, hope surged within her that perhaps at long last Aubrey had met a young lady who might charm him. If only the lady was not quite so well dowered, she would have allowed that hope to flower. As it was, she decided to temper her feelings until she saw precisely which way the wind blew.

She was about to make her way to the drawing room, from which chamber she could hear a great deal of chatter, when she was addressed by a man with a booming voice.

"I say!" he called to her as she turned toward him. "What a great beauty you are! You must forgive me if I do not recall precisely having met you earlier, for I fear I am advancing so rapidly into a state of decrepit old age that my memory now fails me more often than not!"

Fenella could not help but smile and then laugh. "You must be Sir Edgar. May I say you were not mistaken. We have not met, nor do I think it at all possible you could be advancing into such a state as you have described." Sir Edgar Burnhill was a large man, powerfully built, who exuded a tremendous energy. His years were evidenced only by a head of shockingly white hair and a scattering of wrinkles over his broad face. She liked him at once, in particular his open, friendly manners. "I am Miss Trentham. I fear I arrived very late with the Marquess of Perryn."

"So Richard is come! I used to know his father. Come, take my arm and we shall make a great fuss at the entrance to the drawing room. Nothing warms a man's heart so much as having a beautiful lady on his arm when he enters a room."

She could not have refused him even had she wanted to. There was so much command tempered with an infinite quantity of goodwill that it was with some pleasure she accepted his invitation.

Sir Edgar was as good as his word, and their joint arrival occasioned a great deal of notice. Her host's voice soon commandeered the attention of the entire chamber as he proclaimed he had found a prize in the entrance hall and all because he would arrive late. Damme, was he not a fortunate man?

This speech might have brought a blush to Fenella's cheeks had he not immediately directed an enthusiastic welcome to the entire assemblage with a sincere and quite boisterous hope that they would all enjoy the victuals he had laid out on his terrace for them. "So long as you are under my roof, there will be plenty of food, wine, gaming, and even dancing—if the ladies wish for it."

With such a warm beginning, dinner proved a delightful affair conducted under the careful eye of an expert butler and several footmen. All had the pleasure of partaking of an excellent meal beneath a waning August sun.

The wine, as promised, flowed freely, which soon had the travelers laughing and talking to one another vivaciously, if not always discreetly. More than once, Fenella heard Perryn's laughter. Only with a strong measure of restraint did she keep her gaze from straying to where he was seated at the long table.

Earlier, she had decided on a particular strategy by which she hoped to keep her heart safe. She intended, once each day's collecting was complete, to keep herself at as safe a distance from Perryn as she could possibly manage. Thus far, she had succeeded admirably.

When dinner was concluded, the ladies withdrew to refresh themselves and to enjoy a cup of tea quite apart from the gentlemen. Fenella conversed at length with Lady Burnhill about their shared pleasure of the pianoforte, discussing a great variety of music.

"I should dearly love to hear you play, Miss Trentham."

Fenella demurred. "I am not nearly so proficient as my love of the instrument ordinarily should dictate. I would recommend Miss Almington or Miss Keele if you want to hear a truly superior performance. Otherwise I shall reiterate that I play almost strictly for my own pleasure."

"That I comprehend perfectly, my dear. I was always a

trifle too nervous to perform well publicly." She glanced in the direction of the hall. "I believe it is time to set up the card tables, for I hear the gentlemen coming to us. You will excuse me?"

"Of course."

Fenella removed herself to the windows, which overlooked the vista to the north, in anticipation of Perryn once more being within her sphere. The chamber soon began bustling with several servants engaged in rearranging tables and chairs, which coincided with the arrival of the gentlemen, which in turn offered another layer of protection. The ladies quickly created a third barricade as they began their usual greetings and flirtatious sallies.

No doubt Perryn would find himself accosted by one of his three favorites before ever she encountered him. For that reason, she contented herself with enjoying an exquisite skyline of rolling hills covered in beech trees, all cast in a lavender glow of twilight. She lost herself in the delight of the beauty before her of an evening sky not yet dark and a scattering of twinkling stars.

"Did you enjoy the soup?"

Fenella whirled around. "Perryn!" she cried. However had he managed to navigate past so many servants, chairs, and ladies? She glanced beyond him and saw both Mrs. Sugnell and Mrs. Millmeece were frowning heavily at her.

He smiled in a rather silly manner, which led her to believe at once that he was in his altitudes. He shushed her with a finger to his lips. "I believe I trod on more than one foot coming to you."

"I can well believe it."

"Are you much fatigued from our journey today?" He clasped his hands behind his back and rocked on his heels.

She withheld her smiles. She had not seen him so bosky in some time. "A little, I suppose."

"I have not seen you since this afternoon, and you did

not even greet me before dinner. Have I offended you, Fennel?"

"No, not in the least." She could hardly tell him she had been avoiding him to a purpose.

"I am relieved." He sighed and let his gaze drift over the hills beyond. "Dashed pretty! But, by God, I believe I have had a deal too much wine." He then laughed. "Do I seem half-foxed, in your opinion?"

"Yes," she answered succinctly.

His smile grew lazy once more. "Well, I suppose I am. But before I forget completely, I did have a purpose in addressing you, but what was it?" He thought for a moment. "Ah, yes. Have you perchance devised a suitable idea of our collection? I believe we ought to begin very soon. From what I have been able to glean, the entire party has a march on us."

"How well I know it. But to answer your question, I have been unable to think of anything I believe will suffice. I am hoping a night of sleep will produce an idea of merit. What of you? Have you a notion or two to contribute?" She smiled a little, for she doubted very much he had given the matter a second thought once his coach turned up the manor drive.

He chuckled softly. "Good God, no." He lowered his voice. "I suppose I ought to have exerted myself a little, but the deuce take it, Fennel, I should by far prefer drinking the vile waters of Bath to collecting anything."

She chuckled. "I thought as much."

He turned back to the room, casting his gaze about the chamber, then squinted. "I see Mrs. Sugnell is signaling to me. I am to be her partner at whist this evening."

"You had best go to her at once, then, particularly since she is waving so frantically. If she does not have a care, she will sprain her wrist."

He leaned close to her, far more closely than he ought.

"Jealous?" he whispered, his words flowing over her neck. A spattering of gooseflesh rippled down her side.

She gave him a gentle push, which nearly sent him toppling over. He righted himself, chuckling all the while. "You, my lord, have indeed had a great deal too much of Sir Edgar's port."

"So I have, which will make me very bad at whist tonight." He scowled suddenly. "I only hope Mrs. Sugnell is not carrying her fan, for I am certain every time I misplay my cards she will strike me with it."

"Go to her then, Perryn. She has begun to pout."

"Ah, well, there is nothing for it, I suppose."

She watched him weave his way across the room. An odd shiver passed through her. His present state put her instantly in mind of having encountered him in the center of his yew maze. She found herself drawn back momentarily into all those extraordinary memories, of first being accosted by him and afterward falling into his embraces as easily as diving into a calm lake. She had felt as though she was hurtling toward a fate destined for her from the time he dropped that bottle of champagne on the grass at her feet.

But it would not do to be dwelling on such hopeless things. The sight of Mr. Silverdale waving for her to come to his table was a happy relief. She joined him immediately and found they would be playing against Sir John and Miss Keele.

"There will be the devil to pay," he whispered to her as he helped her to take her seat. "Miss Keele is reputed the finest player of us all."

Fenella nodded to the young lady, who in turn inclined her head. Miss Keele was an attractive, elegant young woman of superior intelligence, and in her hazel eyes was a keenness that she quite admired. She whispered in return, "Then I fear we shall lose, Mr. Silverdale, but not without doing battle first!"

The games progressed, enlivened to a great degree by the introduction of an extremely fine East India Madeira, which further loosened the tongues and the laughter of those assembled. Occasionally, she would glance in Perryn's direction and more than once watched as Mrs. Sugnell reached across the table and rapped his knuckles with her fan.

After a time, Fenella brought forward her own dilemma about a collection. Miss Keele, though refusing to reveal the nature of her own, was willing to offer a great number of suggestions ranging from knives, which might do well at auction, to tatting shuttles. Sir John was about to add to her recommendations, but his attention was suddenly diverted away from the subject at hand when Lady Burnhill, having apprehended his inclinations, placed a sampling of very fine chocolates at his elbow.

"I have perished and am now in Paradise," he announced, surveying the plate. After some deliberation, he chose a piece, which he savored as one tasting the food of the gods. "A hint of almond and rum. What perfection! I vow I am in love with Sir Edgar's wife. Sir Edgar?"

"Yes, Sir John?"

"I am in love with your wife. I intend to elope with her if she is in possession of any more of these chocolates!"

"In which case, man," Sir Edgar retorted in his booming voice as he sorted his cards, "I shall give any remaining to the servants, for I, too, am in love with my wife and mean to keep her!"

A roll of laughter passed about the room, along with any number of complaints from players who took their cards more seriously than others.

Mr. Silverdale laid down a card and Fenella groaned, for she could do nothing with it. At the same time, he said, "What about collecting ribbons or something that could be found in the shops along the way?"

Fenella could only laugh. "My dear Mr. Silverdale, can

you actually see Perryn marching in his strong manner into a local shop and begging to see a display of ribbons?"

Even Miss Keele was drawn away from her cards to laugh heartily at this remark.

Fenella sighed as she glanced again at Perryn, who appeared to be expressing some opinion or other to Mr. Almington in his forceful manner. "I begin to fear there is nothing that will suit the pair of us. Mrs. Almington should not have made us partners."

Miss Madeley chanced to pass by at that moment, for whom Sir John was known to have a mild *tendre*. "I know what I would collect, were I able," he said, pressing a hand to his chest.

"And what would that be?" Fenella queried, arranging her cards in a more comfortable order, for her hand had begun to ache.

"That lady's kisses."

All three of them turned to view Miss Madeley pass from the chamber. She was a completely elegant creature and certainly deserving of the sigh which fell from the lips of both Sir John and Mr. Silverdale.

"I think it wholly unfair so much beauty should have come to nest in but one woman," Miss Keele remarked. She was not herself an antidote, but her indifferent light brown hair and brown eyes were no match for Miss Madeley's exceeding loveliness.

Fenella resumed scrutinizing and arranging her cards. "I only wish it were possible to take your suggestion, Sir John, for I am persuaded a collection of kisses would appeal to Lord Perryn mightily."

Since at that moment Mrs. Sugnell trilled her laughter as the marquess lifted her fingers to his lips, the players at her table added their general agreement.

Four

On the following morning, Fenella awoke to the white ceiling of her bedchamber. The hour was early, only a little past dawn. In the distance, she could hear a rooster crowing strongly as though some of his brood had not arisen swiftly enough. Images flitted past her sleepy mind, yet a strange quickening tensed her heart.

Kisses.

Perryn had teased her once about collecting her kisses, and even Sir John had said he would be happy to collect Miss Madeley's kisses. Of course, gentlemen were prone to think of such things even at the oddest hours and moments, but the notion would not leave her.

She thought of Perryn anew. What would keep a rogue interested for a full fortnight? She could not give him her kisses, as he had so absurdly suggested, and she had no interest in somehow allowing him to collect kisses from winsome village maids. However, what if there was a way to collect them without actually touching lips?

As though she had conjured up the notion from the beginning of time, she knew exactly what to do and what their collection for the auction must be. The idea was so simple and in its way so earthy yet oddly pleasing that she was overcome by a sensation of triumphant delight. Perryn would embrace the notion completely, of that she was certain. Not for her partner to be bored during a trip through lovely Somerset!

She leaped from her bed and summoned her maid. Now that she knew what their collection would be and because she had already lost an entire day, she felt the need to be going.

An hour later, she was completely coiffed and dressed and pacing the chamber. "Are you telling me it is only seven? I had no idea I had arisen so early. Do you happen to know in what bedchamber Lord Perryn is ensconced?"

Betsy chuckled. "There is not a maidservant in the manor who is not in possession of that particularly fascinating information."

Fenella turned toward her and laughed outright. "I hope he never learns of it!" she cried. "For then his conceit would surely know no bounds. Only tell me where I might find him."

She nodded toward the door. "Across the hall."

"You mean *directly* across the hall?" Fenella was dumbfounded.

"Aye," Betsy responded.

"Mrs. Almington is more determined than I had thought possible."

"So it would seem."

"Very well," Fenella said. She could not quite credit what she was about to do, yet at the same time she felt determined on her course. In a swift, firm motion, she crossed the several feet of old, planked flooring and rapped loudly on his lordship's door.

A moment later, the Marquess of Perryn, a questioning frown on his brow, opened his door to her. She was taken aback, for a strip of shaving soap was lathered over a portion of his cheek. The remainder of his face was whiskered faintly.

"What the devil?" he cried. "Are you all right? Fennel, is anything amiss?"

"I am perfectly well, thank you. Actually, I was hoping to

hurry you along if I might. We ought to be leaving quite soon, as quickly as possible, for we have much to do today."

He shook his head, wiping his fingers on a towel slung over his shoulder. "You know, you gave me a start. I am not used to such sharp rappings on my door. I thought perhaps one of the chimneys had caught fire."

"If I gave cause for alarm I do apologize, but it did require some degree of pluck to approach your door. For that reason I may have knocked far too soundly. However, I also thought it likely I would need to awaken you."

"I had intended to ride out for a time before breakfast."

"I fear you will not be able to do so. We must be going."

"You begin to frighten me. I have never seen you in this particular state before."

Fenella peered closely at his left cheek. "You have a very heavy beard, do you not?" She reached up and gently touched his face. "Scratchy."

"Some ladies prefer it," he countered, smiling wickedly.

When he leaned provocatively against the edge of the door, she felt it prudent to draw back, if but a little. Only then did she realize he was wearing but his nightshirt over a pair of breeches. "Do you mean to flirt with me at so early an hour?" she asked, feeling a blush rise on her cheeks.

"You were the one fondling me," he countered.

"I merely touched your face, curious about your whiskers."

"A man generally needs far less encouragement."

She shook her head and groaned. "You are quite hopeless. I intend to descend the stairs and have your coach brought round. Would you care for coffee for the journey and something to eat? I have no doubt whatsoever that Sir Edgar's cook would be more than obliging, excellent creature that she is."

"At the very least you owe me an entire vat of coffee, although how I am expected to drink it safely on these country roads is beyond me."

"What gammon!" she cried. "When your coach is as well sprung as it is! However, I will see you have all the coffee you can desire and a little nourishment as well. Now, do hurry, Perryn." She then smiled. "For I am promising you a vast deal of amusement today if you will oblige me."

"I like the decided twinkle in your eye, Fennel. I vow I am intrigued of the moment and not half so impatient with you as I was. What manner of amusement, if I may be so bold as to inquire?"

She could not keep from laughing. "A great deal of kissing," she whispered.

More than one reaction tumbled over his features—surprise, confusion, and finally disbelief. "I vow I am astonished. And just who will I be kissing—although I tell you now I should be vastly content were it you."

She chuckled. "I shan't tell you, at least not for the present. Now do be quick! We lost an entire day yesterday in our dull wittedness, and I intend for us to make up for it today."

"Oh, very well," he complained. "I shall not be much above fifteen minutes." He then closed the door.

Fenella returned to her bedchamber just long enough to gather up her bonnet, a shawl against the morning chill, her reticule, and Betsy's sewing box. Afterward, she hurried down the stairs to make arrangements for a small hamper of food and a large flask of coffee to be prepared for herself and her companion.

Twenty minutes later, as the coach was bowling down the lane in a general westerly direction toward Burrington, Perryn leaned forward to sip his coffee with great care. Thus far, he had succeeded in not spilling even a drop of the rich brew, for indeed, his coach was extremely well-sprung. However, Fenella still moved her skirts and half boots out of harm's way.

"Excellent coffee—and I do thank you—only tell me,

when is all this kissing supposed to begin? So far I have seen none of it."

"There will be plenty to satisfy even your appetite, I promise you, but you will have to be patient."

He narrowed his gaze at her. Sealing the flask, he removed an apricot tartlet from the hamper. "You mean to keep me in suspense then?"

"Yes, of course, for as long as possible."

"You have determined to be cruel today. I can see it in your eyes."

She chuckled. "Actually, I have little doubt that were I to attempt to explain my particular idea for our collection, *which will involve any number of kisses,* your attention would quickly falter and you would set to yawning at me again as you did yesterday. I think it a far better notion that you participate as the day progresses."

"Now I do feel like yawning."

Fenella merely laughed at him and, opening the hamper, withdrew a slice of bread, soft and fresh from having emerged from the oven early that morning, and overlaid it with several thin slices of ham. She suggested he do the same. The excellence of the fare brought a contented light to his eye. It gave Fenella leave to turn her gaze to the countryside, which was exquisite.

The first part of the itinerary had the supreme advantage of taking the entire party on a circuit at least a third of the way around the lovely Mendips in Somerset. The hills were nearly five and twenty miles in length, Burrington being near the westernmost edge. The road first led to Blagdon through deep woods, a pretty drive enjoyed primarily in silence as Perryn alternately sipped his coffee, savored the ham, and ate a second apricot tartlet.

The hamlet came into view at last, but the coach barely slowed as the equipage passed through the village. "Why do we not stop?" he asked, frowning. "I thought you were most anxious to begin our collection, and I have grown weary of waiting for the first of the kisses you have promised me."

Fenella could not keep from smiling. "You are the most absurd man. As it happens, I gave orders to your coachman only to rein in the horses if there appeared to be a prominent shop in the village. I must conclude he did not perceive one suitable to our needs."

"What precisely are our needs?"

"Supplies for our collection, of course."

"I cannot imagine what supplies we would need for a collection of kisses. I begin to think you have been gammoning me all this while merely to disrupt my ride and my breakfast. What exactly comprises this collection?"

She shrugged. "And since when do you give a fig what we collect?"

"I may think the whole of Mrs. Almington's outing quite tiresome," he countered, scowling, "but I still hope we may not disgrace ourselves."

She chuckled. "Then you will have to trust me a little."

"I think you are being ridiculous in not telling me."

"Drink more of your coffee. You are out of reason cross and I will not be persuaded to tell you merely because you come the crab."

He grumbled but did as he was bid. For the next mile and a half, silence reigned within the coach, but quite soon the coachman began to slow and the village of Burrington came into view.

"Ah, here is an adequate shop," she said.

When the footman had let down the steps, Perryn alighted and turned politely to hand her down. She took his hand, wishing his mere touch would not set her heart to beating as quickly as it did. If only she could be rid of her ridiculous *tendre,* she might actually become accustomed to traveling with him.

The shop, though not large, was supplied with the one article she needed most. Perryn watched, scowling further still, as she began perusing a variety of silk ribbons. Glancing at the grimace overspreading his features, she chuckled. "Indeed, I beg you will trust me, Perryn."

She selected ribbons that were at least two inches in width, which she felt would be sufficiently wide for her purposes. When she was satisfied with the quantity of ribbons, as well as several feet of a very fine, thin paper in which she would need to wrap them once they had been properly adorned, she then inquired of the clerk, "Have you any rouge, perchance?"

The older man behind the counter, of staid demeanor and sporting an old-fashioned, heavily powdered wig, appeared quite shocked. "Of course not," he responded politely, if a trifle stiffly.

Perryn whispered to her over her shoulder. "Good God, Fennel, you will give our poor rustic here a fit of apoplexy. Whatever do you want with rouge?"

"Hush," she responded, frowning him down. To the clerk, she smiled and said, "Then the ribbons and paper will have to do. Thank you, sir."

When she attempted to pay for her purchase, however, Perryn was quickly before her. "Allow me."

"How very kind of you, my lord," she murmured, accepting the tied package from the shopkeeper with a slight inclination of her head. Having used a more formal address to thank Perryn, however, caused the clerk's eyes to bulge anew. Fenella thought it wise to hurry the marquess from the shop.

Once out-of-doors, Perryn sidled up to her. *"Rouge?"* he queried again.

Fenella merely smiled. "Do you mean to frown me down as well?" she asked playfully.

"I would not dare," he returned. As he once more handed her up into the carriage, he inquired, "But what the deuce do you require rouge for? Do not tell me you think your complexion in the least need of it, for you always have the prettiest color to your cheeks even when you are not blushing, although I vow I see your cheeks flooding with color even now. Do my compliments embarrass you?"

"Your flirting does. You are quite notorious, you know."

"You were the one attempting to purchase rouge in so outlandish a place as Burrington!"

"Oh, stubble it!" she returned, settling once more into her seat and arranging her skirts. "You always have some manner of justification for your conduct—as though it is all my fault, or any other lady's fault, that you must flirt so outrageously."

"And by this do I apprehend that you hope to instruct me on just how I should behave?"

"Good heavens, no! You are already perfectly aware that you should be more circumspect. It is merely the *continuing* in your conduct that never ceases to astonish me."

He called to Thomas and the coach once more took to the highway. "You have diverted me again from the point. Only tell me, why do you need rouge? I must believe it is somehow connected to our collection—about which I am beginning to believe you have deceived me, since I have yet to enjoy a single kiss."

She ignored his complaints. "I shall give you a hint," she said, as the coach gathered speed, "if you like."

"Please."

"You gave me the idea yourself yesterday. You have but to search your mind for it."

He was perplexed for some time then said, "I can only recall suggesting spiders and other ridiculous objects."

"Perhaps it is spiders."

"No, that would be impossible. I saw your expression when I but mentioned our many-legged friends. I was certain you meant to swoon, but you disappointed me."

"It is not spiders," she admitted.

"Good," he responded. "For I could not begin to imagine just how you would connect kissing to a collection of spiders."

He tried for some few minutes to discover just which of his other ideas had inspired her, but finally threw up his hands. "You are being abominably stubborn!" he cried.

Still, she refused to tell him. She could see that for all his pretense at annoyance, he was content, perhaps even amused by her restraint. She thought she was beginning to understand him a little.However, as she began to arrange the ribbons in a pattern of color that appealed to her and began making notes on a sheet of paper which she withdrew from her reticule, Perryn eyed her warily. "You are not going to force me to assist you in making up a dozen bonnets, or some such nonsense, are you?"

She opened her eyes very wide. "What an intriguing notion! I begin to think we would do well to overturn my idea entirely and set to making hats! Do but think how very much even a single bonnet would fetch at the auction if it were known that a rogue had had a hand in the design of it."

He snorted. "You are trying my patience sorely, you know."

She merely laughed and continued to enjoy the suspense in which she was holding him captive.

The next several hamlets and villages also confessed astonishment at her request to purchase a jar of rouge, but upon entering the ancient if rather small town of Axbridge at the southern edge of the Mendips, she hoped for a greater success. The town consisted of a very long, winding street opening onto a square. Within a nearby shop, she found the very article she was seeking and decided to purchase two jars, which further astonished her partner.

Returning to the coach, she proclaimed, "Now we may begin."

As Perryn once more took up his seat opposite her, he glanced warily at the articles held in her hands. "Yes, but what precisely are we to do with ribbons and rouge?"

"I will show you. Pray have your coachman hold the horses for the present."

"Thomas," he called out. "We are not leaving just yet."

"Aye, m'lord."

Fenella opened the first jar, wondering what he would think of her idea. After placing a liberal amount of rouge on her lips, she brought a light green ribbon to her mouth a few inches from the top edge and, with careful placement, kissed the silk firmly. She then handed the ribbon to him and showed him the imprint. "Do you remember?" she queried. "You said you wished to collect my kisses."

He took the ribbon and stared at the impression, then laughed. "Do you mean to kiss all these ribbons?"

"No," she cried, laughing as well. "We are both to collect kisses at the villages and towns through which we travel. Each ribbon will represent a place, whose name I intend to embroider at the top of the ribbon as we go along."

He huffed a sigh. "Are you telling me these are all the kisses I am to expect on our journey? These reddish things pressed onto strips of fabric?" He grimaced at the ribbon he held in his hands. "I have been humbugged!"

She pouted along with him. "I fear it is all too true—and I am deeply sorry to offer you so much disappointment."

"You have used me grievously ill," he continued. "And worse—you are making sport of me!"

She could only smile contentedly. "Come! Do you not think it an excellent idea?"

"Your earlier hints held so much promise that I cannot help but be disillusioned. However, if you mean for perfect strangers to kiss these ribbons, I only wonder if you realize how scandalous this is."

"This? From you?"

His smile was crooked. "I am not wholly without scruples."

She lifted her chin a trifle. "Well, I do not give a fig whether our collection is praised or despised. I merely wanted to do something unique which would have an excellent chance of raising a proper sum at an auction and which would not bore you to tears. You have but to tell me you do not find the idea wearisome and I promise you I shall be quite content!"

"I suppose it is better than hunting for beetles or some such nonsense."

"I see you are coming round. But come with me, and I will show you just how the business is to be managed—after which you will be better able to judge for yourself whether my idea has merit or not. If you will be so kind as to instruct Thomas to take us to the inn—The Oak House, I believe—then your servants may enjoy some refreshment and I shall show you just how and why I am persuaded that our collection, contrary to your doubts, will flourish. Besides, I find I am in need of sustenance."

He withdrew a watch from the pocket of his waistcoat. "Good God, Fennel, do you know it is after twelve?"

She could not help but smile. "Admit you have been so well entertained that you have failed to notice the passage of time."

He merely grunted, then gave orders for the coach to be driven to The Oak House.

Once within the inn, and after a fine nuncheon had been ordered, Fenella excused herself to lay her proposals before the innkeeper. At first, the landlord was astonished, but upon placing the idea before his wife—and after she had had a chance to actually rest her gaze upon the Marquess of Perryn, to whom the ribbon kisses were to be offered—that lady smiled. "I should think it my duty to help the beggars of Bath in any manner possible. Such a pitiful sight it were when I visited my sister there Michaelmas last. I see no harm in a little rouge and kissing of ribbons."

Fenella thanked her warmly then requested that the entire nature of the kissing-ribbons be kept as a great secret from any of their party, who would soon be arriving at Axbridge. She explained the details of the competition and received from that lady her promises that she and her maids would be as silent as the grave. At once, she clucked her tongue and assembled all the serving maids who, in a great flock, descended eagerly upon Lord Perryn.

From that moment, Fenella merely stood back and watched the transformation of her quite silly idea into the perfect entertainment for a rogue. Because he delighted in the attentions of women, the ladies were quickly at ease in his company. Before long, the rouge was being passed about liberally and the first ribbon began wearing its scandalous pattern along the complete length.

When all the ladies had kissed the pretty green silk, Fenella sat down to dine with Perryn. His spirits were elevated and he lifted a glass of claret to her. "I begin to think you the cleverest lady of my acquaintance, for I will confess I have never spent an hour so happily engaged."

"Thank you," she murmured, lifting her glass to him as well.

"And to think I was certain, save for the pleasure of your company, I would have to *endure* this fortnight instead of enjoy it. You have my eternal gratitude, Fennel!"

Upon commencing the next portion of their journey, which would take them to Brent Knoll, Fenella cut the fine, thin paper she had purchased at Burrington into several long strips of the same width as the ribbons. She then carefully wrapped the saluted green ribbon in one of the strips of paper, cut the paper to the same length, rolled it up quite carefully, secured the ends with a silk pin, and stored the whole of it in Betsy's workbox. "I will need a much larger container before we are returned to Bath, of that I am certain."

"You astonish me. From whence does all this enthusiasm arise?"

She merely looked at him and smiled.

At the next hamlet, not far from Axbridge, Fenella descended with a blue ribbon and one of the jars of rouge in hand. She entered the alehouse with Perryn and gave him the ribbon. He immediately addressed the landlord, who brought forward three serving maids and two younger girls who proved to be his daughters. Before long, the ladies were giggling, particularly when Perryn began helping the youngest put rouge on her lips. The eldest serving maid, perhaps of an age with Fenella, begged him to do the same for her.

What rogue, desirous of keeping his reputation, would refuse so pretty a request? Fenella watched him touch her lips and the oddest sensation pierced her, a feeling she was loath to put a name to except that she knew a sudden, intense desire to pull caps with the audacious female who was even now smiling provocatively into Perryn's eyes. Worse still, his expression became quite knowing. Oh, dear.

When the young woman whispered into Perryn's ear, Fenella could watch no more. The nature of the sensation she was experiencing was so profound that she felt obliged to leave the inn. Once outside, she drew several deep breaths. For all her foresight in having conceived of and planned the execution of their collection, she had not contemplated even once just how she would feel were the requests for kisses to become in any manner flirtatious. She felt foolish for so many reasons, not least because she could never have a true interest in Perryn. So why must she be overset by the sight of some country miss attempting to engage him in a flirtation?

She glanced up and down the High Street and saw several young men, local bucks by all accounts, had gathered at the smithy's. The familiar sound of a hammer falling on iron rent the air time and again. A new notion presented itself. She had at first thought she would assist Perryn in collecting the ladies' kisses exclusively, but she now realized there was no particular reason why she could not acquire a few herself.

With this happy thought in mind, she returned to the coach and secured another blue ribbon, of a slightly darker shade than Perryn's, and the second pot of rouge.

* * *

After another quarter hour had passed, Perryn grew fatigued with the attempts of the eldest of the ladies to steal him away to a private parlor and finally disengaged himself completely from all of the females present. He bid them good day, but upon quitting the alehouse found Miss Trentham absent from his coach.

Gently laying the ribbon on the seat, he called to his coachman. "Thomas, do you know where Miss Trentham has gone?"

"I can see her from the box, m'lord. She is but a hundred yards, at the smithy's."

"What the devil is she doing there?" He, of course, did not expect his coachman to answer, but instead rounded the back of the coach and was astonished by the sight before him. He saw only the top of Miss Trentham's pink bonnet, for she was completely surrounded by gentlemen and local rustics. But to what purpose he could not imagine, unless—

"Good God," he murmured.

He hurried down the dusty street. The laughter of the gentlemen rolled in waves to the sky. There seemed to be an uproar of merriment the like he had never before heard.

When he arrived and begged to be admitted into the deep circle of spectators, he found Miss Trentham in the very center, putting a generous amount of rouge onto the lips of a handsome buck who was staring quite rakishly into her eyes. Miss Trentham, to either her credit or her naïveté, seemed completely unaware of his roguish interest in her, and was concentrating quite studiously on the application of the rouge.

He glanced at the ribbon which the rather burly smithy was holding daintily in his hands, and saw Miss Trentham had collected an entire row of kisses thus far. A further scrutiny of the crowd of men proved what he suspected. She had been putting rouge on each of them, to a man—

including the strongly muscled smithy—all of whom appeared as though they had been eating raspberries! In other circumstances, and had he not been acquainted so nearly with Miss Trentham, he might have been amused or even hugely entertained by the sight of a beautiful lady having come a-begging for kisses for her charity ribbon. However, he *was* acquainted with *the lady,* and he knew quite well what the young buck was doing whose lips were now ready to make the imprint. Taking the ribbon from the smithy, he overlaid Miss Trentham's hand with the ribbon then placed his rouged lips on the cornflower blue silk.

Damme! He was kissing her fingers through the silk!

And if he did not much mistake the matter, giving them an encouraging squeeze as well. How did he know? He would have done the same thing!

What the devil was she thinking to have so exposed herself to the improper attentions of at least a score of men?

Once the buck released her hand, ever so slowly, Perryn stepped forward. "There you are, Miss Trentham!" he called out forcefully. "I see you have succeeded in your efforts here, but I came to tell you we must away. We are expected at Brent Knoll by three."

A disappointed groan rose from the assembled bucks who had not as yet had the pleasure of wearing her rouge, but Miss Trentham thanked them all quite graciously and said the gentlemen of Weare would be forever remembered for their generosity in helping her to raise money for the beggars of Bath.

"Yes, yes," he said, taking strong hold of her arm. "But we must be going."

"Why do you hold my arm so forcefully?" she asked, as he drew her quickly away from the crowd. "You cannot be thinking I was in the least danger?"

"Did that man, or did he not, squeeze your fingers after he kissed your ribbon?"

"Of course he squeezed them. I would have expected

nothing less, since I was so scandalously patting rouge onto his lips."

"And you are not disturbed?"

"Were you disturbed when the eldest of your admirers whispered in your ear what I can only presume was an invitation?"

"I was annoyed."

"Not flattered? I believe you are telling whiskers, m'lord, for I saw your expression. You fairly *leered* at her."

By now they had reached the coach and he handed her up. "Very well, I was flattered," he confessed, following after. He retrieved his kissing-ribbon from off the seat before sitting down. "But the cases are different—quite different! It may not be in the least fair, but what a man might do with impunity a lady may not!" The coach began to move forward again.

She had been attempting to lay out another strip of paper, but at these words she paused and stared at him. "You cannot be serious?" she cried. "I vow, Perryn, you speak as an old woman might. These are modern times. Ladies are not so greatly constrained as once they were."

"I would not quarrel were you an older, married woman, but you are yet a maiden. You risk much in such conduct."

"I believe all I am risking of the moment is having to listen to your strictures on the subject. I never felt for a moment in the least danger, partly because your servants were but a handful of yards away. In addition, I knew quite well you would not be spending the entire afternoon in the inn, even if the company was charming. I saw an opportunity and I took it. That a party of young men who had been hunting nearby chanced to arrive at the smithy's because one of their horses had thrown a shoe was unexpected, but quite manageable."

With this, he realized, he must be satisfied. She was right. He did not truly believe that even for a moment she had been in the least peril. "I suppose it is a little different for you," he responded, "since you are not in the first blush of youth and you certainly have a great deal of town bronze about you."

"Do you mean this as a compliment?" she queried.

"I suppose I do."

"Then I tremble at the notion of hearing a criticism if this is your idea of a compliment—*not in the first blush of youth.* Cowhanded, Perryn—and this from you!"

He knew his mouth had fallen agape. For a moment he had thought himself in the midst of a terrible row. Instead, he could see by the twinkle in her eye that however much she appeared to be quarreling with him, she had instead been teasing him.

He chuckled. "Good God. That was quite unpardonable, and I do beg your pardon. I hope you do not mean to make it generally known that my ability to do the pretty has fallen so flat."

"In turn," she added, smiling ruefully, "I hope you will not make it generally known that I passed a good part of our journey putting rouge on the lips of several quite handsome young men."

He met her gaze and offered a smile in return. "I will say this much—I believe I am indebted to you, for between Axbridge and Weare I have come to thoroughly enjoy our caravan."

"I for one have not seen you so cheerful since you were kissing Mrs. Sugnell's fingers at cards last night."

"Do you watch all my follies?"

"No, just the ones to which I am directed by several others equally struck by your audacity."

Perryn could only laugh. He watched her once more begin the delicate process of protecting the kissing-ribbons by rolling them up in long strips of paper and felt his admiration for her swell. Damme, he liked her. He liked that she teased him instead of coming the crab, he liked that she had taken such pains to concoct a collection that would appeal to him, he liked that she had not hesitated in approaching the local men with a ribbon of her own. Perhaps he had felt a bolt of jealousy at the sight of the men crowded about her, but he had also felt proud that she had commanded them all so easily.

He liked that last night, whenever his attention had strayed to her table so very far removed from his, she was always much animated and, as a result, those around her were as well. Worst of all, he liked that not only had she intruded on his shaving regimen this morning, but that she had felt so comfortable with him she had actually reached up to touch his face. There had been nothing flirtatious intended on her part, save a curiosity about his whiskers, but the openness and simplicity of the act had worked in him strangely. He had in that moment experienced the most ridiculous and wicked impulse to drag her into his bedchamber and to kiss her anew.

Good God! When had he become such a moonling to have his head turned so easily by her? This would not do, not by half. He had no intention of singling her out merely because he felt drawn to her. He knew what love was, for he had loved once before, and this was not it! All these silly, moonling sentiments were transient, he was sure of it! Only why the devil must she be so pretty?

Five

"What a lovely house," Fenella remarked as the coach drew before Woodseaves, the home of Mr. and Mrs. Chebsey, their hosts for the evening. "I suppose we must be somewhere between East Brent and Brent Knoll." She felt weary from traveling, even though the day had been pleasant in every respect. The weather had smiled on their journey, for the sun had shone most of the morning and early afternoon, and the roads had been dry for five days straight.

"I believe you are right," he responded, releasing her hand once she descended the coach.

She turned to one of the liveried footmen and asked him to retrieve Betsy's workbox. After receiving the box from the servant, she was about to bid Perryn a good afternoon when the front door opened and Miss Madeley stepped across the threshold.

"Oh," she cried, evidently surprised. "I heard a carriage on the drive and thought Miss Keele had arrived at long last. Your carriage and hers were to be the last two to reach Woodseaves."

"We are rather late," Fenella said.

"Working diligently on your collection?" Though she addressed the gentle query to them both, her gaze rested upon Perryn. Her smile was lovely, her expression all innocence. She carried a yellow parasol over her shoulder and twirled it playfully. Fenella had a sudden intuition that she had not been waiting for Miss Keele at all, but rather had found her prey—just as she had known she would.

Fenella glanced at Perryn, whose gaze was fixed on The Incomparable. A smile played at the edge of his lips and an experienced light entered his eye. She could see he was of a similar opinion. "Yes," he said in response to her question, "Miss Trentham is a difficult taskmaster and would keep me in drudgery these many hours and more."

"Indeed?" Miss Madeley flicked her gaze to Fenella, then reverted it immediately to Perryn.

Fenella lifted her brows accusingly, which caused Perryn to laugh suddenly. "Not by half, I assure you, Miss Madeley."

"You risk offending your partner, my lord," she said, smiling coquettishly. "Most impolitic. You ought to beg her forgiveness even now."

Perryn turned to Fenella with something of a flourish. "I most humbly apologize."

Fenella huffed an impatient sigh. "Oh, do stubble it, Perryn! Save your absurdities for your favorites." To Miss Madeley, she inclined her head. "If you will excuse me, I am longing to rest a trifle before dinner. However, I am very certain my Lord Perryn will be happy to continue in this strain until the early hours of the morning." She dropped a slight curtsy and moved past them.

Fenella heard a faint protest from Perryn's lips and could only smile for she had succeeded in leaving him alone with Miss Madeley—which she doubted, after journeying for so many hours together, he much fancied. However beautiful she might be, when a man was fatigued, he would not want to be standing about engaged in conversation with a hopeful young lady. A flirtation was one thing with Mrs. Sugnell or Mrs. Millmeece, but quite another when the lady before him had an eye to matrimony.

She was not surprised, therefore, when he caught up with her halfway up the stairs.

"Unhandsomely done!" he cried in a hoarse whisper. "You left me alone with her, and I had the deuce of a time excusing myself. I actually had to proclaim my fatigue."

"And are you fatigued?" she queried, continuing her ascent.

"Only a little. I had hoped to ride out for a time. I am in great want of exercise. Only now, if I am seen doing so, I shall be called to book for it!"

She chortled her glee. "Well, it was you who decided to charm her by insulting me. What did you expect me to do, ridiculous man?"

He ground his teeth in response.

"She was exquisitely attired, however," Fenella remarked. "She most certainly must have arrived several hours earlier, for her gown, of the loveliest embroidered muslin, was wholly uncreased and her blond ringlets, so charmingly gathered into a knot of curls, could not have seen a bonnet in the past two hours at the very least. And to think she had been waiting for her friend. How solicitous, to be sure."

"And you in turn may *stubble it,* Miss Trentham!"

She merely laughed in response as they parted company. A footman directed him to his bedchamber while a maidservant guided her in quite the opposite direction to hers.

"No, Mr. Silverdale, I shan't tell you," Fenella said, walking with her beaus in the garden.

"But you must tell us something," Mr. Aston intruded. "The entire party is agog to know why town, village, and hamlet from Axbridge to East Brent sported any number of inhabitants—both male and female, mind!—with berry-red lips! You and Lord Perryn have been linked with the deed, but we could bribe no one to tell us how it came about!"

"It was most singular," Sir John added. "At first I thought of the plague, but that did not fadge, given that everyone was so cheerful. Which puts me in mind—did anyone chance to partake of the pigeon pie at the alehouse at Badgworth? Quite extraordinary. Tender and flavored with a local herb which I could not quite place."

Fenella laughed, enjoying as she always did the company of her three favorites. She glanced at each in turn, at Beau Silverdale whose costumes designated him a Pink of the Ton; at Mr. Aston, whose light blue eyes were both red rimmed and dark circled; and at Sir John, who had at some point in his life determined that eating was a much less painful pastime than trying to do the pretty among the ladies of his acquaintance. She rather thought her preference for their company was based upon the incontrovertible fact that while each professed an adoration for her and would offer for her given the smallest hint in that direction, not one of them was even the smallest bit in love with her. She could be at ease, therefore, knowing she would not find love-billets beneath the door of her bedchamber, offerings of flowers, or the overt admiration generally bestowed on objects of pursuit.

As a group, they were taking a stroll beside Mrs. Chebsey's maze in the late afternoon, awaiting a call to dinner, when another party appeared at the far end of the garden—Perryn and his three ladies, Mrs. Millmeece, Lady Elizabeth, and Mrs. Sugnell. Her swains each had a succinct comment to make.

Sir John sighed almost painfully. "He has no need of stays as some of us do." His expression was mournful as he pressed his hands to his bulging stomach.

Mr. Aston grimaced. "We each drank a bottle of claret last night. He looks none the worse for it, while I vow I appear to have been shot from a cannon!"

Mr. Silverdale lifted his quizzing glass. "I daresay he has no need of buckram wadding. I do not believe I have seen so broad a pair of shoulders in my entire existence. Quite lowering!"

Fenella could only laugh. "All three of you are being quite absurd. Whatever his appeal to the married ladies of his acquaintance, do you see any of the unattached ladies, even myself, pursuing his company?"

Her beaus cheered up instantly.

"The devil, but you are right!" Sir John cried.

The parties drew near one another, and Fenella could not keep from shaking her head at Perryn. He disengaged his arms from Mrs. Sugnell and Lady Elizabeth long enough to make his bow to her.

Fenella and her swains would have passed by, but Mrs. Millmeece cried out that her demi-train was caught in the bramble, a straggling vine having invaded the finely clipped hedge. Mr. Ashton and Mr. Silverdale, being closest, began immediately to work at the delicate silk, removing thorn after thorn. Mrs. Sugnell also joined the effort, and finally even Sir John became intent on the business. Lady Elizabeth stood beside Mrs. Millmeece and gave instructions. "Sir John, do not tug on the fabric, the thorns will split a hole in it. Fanny, do stand still. Every time you move, you jerk your train in the wrong direction. Mr. Silverdale, have you pricked your finger?"

Fenella wanted to offer her assistance, but there were already too many persons engaged in the task. She took the opportunity therefore of whispering to Perryn, "I vow your ladies appear to great advantage this evening, all to please you I would suppose. There is not a head that has not been intricately coiffed, I see."

He smiled and sighed with some satisfaction. "It is a delight, is it not? They do take pains to make themselves agreeable to me, which I promise you is something of a relief from the society of a certain young lady I know who prefers to argue with me one word out of two."

Fenella laughed, but decided to press him a little. "Why do you not seek out the unmarried ladies? Do you not desire to take a wife?"

He was silent, then said, "I loved a lady once and desired more than anything to wed her, but it was not possible."

Fenella was stunned by this unexpected revelation, for in all the gossip concerning him over the years, not once had she ever heard that his heart had been touched, and that so profoundly. "Indeed?" she murmured. "What happened? I mean, whyever did you not marry her?" She saw the reluctant light in his eye and wished she had not asked him so direct a question. When he looked away from her, she knew she had trespassed upon forbidden ground.

He laughed suddenly. "Are we to begin exchanging histories now, Fennel?"

She regarded him thoughtfully. "To what purpose?" she inquired. "For myself, I believe much of the past ought to be forgotten." She hoped by saying this he might grow more comfortable. At the same time she was giving voice to her foremost concern. She would like very much to forget a certain event she had wished undone a thousand times. Perhaps he was trying to do the same.

"You are wise," he said.

Mr. Silverdale suddenly upbraided Mr. Aston. "Silk!" he exclaimed, as though instructing an imbecile. "You are removing thorns from silk! Must you be so brutal? Have you no knowledge of the general delicacy of the fabric?"

Fenella could not help but laugh, which Perryn did as well. He then turned toward her slightly. "You should marry. I vow your children would be uncommonly pretty."

She chuckled anew. "It is decided, then, that we both would be wise to enter the married state. However, I begin to wonder if we each suffer from some defect that will serve to prevent it entirely."

"You may be right," he said. Afterward he sighed, quite heavily, "Though I ought to take a wife, if for no other reason than that I must have an heir."

"You certainly will have no lack of ladies interested in assuming that particular role."

He snorted his displeasure at the thought of it.

She smiled at him. "I believe Miss Madeley, for instance, would most willingly oblige you and, really, I think it would do you a great deal of good to have children—perhaps a dozen of them."

He caught her eye, his expression challenging. "I will give *you* a dozen children if you are of a mind," he whispered.

She rolled her eyes. "Must you always play the rogue? Do you not grow fatigued with being ridiculous?"

He merely laughed as the rest of the party suddenly exclaimed their victory over the thorny vine. Fenella's beaus, upon observing how closely Perryn was standing next to her, immediately surrounded her as though to offer their protection. Perryn restrained his obvious amusement at their belated gallantry, bowed in a facetious manner, then moved away to offer his arm to Mrs. Millmeece.

As Fenella and her court began walking the opposite direction, she complimented them on their gentlemanly conduct, but Mr. Silverdale would have none of it, having another matter to address entirely.

"What did he say to you? I vow I have never seen you so mortified. Your complexion is still much heightened."

"Indeed!" Sir John cried. "Did he insult you? Even as I saw the last of the thorns from Mrs. Millmeece's gown, I heard you asking him why he must always play the rogue. What did he say?"

"Indeed, you must tell us, for I am of a mind to call him out!" Mr. Aston exclaimed.

"What?" she cried, laughing. "Mr. Aston, I did not know you were skilled with swords or pistols."

"I fear I am not," he retorted, the color receding from his usually ruddy features. "But I vow I would take a lesson or two merely to avenge your honor."

"A lifetime of lessons, I fear, would not prepare you to face Lord Perryn across a misty green at dawn. Or did you not know that he is the finest shot in England and equally as skilled with the sword?"

"Regardless, honor is honor!" Mr. Aston scoffed. However, he began tugging rather desperately at his neckcloth, which appeared to be fairly strangling him of a sudden.

She chuckled again. "I beg you will pay no heed to the Marquess of Perryn. If he appears to be tormenting me, it is to no purpose, I promise you. I fear I am to blame, since I taunt him mercilessly, not less so than when we are locked up in his coach together for hours on end."

"If you are certain," Mr. Aston said, although he began at once to breathe more easily.

"Quite certain. I make it a point never to take anything Perryn says to me seriously, nor should you. It would seem we merely enjoy plaguing one another."

After dinner, Perryn took another sip of wine. "Your port, Chebsey, is remarkable."

Mr. Chebsey was a short, rotund man whose expressive eyes bespoke his intelligence. "Your praise pleases me, for I noticed at dinner you scarcely touched the Madeira. Bad stuff, what?"

Perryn responded only with a faint smile.

"You need not spare your opinion. You cannot offend me. I should have sent to Plymouth, but m'wife did not give me notice of the party until a sennight past. Ah, well. As to the port, you have spoken correctly. Nothing finer from here to London."

Though several of the gentlemen had already returned to the ladies, five yet lingered in the dining room with their host, taking an occasional pinch of snuff from a large jar which Chebsey kept circulating around the table, and drinking as much wine as the good man brought forward. Mr. Leycott, Mr. Millmeece, and Mr. Hanford in particular were much taken with the quality and blend of his snuff. Colonel Bedrell, however, passed it quickly enough, as did Perryn. Mr. Chebsey helped himself once more to a hefty pinch, then sneezed loudly.

The subjects ranged from the twenty-year war with France that had concluded on a battlefield near the village of Waterloo to the troublesome Corn Laws, which erupted into riots now and again throughout the kingdom to the effects, both good and bad, of the radical element in the country.

Mr. Leycott turned to Perryn. "You should take a wife and set up a proper domicile in London. We need another drawing room inclined to Tory interests, and more seems to get resolved in such domestic settings than ever was concluded in Parliament."

"Believe me, Leycott, I should never take a wife for such a reason. The business of marriage appears to me to be hard enough without confusing the purpose of it."

He could only laugh. "I have but one suggestion—make certain any woman who accepts your hand is platter-faced. Otherwise she will learn all your foibles and become convinced she could have done a great deal better in her choice of husband."

Perryn once again smiled but faintly and, rather than offering a rejoinder, took a hearty swig of port. Leycott's wife, Lady Elizabeth, was a great beauty in possession of exquisite auburn hair. She had already hinted that his advances would be welcomed were he inclined to invite her into his bed. He enjoyed her sprightly if vain company, but he had no interest in taking a mistress. He was past the years of complicating his life by risking the wrath of a jealous husband.

"Is that the hour?" Chebsey cried, as the clock struck nine. "M'wife will have my head if we do not join her forthwith. She has planned a little dancing for the party tonight, but I tell any of you who wish for it I would not pass up a game of hazard or vignt-un when the ladies retire for the night."

He rose, and with that the gentlemen made their progress to the nearby drawing room from whence a pretty tune on the pianoforte could be heard being played, if but in odd fits and starts.

When Perryn reached the threshold he saw four couples were attempting to dance the quadrille—or, rather, Miss Trentham was helping Miss Keele and young Miss Almington to perfect the movements of the dance.

His gaze became fixed to the sight of her as the dancing became riotous. Mr. Aston was soon in whoops along with Miss Keele, while Miss Adbaston kept trying to bring the dancers more seriously to the task. Miss Trentham was the true force, however, as she moved from gentleman to lady and in the midst of their laughter or consternation instructed each.

He found himself charmed, doing the very thing he had meant not to do in directing his attention toward her even in the smallest possible manner. Such had been his object since having parted from her in the garden earlier that afternoon. He realized he had grown so comfortable in her society that he had almost told her a portion of his past of which very few had knowledge. An intimacy of this kind was not to be shared with a mere Miss Trentham, whose sole purpose in existence seemed to be to provoke him at every turn. Just why he had been ready to open his budget he would never comprehend, but he was determined not to let it happen again. For that reason, once he had left her to the amusing protection of her three swains, he had resolved to keep his distance from her as much as possible.

He had been succeeding quite well thus far—certainly

throughout dinner, for he had kept his gaze directed away quite purposely from that part of the table where she was sitting. He had devoted himself almost exclusively to the concerns of his hostess, who had been an amiable if rather dull dinner companion. When the ladies had risen from the table, he had studiously ignored Miss Trentham, all the while keeping his attention firmly upon Mrs. Sugnell, who did not hesitate to smile and wink at him as she left the expansive dining hall.

He had therefore thought himself safe. However, in this moment, when Miss Trentham appeared to such advantage in a gown of light pink silk with so many gathers at the back of the high waist that the entire skirt seemed to float when she moved, he found himself caught anew. Perhaps it was her smile which snared his attention as she gently encouraged the considerably younger Miss Almington to move her arms in a less elevated position, or the manner in which all of her dancing movements were an epitome of aesthetic perfection, or perhaps how attentive and animated each of the gentlemen were as she offered her instructions. Whatever the case, he realized he loved to watch her. She possessed a lightness to her spirit reflected in her graceful steps and easy manners that simply pleased him.

His present captivation drew his thoughts backward, to the hour of midnight when he had all but accosted her in Mrs. Almington's rose garden—was it only two nights ago? This same lady, who was so gently teaching Miss Almington the correct steps, was the very same one who had so scandalously slung her arm about his neck and kissed him. Even now he could not quite credit it had actually happened, particularly when she disapproved of him so strongly as she did.

A greater question rose to his mind: why was he pondering any of this? He could have no real interest in Miss Trentham beyond a light and what was proving quite uneven flirtation. No, he was far too old, his experience of womankind too vast, to be taken in by Cupid at this late hour. At seven and thirty, a full ten years Miss Trentham's senior, he had seen enough of the world to be convinced affairs of the heart were mostly humbug.

He was reminded in this moment, for reasons he could not explain, of his angel, the lady who had come to him at a time in his life when he had been at his lowest ebb. He wished he was able to recall the occasion, for he felt instinctively that were he to know more of the particulars, he would be better able to find her.

As his gaze followed Miss Trentham's weaving among the dancers, however, a new, forgotten image came to him in stunning clarity. He remembered now that he had been lying on his back, the grass cold beneath him. His angel had appeared, kneeling beside him and bending over him in such a way that the riot of curls about her face had been set in a glow by the full moon behind her—which was what had always made him think she had been an angel. Unfortunately, the same moonlight had cast her face in shadow so that even in his sudden remembering he could not distinguish a single feature clearly. Earlier recollections blended with this new one, for his very first memory of the occasion was that she had leaned down to whisper to him and to place soft, gentle kisses on his lips.

Where is your heart, my lord, that you are letting your life drift through your fingers? Do you not long for more than the mere pursuit of pleasure? I beg you will open your eyes.

Then she had disappeared or the dream had ended—or, worse still, he had simply fallen into an inebriated state of unconsciousness. Regardless, her presence that night had altered forever the course of his life. What would happen, he had often wondered, were he to find her?

In the ensuing years, he had searched for her at the local Somerset assemblies, in Bath, and in London, although what precisely he was looking for he could not say, since he had been unable to determine what she looked like or even the color of her hair. He had hoped, however, that upon meeting her or conversing with her he would know her instantly, either by the tone of her voice or her bearing, but no such good fortune had come to him. The only lady of his acquaintance who had ever remotely summoned memories of his angel was, quite surprisingly, Miss Trentham. The thought that she could be his angel, however, was ludicrous in the extreme. Where there had been infinite tenderness in his encounter with his angel, Miss Trentham had been as prickly as a pincushion.

When the impromptu practicing of the quadrille drew to a close, a country dance was announced and the process of acquiring partners began. Miss Trentham drew near at that moment, and he wondered if she might have done so because she wished to dance with him.

"I saw you staring at me," she began in her lively manner, "but I thought it best to inform you I would take it most unkindly in you if you dared to criticize my dancing."

He could only smile. She could not know how enlivened her expression was, how arch and charming, when she pretended to come the crab. Her smile betrayed her completely. "I have already been at the wrong end of your displeasure today on the stairs, if you will remember?"

"Of course. You had spoken quite abominably about me in front of Miss Madeley—taskmaster, indeed!"

"Just so. For that reason I would not dare to criticize my charming caravan partner, even if in jest. Such an offense committed once in the course of a day might be forgiven. Twice could only be considered a capital offense. I know the general temper of women to be such that I would pay for such an indiscretion the whole of tomorrow."

"I am shocked!"

"What, that I hold such an opinion?"

"No," she countered, "that you have actually been able to divine so simple a truth. We may not be as bold as your sex, but we do know how to drive a point home."

"To the hilt, at times. To the hilt."

She laughed and moved away as Sir John waved to her to take her place opposite him.

The sensation this small and quite insignificant exchange provoked within his chest, as though some great feeling were attempting to escape by means of expanding his heart, forced him to recognize his very pressing need to be anywhere but near Miss Trentham of the moment.

He espied Miss Madeley nearby and, approaching her, asked her politely to go down the dance with him. The reasons for his choice were simple: he desired neither the effusive flirtations of Mrs. Sugnell, Lady Elizabeth, or Mrs. Millmeece, nor did he wish to raise the hopes of any of the other single ladies. Miss Madeley he believed he understood to perfection.

When, however, the dance drew to a conclusion and he saw a very familiar light of triumph enter his partner's eye, he suddenly felt bored to distraction. Between Miss Trentham's ability to arouse an interest which he held in profound distrust and Miss Madeley's hunt for a handle to her name, he wished he could cry off from the entire expedition and return to Bath—or, better still, to his estates just a score of miles south of Brent Knoll. The game was too hackneyed and the one woman who intrigued him intrigued him far too much for his own good!

Later the next morning, Fenella once more took up her seat opposite Perryn in his fine coach. She held in her hands a long yellow ribbon kissed most delightfully by a dozen young gentlemen who had been hiking Brent Knoll earlier and who had just arrived at the village of Burnham-on-Sea. They had been quite happy to oblige her. She displayed the ribbon for Perryn to view, holding it wide between extended hands.

He sat down abruptly. "Yes, yes, you were more successful than I," he complained.

"How many?" she countered, demanding to see his ribbon.

He held his up, all the while grimacing.

"Two?" she exclaimed laughing. "Paltry, indeed, Perryn, particularly for a *man of your abilities.*"

"I can hardly be blamed. There were far too many protective and quite prudish *mamas* about. Once I had produced the jar of rouge, I promise you the gasp in the dining parlor was quite audible."

"Then it would seem, that for all your charm, I may have the advantage of you yet."

"You need not seem so very pleased. These same ladies could not stop speaking of you in the worst of terms. I believe one of them hinted you might even be an actress in disguise!"

"Good God," she returned, but she would not allow him to dim her triumph even in the least. "Fourteen." She waved the ribbon beneath his nose, then set to rolling it in a strip of paper with great care.

"Insufferable," he murmured, but she saw his smile.

"I have every confidence you will do better at Bridgwater. Besides, according to the itinerary there are at least two, possibly three, hamlets betwixt. Your fortunes could turn at any of these."

At the hamlet of Huntspill, Fenella emerged from the smithy's, where she had been able to gather kisses from not only the stalwart owner of the forge but his four sons as well. She hurried in the direction of the waiting coach, preparing in some delight to gloat over her success, when she noticed Perryn seated beneath a tree, surrounded by schoolgirls of a broad range of ages. The youngest, perhaps four, sat on his lap under the auspices of a plump, older woman who appeared to be in charge of the children. She was beaming and encouraging the girl, who was permitting Perryn to put rouge on her lips.

Fenella moved slowly in his direction, her desire to express her triumph dissipating entirely as she watched the confirmed rogue use his considerable charms to engage the girls and make them comfortable. When the child kissed the pretty lavender ribbon and saw the imprint of her lips, she squealed in delight as the rest of the girls clapped their approval.

Fenella felt as though her heart might burst at the sight of so much tenderness. Sudden tears started to her eyes. Was this the man who flirted so brazenly with her, who had teased her in Mrs. Almington's garden until she had kissed him, who seemed to have but a handful of redeeming qualities?

As she drew closer still, she could hear his conversation.

"What of you?" Perryn said, addressing a shy young woman who appeared to be about thirteen.

Fenella watched her blush. She was a plain girl, with hardly a feature to recommend her. "Oh, no, m'lord. I could not."

More than one of the schoolgirls snickered at her reticence, but Perryn was not so easily deterred and called her forward. "I beg you will do so, not for me nor for your friends here, but for the poor and suffering of Bath."

This gave the child pause. She considered him and his words, the struggle within her obvious in the several changes of complexion which she underwent. Finally, she squared her shoulders and stepped forward. He gave her the rouge and a small looking glass. With trembling fingers, she applied the creamy red substance and quickly but firmly placed her lips against the ribbon.

She smiled proudly through her blushes when she had completed the task.

"Well done," Perryn murmured. "And what a beautiful smile you have. I daresay I have not seen such perfect teeth in all my travels."

The blush, which had been pink enough, now turned a

fiery hue, but she summoned the courage to drop a curtsy
and to thank him for his compliment.

After bidding his audience farewell, he joined Fenella
who walked beside him to his coach. "That was a great
kindness, Perryn. You can have no notion."

"I think I do, if but a little."

She stopped him, however, and made him meet her gaze.
"You cannot know how much your encouragement will
mean to her, not just today but perhaps throughout the entire course of her life. Gentlemen center their attention
upon precisely how a lady appears. That has always been
true and always will be. But do you know what a burden
it is to us? I think not, yet I do not mean to complain, for
gentlemen have their share of trials as well. Your words to
this girl today, Perryn, will carry her farther than you can
possibly ever imagine. I am proud to call you friend in this
moment."

He seemed to struggle within himself, as though he desired to say something to her but could not find the words.
At one moment, he seemed almost angry, at another frustrated. "I believe you," he said at last. "Now, do get it into
the coach. We must be going."

She must have offended him, and yet truly she had not
meant to. However, once within the conveyance, she busied
herself with storing and labeling the ribbons so as not to
forget their origin and the subject—nay, the difficulty between them—was let drop.

Whatever his aggravation with her, for her part, Fenella
was sorry he had shown so much thoughtfulness toward
the schoolgirls, for now she must think more kindly of him
than she wished to. Indeed, since last night, when he had
danced with Miss Madeley, then Miss Keele, Miss Almington, Miss Aston, and his own court of married ladies,
she had begun wishing herself anywhere but on this caravan. She found herself longing to dance with him, but he
never asked her. He kept to his part of the room, which

was always opposite hers, and which she could only conclude was done purposefully. She should have been grateful, but it was one thing for her to decide she must stay
away from him but quite another that he should deem her
society unwelcome.

And now, to have seen him holding a child so tenderly
on his lap and then showering the homeliest girl in the
kingdom with compliments on her smile and her teeth!
Well, she felt entirely undone as she carefully stowed his
well-wrapped ribbon in Betsy's sewing box. Just as well
she had somehow offended him, for she could feel her
heart beginning to warm to him.

At the hamlet of Pawlett, Fenella collected no fewer than
thirteen kisses and was happy to tease Perryn about the
obvious failing of his charms that she should once more
be collecting more kisses than he. He cast her a challenging
glare and quit the alehouse where she was enjoying a cup
of tea and he had just finished a tankard of ale. She could
only suppose he meant to try to gather a few more kisses.

He had not been gone above five minutes when a coach
drew into the yard. A moment later, Mr. Leycott emerged
and turned to help Mrs. Almington alight. With a napkin,
Fenella carefully covered the kissing-ribbon on her lap before they arrived at the threshold. Their conversation was
much animated as they entered the room. They seemed to
be discussing roses at some length, in particular the best
way to press them.

"Say no more," she called to them, halting their conversation instantly, "Lest you inadvertently reveal the nature
of your collection to me."

"Miss Trentham," Mrs. Almington responded. "How do
you go on? I did not see you at breakfast. How does your
collection fare?" She glanced about the small table at
which Fenella was seated as though trying to discover some
evidence of it.

"Our collection is progressing very nicely, if slowly as

collections tend to do. Perryn is even now hunting for those objects which will add to it."

"I see. Oh, but a cup of tea is precisely what I require as well."

"Do join me."

Mr. Leycott ordered a tankard for himself and tea for Mrs. Almington, then excused himself. "I would have a word with Perryn. I will not be gone above a minute or two."

The ladies inclined their heads to him. Fenella was about to ask if Mr. Leycott was enjoying the journey when Mrs. Almington lowered her voice. "My dear, I am grateful he is gone, for there is something he told me earlier about which I feel I ought to warn you. It concerns Aubrey."

Fenella's heart sank. She knew precisely what her kind hostess and friend meant next to say. "How badly is he dipped?"

"Then you know?"

Fenella shook her head. "But I can guess, quite easily."

"A hundred pounds."

"Oh, dear God," Fenella murmured. "Are you certain? When? How?"

"Mr. Chebsey has a certain passion for vingt-un. Apparently your brother does as well, and several of the gentlemen did not retire to their rooms until three o'clock this morning." The tea arrived and Mrs. Almington spooned in a little sugar and cream. "He is not changed, then?"

"He has good weeks, sometimes months. Then for no apparent reason he forgets his intention to regulate his appetite for gaming and loses upward of a hundred pounds. Generally, I believe he has improved considerably, but I am quite sick at heart that just such a lapse must occur during your party."

"Was I wrong to have said anything?"

"On no account!" she cried. "I am grateful to be warned,

for now I will know what to expect the next time I see him."

Mr. Leycott, who must have merely looked up and down the street before deciding to return to the taproom, joined them at the table. "He is nowhere to be seen," he announced, then took up his place before his tankard and set to work with some enthusiasm on seeing the bottom of it.

"Where were you?" Fenella inquired, as Perryn rounded the corner of the alehouse.

"I had to wait until they were gone," he said, unfurling his ribbon quite proudly.

She scanned the ribbon and blinked in some astonishment. "Why, there must be a score of kisses here!" she exclaimed. "You have bested me, and I take it most unkindly in you."

"You shamed me. What else was I to do except pick up the gauntlet?"

"I shall remember that," she said, narrowing her eyes playfully.

"I hear a coach approaching," he said, directing his gaze to the north. "We should leave."

"I could not agree more. I sat sipping tea with Mrs. Almington and the whole time I could not move because I was hiding my ribbon on my lap!"

He led her quickly to his coach, which was awaiting them on the other side of the High Street. The equipage about which he was concerned, however, was traveling at a spanking pace and they had just climbed within, their ribbons kept out of sight, when Colonel Bedrell's coach and four pounded through the hamlet. Miss Madeley's blond curls could be seen peeping from beneath her bonnet as she turned in their direction and waved gaily at them both.

Fenella noticed that Perryn's gaze lingered. "I would

suppose, then, that you wished yourself in *another* coach at this moment?"

"Not by half. You cannot be supposing I was flirting with Miss Madeley just now? I promise you it was no such thing. Bedrell has Almington's pair of blacks, and they are so beautifully matched I could not help but admire them anew. Did you not notice?"

"What a whisker!" she cried, once more bringing forward a strip of paper and gingerly rolling up the kisses. "If you truly were looking at the horses, I vow I will eat my bonnet."

He glanced at her hat and nodded. "You may begin, for I was indeed doing just that—although you may wish to wait until we arrive at the next village. At the very least you will require a pot of tea to aid in the digestion of what I must say is a very pretty confection."

Fenella chuckled. "You can be so very absurd. However, you do realize this is no great compliment to Miss Madeley. She would certainly not like to hear you found Mr. Almington's horses more interesting than she. I think I might tell her you said as much the next time we meet— unless, of course, you own the truth." She lifted her gaze to him and waited expectantly.

He crossed his arms over his chest. "Oh, very well! I can see you are determined to force my hand. Of course I was gaping at Miss Madeley. Only a complete gudgeon would actually look at a horse when The Incomparable is about."

"I thought as much." She smiled in some pleasure. "I would give you a hint, though, unless you have some objection to hearing me, for it concerns your having danced with her last night."

"Not in the least."

"I could not help but notice that you went down two sets with Miss Madeley. Your having done so will certainly foster any number of hopes I believe that lady cherishes where you are concerned, not to mention giving rise to a more general speculation because of it as well."

"You were keeping so close a watch? I had no notion. But I fear I do not understand your scruples on the matter. Yesterday you scolded me for not making the single ladies the object of my attentions and now you are reproving me for my having done so—or so it would seem. Are you never to be satisfied?"

"But I was not suggesting you transfer your flirting charms to unmarried ladies, singling them out indiscriminately. I would never encourage you to do so. I meant for you to converse with them, discover their tastes, their opinions, their—" She got no further.

He protested with a raising of his hand and a deep yawn.

"You are utterly hopeless," she said, and the subject was let drop.

At Dunball, a village north of the town of Bridgwater, Fenella was just returning with Perryn to his coach after having collected a paltry five kisses apiece when the marquess was suddenly addressed in none too polite a tone.

"M'lord! Be ye the scoundrel what kissed my Alice?"

Fenella turned with Perryn in time to observe a large, muscular man wearing a farmer's smock bearing down on the marquess. Though Perryn was also tall and strongly built, the farmer was a veritable giant. Running after him was his wench, Alice, whose ruby lips gave evidence of Perryn's recent effort in gaining her support for their collection.

Alice hurried to place herself between the two men. Perryn did not hesitate to brace himself as he raised his fists and planted his feet an appropriate distance apart, for there could be no two opinions as to the man's intent.

"Mr. Burtle!" Alice cried. "I beg ye will heed me! His lordship did not kiss me, indeed he did not!"

"Do ye take me fer a gudgeon, Alice? I can see that ye've been kissed."

"Nay!" she cried, laughing as she turned to Perryn. "M'lord, I beg ye will show Mr. Burtle yer ribbon and the rouge."

Since Mr. Burtle's complexion was a fine shade of purple and every aspect of his countenance still menacing, Fenella felt compelled to intervene as well. "Indeed, Mr. Burtle. I am traveling with his lordship and can verify what your lady has said is true." She quickly lifted her ribbon for him to view, as well as the pot of rouge she also carried with her. "These last two kisses were from friends of yours, I believe. This from Mr. Startley, third from the bottom, and the last belongs to Mr. Charlinch."

"Be that so?" he inquired, lowering his fists and cocking his head to view the lip prints. Mr. Charlinch approached them at that moment from the direction of the alehouse, his lips as red as Alice's. He was able to corroborate his lady's assertions, and a bout of fisticuffs was consequently averted.

When Mr. Charlinch had returned to the alehouse and Mr. Burtle had offered a thousand apologies before ambling into the countryside with his dear Alice on his arm, Perryn addressed Fenella. "What do you say to a short stroll, Miss Trentham? I vow I am beginning to feel the lack of exercise, and it will not do. You are wearing half boots, so I think trailing briefly along a path or two in this pretty country would not be impracticable."

Fenella agreed readily. Hour upon hour in his coach had indeed left her limbs feeling stiff. She was herself used to riding out frequently and enjoying the pleasures of a long country walk. After stowing the ribbons carefully in the coach and informing the coachman of their intent, Perryn directed her to a path east of the inn.

They had not gone far in their attempt to explore a stone outbuilding that loomed in the near distance, when, upon turning a bend in the path, Fenella caught sight of Mr. Burtle holding his lady fair and kissing her quite passionately. They were some twenty yards distant and but half hidden by shrubbery.

"Oh, dear," she murmured. She whirled around, fairly colliding with Perryn as she begged him in a hushed whisper to retreat immediately.

"What is it?" he returned, also whispering. "What has brought such a blush to your cheeks?"

She could say nothing, but fled past him, her heart thrumming in her ears. The sight of the couple embracing so amorously had flooded her with all manner of feeling that quite stunned her. She continued quickly down the path, although she suspected Perryn had pressed on to see for himself just what had overset her.

When she had gone a considerable distance, she turned to wait for him, although some instinct told her she would be much wiser to take the remainder of the path at a run until she had gained the village once more. She tried to calm herself, but she was miserably engulfed in a longing so profound that she could not order her feet to move or her heart to slow in its fantastic pace.

Perryn emerged at last, his own expression somewhat inscrutable, although his gray eyes appeared quite dark. As he drew near, her senses sharpened. She met his gaze fully and realized he had become taken with a wholly roguish notion. She turned away, frightened, exhilarated, tense, but he caught her hand and in a strong movement whirled her into his arms.

"No protests now, my dear Fennel," he whispered. "The day is far too beautiful for that!" He was smiling crookedly as she lifted her face to his.

She closed her eyes and received the kiss as though she had been hungering for nothing else for the past three days since he had last kissed her. Wicked, wicked, wonderful man.

Perryn could not credit that he was actually kissing Miss Trentham again, and she so yielding in his arms. He found her complete surrender to the moment utterly intoxicating. But how had it happened?

The beauty of the day, the gentle exertion of the walk, the residual heat of nearly coming to cuffs with Mr. Burtle had all worked in him. When he had seen Alice embracing her farmer, he had remembered Miss Trentham's kiss of Sunday evening. Still, he had had no intent but to return to the coach with her.

Then he had seen the look in her beautiful green eyes, as though she had found herself lost within a vast ocean and only he could take her safely to shore. Only then, when he had seen her desire, had the searing need struck him to once again take her in his arms. So it was that he gathered her into a full, warm embrace, holding her as though she was the greatest treasure in the world as he gently drifted his lips over hers. He felt her breath pass from her lips to his in light puffs accompanied by barely audible moans.

What would it be like to take her to bed? he wondered. Heavenly.

He touched his tongue to her lips which served to part them invitingly. In a moment more, he was plumbing the sweet depths of her mouth, savoring the intimacy of a kiss he still could not credit she was able to give and to receive. How she surprised him and charmed him, made all the more delicious by the fact that he knew he held a maiden in his arms. A question rose in his mind. Was it possible he was tumbling in love with her?

Fenella felt the tightening of his arms about her waist. She leaned into him, ignoring the gentle warnings from deep within her mind that she should not be kissing Lord Perryn, that he would get the worst notion from her having permitted such a degree of intimacy again between them. Yet just as she attempted to lecture herself on the horrid nature of her present conduct, her arm seemed to slide of its own volition about his neck, an act which was rewarded by a faint growling sound issuing from his throat. Shivers snaked down her back, and she kissed him hard in return. His kiss became so sensual in that moment, so portentous of a wedding bed, that she felt weak all over, as though were he to demand anything of her in this moment she would acquiesce.

He whispered her name against her lips. She longed for him to possess her again. A hunger for him, repressed for days, enveloped her.

Only the sound of laughter and rustling leaves snapped her from the trance in which his roguish embraces had held her.

He drew back slightly, still holding her fast in his arms. "Mr. Burtle and his *amour* appear to be walking this way. We should go."

Fenella nodded, but she could not speak. When he released her, she took a deep breath, as though breathing for the first time. She felt dazed, unsteady, and gratefully took his arm as he guided her back down the path in the direction of the village and his waiting coach. In slow stages her head began to clear. When the enormity of what she had done settled into her brain, she drew her arm from about his. "You have tricked me somehow!" she cried, staring at him in horror.

"What the deuce?"

"Yes, that must be it." She felt rather hysterical. "For I cannot account for having allowed you to kiss me so forcefully as you did. I . . . I cannot credit that I once again permitted you to seduce me! Wicked, wicked man!"

"Fennel," he returned quietly, "we did nothing wrong. A little kissing hurts no one."

At that, she paused in her steps. "What?" she asked, dumbfounded. "Is this truly what you believe?"

"Yes . . . no," he responded. "I do not know. I can only tell you that—"

"It is our foolish kissing-ribbons!" she cried distract-
edly. "I meant for them to entertain you. Instead they have
inspired your most roguish conduct."

"You were not disinterested," he returned sharply, "yet
you seem to be blaming me. Why, pray tell, did you kiss
me in return? Why did you not pull from my arms and
strike me across the face in protest—or is it that you fancy
yourself in love with me?"

His words stopped all her foolishness. In that moment,
she grew very quiet and shook her head. "I could never
love a rogue," she stated, her expression horror-struck.

He stared at her almost disbelievingly. When she began
her march anew, he did not prevent her.

Perryn followed behind. The scorn in her eyes and
cloaked in her words cut him to the quick. *I could never
love a rogue.* There had been venom and distaste in her
statement, yet she had happily kissed a rogue.

What was he to her, then, that she gave her kisses so
readily, so completely, so freely? He felt all the hypocrisy
of her statement and resented her for it. Very well. If she
could not love him, he wondered just how soon he could
seduce her into a third kiss.

Six

Once established in a bedchamber at Croxton Lodge, Fenella sat on a chair before which rested a worktable. She had laid out those ribbons quite carefully which reflected their day's effort, but she could not work. Instead, she leaned back in her seat, fearful that were she to bend over the ribbons, made of a fine grade of silk, she would endanger the delicate fabric from the ridiculous teardrops that would simply not cease falling from her eyes.

The journey from Dunball to the large Elizabethan house northeast of Bridgwater had been conducted in silence. Perryn had tried to speak to her, but she had forbade it. In response, he had crossed his arms over his chest and endured the remainder of the drive in stony silence. For herself, she had had but one purpose—to keep from becoming a watering pot in front of him.

Now that she was ensconced in her chamber, however, she could not stem the tears in the least.

Ridiculous, ridiculous girl!

How was she to complete the remainder of the expedition now? A second kiss! And she had enjoyed every stolen moment of it. How wicked she was, for she had no intention of giving her heart to such a scapegrace, yet she would happily enjoy his embraces. What must he think of her? A second kiss!

Wretched, wretched kiss!

Only what to do?

After an hour of just such self-recrimination, she finally grew calm. She had erred, terribly so, but now she must make amends for her horrid conduct. Above all, she must somehow alter the impression she had surely given him that she in any manner now welcomed his advances.

So it was that she was able at last to summon her maid and begin the process of bathing and dressing for dinner. Betsy arranged her hair in a knot of curls atop her head and assisted her in donning a gown of light blue silk trimmed in Brussels lace, all the while eyeing her from concerned hazel eyes. Fenella shook her head at her and smiled. "I am quite well, just a little fatigued from the journey."

"Aye, miss, and next you will tell me you mean to tie your garter in public!"

"Betsy!" Fenella cried, much shocked.

Betsy merely sniffed and went about her business.

Fenella composed herself as well as she could under the circumstances and at last descended the stairs to the drawing room. She had succeeded so well in governing her sensibilities that she found she was able to nod politely to Perryn when she entered Sir Alfred and Lady Croxton's most excellent receiving room. Not wishing to converse with him, however, she immediately sought out the company of Mr. Silverdale, Mr. Aston, and Sir John. They, in turn, were happy to entertain her, and soon she was caught up in a lively discourse which involved both Miss Keele and Miss Almington. Perryn—just as she thought he would—made a great point of seeking out his favorites, Lady Elizabeth, Mrs. Sugnell, and Mrs. Millmeece, and greeting them by kissing each of their proffered hands. She chose to ignore his wretched, provoking conduct.

At dinner, however, she was alarmed to find herself seated opposite him. If he wished for it, he could certainly make her miserable with any unwanted attention, and she would be powerless to ignore him without setting tongues to wagging. To her relief, he chose discretion and restricted his remarks almost exclusively to the ladies on either side of him, Miss Madeley to his right and Miss Keele to his left. The latter, however, was much engaged with Mr. Aston in sampling the claret, so Perryn's conversation belonged almost exclusively to The Incomparable. Fenella found therefore that she could enjoy her meal and after a time was able to forget the morning's most horrid impropriety.

Sir Alfred Croxton had a superior buttery, and from the sherry served in the drawing room to the claret brought forth at dinner, compliments flew quite steadily in his direction in praise of the excellence of his wines. He informed everyone that the Madeira to be served later with an orange pudding was quite exceptional, as was the port, but his favorite was the ancient brandy he intended to lavish upon any of the gentlemen wishful of a game of cards later in the evening.

Fenella could not keep from glancing at Aubrey to see how he received this news, but he was quietly engrossed in listening to something the usually shy Miss Adbaston was saying, next to whom he had been seated. She could not be content, however, for though he may have appeared disinterested in Sir Alfred's hopes for an evening of gaming, his present interest in Miss Adbaston could not make her easy. If only the plain young lady was not so well dowered.

As the second course was brought forward of a succulent roast beef, Yorkshire ham, trout in a lemon sauce, broccoli, beets, an elegant array of artichokes, and salad, Fenella heard Perryn address Miss Madeley. "I am persuaded the seeking and taking of pleasure is everyone's most constant object. We, all of us, work to that end, whether it is enjoying a fine glass of claret"—here he inclined his head to his host, who responded by smiling broadly at the compliment—"or creating a collection to be auctioned at the end of a fortnight."

Miss Madeley nodded enthusiastically. "I vow I could not agree with you more. I, too, believe pleasure is our daily object. The collections in which we are presently engaged give us delight because we know that in the end we will be helping a great many of the poor."

As Fenella took a sip of claret, she glanced at Perryn over the rim of her glass. She rather thought she detected in his sharp gray eyes a flicker of annoyance that The Incomparable had agreed with him so readily.

"I think the notion absurd," she heard herself say before she could check the words.

He glanced at her, also quite sharply. His brows rose. "You disagree, Miss Trentham?" he queried, a smile just touching his lips.

By this time, her sudden pronouncement had caught the attention of the table. "Yes, as it happens, I do. There must always be a certain amount of satisfaction in creating a suitable collection for so worthy a cause, but I would not call the activity a pursuit of pleasure. Far from it. The work required, coupled with the exigencies of having to accomplish the task in the company of another creature whom one must strive not to offend in the course of each day, can be considered nothing less than an act of supreme labor."

Since at this moment at least two of the gentlemen murmured, "Hear, hear," she knew she was not far off the mark.

She smiled as she continued, "I am greatly satisfied with our collection, my lord, as well as with the effort we are making, but I daresay more than once during our journey you have wished yourself anywhere but in my company. Admit it is true."

His smile was utterly rueful. "I shall do no such thing, Miss Trentham, for the moment I should utter such a statement, the ladies at this table as one would fly into the boughs for my saying anything so ungentlemanly."

A general round of laughter passed about the table.

"So do you truly believe," she continued, still meeting his gaze, "that one should make pleasure the object of one's life?"

Miss Madeley took exception to this. "You have misunderstood Lord Perryn, I am sure of it. I believe he only meant to indicate how much pleasure can be found in any activity."

Perryn thanked Miss Madeley for taking up his cause, but addressed his next remark to Fenella. "The object of this entire caravan is a noble one," he said, "and there has been a certain amount of toil involved, but even you must admit we each have taken a certain amount of pleasure from it."

She eyed him shrewdly and thought she understood his meaning. "Some more than others, I suspect," she countered readily.

A soft smile touched his lips. "I suspect the pleasure thus far has been shared equally—or at least that is my opinion."

She could not help but shake her head at him and thought him wholly incorrigible, but at least he was smiling, if but a little. Miss Madeley, disliking intensely that she had been overtaken in conversation by another lady, immediately changed the subject by desiring to know of what Perryn's collection consisted. Her arch inquiries needed rebuffing, which Perryn accomplished quite gently, but in so doing his attention became fixed, much to Fenella's relief, wholly upon Miss Madeley.

Though Fenella was not entirely satisfied with this exchange, for indeed it violated her whole purpose in attempting to avoid Perryn throughout the evening, she had to admit somehow it had softened the aggravation the experience of the morning had afforded her. She even thought

Lord Perryn's temper had been softened a little by their cloaked argument.

Later, while Miss Aston and Miss Keele were performing a clever duet on the pianoforte, he approached her. "I was happy to see you smile at dinner."

"I am still quite vexed, Perryn," she countered, speaking a half-truth. "You had best not speak to me until the morrow."

"As you say," he murmured, leaning close to her as he spoke, which was his way. However, his warm breath chanced to drift over her bare neck in a familiar manner, and a spate of gooseflesh once more rolled down her side.

"Insufferable," she murmured quite to herself, all the while smiling.

After the ten o'clock hour, Fenella was ascending the stairs to her bedchamber, admiring the scarlet carpet overlaying the wooden steps, when Aubrey came up behind her and caught her by the elbow.

"I shall say good night then, Fen," he said, smiling, but his movements were nervous.

"Good night," she responded pleasantly.

"Allow me to escort you to your chamber. I will carry your candle for you, if you like."

"Thank you." She paused in her steps and carefully handed the candlestick to him.

She would have been gratified by such gallant conduct, particularly in a brother, had she not been certain he was attempting to turn her up sweet. She opened the door to her bedchamber, thanked him for the escort, and would have closed the door quickly had he not placed his foot in the way. "Fenella, I need a few pounds. Croxton is getting up a game and . . ."

"We have already discussed this matter, Aubrey. I will no longer lend you gaming money."

"I need only ten pounds or so to begin. Then I shall be as right as rain."

"How can you say this when I already know you owe good Mr. Chebsey a hundred pounds? When will this stop?"

"You do not understand in the least."

At that, she drew in a deep breath. "Unfortunately, Aubrey, in this you are quite mistaken. I understand the whole of it a great deal better than you imagine. Now, if you please, I beg you will remove your foot and allow me to retire."

Without warning, he snatched at her arm and held it firmly. "You owe me this, Fenella. Toseland should have been mine, not yours. Give me what is my due."

She was startled as much by the forcefulness of his address as by the rather wild, desperate light in his eye. She had heard his arguments a score of times, how he felt ill-used because the estate was not entailed to male heirs only. "I have nothing further to say. If you do not remove your foot, I shall shut the door anyway."

"This is not finished," he whispered, sliding his foot backward into the hall.

With her heart racing, she closed the door with a snap. She waited for a full minute, intending to lock the door, but she knew he had remained standing where he was. She did not feel she could lock the door without summoning some manner of reproof from him. Finally, she heard him move down the hall. Slowly, she inserted the key and heard the proper click. Her heart was hammering in her throat. He had seemed so threatening, as though he would have done her harm had he been of a mind.

When Betsy arrived at her summons, she laid the whole of the exchange before her.

Betsy listened intently then clucked her tongue. "Poor master Aubrey," she murmured. "He can in one moment be so sweet tempered, and the next . . ."

"Do you think he would have hurt me?"

"Nay," Betsy cried. "I would not go so far as to say that.

Certainly his conduct can move from one extreme to another without the smallest warning. But I've never seen
him go beyond the pale."

"I suppose you are right," Fenella returned, troubled.
"He is in debt again, you see. Mrs. Almington warned me
of it only this morning."

"That would explain the whole of it then, I think. And
he had been doing so well of late."

"Yes, I know. It is most distressing."

"Well, tomorrow I daresay he will be sick at heart to
have spoken to you as he did and will apologize, as is his
way. Now, come, let me brush out your hair."

Fenella went to bed that night distressed on two fronts.
Aubrey had taken to gaming again, or so it would seem,
and she had permitted Perryn to kiss her for the third time.

Aubrey, she decided, was probably even now repentant
and would do as Betsy said. He would offer her an apology,
she would forgive him, and hopefully all would be well
again.

The matter concerning Perryn was far more disturbing.

She arose therefore on the following morning knowing
she must speak with him about the unfortunate kiss of the
day before. She had decided she could be neither content
nor easy until she had extracted from him a promise that
he would never attempt to kiss her again. She was far too
vulnerable to him, which she doubted he could comprehend, but somehow she must try to make him see how
much his mere presence troubled her, nonetheless a roguish
embrace followed by a kiss. The very thought of either of
these delights so set her heart to pounding and her limbs
to trembling that it was with some difficulty she managed
to tie the ribbons of her bonnet.

As she descended the stairs slowly, she pulled on her
gloves, her mind trying to form exactly the right words to
say to the marquess when suddenly, as she reached the

bottom step, her brother was speaking to her. "Hallo, sister," he called out cheerfully.

"Oh!" Fenella cried. "How you startled me. I fear I was air dreaming again."

He moved toward her rapidly, his expression decidedly cast down. "Fenella, I am so sorry," he began, speaking rapidly. "I should not have spoken to you as I did last night, particularly when you were only trying to help me curb my tendency to dip far too deeply when gaming. I beg you will forgive me!" He took both her hands and squeezed them quite firmly.

Her heart melted, as it always did with her dear Aubrey. He would forever be her little brother, and she could not look at him without remembering how they used to play all their childhood games together and, when he was very young, how he used to trail after her wherever she went. He had the look of a child even now as he offered his apologies. How could she not forgive him? "Of course, dearest, but I must say you quite overset me last night."

He shook his head, looking down at her gloved fingers. "Sometimes I feel as though I am two different people entirely. I still cannot credit that I spoke to you as I did. It was very wrong of me."

"Yes, it was," she agreed, smiling.

At that, he met her gaze and could not keep from smiling, if ruefully, in response.

Since Miss Adbaston called to him from the front door saying that their coach had been brought round, he bid her farewell and even went so far as to place a kiss on her cheek. "I am sorry," he reiterated as he moved away.

"Enjoy your journey today," she returned.

With that, he disappeared outdoors.

From the landing above, Betsy called to her. "Miss, you forgot your bandbox."

Fenella glanced up. "So I did." The small sewing box had not been sufficient to store all the neatly packaged and rolled ribbons, so Betsy had borrowed from Mrs. Almington's maid one of her mistress's little used bandboxes.

Betsy hurried down the stairs and gave the box to Fenella. She lifted the lid and saw that Betsy had placed within it an embroidery hoop, a variety of threads, a needle, and a pair of scissors. "Thank you. I believe this will suffice."

"Very good, miss, and we shall see you at Milverton." Betsy gave her a polite curtsy and ascended the stairs.

She was just closing the lid when Perryn rounded the corner and was upon her. She was so startled by his sudden appearance and by the fact that she had yet to truly address the difficulty between them that the box simply slipped from her fingers. She struggled to grasp at it, but it fell to the floor.

Perryn hurried forward, insisting upon retrieving it for her.

"You are very kind," she responded nervously. She felt certain a blush was climbing her cheeks, for her face felt suddenly quite warm.

He frowned slightly at her, as though perplexed. He opened his mouth to speak, but Mr. Almington, in charge of the procession of coaches, informed him their coach was ready.

Fenella sighed with relief and immediately quit the manor. Perryn, as was his habit, waved the footman away and handed her up into the carriage himself, an attention which further increased her agitation.

As the coach turned down the avenue, Perryn, who was sitting forward, leaned close to the window. "Both Aston and Sir John are driving their curricles out today. How I envy them."

"I as well, with the weather so pleasant."

Fenella was grateful that so innocuous a subject should be introduced. With her own intentions of bringing forward so painful a subject serving to rattle her nerves one minute

out of every two, the benign act of speaking of the weather
and open carriages had a happy effect on her disquiet. Perhaps she could not be entirely at ease, but for the present
she was not nearly so distressed as she had been but a few
moments earlier. Only, just how was she to place before
him so delicate a request?

Hamlet succeeded village, which succeeded town, and
still she could not summon the courage to make her request.

The collecting of the kisses, however, progressed nicely
from Bridgwater to North Petherton and Thurloxton. At the
latter hamlet, Fenella decided she must address the subject
with him, perhaps over a cup of tea. However, she had just
secreted their ribbons within the bandbox when Mr. Aston
and his partner, young Mrs. Millmeece, drew up beside the
coach.

"Ho, Perryn! Care for a race? Sir John and I were toss-
ing coins to see who might have the right to challenge you
to the next quarter mile. I won."

"Did you?" Perryn returned. "And will I then be using
Sir John's curricle?"

"Unless you prefer mine. I would venture that mine is
better sprung, but Sir John's has a fresher team. I do not
give a fig which one I pilot. My hands are a great deal
lighter than yours and I shall beat you in a trice, see if I
won't!"

Perryn chuckled throatily. "By God, you've a race!" He
turned to Fenella. "Will you join me?"

Fenella was completely taken aback by the request.
Whatever did he mean by it? She could see by the light in
his eye that he was challenging her as strongly as Mr. Aston
had just challenged him. There was only one answer she
could give him.

"Of course I will!" she cried.

"You trust me, then?" he asked, narrowing his eyes.

"Without the smallest shade of doubt!" she responded

firmly, thinking that a discussion of yesterday's infamous kiss would apparently have to wait a little longer still. "You have a fine reputation where horseflesh and vehicles of any matter are concerned."

He leaned close to her. "That is by far the kindest thing you have ever said to me. Come, then! Let us show them how a race is to be won!"

Mrs. Millmeece, descending Mr. Aston's curricle, called out, "Miss Trentham, do you mean to attend Lord Perryn?" She was clearly shocked.

"Indeed, I do," she responded brightly. At that moment, Sir John arrived with Miss Almington. Her face was rather pale, and as Perryn moved gallantly to hand her down from the seat, her relief at touching the earth after the past several miles of travel was quite palpable.

Mr. Aston, prompted by Fenella's bravado, begged of his partner to take up her seat once more. Mrs. Millmeece, however, planted her hands on her hips, scowled at Mr. Aston, and said, "If you think I would risk my neck one more quarter mile in your care, I vow you have windmills in your head! Besides, I can see Miss Almington is in need of a little sustenance before we continue our journey."

"Perhaps I should go to her as well," Fenella said, glancing at Miss Almington.

Perryn, having already climbed aboard Sir John's curricle, extended his hand down to her. "Mrs. Millmeece will tend to her. Come. The race will be of short duration. Then we may all see to her comfort."

Fenella did not immediately acquiesce. "I am thinking we ought to take her up in your coach for the remainder of the journey. Mrs. Millmeece as well. Would that be agreeable to you, Perryn?"

"Of course." She saw the sincerity in his expression and was struck by it.

"You are very kind," she returned. When he placed a hand on his chest and pretended to swoon, she could not help but laugh. She continued, "Allow me at least to inform both of the ladies of your offer, although if you dare to conduct your race without me, I fear you shall hear me complain of it the remainder of our journey to Milverton!"

"I would not risk your wrath for a kingdom," he responded, his features warmed by a smile. "I shall await your return."

Fenella entered the alehouse, where Miss Almington sat sipping a small glass of brandy. She wore the bleakest expression Fenella had ever before seen.

"It is no wonder you are feeling so poorly," Mrs. Millmeece said, wrinkling her nose. "Sir John cannot manage his cattle. I vow even I could do better, and all I have ever driven is Lady Elizabeth's small pony phaeton up and down her drive."

"Pray, do not even speak of carriages of the moment," Miss Almington adjured her.

Mrs. Millmeece covered her hand with her own. "Poor thing. Have another sip of your brandy. I am persuaded you will feel a great deal better in but a few minutes."

Miss Almington swallowed very hard and once again brought the glass to her lips.

"I have good news, Miss Almington," Fenella said. "Lord Perryn requests that you join us for the remainder of the journey. Both you and Mrs. Millmeece. Would that be suitable, do you think?"

Since Miss Almington's lower lip quivered ominously, and tears started to her eyes, Fenella was not surprised when a watery, "Yes, thank you," passed her lips. However, this was followed by, "Oh, dear! Mrs. Millmeece! I fear . . . that is, I believe I am going to cast up my accounts!"

"Goodness! Hallo there!" Mrs. Millmeece cried out, summoning a servant.

Fenella thought it wise to allow the young lady a little privacy.

As she quit the inn, she could see the carriages had already been aligned side by side. Mr. Aston was clearly ready to be going, his whip in hand and his reins properly looped about his fingers. Hurrying to Sir John's curricle, Perryn extended his hand to her and quickly assisted her in climbing aboard.

"Miss Almington thanks you for your generosity," she said. "She is also of the moment being quite ill, so I thought it a propitious moment to absent myself."

"A very wise decision."

The teams were restive and clearly ready to be galloping. "I have sent a lad ahead," Perryn said. "You can see him in the distance. He will be our judge. Are you prepared for this?"

Fenella met his gaze and nodded.

"Excellent."

"Are you ready?" Sir John called out. He stood to the side of the coaches, a handkerchief in hand.

"Ready!" Perryn returned.

"Aye, Sir John!" Mr. Aston shouted happily.

With the highway clear, Sir John did not hesitate to lift his kerchief high in the air and cry out a resounding, "Off!" as he swung his arm to the earth.

Perryn cried out loudly to his team and Fenella instinctively took strong hold of the side of the carriage, planting her feet firmly on the floorboards. The initial uneven leaps and starts of the horses were quickly replaced by long, firm strides. She glanced at Mr. Aston to her left and saw that though Mrs. Millmeece might have disparaged her partner's driving, presently he had the aspect of a man intent on winning a race.

The wind buffeted her face, tugging at her bonnet and increasing the sensation she was flying through the air. Her chest swelled with the excitement of the race as the lad at the finishing line loomed closer and closer.

Horses' hooves pounded the earth. Perryn held himself

in a taut, tense line, calling to his team and slapping the reins hard. He began to inch forward. Fenella heard Mr. Aston's shouts.

The roll of the wheels, the jingle of the traces all blended into the most exhilarating cacophony of brilliant noise. Fenella cried out her own encouragement.

Perryn took hold of the whip and twirled overhead. A sharp crack split the air. His team lunged forward in a burst of speed. With but inches to spare, he passed first over the makeshift line in the dirt road.

Perryn strove to ease the horses into a walking gait and soon found a lane by which he might turn the equipage about in order to return to Thurloxton. At the same time the village lad, by his invitation, hopped up behind. Mr. Aston followed suit, and before long they were returned to the village, the young man proclaiming Perryn's victory the entire distance.

The baronet offered his congratulations, after which Perryn confessed that had he not had the use of his excellent whip, he doubted he would have carried the day. "Quite an excellent feel to the leather."

"A gift from m'father two years past upon the occasion of my birthday," Sir John responded, congratulating him again. He then turned to seek out and console Mr. Aston, who would in no manner be content that he had lost the race.

Perryn leaped from the curricle and handed Fenella down. She was careful to make use of the proper steps, but still her skirts caught on something or other. She gave a slight tug, but the fabric freed itself so suddenly that she fell forward, landing squarely in Perryn's arms. She came up laughing and begged to know if she had injured him.

"On no account," he returned, also laughing . . . except that he did not let her go.

"You were magnificent," he whispered.

Fenella looked into his eyes and realized he was in a state of some exhilaration.

"You should let me go," she whispered. Once again, as always, she could not breathe.

The horses kept them from the view of Sir John and Mr. Aston, a circumstance which caused Fenella the greatest concern. She felt herself yet again to be in the greatest danger, even after a night of suffering!

He did not hesitate, but leaned forward, his lips nearly upon hers, his intention clear.

"No," she murmured, averting her face.

His lips touched her cheek and she tried to pull free from his embrace, but he would not entirely release her.

"You must not," she whispered.

"You desire a kiss as much as I. The moment is ripe, and how much harm can there be in one kiss . . . for the victor?"

She met his gaze directly, a hand pressed strongly against his chest. "Perryn, there is nothing harmless in your kisses and for that reason—ah, Sir John!" She stepped easily away from the marquess, who released her abruptly.

Perryn spoke loudly. "You should have more care with your skirts, Miss Trentham. You nearly tore the hem upon descending. Are you certain you are not hurt?" He turned to Sir John. "She fell almost from the top of the wheel."

"Good God," Sir John remarked. "Have you suffered an injury, Miss Trentham?"

"Not in the least. I only wish you had been able to see the finish to the race. It was most thrilling. Mr. Aston would have surely won, save for the horses having been spurred on at the very last moment by the use of your whip."

"Yes, I wish I had seen it as well. As I was telling Perryn earlier, an excellent whip, a gift from m'father."

Mr. Aston called to him.

"Eh? What's that, Charles? I see." He turned back to

them. "Do excuse me. Aston thinks one of his horses is come up lame. Probably just a pebble in the shoe."

When he was gone, Perryn took her elbow. "Come," he said. "I must have a word with you." He guided her away from the coaches to the green not far distant so they might continue their conversation. "So you do not think my kisses harmless?" Again, there was a challenging light in his eye. She wondered what he could mean by it.

"Hardly, but you can scarcely be unaware of that. However, I was hoping I might have a chance to speak with you on this very subject. I have something I wish to ask you in every seriousness. Will you hear me?"

He met her gaze and frowned slightly. "Of course I will."

"I must speak to you about yesterday—at Dunball. I wish so very much that I had not succumbed to that dreadful kiss."

Perryn was silent. "Dreadful? As bad as that?"

She heard the anger in his voice and tempered her words. "No, to be sure it was not."

"Thank you for conceding as much."

"Perryn, I beg you will not be sarcastic. If you can refrain from such comments, I promise to do better in how I speak of our encounter of yesterday."

"Very well. Agreed."

She met his gaze squarely once more and drew in a deep breath. "I must ask you to promise me, to give me your word, that you will never kiss me again."

"I beg your pardon?" he queried.

"I am asking you to promise, upon your honor, never to kiss me again." She swallowed hard. Now that she was standing in front of him and his gray eyes had grown quite dark as though he was angered anew, as he had been on the day before, much of her courage began to fail her. Still, she was resolved. He must comply, or she would never have a moment's peace again! "Please, Perryn."

At that, with her voice having dropped to a whisper, some of the hostility left his features. "If this is what you truly wish," he responded, if brusquely. "I promise, upon my honor, never to trespass your lips again."

She released a great sigh of relief. "Thank you. You can have no notion—"

He interrupted her. "You did not permit me to finish, Miss Trentham. I will make you such a promise, but shall keep it only until the moment you release me from it."

"I never shall," she countered readily.

A smile touched his lips. "Nevertheless," he pressed her, "the moment you but speak the words and tell me this vow is revoked, I shall consider myself not in the least bound to honor it. Do you understand?"

"Of course. But there will be no such occasion, I am certain."

His smile broadened. She had the distinct impression she had made matters worse, but in what way she was not at all certain.

"Perryn! I beg you will be serious!"

"I am serious," he countered. "As serious as one can ever be on such a subject, as I have said before. No, no! Do not distress yourself further. I have given you my word and you may rely upon me to keep it."

"Then I thank you."

"I suppose this means you will not even give me a kiss for having been triumphant in the race."

The teasing tone had returned to his voice. She felt relieved beyond words. "It would be far wiser for me, I think, to handle a hundred poisonous serpents rather than to oblige you in such a manner."

At that, he shook his head. "Come then, Fennel. Let us see if Miss Almington feels capable yet of climbing aboard my coach."

Upon entering the inn, Perryn was happy to discover both Sir John and Mr. Aston were involved in savoring the local ale and that a tankard had already been drawn for him. He moved to the bar, joining the gentlemen readily. From his station, he could watch the ladies and was relieved to find that Miss Almington had recovered, that she was even nibbling on a biscuit.

Mrs. Millmeece addressed his partner. "Have you not noticed, Miss Trentham, that at every village since Axbridge, the inhabitants, both male and female, have sported the reddest lips? I find it astonishing and at first thought perhaps a peculiar illness had infected the west country, but everyone seemed so generally content and even rosy-cheeked that I quickly knew I was mistaken. How do you account for it?"

Perryn watched Fenella shrug. "It is the berry season," she responded. "Perhaps the local berries stain more deeply here than in other parts of the country."

"I find it singular," Mrs. Millmeece said, her eyes narrowing suspiciously.

Perryn took a pull from the large mug, his senses warmed as much by having won the race as by the rich ale. What lucky impulse had prompted him to invite Miss Trentham to enjoy the contest with him? It had given him the excuse he had been seeking to attempt a third kiss. He was certain that had circumstances afforded a greater degree of privacy, he would have succeeded in his objective. Since their brangling of yesterday, he had not forgotten the harshness of her words to him. *I could never love a rogue.* Whatever her protestations, however, she was certainly inclined to share her kisses with him, regardless of all this silliness over making him promise not to do so again.

He could not help but smile. She could not know that such a promise had made him all the more determined to wrest another kiss from her.

As he watched her now, her lively expression, the manner in which she concentrated on the speaker so completely, and the sparkle of her green eyes, he realized that however much he was out of patience with her hypocritical attitude toward him, she was certainly an original. He tried to recall the earliest occasion when he had noticed how different she was from the ladies of his acquaintance. A short review of his quite varied relationship with her took him back to a London Season some four years past, when he had first made her acquaintance.

He had been in attendance at a ball, an odious 'squeeze' in which he had been far too bored to do more than wish himself anywhere but at that particular fete.

Suddenly, he had felt himself watched and, glancing about the ballroom, found a young lady, quite unknown to him, scrutinizing his face, her expression entirely unsmiling. He had been struck by her odd conduct even then, particularly since though she had been discovered in the act of gaping at him, she had not looked away when found out.

Her gaze had been measured, judgmental. This alone had caught his interest, since the usual mode of young ladies was to offer him a blinding smile in hopes his interest might be caught. But not Miss Trentham. She had regarded him with a level, appraising gaze until he had simply turned away from her. Who was she to stare at him in what he had felt at the time to be a rude fashion?

Except . . .

Except that he had never forgotten that odd encounter. How it haunted him in the strangest manner. From that moment, whenever a lady smiled at him or made every effort to secure his interest, he thought of Miss Trentham and how she had simply looked at him. In the course of his acquaintance with her, he had never known her to accommodate him, unlike Miss Madeley last night, who had agreed with an opinion he had put forth during dinner, one he had not especially believed. Poor Miss Madeley, hungering after a title. She had failed his little test, just as he had expected her to, but how very much like Miss Trentham to call him to book for his ridiculous ideas.

He was still watching her as she continued to deflect Mrs. Millmeece's attempts to discover the nature of their collection, when, during a pause in the conversation, she glanced his direction. "Are you anxious to be going?" she called to him across the small, dark chamber.

"Only a very little." He might have encouraged her to remain a little longer, but his thoughts were disrupted entirely when the door opened and a charming, rather petite village maid chanced into the room. She was the prettiest thing, with fiery red hair, yet not a freckle to be seen on her smooth, creamy complexion.

Even Sir John drew in a sharp breath. "A diamond of the first stare," he murmured.

The lady, probably one of the serving maids, lowered her gaze and passed quickly into the nether regions.

When Perryn turned around, it was to discover that Miss Trentham had gathered up her reticule and gloves and was even now crossing to him. Once beside him, she queried, "Must a rogue ogle every pretty face?"

"My dear Fennel," he returned in the same manner, "that particular activity is hardly restricted to rogues."

She turned and caught the entranced expressions of both Sir John and Mr. Aston who were nearly swooning in admiration as the young lady returned to the taproom and moved briskly up the stairs.

"So it would seem," she responded, laughing.

Ah, Fennel, he thought, *how soon will it be before I possess your lips again, promise or no promise?*

Seven

For the next portion of the journey, Mrs. Millmeece and Miss Almington took up a place in Perryn's coach, while Sir John and Mr. Aston followed behind in their curricles. When the thriving town of Taunton was reached, however, a change occurred. Sir John and Mr. Aston felt obligated to hire a post chaise for their partners to take them the remaining distance to Milverton, since both ladies felt it was unfair that Lord Perryn and Miss Trentham be deprived of the opportunity to increase the size of their own collection merely because, as Mrs. Millmeece had put it, the gentlemen were wont to be self-indulgent cretins.

Fenella had been grateful to Mrs. Millmeece in particular, for it was through her efforts primarily that the necessary change was made. Perryn, as a point of gentlemanly conduct, never would have thrown the ladies from his carriage. But her beaus, however delightful their attentiveness to her in a drawing room or ballroom, were hopelessly addicted to the pursuit of their own pleasures and beyond even the broadest of hints.

So it was that she was once again alone with Perryn as the coach wended its way around the southern prominence of the Quantock Hills. The ease she had begun to feel in his company following the race continued, much to her relief, and there was every indication he meant to be as good as his word where his recent promise to her was concerned. If she found herself caught now and again by her own powerful sentiments, these she suppressed as being wholly impracticable. She knew what Perryn was, and that was that!

The bustling market town of Taunton was a welcome diversion from the villages and hamlets that had characterized the journey from Bridgwater. The high slender tower of the church appeared to Fenella to rise to over one hundred and fifty feet and was constructed of a red stone which Perryn, as a long resident of Somerset, informed her had been quarried from the Quantocks themselves. The windows, on the other hand, were framed in a beautiful, contrasting yellow stone.

"What a lovely street," Fenella remarked as she stepped down from the carriage. The buildings were in the modern Georgian style, primarily of deep red brick and set to remarkable advantage with white porticoes. The streets were crowded with every manner of conveyance from gigs to traveling coaches to gentlemen on horseback to carts and wagons.

"Shall we walk in the direction of the church?" she queried.

"What? Do you suppose the vicar will add to your kissing-ribbon?"

She regarded him, laughing. "Well, I suppose he just might if I were to explain the purpose of our collection." He laughed in turn, and as they began to walk toward the tall spire, she added, "You must know Taunton well, for your house, if I recall, is situated between here and Ilminster."

He frowned slightly. "So you are familiar with Morchards?" he asked, clearly surprised.

"Yes, of course. My father and I called on you once, but that was several years ago."

He appeared as one struck dumb. "How is this possi-

ble!" he cried. "I have no recollection of the event. Surely
I would have remembered so singular an occasion!"

Fenella shook her head. "I fear not, for you were decidedly in your cups. Quite bosky, as I recall."

"The deuce take it!" he cried, almost triumphantly. "I
comprehend it all now, in particular your ill opinion of me
from the very beginning of our acquaintance—only it was
not the beginning, was it?"

"I do not take your meaning," she responded as Perryn
guided her away from a horse skitterish in harness.

"I thought I had become acquainted with you four seasons past, but it is no such thing, is it? How long has it
been?"

"Five years."

He shook his head ruefully. "And you have held me to
book for my conduct all this time. I must have behaved
very badly for you to have glared at me that first Season
in London after your visit to Morchards."

Fenella was entirely disconcerted that her casual remark
on the location of his home would lead him to bring forward a most troublesome subject. At best, she had difficulty remembering with even the smallest degree of
equanimity her experiences at his home so many years ago,
but to hear them discussed so lightheartedly by Perryn
threatened to undo her completely. "You were not so very
bad," she responded uneasily. "Papa laughed heartily at
you, for though you were in your altitudes, you insisted on
receiving us. Not even your quite worthy butler could prevent it. We were gone the next morning before ever you
stumbled from your bed."

"Only tell me how I offended you that you have set
yourself against me on every possible occasion since."

Fenella did not want him to know he had actually kissed
her, and she certainly had no intention of telling him she
had returned his kisses with great fervor. Instead, she addressed the heart of the matter. "I was left with the im-

pression you took your duties lightly, and that gave me a measure of disgust. I was angry that such a handsome man, endowed with fortune and rank, was so much given to drink and flirtation and in so many respects appeared to be such a useless creature. I trust I do not give you pain in speaking so bluntly."

"Miss Trentham!" he cried facetiously. "I perceive you are restraining yourself. Do not hold back, I beg you. Let me hear what you truly think!"

She slipped her arm about his. "I beg pardon for having wounded your sensibilities. But come, tell me a little more of Taunton." A wagon, heavily laden, passed by, the wheels clattering loudly.

He shook his head and sighed. "You are come to torment me. I vow you are my nemesis after all. I remember thinking as much more than once over the past several years, but now I am convinced of it."

"You are being quite nonsensical again. Pray, what else do you know of this pretty town?"

"That of the moment it is aptly named *Taunton.*"

She could only laugh.

"Very well. I recall as a lad when many of these buildings were being erected. Sir Benjamin Hammet, a local M.P., laid out the streets in 1788. Not so long ago."

"No, indeed. And there is always a freshness to a town so recently built, yet I have little doubt the site is quite old."

"You are not mistaken. The wool industry has thrived here since the early eleventh century, when the town built its first fulling mill. Wool has been a prime industry these many centuries and more." When the mail coach appeared at the top of the street, several boys nearby set up a whoop and ran in the direction of the equipage, which was being drawn by three teams of strong horses.

Once at the church, Fenella spent several minutes viewing the structure, particularly in craning her neck to gaze up at the exceedingly tall spire. "Impressive," she murmured. "Shall we go inside?"

He nodded. "If you like."

The church was cool and quiet within and instantly ended their discourse by the very solemnity of the wooden pews and high, vaulted ceiling. She let her gaze drift about, enjoying the work of centuries past. "How old do you suppose this church is?" she asked quietly.

"Fifteenth century, I believe, and in some need of repair."

"I suppose it would be. It is certainly quite beautiful."

"Indeed, I could not agree more."

She turned toward him and saw that he was looking not at the fine architecture, but at her.

She smiled and shook her head at him. "Incorrigible," she murmured. "I believe it is time to go."

He smiled broadly as she turned to walk back up the aisle.

Once outside, she looked up and down the street. "Where would you advise we go to collect our kisses?"

He leaned close to her. "My coach," he whispered. "Forget the maids of Taunton. Your lips would serve as well, one after the other."

She looked at him, aghast. "Perryn, you promised!"

"I promised not to kiss you, but you said nothing of teasing you a little. Besides, you wounded me terribly in telling me earlier of your opinions. I fear my lacerated feelings need a little soothing of the moment!"

"What a rascal you are. Come. Let us see what might be accomplished at the Market House before any of Mrs. Almington's party arrives to expose our deeds."

"As you wish," he said, turning her in the proper direction.

As he walked beside her, however, he felt oddly content and could not keep from smiling. Her harsh speech damning his character, for some reason, did not prick him in the least. Rather, a powerful feeling had seized command of his chest. The Duchess of Cannock had also taken him readily to task for his flaws, and he had suffered no lack of admiration for her because of it.

"What a triumph!" Fenella cried, holding several ribbons on her lap as the coach set forth on the remainder of the journey. "Together we must have collected no less than three score of kisses among all these ribbons!"

"Does so little frequently charm you?" Perryn asked.

"Always," she responded, once more retrieving several strips of paper from her bandbox and beginning the careful process of protecting the rouged kisses. "If one must be charmed by only that which is magnificent and stunning, then one waits forever to be charmed. I much prefer to be delighted every day."

He merely smiled rather enigmatically at her comment, and Fenella felt no need to elaborate on her thoughts. Instead, she concentrated on properly storing the ribbons, after which she retrieved her embroidery hoop and began the more tedious process of stitching the name of each place at the top of the ribbons.

When Perryn suggested they travel straight through to Milverton without stopping at any of the local villages or hamlets betwixt, Fenella glanced out the window. "The hour must be nearing three o'clock, we dawdled so at the Market House."

"The ale was excellent."

"As was the tea, and I do not think I have tasted a more tender apple tart in my entire existence. I only hope Sir John discovered them."

"I daresay he did," Perryn responded, smiling.

"As to your original notion, I believe it would be best that we press on."

By the time the coach drew before the door of Lord and Lady Kingsland's grand home, just two miles past Milverton in the eastern portion of the Vale of Taunton Deane,

Fenella confessed to Perryn her relief that the day's tasks were nearly at an end.

"Will you be able to complete so much embroidery?" he asked, handing her down yet again from his coach.

"There is that," she agreed. "I fancy I will need to employ Betsy in some of this particular labor. She is a most skilled needlewoman."

As they entered the house, Lord Kingsland greeted them warmly, expressing his delight that Mrs. Almington's party should have the use of his home for the night. "And how do you go on, Perryn?" he asked. "I had expected to see you at The Pavilion in July."

"Mrs. Almington was before Prinny and invited me to Whitmore. However, I expect to be in Brighton before summer's end."

"Excellent. Well, I will not keep you. What maggot got into Mrs. Almington's head to send you all on such a fool's errand, I shall never know. Better to have made a large donation to her charitable fund than to have bound you all to a fortnight of slavery, what?"

"I might have had cause to complain, but she chanced to pair me with such a beautiful young lady that I fear I would sound like a complete gudgeon in doing so. Are you acquainted with Miss Trentham?"

Lord Kingsland turned to her. "Indeed, I am. How do you go on, Miss Trentham? I had the pleasure of dancing with you at Almack's this past Season, on more than one occasion." He was all smiles as he bowed to Fenella.

"And you, my lord, were a most excellent partner," she returned, curtsying slightly.

He laughed. "Yes, I was, as I recall. Most gracious. I trod on your feet only twice!"

Fenella chuckled. She liked Lord Kingsland very much.

"Ah, here is one of the servants now to show you to your rooms."

"Thank you," she said and did not hesitate to take Per-

ryn's arm when he offered it to her. She was suddenly quite
fatigued.

He parted from her at the hallway leading to her bedchamber by saying, "Thank you, Fennel, for a delightful
day—in particular for sitting bravely beside me during the
race at Thurloxton."

"I enjoyed every moment of it, as well you know."

He bowed to her and moved in the opposite direction,
where his own room had been prepared for the night.

Fenella watched him go, a soft sigh passing her lips.
Truly, he did move like a soldier, as though he was marching over a battlefield instead of down a very fine hall. Old
feelings surfaced quite readily, as well as memories, but
this would not do by half! She gave herself a shake and
followed the maid to her room, where she decided she
would rest until the dinner hour.

"A ball!" Miss Madeley cried. "At Morchards tomorrow
night! But how wonderful!"

"Yes," Mrs. Almington said, smiling broadly as she addressed the entire party now gathered in Lord Kingsland's
drawing room before dinner. "And nearly three hundred
guests are expected to welcome us in what is nearly the
halfway mark of our journey."

Fenella glanced at Lord Perryn, who was wearing an
exceedingly satisfied expression. Somehow he had been
able to keep his great secret to himself for a full four days
since the journey about Somerset began. Longer still, she
thought, since a ball was no small event and he would
surely have had to give his staff notice as much as a fortnight in advance. Fenella found herself wondering about
Perryn yet again. There were times when he was not so
very bad, and the giving of a much-needed ball in the midst
of their journey was a kindness indeed.

She might have continued in her momentary good opinion had his favorites not descended upon him in that moment—Mrs. Sugnell on his right, squeezing his arm and squealing, while Lady Elizabeth on his left was jumping in small leaps and clapping her hands. As Mrs. Millmeece also approached Perryn, rapping his cheek lightly with her fan, she turned away in something near disgust. All three ladies fawned over the man at every opportunity, and he in no way appeared inclined to discourage them.

On the following day, just past nuncheon and with their day's labor complete, Fenella once more drew her embroidery from the bandbox beside her and set to work on a ribbon from East Brent. She glanced at each kiss and marveled at how much had transpired and how many kisses had been collected since their initial efforts at Axbridge.

"Are you as pleased with our progress as I am?" she queried, sinking the needle into the delicate fabric. Perryn as usual was seated across from her.

"Not by half," he remarked. "These kisses are still not at all what I would have wished for!"

Fenella pricked a finger in surprise as she glanced up at him. This was not the answer she had expected. Noting, however, the teasing smile on his lips, she drew in a sharp breath. "Why are you smiling? Oh . . . oh, Perryn! I doubt I will ever become accustomed to just how early in the day you can begin a flirtation. You quite astonish me."

He chuckled. "To answer your question, of course I am pleased. You are doing most of the labor, you were the one to concoct the notion in the first place, and all I seem to be required to do is to exert a little charm on a handful of village maidens now and again. Yes, I am well pleased, indeed."

"If you feel you are not making a sufficient contribution," she said, setting a stitch, "I could always teach you to embroider."

He scowled at the hoop and thread in her hands. "I had rather stick that needle in my eye."

She laughed outright. "What a hand you are. Of all the things I ever imagined you to be, I never suspected you would have possessed the ability to make me laugh so very much."

"I hope you mean to make the most of it, since you have found my character so wanting in most respects."

She lifted a brow. "Your *court* last night," she began, tightening the hoop on her lap, "seemed *aux anges* that you were to give a ball at Morchards."

"Is there a lady alive who does not love a ball?"

"This much is true." She glanced at his elegant coat of Spanish blue superfine, as well as his buckskin breeches and polished top boots. "Did I perchance mention that I think you quite nattily attired this morning? Blue suits you, I think."

"That was very kindly said. Thank you."

Together they had already scoured several villages en route to Morchards, from Oake, Rumwell, and Trull, all near Taunton, to the more southeasterly hamlets of Stoke St. Mary, Wrantage, Hatch Beauchamp, and Ashill. They were not far from the marquess's estate near Ilminster. "But to revert to our earlier topic," she said, "as for myself. I could not be happier with how well our collection is progressing."

"And how do you mean to display the ribbons?" he asked.

"I have been thinking of a sort of maypole, the embroidered ends of the ribbons attached to the top of a pole. With so many ribbons and a slight spinning of the pole, the effect would be quite playful."

"And impressive."

"Are we just now departing the village of Ashill?" she inquired, trying to gain her bearings.

"Yes," he responded, glancing out the window. "We are but two miles from Morchards."

"I forgot to mark the ribbon." She was about to redress her oversight, when movement at the side of the highway caught her eye. "Oh, dear! Perryn, do you see that! Stop the coach, at once!"

"Abominable!" he cried. "Thomas! Draw the horses!"

Before the coach had rolled to a stop, Perryn was opening the door and letting down the steps in one swift movement. "You there!" he called out as he leaped onto the street. "Desist, before I have your hides!"

Several boys immediately scrambled in all directions away from a whimpering, trembling mass of ruddy fur.

"Is it hurt?" Fenella cried, picking up her skirts and following swiftly in Perryn's wake.

Perryn reached the dog and began speaking in soothing tones. The small creature, a female, sniffed his hand, and with what seemed a great deal of courage, rose to her feet. "Poor thing. I wonder who she belongs to." When a farm laborer came running up as well, in smock and limp hat, Perryn queried, "What do you know of this dog?"

"A stray, sir. The baker's wife feeds her scraps from time to time and she is let run about wild-like because she enjoys hunting rats. Otherwise, hers is a sorry life. I've three dogs of my own or I'd have taken her home 'afore now."

"Perryn, we must take her with us," Fenella said.

He frowned as he gently began checking her sides and limbs. "Of course," he said, his voice somber.

"I did not mean to foist her on you, and I shall certainly transport her to Wiltshire when I take my leave of Bath later this month. Toseland is not so far from Morchards, after all."

Perryn retrieved a carriage rug from the coach and wrapped the dirty creature within. She grew very quiet in his arms as he handed Fenella up. "We can certainly make that decision at a later hour. For the present, we shall care for her together."

Once within the coach, Fenella took the dog, still swaddled in the carriage rug, onto her lap.

"Do you wish me to hold her? I fear you will soil your gown. Indeed, already her muddy paws have left several streaks."

"What do I care for that? Betsy may complain a little, but this will not be the first time she has removed dirt from a gown of mine. If I recall, she caterwauled quite significantly after that little excursion we took into the woods near Dunball."

He lifted his brows and his smile grew rather crooked. "I suppose your gown would have been a trifle soiled. I only wonder that you mentioned the matter at all, since it can only bring forward certain significant recollections."

Fenella chuckled. "We ought to laugh about things— quite a lot, I think. Even unfortunate kisses in a wilderness."

"Never unfortunate," he exclaimed. "A kiss can never be regarded as a misfortune."

Fenella might have laughingly agreed with him had she not suddenly been reminded of the very first kiss she had shared with him—at Morchards in the center of the maze. How odd that but a few careless words would cull forth the memory so quickly and so strongly. However, in this moment it seemed to her while she patted the dog's head that she was there once more, with the mist of the night rising up from the grass at her feet. She had heard him coming long before his arrival at the heart of the maze, for he had been laughing, singing, and falling into the shrubs for the prior twenty minutes. She would never have credited he could have actually found the center, but then he had been working the maze since a child, so undoubtedly the path was as familiar to him as his reflection in a looking glass. He had carried a bottle of champagne with him.

"I saw you," he had called to her. "My little angel, though I vow . . . hiccough . . . I have not the faintest notion who the devil you are, but my angel you shall be, for you have saved me from the worst of fates—a night of boredom!"

She had not been flattered. If anything, her disgust of him had risen to new and awesome heights. How could a man, given so much by the pure chance of his birth, be such a useless, vulgar drunkard? She had moved quickly, intending to leave the maze, but he had opened his arms apparently convinced his advances would be welcome.

Appalled, she called out, "Stand aside, my lord!" She should have been able to move easily past him, but somehow he had captured her, the open bottle of champagne landing in a soft clunk on the grass at his feet, as he caught her swiftly about her waist. Then, as though she had been but a leaf in a breeze, he whirled her into his arms.

"Oh!" she had murmured, her hands planted on his chest. "You must not!"

"A protestation from these beautiful lips," he slurred. "How delightful! How intriguing! I must take a kiss!"

That kiss had been her undoing. Even if champagne was on his tongue, a fiery passion was what drifted over her lips. He held her so tightly, yet his kiss had been so very gentle. She had meant to struggle against him, but he was too skilled in his seductions. Before long she was leaning into him, sliding her arms over his shoulders and wrapping them about his neck. The groans which had issued from his throat had further ignited the completely rakish assault until he was dropping her to the grassy turf, pulling at the front of her gown until he had rolled her on top of him, and kissing her again. She could have easily left him at that moment, since he was pinned beneath her . . . yet she had not.

Fenella still could not think of the wickedness of it without shuddering. Why had she not in that moment done him some injury and sped on her way? Instead, he had begun sliding his hands into her hair and pushing her brown locks away from her face. Moonlight had spilled over his face, and there was something in his illuminated expression that made her pause. She had never been quite certain, but for a moment it had seemed as though tears had filled his eyes. Regardless, she had felt as though she had peered into his soul and seen both the joys and agonies of his life.

"Who are you?" he murmured. "Have I imagined you? For you are like no other lady I have ever known. Faith, but I have drunk too much wine."

"Indeed, you have," she had responded on a whisper.

"And yet there is something about you . . ." He scowled slightly. "Have you come to punish me?"

Fenella thought this quite odd, but then he was completely foxed. "Not precisely," she said, placing a gentle kiss on his lips. "Merely to ask where is your heart, my lord, that you are letting your life drift through your fingers? Do you not long for more than the mere pursuit of pleasure? I beg you will open your eyes."

He had chuckled then. "So you think all I care about is the pursuit of pleasure? You are mistaken. I desire a wife more than anything, I think, and a score of children, perhaps, racing about these halls." He had lifted a limp arm in the direction of the house.

"Indeed?" she had murmured.

"You have been sent to me," he whispered. "My angel."

"Yes" she had responded, not knowing what he meant, but thinking there could be no harm in agreeing with him.

"What would you have me do?" he had asked.

"You take your wine too liberally, m'lord. You do not honor your ancestors who gave so much to you. What of your estate? Your lands? Tend to them." Without understanding the impulse, she once more kissed him, again and again.

After a moment, she had drawn back. "Will you remember me when I am gone?" she had asked, her voice barely a whisper.

"There is something I would say to you," he responded, frowning. "I did not always . . . that is . . . I was not always so very bad, but . . ." He struggled for a moment as though he could no longer see and then fell into a state of unconsciousness.

She had slid off him, but had chosen not to leave. Instead, she had knelt beside him, taking his hand in hers and bringing it to her cheek. She had remained there for perhaps an hour, looking at him as the moon trekked across the night sky. She had wondered and wondered about him, who he was, why he was such a rogue, and mostly why not only she had enjoyed his kisses but why she had so wantonly kissed him in return. These were mysteries she did not think she would ever truly comprehend.

Now, as she smiled down at the hapless dog, hoping Perryn had not noticed her silence, she pondered his remark that no kiss could be considered a misfortune. How sadly he was mistaken, for his kisses had brought her the worst misfortune in the world since, for reasons she could not explain, he had spoiled her forever for the attentions, the advances of other gentlemen. Nothing would do for her, it would seem, except a rogue—and yet she had vowed she would never, never give her heart to so unworthy a creature. She had been keeping her vow quite nicely until this wretched fortnight had been thrust upon her by a misguided matchmaker. Mrs. Almington had a great deal to account for!

Within half an hour, Perryn's house came into view, well laid back against a verdant, hilly landscape. Fenella recalled first seeing the house so many years ago and how she had felt as though she had stepped into another time, so ancient did the weathered stone make the house seem.

She glanced at Perryn and saw there was a curious smile on his lips as he, too, viewed his grounds and his home.

"What are you thinking?" she asked him, the dog now asleep on her lap.

He shrugged faintly. "How fortunate I am to be master here."

She was surprised. "Were you always used to feeling thus?"

"No," he responded, chuckling. "Not by half, I fear. But that changed some years past, and now I cannot but look upon the magnificence of this dwelling without a sense of awe and gratitude, which is one of the reasons I agreed so readily to Mrs. Almington's scheme to hold a ball for her. Such a vast and truly beautiful home deserves to be enjoyed by a multitude."

"Are you expecting as many guests as Mrs. Almington indicated last night?"

"Word from my housekeeper indicates that we are— nearly three hundred, just as she said. All the primary receiving rooms will be crowded and the ballroom stuffy."

"In short, your fete will be a resounding success. But were you not anxious in having to be gone from home until today?"

"On no account. If you knew my housekeeper, Mrs. Wimbish . . ."

"I have met her, of course. She seemed most capable, and there was a certain warmth of temper that I particularly enjoyed in her."

"Ah, yes, when you visited Morchards five years ago. You are right, though. I do not believe anyone to have so excellent a staff as myself. Mrs. Wimbish and my butler, Clive, are extraordinary servants."

The coach turned up the drive, and most of Fenella's view of the house was lost in the angle of the equipage. A spattering of gooseflesh crept along her neck. She had the oddest sensation she was somehow traversing sacred ground.

"What is it? You are shivering."

"I cannot explain what I am feeling of present—as though I have entered a church, which makes no sense, of course. I wonder . . . do you have many ghosts at Morchards?"

"Several," he responded with a smile.

"Anyone I should be particularly wary of?"

"Only the priest. Once seen, it is rumored you will marry within a twelvemonth."

"I can only presume you have never seen him."

"Oh, I have seen him, but he runs the other direction when he espies me."

She laughed as the coach drew to a stop. "Do you know," she said, following him from the coach, the dog still cradled in her arms, "that I never truly comprehend how greatly fatigued I am until I set foot at the door of our next abode? Then I am astonished to find I want only my bed for a lie-down."

"A bed you shall have. Those I possess in abundance."

He took the dog from her and led her to the door, where his butler smiled a warm greeting. "How are we situated, Clive? Has Mrs. Wimbish thrown anything at you today?"

"No, my lord," he said, glancing at the muddied snout, ears, and face of the bundle in his arms. "She is never happier than when there is a ball at Morchards. But what have you here, m'lord?"

"Ah, yes. A sad little thing, I fear. Will you be so good as to have her bathed? I will inquire after her later."

"Of course, m'lord" He signaled to a footman, who at once took the dog from Perryn. The poor animal whimpered at being separated from her benefactor, faint yelps being heard as the servant disappeared down the hall.

"You remember Miss Trentham?" he said.

Clive bowed to her. "Of course. You visited his lordship with your father some four or five years past, I believe."

"You have an excellent memory, for we stayed but one night."

"But a memorable night"—he glanced at Perryn—"or so I recall."

Fenella laughed outright. When Perryn seemed at a loss to understand the conversation, she explained. "You were badly foxed, if you remember, and I had to fetch poor Clive and two or three footmen to haul you to your bedchamber."

He frowned at her. "I begin to fear learning anything more of your visit. To think of your having to tend to me in such a manner, and that upon a first acquaintance, is quite beyond the pale. I offer you a thousand apologies."

Fenella smiled. "One will do. And now, if you please, I long for nothing more than my bedchamber."

"Of course."

"Oh, no," Fenella murmured some five hours later as she regarded her reflection in the looking glass.

"What is it, miss?"

The gown, her coiffure, even the lovely gold and pearl necklace dangling prettily about her neck conjured up sudden memories which brought the most ridiculous blush to her cheeks. She had been wearing this same gown and jewels the last time she had waltzed with Perryn at Mrs. Almington's town house in London. She felt certain he would recall her ensemble, since he had praised her appearance so warmly that evening.

She wondered if Perryn had even the smallest notion in how dramatic a fashion that waltz had changed the course of her life. By May of that Season, she had believed herself in love with a wonderful young man by the name of Mr. Darius Clavering, tall, blond, blue-eyed, handsome, and of so sweet a temper she had been completely at ease in his company. He was attentive, kind, welcoming in every respect, and would make a most admirable husband. She had been convinced of her sincere attachment to him.

The entire *beau monde* had supported their interest in one

another, for he was a beloved younger son of Viscount Clavering, with scarcely a farthing to his name, and she a great heiress. She had felt on such solid footing for the first time in her life that even the infamous kiss in the maze had ceased plaguing her dreams. She had had every confidence she would very soon be betrothed to her dear Darius.

For that reason, she made the worst of mistakes in softening her attitude toward Perryn. She even deigned to offer him a smile on one occasion which led, most unfortuitously, to the waltz at Mrs. Almington's house during the last week of the Season. She had been surprised he had asked her, but she felt perfectly safe in accepting him. After all, she was nearly betrothed to Mr. Clavering.

He led her onto the ballroom floor. The music began all so innocently. He took her in his arms, and from that moment, she had been lost. She had felt so odd—as though a song was being sung in every fiber of her being, to which Perryn alone knew the melody. He did not speak, she scarcely lifted her gaze to him, yet the whole while she knew herself to be desired.

"Do you love him?" he had asked on the third revolution about the floor.

She finally had the courage to meet his gaze. She had intended upon answering lightly, to toss her head, to smile, to laugh, to pronounce her deepening affection for Mr. Clavering. But the expression in his eyes was serious, more than she had ever known it to be. She had meant to speak firmly of her love. Instead, she responded in a quiet voice, "I do not know."

There, the truth had been spoken, a truth she had not known existed. How was this possible? She had been so certain of her love for Darius. Why had Perryn's simple question caused her to doubt?

She had expected taunts or quips or even reprimands to fall from his lips. Instead, he had said, "Be certain, Miss Trentham. Be very certain. Mr. Clavering is an honorable man, well-respected, and as your husband would deserve nothing less than your most passionate love."

Tears of frustration touched her eyes. She remembered having thought, *I could love him were it not for this man always reminding me of what I long for in the deepest parts of my dreams*. The remainder of the dance was conducted in thoughtful silence, at the end of which she extended her hand to him. He placed an impulsive kiss on her fingers, yet why he did so bemused her entirely. She withdrew her hand, feeling as though her skin was on fire even beneath her gloves.

"Why did you do that?' she asked.

He smiled. "I suppose I shall always be a rogue."

Mr. Clavering had left London the next day after a brief conversation with her, when she confessed, before ever he offered for her, that she had come to understand that though she greatly esteemed him, she did not love him.

"Miss?"

Fenella's thoughts trickled back to the present.

"Miss?"

She turned to her maid. "I wore this very gown, these very jewels, and my hair in precisely this fashion the night I waltzed with Perryn."

"Oh, miss," Betsy commiserated.

"Do you think he will take notice of it? I fear encouraging him in this wretched oversight."

"I have not unearthed any of your other gowns. I am that sorry. To see a new one properly pressed would require an hour at the very least. If only I had not let you sleep so very long."

"Do not fret yourself. I did not think of it until I looked in the mirror, and I daresay Perryn will be so very much engaged with his many guests that he will take little heed of me."

Eight

Perryn stood before the mirror in his bedchamber, his shaving gear spread before him, his whiskers soaped, the blade of his razor poised against his cheek. He barely noticed his reflection, however, for his thoughts were drawn inward, his mind caught up in a dozen images at once.

From the time he had given the poor dog into the care of one of his footmen and listened as Fenella teased him about being carted to his chamber, she had been fixed in his mind. He did not comprehend precisely why his thoughts had become so full of her, except that he had seen approval in his butler's expression.

He should not give a fig for what any of his servants thought of his guests. However, he had known Clive his entire life and understood how very particular he was in his opinions about young ladies. His approbation of Miss Trentham seemed to be working in Perryn strongly.

He wondered again if it was possible he had formed a *tendre* for Miss Trentham—only that seemed impossible, since she challenged him frequently and had no interest in pleasing him in any manner, except—here he lowered his arm, which had begun to ache—except that she had designed their collection strictly with his entertainment in view.

He smiled faintly. She was such an oddity, and he still could not credit that she had actually hinted at a rather embarrassing situation to his butler after not having seen the man for five years. An oddity, indeed.

She was more, however. She had taken part in the race at Thurloxton with great pluck, which had pleased him very much. There was always in her countenance and in her conduct an attitude of concern and caring, save of course where his own pride was concerned.

However, in her general concern for others, her simple, thoughtful actions frequently rendered otherwise unpleasant situations perfectly innocuous, just as her attentions to Miss Almington yesterday had saved the young woman from a day of unmitigated suffering. Her disposition toward what he considered a complete trial of a journey was one of determination, enthusiasm, and even a measure of competitiveness. He realized he valued quite deeply all of these qualities, which it would seem she possessed in abundance.

Then there were the quite forbidden kisses he had shared with her. Here he settled his razor on its tray and braced his hands on the chest of drawers as he recalled the kiss in the garden at Mrs. Almington's, and most recently the one in the woods at Dunball. Even now he could barely recollect these experiences without a profound desire to seek her out yet again, drag her into his arms, and repeat the tender assault anew. What troubled him was that he had found kissing her to be an oddly familiar experience, and yet he knew until a few days past the closest he had ever been to doing so was when he had been holding her in his arms during the waltz they had shared at a ball recently in London.

He wiped the soap from his face, moved away from the shaving stand and began pacing his bedchamber. If his valet lifted a brow, he ignored him. Something within his mind needed to be settled where Miss Trentham was concerned. What precisely, he could not say.

She had taken possession of his mind, something no

lady, not even the Duchess of Cannock, had done before. The sensation was disturbing, even vexatious, yet at the same time oddly pleasing. The whole of it was a complete mystery to him. He ought to have been a great deal more captivated by the beauty and charm of Miss Madeley, who sought to please him at every turn, than he was with Fenella Trentham, who would bite his head off did he speak the smallest word of offense to her.

He chuckled and finally decided he should complete his shaving, since his several hundred guests would be arriving soon. Many would be joining the party early for dinner. Once more soaping a portion of his face and taking up his razor in hand, he could not help but laugh at himself a little for all his concerns.

The journey would end in little more than a sennight. He would probably not see Miss Trentham again until the following year in London, and this little season of flirtation and squabbling would draw to a close, as all things did. Although, he thought, as he scraped his cheeks carefully with the sharp blade, he intended to kiss her again, promise or no promise.

"Damn and blast!" he cried out. A small rivulet of blood welled in a minuscule line across his cheek. Better not to think of kissing Miss Trentham while shaving.

When Fenella arrived on the threshold of the drawing room, at least fifty guests had assembled for dinner—a score from the charity caravan party, the remainder neighbors and friends of Lord Perryn. However, even with so many gathered in the grand salon, her gaze still became instantly fixed on the marquess. She felt a shudder of something she had rather not have felt pass through her.

He was unutterably handsome this evening in his tailcoat of black superfine, an embroidered burgundy silk waistcoat, black breeches, traditional white stockings, and black slippers meant for dancing. Would he dance with her this evening, she wondered? How wise would that be?

She knew very well there would be no wisdom at all in such a course, since of the moment she was feeling quite vulnerable to him. The rescue of the little dog alone had been sufficient to arouse her more ardent sentiments, but somehow being fixed in his home and seeing him thus surrounded in the warmest of atmospheres by his friends worked strongly on her poor, aching heart. There was only one thing to do if she was to survive the evening, the same thing she had done for the past several nights—she must keep at as great a distance from his lordship as possible. Drawing in a deep, resolving breath, she moved forward into the chamber. With so many guests to whom he must attend, she did not feel the task to be at all insuperable.

For Perryn's part, from the moment he had arrived in the drawing room he had been keeping watch for Miss Trentham. Hopes of kissing her again had quite taken up residence in his mind, and he had decided he would do what he could to steal another from her—tonight! To that end, he had orchestrated a little surprise for her during the course of the evening.

When he finally saw her, wearing a gown that was all too familiar to him, for she had worn it during the only waltz they had ever shared, strange, odd twistings tightened his chest. He vowed she grew prettier every day, even though she seemed in some manner distressed. He wondered why and wished he was free to cross to her, take her arm, and demand she tell him her troubles. When had her contentment become so important to him?

She was quickly besieged not by just her usual beaus but by several others as well, and his desire for her contentment transformed into a pulsing need to land each of the gentlemen surrounding her a powerful leveler. They crowded her and winked at her and attempted in every manner possible to ingratiate themselves into her lovely society. She said something and they all laughed uproariously. He despised them one and all.

"I suppose you will lead out the Countess of Brockley for the first set."

His attention was drawn back to Mrs. Sugnell, with whom he had been flirting. "Eh? Oh, yes, of course. Propriety demands it, since she is the principal lady in the room."

"I wonder with whom you will dance after that."

Though his attention again strayed to the far side of the room where Miss Trentham was engaged in dazzling her court, he did not misunderstand Mrs. Sugnell's hint. Turning to her, he smiled. "With you, of course, Mrs. Sugnell, if you will have me." He then caught up her hand and kissed her fingers lightly.

She blushed rather deeply, a circumstance which took him aback. What was she thinking? he wondered. Did she fancy herself in love with him? His conscience strained at its moorings as he recalled Miss Trentham's animadversions on the subject of his flirtations. He began to wonder if he was using her ill, keeping certain impossible hopes alive while his only intention of the moment was to stave off the jealousy he was feeling. If only Miss Trentham had not formed part of Mrs. Almington's caravan, how differently he would be feeling in this moment.

Fenella felt ill at the sight of Perryn kissing Mrs. Sugnell's fingers *again*. A rogue was a rogue. She turned her back on his part of the room and concentrated instead, although with a mounting sense of boredom, upon Mr. Silverdale's description of how many folds he felt was necessary to properly arrange and tie the Mathematical neck cloth.

Dinner was soon announced, and Fenella began to feel a little more at ease. With fifty people sitting down to enjoy two removes in Perryn's grand dining hall, and her seat situated quite distant from his, she had little to fear. She became acquainted with those around her and the conversation became quite lively, particularly with the gentlemen to her right and her left. If occasionally she permitted her gaze to stray to the head of the table, who could blame her? She only regretted doing so when finally Perryn caught her eye and raised his glass to her.

Her heart seemed to swell at the sight of his smile. She took a sip of wine. He did as well. The silent toast somehow affected her as much as if he had just whispered something improper into her ear. She felt warm to her toes.

The gentleman to her right asked her if she had been to Morchards before. Gratefully, she turned her attention to him and tried very hard once more to ignore her host.

The ball progressed for her in much the same manner. She maneuvered carefully to keep herself at a strong distance from the marquess, at the same time taking delight in her various partners and the variety of dances which presented themselves hour upon hour. The practicing of the quadrille just three days earlier had resulted in the gratitude of both Miss Almington and Miss Keele, who each exclaimed they had gone down the set with perfect ease. So happy was Fenella because of being at a ball, dancing every dance, and enjoying the society of her friends that she lost track of Perryn. A waltz was next and she had been hunting for Mr. Aston, to whom she had promised this dance, only to discover him quite foxed in the billiard room.

"I fear I cannot oblige you, Miss Trentham," he slurred, and then hiccoughed. "Too dashed bosky by half!"

She laughed and turned to leave when she found herself confronted by Perryn.

"Oh!" she cried, a quick distress overwhelming her. "I was just . . . that is, you will excuse me?"

"You have been avoiding me the entire evening," he said, "and pray, do not pretend otherwise, for I have watched you carefully. Come, let me escort you back to the ball-room."

He offered his arm and she stared at it, fear seizing her heart.

"Have I offended you somehow?" he asked, his expression faintly stricken. "I will apologize now if I have."

She shook her head and took his arm. "I do beg your pardon. I did not intend to seem ungrateful or vexed, for I am neither."

"Then what is troubling you? I noticed your discomfiture the moment you entered my drawing room earlier."

She could hardly tell him that he was the cause of her disquiet. She released a sigh. "I can hardly say," she responded truthfully. The halls were filled with guests nodding to Perryn and occasionally to her, not precisely the most appropriate place for such a conversation.

"Then I will not press you. May I have the pleasure of dancing with you, Miss Trentham? I could not help but apprehend that your partner was unable to fulfill his duty to you."

At that, Fenella smiled. "Poor Mr. Aston. I fear he grows daily more heavily inclined to wine than he ought to be. Of course I shall be delighted to dance with you, my lord."

Fear, however, once more sliced through her heart. She felt so close to tears that she averted her gaze and commented on how beautiful the wainscoting was in the blue antechamber as they passed through. He responded in kind. When conversation threatened to languish, she brought forward what she felt was a harmless subject. "Have you perchance seen yet the little dog we rescued? I imagine she will look very pretty bathed and brushed."

"No, I did not have time to go to her. I believe she is in the kennels, but you may trust me she is being well cared for."

"I have little doubt of that."

"Perhaps tomorrow we can decide what to do with her. We still have a sennight before we return to Bath."

"Tomorrow will be soon enough."

Once arrived at the ballroom, she felt a little more at ease, but not entirely.

"I fear you are trembling, Fennel," he said. "Are you certain you are well? Perhaps you wish to retire." He seemed genuinely concerned for her.

This use of his favorite sobriquet, however, coupled with his sincerity, seemed to give her a little strength. "I am suffering only the mildest fit of the nerves, undoubtedly from so many days of travel, collecting of kisses, and general merriment. However, I feel perfectly capable of dancing a simple waltz with you."

"Excellent," he responded, guiding her onto the floor. "Faith, but it seems only yesterday we were dancing thus. Did I tell you how lovely you look this evening? Gold suits your coloring, I think, quite enhancing the green of your eyes."

"Thank you," she murmured, meeting his gaze fully at last. This was a terrible mistake, for he smiled warmly and her heart turned over in her breast. Her trembling increased as he made his bow and she her polite curtsy. The music commenced. In his commanding manner, he swept her into his arms and began guiding her into the marked rhythmic moves about the floor.

"You are still trembling," he murmured.

"I cannot seem to stop, but perhaps if we keep dancing the sensation will subside."

"Do you wish it to?" he asked.

The powerful expression in his gray eyes flooded her with that which she had been attempting to avoid. "I suppose not," she said, smiling faintly.

"You are so beautiful," he whispered, his arm tightening about her waist. The words teased her cheek, since he leaned daringly close to her.

She began to feel wonderful and dizzy as he turned her around and around, up and back. She forgot her earlier intentions in that moment and let herself take the delight she always did in being so close to him. Her mind became a mingling of several of the more pleasant experiences with him, of holding his hand to her cheek the first night she met him, of kissing him in Mrs. Almington's garden at midnight, of seeing him with a child on his lap at Huntspill, of receiving his wicked kiss in the woods near Dunball, of having all the pleasure of watching him tend to the injured dog earlier today.

Perhaps his tender care of the dog had been her final undoing. And yet, for the present, she did not care. She was waltzing with Perryn and she would waltz a little more and she would let herself love every moment of it. After all, the fortnight would soon draw to a close, she would return to her home in Wiltshire, and he would go to Brighton. She doubted she would see him again until the following spring in London. Or maybe she would not even go to London in the spring. Now that the war with France was two years past, she could easily travel to the Continent, where she might just be able to forget him entirely.

Around and around, up and back. How dizzy. How delightful.

Perryn could find no words with which to converse with the lady he held in his arms. Indeed, he did not desire to speak at all. He felt completely satisfied in merely being able to look into Miss Trentham's bewitching green eyes and to lose himself for a time. He had felt this way in May, when he had last danced with her, as though in the ease of their movements and the powerful sensations that flowed between them there was no need to utter mere words. The conversation they were having was in touch and thought and dance.

He had been plotting this moment all evening, waiting until he could secure a waltz with her, having but one objective—a third stolen kiss, a kiss she would have to bestow upon him because he had vowed not to kiss her again. He was still smarting under her ill opinion of him and knew the most perfect revenge possible would be to expose her hypocrisy.

At the same time, he could not quite credit the pleasure he felt in simply dancing with her. Though his motivations were not honorable, he was surprised by how extraordinary he felt in this moment. Not for the first time he felt obliged to ask himself, *Am I tumbling in love with Fenella Trentham?*

The time had come, he thought, to give her the surprise he had prepared for her. The moment the dance ended, he queried, "Will you come with me? There is something I must show you." Once more, he offered his arm to her.

Once more, she accepted—this time without the least hesitation.

Fenella was no longer trembling, but her limbs felt fuzzy, almost disconnected. She could not quite feel her feet. She was walking, she could see the carpet and wood floors as she moved through the various halls and antechambers, but she had not the smallest sensation that her embroidered gold and pearl ballroom slippers were actually touching anything but air.

"Where are we going?" she inquired.

"The library." Once again, as when he led her from the ballroom to the billiard room, he nodded to guests and called out appropriate greetings from time to time. If Fenella knew herself to be watched with interest, if Perryn's conduct toward her in taking strong hold of her arm and piloting her through his mansion gave fodder to the gabblemongers, again she did not care. He had something he desired to show her. She wondered if he was merely being sly and that he meant to attempt to kiss her again once within the library. Would he break his word to her? Would she encourage him to do so?

She could not think seriously about anything of the moment. Her heart was as light as downy feathers caught on a breeze.

Mounting the stairs, she felt certain she was ascending not to the first floor but rather to the clouds. He turned to her, looking down into her face, and smiled. She smiled in return. He was so deuced handsome. On impulse, she overlaid his arm with her hand.

"Do you fear falling?" he inquired, his smile teasing.

"I believe I do," she responded.

Once at the library, he released her arm, opened the door, and guided her within. Betsy stood by a glowing fireplace, grinning, a long cord held in her hand. Fenella followed the line of the cord, but could not see the object attached to it for the numerous chairs and tables hampering her view. She took a few steps, peered around a vase of flowers, and saw the most adorable dog, bathed, groomed and lying flat before a warm blaze, her head supported on her paws. Her tail began to wag.

"Is this our pup?" she cried.

"Indeed it is."

"Oh, Perryn, she is utterly adorable. I would not have known her." She moved forward at once, hastily removing her long silk gloves, and in full ball dress dropped to her knees before the beautiful little dog that was part cocker spaniel and some smaller but unrecognizable strain suggested by her long, thin fur of a coppery hue. Her forehead bore a white mark and her ears hung well past her muzzle. "She is inordinately charming. What a wonderful surprise, Perryn! Thank you. I believe I shall have her with me always."

"I shall leave you, miss," Betsy said. "Ring for me when you need her to be taken away."

"Thank you, Betsy."

As the door closed softly upon her maid, Perryn drew a chair forward and planted himself next to Fenella, who was still kneeling beside the dog. "What will you name her?" he asked.

"She has the delicate look of a Missy, I think."

Since at that moment, the little dog turned her large brown eyes to Perryn, he laughed. "I believe you are right, and certainly of a temper that would be in keeping with such an obsequious name. I believe she is attempting to ingratiate herself into my good graces with such an imploring expression. I only hope your maid does not leave your employ because of having to attend to her."

"Missy will become the object of her coddling before the night is far spent, though I daresay she has already begun working her wiles on my poor abigail."

Perryn looked at the little dog, who again wagged her tail. "She does not seem big enough to be of use on a farm."

"You forget that she has an excellent reputation for chasing rats. I am persuaded her size means nothing in this instance and that her spirit is large enough to fend off a bear were she of a mind to attack anything so large."

Perryn laughed.

As she rubbed Missy's ears, Fenella sighed. "Indeed, Perryn, thank you so much. This was an unlooked for kindness and the very best surprises."

He leaned forward, settling his elbows on his knees. The glow from the hearth covered his features in gold and red hues. He appeared unearthly, his face lit with fire. His voice was soft, beckoning as he spoke. "The least I could do for a partner who has made what I thought would be the most tedious of journeys something of a joy."

Fenella's heart skipped a beat. He was so close to her, but inches away. Her gaze drifted to his lips and back slowly to his eyes. A warning sounded somewhere deeply in her mind, but then disappeared entirely.

He caught up her hand and kissed her fingers, not as she had seen him salute Mrs. Sugnell's fingers with grand flourishes and broad smiles, but quite slowly, one at a time. She stopped petting Missy, her attention solely for the sight of his lips inching past her fingers until he gently turned her hand over and kissed the inside of her wrist. She found she could not breathe.

"You promised you would not kiss me," she whispered.

"I have not kissed you—or did you mean to include your arm in the vow you forced on me?"

She said nothing in response, for he had begun making a very slow, deliberate progress up her arm. After a time, he slid from the chair so that he was kneeling beside her. In a very gentle movement, without once releasing her arm, he picked up Missy with his free hand and shifted her carefully onto the hearth. Once more he settled his lips on her arm, though for the life of her she could not understand precisely why she did not utter even the faintest protest, except that she believed nothing in her experience had ever felt so exquisite as the trail of soft kisses he was placing against the bare skin of her arm. When he reached the puff of her gold silk sleeve, he moved behind her and began kissing her neck.

A spattering of gooseflesh raked down her back and side. "My lord?"

"Do not fret. I will not kiss you. I vowed I would not and I will keep my word, unless . . ."

Unhappy word. *She* must decide. She should tell him to stop. Indeed, she should. This was most scandalous. He kissed the small space behind her ear and once more settled several down her neck. "Perryn?" Nothing followed, not a single word either of acquiescence or encouragement. She must decide.

She felt so very weak, as though a sudden illness had taken hold of her, robbing her of all strength. In her debility, she began to slide away from him. He caught her waist and supported her. She rested her head against his and the kisses on her neck became almost urgent. A faint, unexpected moan escaped her lips.

He moved upward, kissing just behind her ear once more. "Fenella," he whispered, speaking her name for the first time, his breath drifting over her cheek. More gooseflesh. The room had grown so warm. He began settling kisses on her cheek, drifting downward until he was just touching the corner of her mouth. "I will not kiss you, unless . . ."

She should not do what was in her heart to do, but heaven help her, she wanted his kisses so very much! Her lips parted. She had but to turn into him, just a little.

"Beautiful Fennel," he whispered against her cheek. "Allow me one kiss. Just one."

Her lips parted. "I should not, but oh, Perryn . . ." She turned willingly into him, and his lips were on hers in the most blissful meeting she could have imagined. The room, gently lit as it was, now disappeared entirely. She was in a mystical place of everlasting dreams, hopes, and desires. She slid her arm about his neck, accepting the gift of his kiss with deep gratitude and wonder.

Perryn had kissed a great many ladies in his life, but never had a woman so captivated him as Fenella Trentham. He had accomplished what he had set out to do—to take a third kiss from her against her expressed wishes and a most hateful promise. He remembered somewhat hazily that he had been angry and that this kiss was supposed to be a sort of retribution for her hapless statement, *I could never love a rogue.*

However, at the moment vindication was not what he was experiencing, but rather a passion that shocked even his own roguish sensibilities. He explored her mouth, his own longings taking hold of him. Images of a marriage bed rose in his mind. What would it be to take Fennel to wife?

The feel of her lips beneath his own was heavenly. He

was reminded suddenly of his angel, the unknown lady who had visited him so long ago and spoken to him of wonderful things and turned the course of his life. If only he could combine the lady in his arms with his angel, he would have something beyond speaking.

"Perryn." Her voice floated through his thoughts. What did his angel matter when Fennel was held captive in his arms?

He kissed her again and again until she spoke his name in a continual soft murmur against his lips. He gathered her more closely to him, slanting a hard kiss across her lips. She clung to him, responding to each shift of his body with a languorous slither as she moved to fit herself against him. Was this indeed Fenella Trentham who pinched at him one word out of two?

Fenella could not know what he was thinking. She was not certain of her own thoughts—or even if she had any. She was still caught in that other, mysterious world where only Perryn existed. She had tried to avoid his embrace as well as the ensuing assault on her lips, but even as he kissed her more recklessly, she knew it was a hopeless case, certainly from the moment he placed his lips on her wrist. That light touch had been her undoing and if not that, certainly when he kissed her neck so seductively. What was this power he had over her, that with a few assaults on her fingers, arm, or cheek she had but the strength of a bowl of pudding?

In the distance of her mind, a frayed nerve began to wink at her. *Think, Fenella.* Oh, but thinking was not nearly so delightful as . . . his tongue pierced her mouth anew and she fell again deeply under his spell. Was she upright or lying down? she could not say. All she knew was her body felt pinned to Perryn's as though by ancient design. The world had conspired against her from the beginning of time that she would so readily give her kisses to the very man she had been determined to hold at bay.

Once more her mind called to her from deeply within. Doubt in odd, quick streams began to swirl over her eyes. Whatever was she doing? She felt him draw back.

"What is it?" he asked, stroking her cheek with the back of his finger.

"Perryn, whatever does this mean?" she asked, her heart tightening. Missy scooted close once more and whined. Somehow the sight of the little dog brought her closer to the truth. She withdrew her arm from about Perryn's neck and pulled Missy onto her lap.

"I do not know, Fennel," he murmured, an arm still slung about her waist. "Faith, but you are so beautiful."

He leaned forward as if to kiss her again, but she stopped him with a hand on his chest. "Dear Perryn, this cannot be." She smiled, if sadly. "You must return to your guests."

"Of the moment," he said quietly, "I do not give a fig for my guests. I vow I could remain here with you forever."

Fenella looked at him, her heart leaping in hope. What did he mean by saying such a thing to her? "Perryn, I do not comprehend in the least what it is you might be feeling. Indeed, I hardly know my own sentiments or . . ." She could not complete her thought, for at that moment the door opened quite abruptly. Mrs. Sugnell stood on the threshold. Perryn released her gently and rose to his feet.

Fenella had the worst feeling about her sudden appearance.

"Hallo, Perryn," Mrs. Sugnell called sweetly. "I am sorry I arrived so very late, but at least you have had Miss Trentham to entertain you—and there is that dear little dog you were telling me about! How very pretty she is."

"If you will excuse us for a moment, Mrs. Sugnell?"

"Why yes, of course." She withdrew, but not without offering a knowing wink before she closed the door.

Fenella glared at Perryn. "How could you?" she whispered. "A tryst with two ladies in the same place at the same hour? Quite lacking in finesse, do you not think so?"

Perryn appeared shocked. "You cannot possibly think—!"

Fenella did not wait to hear his explanations. She gathered up Missy, as well as her gloves, and hurried from the chamber.

Perryn's voice followed her. "Well, of course you would think something so contemptible, since you believe me devoid of every proper sentiment. Go, then, Miss Trentham! I am well rid of you!"

Perryn glared at the doorway, beyond which he could see a rather smug Mrs. Sugnell waiting to be beckoned forward. How dare Miss Trentham accuse him of anything so vile as inviting two ladies to an assignation?

Her wretched opinion of him once more scraped at his nerves. In this moment he almost despised her. In truth, he should have felt triumphant for he had succeeded in his objective—he had secured a kiss from her which she had made him promise never to take. Hah!

Except, by God, he had enjoyed that kiss, holding her, pressing his lips to hers, her mouth so yielding, her kisses utterly delectable. His thoughts drew to a sharp halt. He wondered what it was she had meant to say to him before Mrs. Sugnell's unexpected arrival. His mind took another leap. What would he have said to her had that lady not interrupted them?

He felt sobered suddenly. Good God, he never should have kissed her! What the deuce was he thinking—retribution or not!—to be trifling with a maiden?

"Perryn?" Mrs. Sugnell was standing in the doorway smiling at him.

"Mrs. Sugnell," he returned, wondering just how he ought to deal with this lady. He did not, however, begin by inviting her into the library. Instead, he went to her. "I hope you are pleased for the mischief you have brewed just now."

"I do not take your meaning, m'lord."

He shook his head. "And yet you will pretend your innocence. Do you take me for a simpleton?"

"On no account."

"Only tell me why you announced you were sorry to have arrived so late."

"I thought it the quickest means by which to save you from being entrapped by a young lady who is yet unmarried and who should not be cloistered with any gentleman in private for so long a time. She could easily accuse you of ungentlemanly conduct, and you would soon find yourself in the basket!"

Perryn did not feel inclined to argue the point. Indeed, of the moment he found himself grateful Mrs. Sugnell had arrived when she did to disrupt the tryst. Though he doubted very much that Miss Trentham was just such a manipulative creature as Mrs. Sugnell had described, he had been far too forward with her for his own good. She could easily claim he had taken sore advantage of her and force a marriage if she wished for it, because indeed he had used her quite ill.

Had he gone mad, he wondered, that he would be so reckless, so heedless as to have kissed Fennel as he had?

Fenella carried Missy to her bedchamber, which she entered by slamming the door shut quite hard. She was furious, not more so with Perryn than with herself. She settled the small dog on the carpet and watched her begin a progress about the room, sniffing into each corner and beneath the bed.

Fenella paced the chamber herself, pausing once in her hasty strides to check her coiffure. At least in that regard, Perryn had not been overzealous—her ringlets were still in place.

She tugged on the bellpull to summon Betsy and once more set to pacing her room. She did not think Mrs.

Sugnell was much given to gabblemongering, but the mere thought that it could become known that she had been closeted with Lord Perryn so very scandalously brought a fiery blush to her cheeks. What had possessed her to behave so imprudently?

In due course, Betsy arrived. "Whatever happened, miss? I was awaiting your summons, expecting to attend you in the library, and then learned you were now in your bedchamber. Ah, there is little Missy." She scooped the dog up in her arms and met Fenella's gaze. "Oh, miss, what has happened? I can see that you are overset."

"If you must know I . . . I quarreled with Perryn. His conduct—"

"He did not—"

"He did, if you must know—"

"Oh, miss . . ." Betsy's eyes drooped suddenly with longing. "He is that handsome. Was it wonderful?"

"Betsy!" Fenella cried, aghast. "Take command of yourself! He . . . he insulted me in the worst manner possible."

Betsy, who knew something of the world, merely rolled her eyes. "I shall take Missy for a walk and then return her to the kennels."

"No!" she cried. "I intend for her to remain with me. Of course she should spend a little time in the gardens, but then bring her here for the night."

"As you wish. Then I shall stay with her until you retire to bed for the evening."

"Thank you."

Fenella turned to leave the room when Betsy continued, "I do so love Morchards. Should you decide to marry his lordship, I would not be averse to spending the rest of my days here."

Fenella, who had been opening the door upon this speech, turned to glare at her maid. "You had best make the very most of your last night here, for I tell you now it is very unlikely either of us will ever see Morchards again!"

Ignoring Betsy's quite doubting expression, she passed into the hallway and found herself in near darkness. She could smell the freshly extinguished wax and wondered if someone from the ball had been playing pranks.

She walked carefully in the direction of the staircase leading to the first floor, but found both the stairs and the lower landing also to be in near darkness. Her bedchamber was so far removed from the receiving rooms that there was scarcely anyone about, although she could see a faint, flickering glow to the left of the landing below her. She felt her way to the banister and began to descend. She eased down the first and second steps, but on the third step she tripped on something and with a cry began to tumble. Fortunately, the angle of her fall brought her colliding with the stairwell wall and she found herself upright—a little bruised, but perfectly sound.

The glow of light below grew brighter and brighter until Aubrey appeared at the bottom of the stairs.

"Fenella?" he called out, lifting his candlestick aloft. "Good God! Whatever are you doing there? I heard a cry. Do not tell me you have fallen!" He began mounting the stairs swiftly. "Are you all right?"

"I did fall," she responded, nodding. "But I believe I am uninjured." She tested her wrists and ankles and rose to her feet. "Just a little bruised, I think."

"But what happened?"

"It was very dark and I stumbled over"—she turned around—"these books." She pointed to them and immediately thought of Mrs Sugnell. "I cannot imagine why they were on the stairs or why the candles were extinguished. Anyone might have been hurt."

Aubrey moved to quickly retrieve the books. "Morchards is so very sprawling, and I had returned to my own bedchamber only to find the hallways in near darkness myself. I cannot account for it at all. So very unlike Perryn to allow any of his home to be without quite generous illumination." He turned to her. "My only present concern is that you could have been seriously injured in such a fall."

"I promise you I am perfectly well, if a little shaken. However, I feel I ought at the very least to inform Perryn's butler so the candles might be relit immediately."

Aubrey escorted her in search of Clive and found him in the entrance hall. Once there, he quit Fenella's side, leaving her to lay her concerns before Perryn's retainer. Clive was surprised to learn all the candles in that particular hall had gone out, but said he would tend to the matter at once. She was about to return to the ballroom when Perryn found her.

"Your brother has just told me. Are you certain you are not injured?"

"No, not in the least, I promise you."

Perryn took her arm but addressed his butler. "Thank you, Clive. I know I can rely upon you to tend to this matter."

"Of course, my lord," he responded, hurrying down the hall toward the nether regions.

Perryn led her away from the primary receiving rooms, and Fenella soon found herself sipping a glass of sherry in what she realized was Perryn's study. "Who would leave books on the stairs?" she queried, still feeling shaken.

"With so many guests about and so much champagne flowing through my halls, I daresay any number. I am sorry, Miss Trentham."

She looked up at him and in a quick gulp finished her sherry. He had spoken her name so formally that she was reminded of the fact they had just quarreled. He was seated on the edge of his desk, one leg swung over the corner, and watching her carefully.

After a moment, she rose to her feet, feeling as though

a century had passed since he had last kissed her instead of an hour. "I am much better, thank you. I should like to return to the ball now."

His gaze was still quiet and appraising. "I should be happy to escort you, but only if you are to tell me you do not believe I actually invited Mrs. Sugnell to the library. She was telling whiskers, you know."

"Indeed?" she responded on little more than a whisper. She frowned, for she had not thought he would address the matter with her. "Well, I am not certain it is important whether she was telling the truth or not, because I believe it is not so much that you and I might disagree as to particulars of what just happened but rather as to the substance. Was there anything in your conduct earlier, for instance, that might have led her to believe you wished for a tryst?" She could see by his expression he knew precisely what she meant.

"You mean to be harsh with me, I see."

I mean to protect my heart, what little of it yet does not already belong to you. Aloud, she said, "If that is how you perceive what I have said, then yes, I mean to be harsh."

"Very well. Allow me to escort you back to the ball."

Perryn gave her into the hands of Mr. Silverdale and watched him lead her out for a country dance. He felt frustrated and grave, for, damme, the chit had a point!

Nine

On the following morning at Crewkerne, with the caravan resumed, Perryn stood in the open doorway of the inn, taking pulls from a tankard and watching his partner, who was presently surrounded by several young schoolgirls. She was helping each of them to place kisses on a light pink ribbon.

His former pique at her opinion of him had been replaced by a concern, the depth of which surprised him, as to just how right she was about his character. He was troubled on so many fronts that it was no wonder the entire day's journey thus far from Morchards, in a southerly circle through Chard and Cricket St. Thomas to Crewkerne, had been conducted in near silence. She had feigned a complete preoccupation with embroidering the place names on the ribbons while he sat cross-armed and in crab street for all the vexation he felt at last night's accusations. What right did she have to condemn him on any point? What did any of her opinions matter? She was, after all, just another lady of his acquaintance in whom he had no particular interest other than a pronounced desire to kiss her. He should be able to conclude the whole business in the simplicity of these thoughts.

However, the sight of her thus engaged, charming the village girls and putting rouge on their lips, brought a rush of affection to his heart. So profound was the sensation that he had to acknowledge again that his experience with her was different from anything he had known before.

"Good God," he murmured to the empty room, his gaze still fixed beyond the window. "You are tumbling in love with this chit." Only, she was no chit. She was seven and twenty, a lovely woman, intelligent and kind.

Two coaches entered the village, each containing members of the caravan, among whom Mrs. Millmeece and Lady Elizabeth were numbered. Miss Trentham hastily secreted the jar of rouge in her reticule and hid her ribbon from view. He could not help but laugh as he watched her fairly run in the direction of his coach in order to conceal the nature of their collection from several interested parties. He called to his fellow travelers, intent on distracting them from her surreptitious activities, and escorted the ladies into the inn at the same time. He was relieved by their presence, for at least in the ladies' unrestrained attentions to him he could forget for a moment his unsettling thoughts about Fenella Trentham.

Having succeeded in hiding the pink ribbon, Fenella crossed the High Street just as another coach arrived, this one belonging to her brother and Miss Adbaston. She greeted both warmly, but noted with some concern that Miss Adbaston possessed herself of Aubrey's arm the moment she descended the coach. By the smile she gave Aubrey at the same time, Fenella could see at once that the young woman had developed a considerable attachment to her brother. She wondered if Aubrey was aware of Miss Adbaston's interest.

"Hallo, Fenella!" he cried cheerfully. "How do you fare this morning? I have fretted about you since last night."

Fenella was happy to report she had not felt even the smallest twinge of discomfort from having fallen on the stairs.

"I am happy to hear as much," he said sincerely. "And I have happy news of my own to report."

For a moment Fenella quailed, thinking perchance he meant to announce his betrothal to Miss Adbaston "Oh?" she queried.

"Indeed and I think you will be happy to learn of it. I recovered my losses of several nights past. Mr. Aston and some of the others got up a game of hazard once most of the guests had departed Morchards. Of course"—and here he looked down at Miss Adbaston and smiled—"I had the advantage over them all, for Miss Adbaston charmed the dice for me."

"You are being absurd, Mr. Trentham," his partner murmured, blushing. "You know very well I did no such thing."

"But it was you who made the loan of ten pounds to me. I am persuaded my winnings were all on your account."

Fenella thought she could not have heard anything worse than these revelations. "I hope at the very least," she said, addressing Miss Adbaston, "my brother repaid you."

"I would not think of letting him do anything so coarse!" she cried emphatically. "The money I gave him was a gift, which I extended to him most particularly because he has proven such an excellent friend and partner on our expedition."

Fenella glanced at Aubrey, wishing to catch his eye to see if he comprehended to the smallest degree just how violently in love this young lady was with him. He, however, chose at that moment to conveniently cast his gaze at all the various assembled coaches. "Who else might we find within? Miss Adbaston wished for a glass of lemonade before we continued, and now I see a veritable party has gathered."

"Mrs. Millmeece, Lady Elizabeth, Mr. Hanford, and Mr. Aston."

"Indeed," Aubrey cried. "But how delightful. Come, Miss Adbaston, Fenella."

He offered an arm to each of them. Fenella accepted his escort, though barely suppressing a sigh. She wished very much she could offer a warning to Miss Adbaston, but such interference seemed quite beyond the pale.

When she entered the inn, her gaze was drawn at once to Perryn, who was seated between his two favorites and laughing riotously with them at some joke or other. Aubrey and Miss Adbaston joined them. She turned away and moved to seat herself near Mr. Aston and Mr. Hanford, the former of whom seemed rather bored.

"I am sick to death of chasing after butterflies," Mr. Aston complained as he drew his tankard to his lips.

"Mr. Aston!" Fenella cried playfully. "You are not supposed to reveal the nature of your collection."

He snorted. "What collection? We have managed to capture but two of the winged creatures thus far. At the last village, I accidentally trampled a third, after which Mrs. Millmeece struck me with her parasol and called me a dolt."

Mr. Hanford took a pull from his tankard and chuckled. "My friend here," he explained to Fenella, "is disconsolate because he was relieved of two hundred pounds in Perryn's billiard room—hazard, you see."

"I heard there was a bit of gaming last night."

"Your brother had the luck," Mr. Hanford added. "In more ways than one. He would be wise to offer for the chit. She was of particular use in taking him from the table after he had won."

"Indeed?" Fenella turned and watched her brother for a moment. "Such influence I have observed, however, frequently does not last much past the speaking of vows. Once love and attachment is secured, the partners feel free to behave as badly as their characters otherwise dictate."

"I did not know you were such a cynic," he cried. "You do not believe in the efficacy of love, then?"

"I suppose I do not."

"What do you believe in?"

Fenella thought for a moment and responded with a smile. "Good manners."

Mr. Hanford laughed heartily. "It is no wonder he is so taken with you."

Fenella did not pretend to mistake his meaning. Perryn's attentions to her, particularly where Missy was concerned, had given rise to all manner of speculation. Only this morning, she had overheard Miss Keele and Miss Aston agreeing that the Marquess of Perryn had actually tumbled in love at last, and not with Miss Madeley, as that lady so fervently hoped.

"But where are *my manners?*" Mr. Hanford said, "for now I have brought a blush to your cheeks." In a quieter voice, he added, "You could not do better."

Fenella turned to stare at him. Mr. Hanford was a man whose opinion she quite respected. He was an older gentleman, perhaps sixty in years but nearer thirty in spirit. A fringe of white unruly hair surrounded his balding pate and a twinkle was never far from his kind brown eyes. Of Mrs. Almington's entire party, his sentiments on any subject seemed to her to be of great sense, offered only after careful deliberation. Yet he would tell her this? His words stunned her.

"You cannot mean what you are saying," she returned, her voice dropping as well. "Do but look at him."

Mr. Hanford shifted his gaze slightly and chuckled. "The attentions of pretty women will always please a man, and given the opportunity he will flirt rather than not, but I would encourage you to look to other considerations before rejecting entirely any gentleman."

"Such as?"

"First, I do not know of many men who would stop a coach to rescue a dog."

Fenella smiled faintly. "I believe you have the right of it."

"How does the dog fare?"

"Quite well. My maid is in charge of her, and she will eventually return to Toseland with me."

He nodded and smiled, if knowingly.

"Very well," Fenella said, "I will concede this much—aiding my dear little Missy was quite gentlemanly."

"Beyond this kindness," he continued, "I would recommend you look to Perryn's conduct in a broad range of settings and circumstances, his opinions on a variety of subjects, and most particularly the affection and respect in which he is held by his closest friends. This"—he waved a hand at the two giggling ladies—"is but nonsense."

"Nonsense?" she cried. "In that, I feel you are greatly mistaken. I think . . ."

He would not permit her to complete her thought, but rather lifted a hand. "No, no, Miss Trentham. I cannot allow an argument on so pretty a day. Suffice it to say that these are my opinions. You may tell me to go to the devil if you like, but I will not be reasoned out of them. Let me therefore bring forth a much more agreeable subject. Do you intend to perform for us this evening? Our hostess at Tewins Court, Mrs. Fielding, is a very great friend and told me not a month past she purchased a most excellent pianoforte in honor of Mrs. Almington's caravan.

"Mr. Hanford, you know very well there are at least six other ladies among us far more accomplished than myself."

"Perhaps," he returned, smiling. "Yet for some reason I seem to take delight in your performances above them all."

"How on earth do you account for that?" she cried. "I am always apt to misplay at least one note, usually more, throughout my performance."

"Yes, but you do so quite charmingly."

"And you, sir, speak as much nonsense as any gentleman I know."

He laughed heartily.

"Miss Trentham."

Fenella turned to find herself addressed by Perryn. "Oh,

I beg your pardon, Perryn. I did not see you. I expect you wish to be going?" When had he left the ladies, now sulking, to approach her, and why the deuce were his eyes flashing, unless . . . was it possible he was *jealous?*

She glanced at Mr. Hanford and saw he was barely repressing a smile. It was evident to her he shared her suspicion.

"As it happens, I am," Lord Perryn said, rather coldly. "But only if you are willing to be drawn away from such agreeable company. I hate to think of your suffering even the smallest ennui for the next portion of our journey when you could be so charmingly entertained here in Crewkerne."

Fenella rose, something within her heart beginning to hum. "Mr. Hanford is always charming and agreeable, but you have the right of it. We should be going." Given Perryn's aggravation, she could not resist turning to Mr. Hanford, who had risen politely to his feet as well, and extending her hand to him. In keeping with her intention, he made a great fuss, raising her hand to his lips and kissing her fingers with something of a staged flourish—much in Perryn's manner, she thought wickedly. If he winked slyly at her before releasing her hand, she pretended not to notice.

Permitting Perryn to guide her back to his coach, she was oddly pleased that a very harmless though lively conversation with a gentleman far beyond the age of her own father should overset him as it had.

The remainder of the morning's work as the coach ambled its way from Crewkerne to Hinton St. George, Lopen, and finally Martock was conducted in much the same manner as the earlier part of the journey—Fenella concentrated on her embroidery and dark clouds gathered above Perryn's head. She could see he was out of reason cross, but she did not feel in the least responsible for his ill temper.

He was, however, polite to a fault, which made her wonder all the more at the opinions Mr. Hanford ventured at

Crewkerne. What was Perryn's conduct in his larger world, what were his views on numerous subjects, and in just how much affection was he held by his closest friends—Mrs. Almington, for instance, or Colonel Bedrell, who was said to have been at Oxford with him?

On one point, however, she was not in agreement with Mr. Hanford. Though he had been able to dismiss quite lightly Perryn's flirtations, she could not. What a gentleman might excuse easily in another of his sex she was not at all certain a woman could or even ought to.

As the coach drew into the lane leading to Tewins Court, Perryn broke a five-mile silence. "I have been wondering what precisely Mr. Hanford had been saying to you and you to him that you were both so engrossed in your conversation."

She was surprised he had even brought the subject forward, and that after so great a lapse of time.

"Many things," she responded vaguely.

He narrowed his eyes. "You appeared to me to be enjoying a lively flirtation with him. I only wonder at your doing so with a man old enough to be your grandfather."

Fenella put away the last of her embroidery and secured the bandbox. "Not my grandfather, surely. I believe Mr. Hanford is just sixty, and I am a spinster of seven and twenty. For him to have been a grandparent to me would have meant both he and his offspring would have married and born children at about the age of fifteen or thereabouts."

She heard him growl. "You are speaking absurdities," he responded. "What were you discussing—or is my question wholly impertinent?"

"It is," she responded archly, as the coach turned up the drive. "However, I shall answer you just the same. As it happens, we were speaking of you. He hinted I would do well to become the next Marchioness of Perryn."

"What?" he exclaimed. "Hanford never said as much. I would wager my entire fortune against it."

"Then you would forthwith be a pauper. I believe he was attempting to play the matchmaker, although your tone quite offends me. Really, Perryn, you should not have brought the subject forward if you did not desire to hear the particulars. Are you stunned that he would make such a suggestion to me, or do you not yet realize how dear little Missy has given rise to a great deal of gabblemongering in many quarters?"

The coach drew to a stop and Perryn led the way from the elegant conveyance, handing her down, a scowl marring his features. "I trust you laid any such gossip to rest."

"I did not have the opportunity to do so. Mr. Hanford was intent on convincing me that in terms of choosing a husband, I could not do better than to wed you. Only tell me, Perryn," she added as she crossed the threshold of the lovely Tudor mansion, "is that true?"

Perryn met her gaze strongly, his own temper rising sharply. There it was again, that deuced challenging manner of hers.

Then she smiled, rather ruefully, and shook her head. "Come, let us set our squabbles aside and do the pretty with our latest host and hostess."

"Abominable girl," he whispered over her shoulder as she moved forward to greet their most recent host and hostess.

He was, however, far from feeling she was any such thing.

That evening, after enjoying a splendid feast at Mrs. Fielding's table, Fenella moved into the grand salon, where the party was gathering to admire the new Broadwood Grand. Just as Mr. Hanford had said, it had been brought to Tewins Court especially for the occasion. Several of the most accomplished ladies gathered about the instrument and took turns playing short melodies in order to determine the weight of the keys and the general tone of the instrument. Mrs. Fielding had chosen well, and her pianoforte was very soon proclaimed by all to be superior in every respect.

Fenella took her seat before the instrument, as had the others before her, and found their praises not to be exaggerated. However, when the hour arrived for actually performing, she quickly moved to the back of the room, hoping she would be forgotten. Regardless of what Mr. Hanford had said in praise of her skill, she knew herself to be far less proficient than most of the ladies present. In such a society as the one gathered here tonight, she had no interest in exposing her deficiencies.

Miss Keele performed first and played exceptionally well, which was not surprising. She was by far a superior pianofortist. Then Miss Almington acquitted herself wonderfully, to the delight of her parents, who both applauded her performance loudly. Lady Elizabeth Leycott was next, along with Mrs. Sugnell, who performed together a charming duet. Afterward, Mrs. Fielding brought forward a harp for her daughter to play while she, herself, executed the accompaniment.

A respite occurred, in which tea and cakes were served, immediately following which Mr. Hanford noisily begged Fenella to take a turn at the instrument. She declined graciously, and was relieved when he acquiesced politely to her refusal.

She watched, however, in some horror as he then approached Lord Perryn, whispering something to him which caused Perryn to glance in her direction. She caught her breath, for she was fully conversant with the particular light which entered his eye and knew it boded ill for her.

A moment later, Perryn approached Miss Madeley and in the most fulsome manner possible beseeched her to play for them all. Miss Madeley pretended to blush and protest, but at the same time quickly rose to her feet and accepted his arm in escort to the pianoforte.

Miss Madeley, who set every masculine heart to beating wildly with her delicate blond beauty, was no great performer, but she never hesitated to make a spectacle of herself if given the proper encouragement. Perryn released her to the keys by thanking her for playing, but apparently decided he could not possibly leave her side without bringing her fingers to his lips. Odious man!

The entire gentle scene so irritated Fenella that it was all she could do to attend to Mr. Silverdale's conversation. When Perryn returned to his seat beside Mrs. Sugnell, he glanced in her direction, caught her eye, and lifted a challenging brow.

"Rascal!" she murmured.

"Beg pardon, Miss Trentham? Have I given offense?"

She glanced up at Mr. Silverdale. "No, of course not. I was referring to someone else. I am being provoked, and that quite sorely, if you must know."

"How so?"

"My lord Perryn is attempting to taunt me into performing."

"What? By bringing Miss Madeley forward? How would that accomplish the deed?"

"He knows I am competitive by nature and comprehends quite well how sorely it will rankle that she will perform when I will not. There! You see she can hardly find the proper notes, but afterward she blushes so adorably that she wins her audience through her beauty and sympathy. I am all out of patience, I tell you!"

"Well, you should play," he returned quietly. "You do not know how much your performance pleases."

She looked at him, recalling that Mr. Hanford had said something similar. "Indeed?"

"Very much so."

When Miss Madeley had concluded her performance, Perryn took the opportunity to march directly to Fenella, extending his hand to her. "Will you now play for us, Miss Trentham? I know you have refused once already, but will you not perform for your long-suffering partner?"

"Beast," she murmured, taking his hand "Very well."

He chuckled deeply as he led her to the instrument.

Once at the pianoforte, Fenella quickly withdrew her hand from his lest he attempt to kiss her fingers as he had Miss Madeley's. She sat down, positioning herself carefully before the full range of keys.

Just as she predicted, she did not play perfectly. However, once she settled into the sonata and the sweetly familiar patterns of the music, she forgot the room entirely, every bickering jealousy, every struggle, strife, and suffering. She sank into the inspiration of the composer and let the music take her on its delightful journey. She was done before she felt she had even begun. A minute seemed to have passed, instead of fifteen. She rose and took a very small bow, only this time, she listened to the audience and looked at them as she had not before.

There seemed to be a swell of applause and even a few murmurs of praise. "Well done," from Mr. Almington. "Good girl," from Colonel Bedrell. Mr. Hanford was applauding strongly and beaming a smile at her. She felt shy of a sudden and embarrassed. Mr. Fielding took her arm and led her back to her seat. "Excellent, my dear," he murmured. "First rate!"

She truly did not understand such accolades, but for the first time she felt the full import of them and was grateful if for no other reason than that her performance had actually given pleasure to so many. She chanced to catch Perryn's eye and saw a speculative expression she could not precisely comprehend. He then smiled and nodded his approval as well.

She looked away, moving to rejoin Mr. Silverdale.

Though he was fervent in his compliments as well, she felt overwhelmed by the knowledge that Perryn had in some manner approved of her performance.

On the following morning, Fenella walked beside Mrs. Almington and her husband as the entire party made its way to church for morning services. She found herself in a reflective state, as must generally be the proper attitude before church. However, she rather thought the cause had more to do with Perryn than anything of an exalted nature.

After the musicale of the night before, she had finally crawled into bed, fatigued yet unable to sleep. Her thoughts, as they were so frequently, had been drawn to Perryn. If only she had not succumbed to his silent taunting, she would not have performed her sonata, and sleep would have found her readily.

Instead, the image of his face, the speculative look, the approving nod, seemed fixed within her mind—and, worse, had had the effect of softening her heart toward him yet again. She could not explain the back and forth of it all, how one moment she could be so determined against him, but a look, a wag of his head, and her determination faltered.

She could only sigh in some bemusement as she entered the church near Mrs. Fielding's home. Unfortunately, the first sight which greeted her eyes was of Perryn standing to the left of the door and conversing with Colonel Bedrell. She was not prepared for the sudden rush of emotion which swelled over her in that moment, of a rather tense longing to be with him, to converse with him, to challenge his opinions, and to see the crooked smile which often teased his lips when she was with him.

He glanced toward her and his expression sharpened. Afterward, the very thing happened which she had desired—his smile grew crooked, laughter entered his gray eyes and she was certainly standing on the edge of a cliff, ready to fall. Fortunately, Mrs. Almington's voice caught her.

"What a lovely screen," that good lady cried as she gazed in the direction of the pulpit.

Fenella's attention was drawn away fortuitously from seduction and ruin. Well, perhaps not seduction and ruin, but very nearly. She inclined her head to Perryn and kept a proper pace with Mrs. Almington.

After services, there was nothing for it but to take up her place anew in Perryn's coach. She immediately possessed herself of her embroidery as the coach headed away from Tewins Court. It was all too ridiculous, she thought, as she pulled the needle carefully through the pink kissing ribbon from Crewkerne. There was no reason why she should be afflicted as she was. If only this deuced journey was over, she could return to the comfort of her life and be at ease once more. As it was, she dreaded speaking with Perryn for fear she would like what he said, and she feared not speaking lest some remarkable effect be lost to her forever.

"You played beautifully last night," he said, as the coach turned into the lane and began gathering speed.

She lifted her eyes to him as a butterfly might, glancing at his gray eyes in a flutter of movement, only to return swiftly to her embroidery. "I would thank you for the compliment, but I am far too vexed with you."

"What now?" he cried, pretending an affront she knew by the tone of his voice he did not in the least feel. "I have not said two words to you today for fear of just this, that before I had begun you would be miffed. Now I begin to comprehend that even my silence is enough to send you into the boughs."

He exasperated her so, and that so delightfully! "I was referring to last night. You appealed to my vanity by leading Miss Madeley forward as you did. You knew I could not resist playing if she played."

"I knew no such thing," he retorted.

"What a rapper!"

"Very well. I desired to hear you play, as did Mr. Hanford, and since you are generally determined to think so ill of me, and would not have responded to a simple request, I chose to accomplish the task by approaching Miss Madeley. You obliged me quite readily. I was beyond conceit at my cleverness."

"You are very absurd this morning, but you are wrong on one score—I am not determined to think ill of you, not by half."

"Now you mean to shock me, for I do not believe you."

"I have seen much while in your company of which I heartily approve."

"And what might that be? I realize normally that such a question would appear to invite praise for the sake of praise, but I promise you, my pride has been so much lowered since having entered this coach with you a sennight past that I vow unless I hear something good of my character, I shall soon fall into a decline."

"I wish you would not tease me so—for if you must know, I like it very much."

"And I like it that you said so, but I begin to think you mean to avoid the subject at hand. Only tell me, of what in my conduct do you approve?"

"Missy, for one. Not all gentlemen would be so inclined to help a stray as you did, but there was not the smallest hesitation in your actions. If I recall correctly, you were as horrified as I was, or nearly so."

His expression became quite serious. "There can never be even a particle of justification for such cruelty. I trust Missy is prospering?"

"How could she not," Fenella responded, "when Betsy has taken to spoiling her with great zeal?"

"I am glad to hear she is well. No injuries, then?"

"Not a bit. She is perfectly sound." She was silent as

she took another stitch. "I can see you are generally kind to canines, but what of other creatures? Are you, for instance, opposed to bear-baiting as well?" She knew the question to be provocative, for many gentlemen enjoyed the sport.

"Yes, of course," he responded. "Though I believe I may have surprised you."

"Not necessarily," she responded. "Now, were you to censure the degree to which you enjoyed your flirtations, yes, m'lord, you would surprise me, indeed!"

"A flirtation," he countered, "always involves two people, not one. Does your hapless opinion extend to the ladies with whom I engage in such questionable conduct?"

She finished the lettering on the ribbon and began tying off the thread. "That, I believe, is a most excellent question. I am not certain what I think, precisely. You are the only gentleman with whom Mrs. Sugnell or Lady Elizabeth or Mrs. Millmeece flirts. Yet without the smallest differentiation, you shower your attentions on each. There lies the difference, I believe. Perhaps my complaint is with your appetite—you do not seem satisfied with one lady."

He scowled. "I do not like the turn of our discussion, particularly when it began as a categorizing of all the ways you approve of my conduct but has quickly devolved into a reproach of my enjoyment of flirting. Let us return to the previous list, if you please."

She stowed the pink ribbon carefully and withdrew another, unwrapping it from the strip of thin paper. "What is our next destination?" she asked.

He removed the itinerary from the pocket of his coat, which she had long since given to him as his particular responsibility, and perused the list. "Muchelney, I believe, and then to Langport We are headed north, it would seem, but soon east again."

Fenella nodded, her thoughts however turning in a different direction entirely. As she threaded her embroidery needle, she recalled Mr. Hanford's comment of the day before, suggesting she broaden her view of Perryn. "Colonel Bedrell is quite gentlemanly. I believe you have known him since university?"

He shrugged slightly. "Yes, but we have been friends a great deal longer. He grew up near Morchards."

Fenella stretched the lavender ribbon from Huntspill over her hoop. "This morning when I entered the church, you were engaged in conversation most enthusiastically with him. Was your discussion of a profound nature?"

Perryn chuckled. "Quite profound," he returned facetiously. "We were speaking of horses. He has a hunter he wishes to sell, and I am interested in purchasing him."

Fenella smiled as she positioned her needle carefully, pierced the ribbon, and pulled the needle through. "Gentlemen frequently enjoying exchanging views on horseflesh, I have noticed. We can pass a field with the sorriest looking nag, sway-backed, short of bone, and two men will spend half an hour deciphering every aspect of her anatomy."

"While a lady nearby yawns."

"Of course, but I suspect the reverse is true. I daresay you do not delight in hearing the finer points of a new bonnet discussed."

He feigned a yawn in response, but his eyes were laughing.

Fenella added. "I sometimes think it is a wonder we come together at all, man and woman, given the general disparity in our interests and our passions."

"I am convinced it is because there is only so much we can bear of the society of our own sex. The spirited competition one may find among men, as a topic is bandied about with port and snuff after an excellent meal, will always wear after a time. Believe me, the society of women, who generally do not take an expressed opinion as a challenge to one's position and rank in society, becomes a relief."

Fenella smiled.

"So tell me, Miss Trentham, since we are exchanging a little of our histories and views, there is something I have wanted to know for a very long time, and it involves an occurrence of three years ago."

"Three years. That is a very long time, indeed." She looked up at him, eyeing him speculatively.

"Do you recall the night you spilled champagne on me?"

"Of course," she responded, setting another stitch. "And the answer to your question is, yes, I did so intentionally." She heard a faint gasp and lifted her gaze to him.

His mouth was slightly agape. "First, I am astonished that you divined my question and, secondly, why on earth did you actually wish to drench my coat with champagne?"

"I was in the boughs, of course, for reasons I believe I have already given you during our journey through Somerset. With all your abilities and all that has been given to you, your concerns seemed no larger than which lady you might seduce in a ballroom. I was out of patience with you. But you must remember I had already met you at Morchards, and you had no knowledge of who I was or that you had—" She broke off, realizing she had very nearly revealed what had happened between them five years past when she and her father had first called on him at his home.

"There is something you're not telling me. I can see it in your complexion, which has grown rather pink."

She shook her head, feeling deeply frustrated. "It hardly matters. Suffice it to say that for the space of that Season and the Season prior, I watched you wreak any manner of havoc upon the unsuspecting hearts of lady after lady, yet no one seemed in the least capable of making you stop. I believe in that moment you had just given a young miss a rather shocking set down after having engaged her in a quite reckless flirtation. Your conduct disgusted me."

The coach struck a shallow hole, rocking slightly. He shook his head. "And so, merely because you felt strongly, you doused me with champagne?"

She could not help but smile. "Why not champagne? Although I must confess it was entirely a result of the impulse of the moment. I had not actually planned to do so. Merely, you chanced upon me just after I had listened to my friend, Miss Amesbury, speak of your conduct at Almack's toward her the night before, and there you have it."

"Good God," he muttered. "Your audacity never ceases to astonish me."

"I think what astonishes you is that anyone would dare to criticize you on any score, champagne or no."

These words appeared to give him pause. He even shook his head and chuckled. "Well, perhaps you are right, but I was as mad as fire! You can have no notion. However . . . despite whether I deserved to be punished or not, I have since puzzled over what you said to me that night. Do you recall your words?"

She shook her head and rethreaded her needle. "I fear I do not."

"Though I am certain I cannot possibly be quoting you exactly, your words were something to the effect, 'You are so puffed up in your conceit I thought at the very least you should wear a little of the champagne you withhold from others.' The part about conceit I understood perfectly, but what did you intend by the champagne I withhold from others?"

"Is that what I said to you?" she asked, once more poising her needle over the lavender ribbon.

"Yes."

"I am astonished you were able to recall it with any degree of clarity."

"Only tell me what you meant by your remarks."

She pondered his recollection of what she had said. "I suppose I expressed myself very poorly, but my meaning was that you did not share what was finest and best of yourself with others."

"So you threw champagne on me?"

"More like dumping, if I recall, for you were standing quite near to me—as you are wont to do when you are attempting to get up a flirtation—and I was mad as hops. I never would have done so had you actually attempted to converse with me. Instead, I was some wretched object, a thing to be conquered one moment and trampled the next."

He stared at her for a very long moment. "I no longer wonder you run from me when I kiss you."

"And were I not to run, my lord, what then would you do? These kisses we have shared are scandalous in the extreme. Were I to gaze adoringly into your eyes, would you then offer for me? I think not."

"What if I shocked you and said I believe I would?"

At that, she laughed heartily. "I think it far more likely you would go off in a fit of apoplexy than that you would offer for any lady under such circumstances, nonetheless my own charming, agreeable self. Ah, I see we are arrived at Muchelney at last."

The coach drew to a stop. Fenella handed Perryn a white ribbon and kept one for her own use. As she descended the coach, she found herself grateful for their arrival, since the conversation had created an atmosphere of intimacy between herself and Perryn, something she felt would be wise to avoid. Acquiring more kisses for their collection was precisely what was needed to disengage their discourse entirely.

After an hour had passed with the agreeable inhabitants of the village, Fenella was once more seated opposite Perryn as the coach headed in the direction of Langport. She noted with some relief that her partner seemed ready for a respite from their conversation as well. The remainder of the day's journey was spent quietly in collecting more kisses and embroidering place names between villages, hamlets, and towns. By the time the coach arrived at Briars Lodge just past Montacute, where the party would be enjoying the hospitality of Sir Robert and Lady Roxwell, Fenella could think only of her bed. Once resting within her own room, she spent much of the afternoon in her slumbers.

"I have never seen a sadder assemblage in my entire existence," Mrs. Almington said quietly.

Fenella could see she was in something of a quandary as to what could be done to enliven their party. There seemed to be a settling in of the doldrums which not even Sir Robert's suggestion of bringing in the card tables had allayed.

Mrs. Almington continued, albeit in a hushed voice, "Mrs. Millmeece and Mr. Aston have been squabbling from the time their coach arrived at Briars Lodge, none of the amusements I have suggested have aroused the smallest interest, and I have seen practically everyone here offer me a yawn. Our poor hostess is becoming most anxious."

Fenella glanced at Lady Roxwell and watched her wring her hands. "She and her husband are quite the best of people," she said. "They do not deserve our dullness."

Mrs. Almington sighed. "No they do not, but I have not the faintest notion what to do. Along the way, we have danced, played at cards, listened to music, and enjoyed a ball. I cannot think of another amusement that will serve."

Fenella watched as Mrs. Sugnell and Lady Elizabeth fought for the seat nearest Lord Perryn. She thought them utterly ridiculous, particularly since Perryn's attention was wholly engaged by the beautiful Miss Madeley on his right. However, the antics of the jealous ladies gave her a notion and she whispered it into Mrs. Almington's ear.

"The very thing!" she cried. "You have hit upon it exactly. I only wonder that I did not think of it myself." She moved swiftly to Miss Keele, who stood beside the pianoforte. When she in turn told her of Fenella's suggestion, Miss Keele laughed heartily, clapped her hands, and immediately took her place at the rosewood instrument. She began playing a sprightly Scottish air. "Will this do?" she inquired of her hostess.

"Perfectly." Mrs. Almington then approached Lady Roxwell and shared the idea with her. That good lady responded with a relieved smile.

With the advent of the music, the weary travelers began to sit up a little straighter in their chairs, to cease their yawns, and to watch in some curiosity as both Lady Roxwell and Mrs. Almington began moving the furniture about the chamber. Lady Roxwell murmured several orders to her butler, who left the room only to return a few minutes later with several male servants in tow, each carrying a dining chair in hand.

Miss Madeley was the first to guess. "Musical chairs!" she cried out. "How wonderful!"

Not everyone was as enthusiastic, but the notion of an entirely different entertainment at hand, one that would require a great deal of walking, leaping, and scrambling to keep a seat, pleased a sufficient amount of the party to lift the spirits generally.

"Was this your doing?" Perryn inquired of Fenella just before everyone took a place before the tall-backed chairs.

"It was, but Mrs. Sugnell and Lady Elizabeth inspired me."

"How so?"

"I shan't say, because the music is about to begin and I hope to win if I can!"

He laughed at her, which he should have. She was always ridiculous when it came to games and competitions. But winning was so very much fun!

Miss Keele happily played the music, and whenever it suited her she simply lifted her fingers off the keys. The scrambling commenced immediately, accompanied by squeals and laughter and a general flopping on laps that was entirely unavoidable and certainly half the fun.

Again the music began and again it stopped. Each time Fenella was quick to the mark, with Perryn beside her equally as fast. To his credit, he never attempted to take her chair, which she thought chivalrous but entirely unnecessary, since she was faster than he.

"Do not spare me, my lord!" she cried out as the music began again.

Hurrying, scurrying, shoving, and racing. The music stopped. More squealing and laughter. The rafters shook, someone groaned, another chair was removed.

Again and again until only three remained, Perryn, Miss Madeley, and Fenella.

The music began and two chairs sat waiting for elegant bottoms.

Miss Keele picked up the pace of the music, which the contestants were obligated to keep. The audience began clapping in rhythm, hurrying them about the chairs. The music stopped.

Fenella took her seat. Looking over her shoulder she saw Miss Madeley was sitting on Perryn's lap and proclaiming loudly that she had been wretchedly ill used. Fenella did not fail to notice how long Miss Madeley lingered, nor was Perryn in any haste to be rid of her.

The butler moved forward and removed a chair. One remained. The music began. Fenella's heart raced so fast she thought it might burst. Stars played within her head. She felt dizzy, exhilarated, intent.

Faster the music moved, more clapping, and this time shouting from the onlookers. Fenella picked up her skirts, lingering as she passed by the chair, hurrying to race round the back of it, hoping to catch it in time.

The music stopped.

She scrambled, sliding half onto the chair. Perryn's foot landed on her ankle as he, too, took possession of half of the seat. "My foot!" she wailed, more loudly than she needed.

He moved his foot, was put off balance, and she pushed him onto the floor.

Wild laughter ensued. She stared down at him triumphantly.

"You tricked me!" he cried.

"You stepped on my ankle!" she countered.

He stood up and bowed to her. "What a baggage you are!"

He offered his hand, she took it and stood to her feet. She took general bows all around and then moved away, limping.

"You are hurt!" Mrs. Almington cried. "I thought you were only feigning in order to win."

"I fear not," Fenella returned. "However, this trifling injury was quite worth it merely to see Perryn sitting on the floor."

More laughter ensued and the chairs were arranged anew.

Fenella chose to absent herself. She had no choice. Her ankle was indeed bruised, far worse than she had supposed in the heat of the game. She thought it best to quit the chamber and see for herself precisely what damage had been done.

Perryn followed after her. "I thought you were shamming it."

"In part I was—or at the time I thought I was. I mean, you did step on my ankle quite forcefully, and it did hurt. However, I chose to make a fuss over it so that I might win—and so I did! Oh, Perryn, it really does hurt!"

"I know what must be done. Come." He supported her down the hall with an arm about her waist and led her to

Sir Robert's bookroom, where he helped her sit on the sofa by the fireplace. He knelt before her and settled her leg across his lap, afterward gently feeling all about her ankle and foot.

"I do not think anything is broken," he said at last.

"I am sure it is not. I daresay I could not have placed any pressure on my foot otherwise. No, no, it is merely bruised a little."

With gentle strokes he began massaging the injured joint.

She began to relax and eased back into her chair.

"Better?"

"Yes, a little."

He released her foot, but maneuvered her leg carefully so the unhappy ankle would be resting on the sofa. He then moved to the bellpull and gave it a strong tug. A few minutes later, she was sipping brandy from a small snifter and he was still massaging both her stockinged foot and ankle.

After a few minutes, the pain seemed to have disappeared. Whether the brandy had worked its wonders or whether it had been Perryn's fingers she could not say, but she told him he could desist, which he did readily, particularly given the fact that footsteps were heard down the hall. Fenella was not surprised when Mrs. Sugnell appeared.

"I came to see how you were feeling, Miss Trentham. Are you in much pain?"

"Only a very little." She then added quite facetiously, "And how very kind of you to inquire after me."

Mrs. Sugnell all but ignored her as she shifted her gaze to the marquess. "And how sweet of you to tend to your partner so graciously, particularly when she all but cheated you of your victory."

Fenella gripped the snifter firmly and Perryn, seeing her fingers flex about the delicate glass, reached out and took it from her. Fenella thought he was right to do so. Mrs. Sugnell's purpose in coming to the library had nothing to do with concern for her and everything to do with throwing herself at Perryn's head. Another word or two and she would have thrown the snifter at Mrs. Sugnell's black curls.

"Miss Trentham cheated me of nothing," he returned easily. setting the snifter on a table at his elbow.

Mrs. Millmeece and Lady Elizabeth suddenly appeared in the doorway as well. Lady Elizabeth's cheeks were flaming with indignation. "Mr. Aston is quite foxed and fell on me! I tore my skirt."

She showed her friends the rent near the hem. Fenella suddenly felt weary to her bones and whispered to Perryn to help her to her feet, for she meant to retire. She had no desire to remain in the company of his favorites and thought that since the pain had all but disappeared, she would return to her bedchamber. She thought she would be able to put pressure on her foot, but the moment she did so, she buckled. Fortunately, Perryn caught her about the waist once more.

She turned into him and whispered, "I know your admirers will be as mad as fire, but would you please help me up the stairs? Then I shall bid you good night and they will have you all to themselves."

"Of course." Turning to his whining court, he said, "I must see Miss Trentham to her bedchamber."

They gasped, one and all.

He rolled his eyes. "I did not say I would go in, merely that I would take her to her door. She cannot bear the weight on her foot."

As one, the ladies looked at Fenella's ankle.

"Of course, Perryn," Mrs. Sugnell said. "Then you will return to us?"

"Nothing could keep me away," he remarked with a smile.

The ladies parted like water before the prow of a ship, but not without glaring at Fenella. She could only laugh, for she thought they were all being quite ridiculous following Perryn about like a gaggle of silly geese.

Even with Perryn's arm about her waist, however, she could do little more than hobble her way to the stairs. She fared even worse in attempting to mount them.

After six steps, Perryn clucked his tongue. "I fear this will not do." Without so much as a by-your-leave, he caught her up in his arms and continued the ascent.

"Oh," she murmured, sliding an arm about his neck for comfort. He carried her so easily, as though she were but a feather. She was acutely aware of being held so closely against him. Any number of former memories returned to haunt her in this moment—of kissing him with such passion in his library at Morchards, for one.

She felt dizzy of a sudden. She could hardly breathe.

When he reached the landing he paused. "Down which hall?"

"To the right." How odd her voice sounded, like a faint stirring of leaves in the wind. How did he even hear her?

Arriving at her door, he paused and looked at her. "You cannot know how I am tempted in this moment," he whispered. "You are so lovely. I vow only a saint could resist."

At that she smiled. "You are hardly a saint, m'lord."

He did not hesitate, but kissed her in a swift movement that fairly stunned her, his lips warm against hers. Time seemed to slow. The protest which formed within her mind rolled about, misshapen and entirely unheeded, as she allowed the kiss to linger.

After a moment, he drew back. "I should not have transgressed your lips," he murmured. "It was most unchivalrous of me. I had meant only to do this thing for you in helping you to your room. Forgive me?"

She released a sigh which had been locked within her throat. "Of course. You have been so kind to me since playing at musical chairs. Thank you Perryn."

He smiled and opened the door, after which he carried

her to her bed, where he set her down gingerly. He then rang for her maid. When she tried to stand, he said, "Fennel, at least wait for Betsy to arrive. She will tend to you. If you rest your foot well tonight, you will do far better tomorrow."

"You are right. I am always impatient."

He smiled. "You did a fine service to the party tonight," he said, giving the subject a little turn. "I believe that ridiculous romp downstairs was precisely what was needed to fortify the caravan. I was impressed."

"Thank you, Perryn. That was very kindly said and I am grateful." She was, however, still reeling from the kiss. "Perhaps you should go now. I promise I will not move from the bed until my abigail arrives."

He smiled and nodded. "Of course. Tomorrow, then?"

"Yes, tomorrow."

Fenella watched him enter the hall and close the door behind him. Had he truly just kissed her? Had he then actually apologized to her for having done so? Wonder of wonders!

Betsy was not long in coming. Being an excellent nurse, she soon had her ankle wrapped up carefully and in a trice saw her tucked warmly between the sheets.

Ten

"What a whisker!" Fenella cried.

"You offend me," Perryn returned playfully.

The coach hit a rut and Fenella balanced herself until the equipage stopped swaying. She withdrew a gold ribbon from Hinton St. George and carefully began unrolling the fine silk from the strip of paper. "You cannot have discovered everyone's collections," she protested.

"All but one," he announced proudly.

"I confess I am astonished. But how . . . oh, never mind. I know very well how you achieved it. Undoubtedly you approached only the ladies and bewitched each with your considerable charm."

He smiled. "Only tell me, how is your ankle this morning? I could not help but notice that though you descended the stairs carefully, you were hardly limping."

She stretched out her foot and moved the ankle in a circle. "Betsy wrapped it tightly in a bandage last night. I can say only that beyond a twinge now and again I am perfectly well."

"Good. I feared I had maimed you."

"Whatever injury you may have inflicted, I am presently persuaded that your kind ministrations last night, particularly in massaging my ankle, had a quite beneficial effect. So I thank you for that." Her thoughts were drawn quite suddenly to what had occurred later, at the door to her bedchamber, and her cheeks grew quite warm. She was mystified at their odd relationship—that while neither was of a mind to engage the other in any serious manner, they were more apt to end any encounter with a kiss than not! Having no interest, however, in bringing such a subject forward, she said, "I trust you mean to tell me what you have discovered. To begin with, what are Mr. Almington and Mrs. Sugnell collecting?"

"Fennel, you are being quite presumptuous. I never said I would reveal what I had learned."

At that her mouth fell agape and she gasped. "What a rascal you are! What a tease! You cannot be serious?"

"I might be *persuaded* to tell you, however."

She eyed him suspiciously. He could be quite wicked, and the notion that he would demand a kiss or two for the information he had acquired flitted across her mind. Her heart fairly raced at the thought, even though she certainly had no intention of obliging him. "And in what manner am I supposed to *persuade* you, though I tremble at the very notion of posing such a question?"

He sighed and a rather moonling expression overcame his features. "I am thinking of last night. I vow were you to allow just such another kiss, I would tell you all instantly!"

"Last night," she mused. "Perryn, do you not think it odd in us, when we are veritable strangers, that we would find ourselves engaged in such a wicked—dare I say pastime?—so very often?"

He smiled, rather boyishly. "There are so many things I could say in this moment, for I cannot believe you would refer to kissing me in such terms. I feel I am quite incapable of choosing with which absurdity I should respond to what you have said. Pastime? So very often?"

She sighed and searched through her embroidery thread to find an appropriate match in color to the gold ribbon. "I suppose you are right, if in nothing more than reminding me you will never be serious on such a subject. Very well, forget that I posed so ridiculous a question. Other than by parting with a kiss or two, or however many you would demand, how else might you be persuaded to tell me what you know?"

"Am I to apprehend by this statement that I have no hope of another kiss this morning?"

She merely lifted a brow and began threading her needle.

He grew quite pensive for a minute or two, then said, "For every collection I have identified, I want to know something unusual or not generally known about you. Would you agree to that?"

Something within her trembled. How strange. She did not know which she thought would be more foolish—to exchange a kiss for information or what he was now suggesting. The memory of the former would always fade, but just what unwelcome connection would be made were he to learn any number of particular things about her? "I cannot agree wholly," she said. "I believe I must hear the question first."

"You do not trust me to stay within the bounds of propriety?"

"I do not think that is the issue. Many questions might prompt ideas or feelings best left alone, if you take my meaning."

He regarded her thoughtfully for a moment. "Perhaps I do. At your discretion then."

"Very well, let me hear your first question, and if you are satisfied with my answer, you will tell me what Mrs. Sugnell's collection entails."

He thought for a very long moment as the coach wended its way in the direction of East Coker. "Will you tell me of your family?"

She did not hesitate. "I have only one sibling, Aubrey, though he is but a half brother. My mother died a few months after I was born. My father remarried, and Aubrey was the result of that union. His mother perished a few years past as well."

"Is your father yet alone?"

"Yes," she said smiling, "but of late he has been calling frequently at The Priory, a manor three miles west of Toseland. At this house resides a very pretty widow of an age with my father. I think the courtship most promising. Does this suffice?"

"Quite agreeably. Mrs. Sugnell and Mr. Almington are collecting roses and pressing them."

"Of course," she said. "I recall now that at the village of Pawlett, when they entered the inn, they were speaking of the very same thing. I think it an excellent notion, for they will have every opportunity for finding specimens. What good housewife does not pride herself on her roses?"

"Very true." He sought about in his mind for a moment. "My next question. Why do you challenge me so frequently as you do—and I do not want a simple answer like, 'because someone should lay down the gauntlet.' "

Fenella thought that were she to delve very deeply into this subject she would soon be quagmired. Still, there might be something she could say that would appease his curiosity. After a moment, she said, "I think it is because of your conduct at Morchards when my father and I visited. I know you cannot remember, but you and I had a conversation, even though you were in your cups."

He frowned and shook his head. "I truly have no recollection of it."

"I know. It is most disheartening."

"Will you at least tell me the nature of our discourse?"

"You revealed to me you had always wanted a home with a wife and children. I suppose I saw in that moment the man you perhaps wished to be, yet for whatever reasons could not. So every time you make me mad as fire with some superfluous, silly action, I cannot help but think not just of your words but of the earnestness of your expression. I suppose knowing as much prompts me to contest you."

He frowned more deeply still. She could not tell what he was thinking and wondered if he might desire to know more. In this she was mistaken, for he finally said, "Mrs. Almington and Mr. Leycott are collecting china cups and saucers."

"That is a disappointment. I would have thought Mrs. Almington would have chosen something far more intriguing or exceptional."

"I suppose, though I do think such a collection would auction well."

"Yes, of course it would. I see her design now." She continued setting her stitches, working her way through the word *Hinton*.

By that time, the hamlet of Montacute appeared, a beautiful village of Hamstone. Fenella descended with great care and found her ankle was still performing quite well so long as she walked slowly. The collecting of the kisses required but a brief half hour and once more the journey continued.

After half a mile, Perryn queried, "Shall I ask my next question?"

"Of course," she responded, threading her needle anew.

"Do you worry much about your brother?"

Here she sighed. "More than I can say. He has shown every evidence over the years of becoming a complete gamester, if he is not already, and yet pursues such a worthless existence on what can only be described as a small competence. You have not heard something untoward, have you?"

"Only the concern that Miss Adbaston is being led a merry dance."

Fenella cringed. "As to that, I would like to think that Aubrey has but the very best of motives toward her, but I truly cannot say what is in his heart. Do I think he has an eye to her fortune? Like most gentlemen who find themselves with but a pittance upon which to build a life, he would be a fool not to consider her prospects. Beyond that, I simply cannot speculate. I trust—I hope—he will treat her kindly in every respect."

Perryn nodded. "You are a good sister to him, then?"

"I try to be, but when a younger brother attains his majority, there is very little one can say to him on any subject without raising his hackles."

"This much is true," he corroborated, "having an older sister myself."

"I had nearly forgot. She is not much in London?"

"No, she has quite a brood of her own in Staffordshire and she prefers a country life."

"Do you see your nieces and nephews very much?"

"I try to visit three or four times a year. I am very fond of them."

"I would imagine you are. I could not help but notice how kind you have been to the children of the places we have traveled through. I think it one of your finest qualities."

"A compliment?" he asked, pressing a hand to his chest. "Have you perchance developed a brain fever, Miss Trentham?"

She chuckled. "I believe I have answered your third question. You now owe me a nice piece of information."

"Ah, yes, let me see. Mr. Charles Aston and Mrs. Fanny Millmeece—"

"Are collecting butterflies and as of the village of Crewkerne had only two in their collection."

He laughed heartily. "You should hear Mrs. Millmeece tell of her sad attempts to interest Mr. Aston."

"She would have done better to have suggested they collect tankards from every alehouse on this journey through Somerset."

"I do not believe Mrs. Millmeece has your ability to be so foresightful, I fear."

"I take that as something of a compliment, but you owe me other information, my lord, since I already knew about Mrs. Millmeece."

"I suppose I could argue the point, but I will not. Very well, Mr. Hanford and Lady Elizabeth Leycott are collecting a variety of crocheted items—tea cozies, mittens, doilies, caps, et cetera. Lady Elizabeth was very enthusiastic about it. Mr. Hanford, as I expected him to be, was both polite and entirely lacking in interest."

She glanced out the window. "We are arrived so soon at East Coker. Also of Hamstone and quite lovely, if a little rugged. How I long for a cup of tea."

"Tea you shall have," he responded. "But I think I shall save the remainder of my questions for later. If I do not much mistake the matter, your brother and Miss Adbaston have just arrived as well. Ah, it has begun to rain."

Fenella accepted his hand as once more he helped her descend the coach. One of his grooms met them with a large umbrella, which he held over their heads as they approached the inn.

East Coker was a lovely village, perhaps one of the prettiest in Somerset, built of golden stone, with many of the buildings beautifully thatched. She peered to the right of the coach and saw that, indeed, her brother was just descending his coach, with Miss Adbaston smiling prettily down into his face as she made her descent on the narrow coach steps.

"Miss Trentham!" Miss Adbaston called to her merrily, moving hastily in her direction to avoid the rain. "Your brother has just told me you handle the ribbons with some skill. I was wondering how you would feel to having a little race between us. I take some delight in the sport myself."

Fenella was surprised. Miss Adbaston was such a small, frail-looking young lady that she could not conceive of her

managing a single horse let alone a team. "One pair or
two?" she responded lightly, as she entered the inn. She
rather thought that the mention of so many horses would
end the subject entirely.

"I have only been practicing with two teams this year
past, so I do not believe myself fully experienced as of yet.
However, a single team, well-matched, is just what I would
like. There are sufficient curricles among the gentlemen,
and I know a race would be the very thing to enliven our
little party. Mr. Trentham thinks we should do so at Wells,
for he is familiar with the lanes about Sewards Manor,
where we will be staying. He says there is one in particular,
quite long and straight and just to the south of the manor,
which would suit our needs to perfection."

As the whole party moved into the parlor, Fenella
glanced at her brother, who wore an oddly conscious expression.

"Only if you wish for it, Fenella," he added, frowning.

"Aubrey, you know me better than anyone. I would
dearly love a race."

"Then it is settled!" Miss Adbaston cried, clapping her hands.
"How thankful I am that I thought to bring my driving gloves—
although I do not think I shall wear my bonnet."

"Will you join us for tea?" Perryn asked. "We can then
discuss the particulars, if you like."

An hour later, Fenella glanced out the window of the
coach as it drew into the next village. The shower had
ceased soon after both coaches pulled away from East
Coker, and presently a gray reach spanned the skies.

"We are just arriving at Queen Camel," Fenella said.
"What a curious name. Do you know of its origin?"

"As it happens," Perryn said, "I do know one theory put
forth by the vicar the last time I visited nearby."

"Indeed?" Fenella queried. "You will have to wait for a

moment to tell me, however, for I do not think I have heard more thunderous church bells in my entire life!"

"Not in all of Christendom," he agreed. When the bells quieted, he continued, "The river is named Camel since the ancient meaning of 'cam' refers to a curve or bend, hence, a curved river. The manor nearby was given to Queen Matilda by her husband William the Conqueror. Hence, Queen Camel."

"How very interesting, although not quite so exotic as I had hoped. For me the name conjured up nothing less than the image of Cleopatra and the possibility we might strike a desert over the next rise. You have completely shattered my air dreams."

"A thousand apologies," he murmured in kind, chuckling.

After they collected a few kisses at the village, the coach rumbled its way into the countryside. Two miles beyond the village, the Tudor mansion came into view where they were to pass the night, also of a fine golden stone like Queen Camel.

"Hallings Hall," Perryn stated, perusing the itinerary. "I have visited here on several occasions. Lady Hallingbury has recently built a large, beautiful conservatory onto the east wing. Quite magnificent. I would be happy to show it to you later, if you like."

"Yes, very much—only when am I to learn of the remainder of the collections?" She was anxious to know them all so that she might best determine if their collection had even a chance at winning the prize. So far, she had heard nothing extraordinary that she felt could compete with the kissing-ribbon maypole, as she had come to think of their collection. "Perhaps we could take a turn about the gardens in a half hour or so."

He shook his head, as the coach lumbered up the drive. "I fear I will not be able to do so."

"Have you already promised Mrs. Sugnell or Fanny Millmeece just such a stroll?"

"Not by half," he countered, smiling. "As it happens, I plan to ride out for a time. I am feeling the want of exercise."

"I have little doubt of it. Musical chairs or a stroll about a garden cannot possibly compete with a hard ride on horseback over a course of several miles."

"No, indeed it cannot. However, I am thinking that the conservatory, sometime after dinner, might be just the hour to continue our exchange."

The coach drew before the front door of the manor, and once more Fenella took Perryn's hand as she descended to the gravel drive. After making the acquaintance of Lord and Lady Hallingbury, Fenella retired to her bedchamber for a lie-down.

She was not prepared, however, for the deep sleep which followed and from which she awakened as one in a stupor. Her dreams had led her into an unknown conservatory, where Perryn had kissed her again. The feel of his lips was still heavily upon her as she blinked several times and tried to awaken more fully.

She rolled onto her back, tears trickling from the corner of her eyes. Even in her sleep she could not be relieved of her *tendre* for Perryn.

"But I promised to show you the conservatory," Perryn coaxed. Dinner had long been concluded and he had finally approached her about the promised visit to Lady Hallingbury's latest addition to her home.

Fenella tried to move past him yet again, but once more he blocked her path.

"Why are you avoiding me again, particularly when I have been striving to conduct myself in the most gentlemanly manner possible?"

She saw the teasing light in his gray eyes, which had become so familiar to her. She could not keep from smiling. "Perryn, I simply do not think it wise." The dreams she had experienced that afternoon were still haunting her, and she was not certain were she to be alone with Perryn she would be entirely of a mind to prevent his embraces.

"Why would it not be wise? I shan't assault you, if that is what you fear."

That was very much what she did fear, but how to tell him? "I am persuaded that in this moment you actually believe what you are saying to me." She lowered her voice, for though they were standing to the far side of the drawing room where the entire party was gathered, they still might be overheard. "However, it seems we have but to be alone for a few minutes together and all caution is scattered to the wind."

"We are alone for hours in my coach and I have yet to enjoy a single kiss from you. I begin to think myself sorely used."

"That is very different," she cried, laughing.

"In what way?" he asked. She could see he was enjoying himself.

She leaned toward him. "Who can possibly kiss to good effect when the coach is bouncing from one rut to another on these country roads?"

He burst out laughing. "I would never have thought you would say as much."

"I am in some ways a very practical girl."

"Come to the conservatory," he urged her. "We shall laugh a little more, and I promise I shan't distress you."

"You always distress me."

"Come anyway. It is lovely, and I have not traveled with you for miles on end without knowing you would delight very much in the beauty of Lady Hallingbury's latest creation. Come."

When she hesitated, he pressed her. "I tell you now I shall only reveal the last of the collections if you come with me."

"What a wicked man you are, appealing to one of my weaknesses." She looked at him, at the devilish, teasing light in his gray eyes, and felt caught anew. After all, she simply had to know the nature of each collection. "Oh, very well—but we will remain but five minutes, mind."

"Yes, miss," he responded obsequiously, but she was not fooled. He appeared very triumphant.

The conservatory was a marvel of workmanship, very tall and made all of glass. The sheer size of the structure made her feel as though she had entered a mysterious forest. Several candelabra on tall pedestals lit the space in a quiet glow. The air was humid and earthy in feel and smell. A number of flowers were in full and even riotous bloom. "You were right to press me. I vow I have seen few things so magnificent. I do love it, Perryn. Thank you."

"Must we remain only five minutes? We have spent half the time already just in gaping."

Fenella shrugged. "Six will do, I suppose."

He groaned. "What a taskmaster you are."

She strolled the entire length of the glass chamber, noting as she looked up through the panels in the ceiling that stars twinkled beyond. There was something utterly magical about being surrounded by plants, flowers and even several young trees, all under glass, as though in an attempt to preserve them for an eternity. The path moved in a circle about the conservatory and every turn brought a new delight. A branch of fern dangled to her nose. She touched the feathery frond and sighed with some contentment.

"You have yet to ask me," he murmured.

"Ask you what?" she returned, speaking to him just over her shoulder for he moved behind her.

"About the remaining collections."

She could not help but smile. "I nearly forgot them in the face of so much beauty. Shall we continue, then?"

"You realize, of course, that we shall surpass the allotted six minutes."

She groaned. "Will you please stop teasing me, you wretched man? Now, whose collections are remaining?"

"First, if you will recall, you must answer another question."

"You will hold me to that when you have somehow finagled my presence here?"

"Of course," he returned, smiling.

She narrowed her eyes. "I begin to think you know me far better than is at all good for me."

His smile broadened to a grin, and in that moment her breath caught. She seemed to be particularly susceptible to him when he was reduced to this boyish expression of innocence. All the hope of who he might have been as a young man appeared to rise within him. Her heart was entirely aroused, and only with some difficulty did she calm the poor, overtaxed organ.

Finally she was able to speak. "Well?" she queried. "Let me have your first question so that we might be done with all this absurdity."

He thought for a moment, then asked, "Do you desire to marry? I cannot for the life of me account for your spinsterhood."

At that Fenella laughed outright. The question was wholly unexpected.

Before she could answer, he continued, "At the end of the Season, I truly thought you would marry Mr. Clavering."

"How can you say that, Perryn, when we had a discussion about him, *while waltzing,* and you forced me, in the kindest way, to realize how I truly felt about him, that my heart had not been fully engaged?"

"Perhaps it is my cynicism, but I thought you would wed him anyway."

She shook her head. "Until that dance and your having addressed the matter with me, I truly had believed myself in love with him. Therein lies your answer. I do desire a husband and a family, more than you will ever know. However, I also desire love and a sense that I could really de-

light in my husband. I esteemed Mr. Clavering, but I did
not truly love him, not as he deserved to be loved."

"Did he love you?"

"Why must I answer you? The question is impertinent!"

"Did he love you?" he asked again, completely unper-
turbed by her complaints.

"Oh, very well . . . if you insist upon knowing." She
recalled her earlier experiences with Mr. Clavering and finally said, "I must confess that when I made my sentiments
known to him, that though I esteemed him I did not love
him, he did not seem in the least overset. I would therefore
have to conclude he was not nearly so attached to me as I
had supposed. All of this, by the way, I feel is worth at
least two revelations from you." She glanced about her.
"However, before you tell me, there is a stone bench across
this little bridge. Would you mind if we sat for a time?"

"Not in the least." He guided her to the bench and sat
down beside her.

"Two revelations, you say?" he queried. "I suppose your
confidences about Mr.Clavering are worth as much. Very
well, two then. Who yet remains?"

"Mr. Silverdale and Miss Aston, for one."

Here, Lord Perryn laughed outright. "I do beg your pardon . . . I know he is a very great friend of yours, but Beau
Silverdale is such a complete fop!"

"I am aware of his inclinations. Only he would not confide in me even though we do understand one another so
well. I apprehend Miss Aston was much more manageable?"

"Yes, but I believe it was because she holds my rank in
some awe."

"She is a bit younger than most of our party, two and
twenty I believe. I daresay she looks upon you rather as a
father."

He feigned being struck a hard blow to his chest. "What
a viper's tongue you have on occasion, Fennel!"

She merely laughed at him. "And their collection?"

"Ah, yes, though I feel you ought to prepare yourself—bits of lace, at his insistence."

She could not help but laugh. "So very much like him. Only I do not know how he will part with the collection once we return to Bath."

"He will probably bid on it himself."

"Undoubtedly."

"What of Sir John and Miss Almington?"

"Recipes for biscuits."

She gasped. "That is the very thing I thought he should collect!"

"Now, Miss Trentham, another question—what is your favorite color?"

"Blue. Now tell me of Mr. Millmeece and Miss Keele. I would suppose their collection might be intriguing."

"Your sharpest competition thus far. A great variety of snuffboxes."

"An excellent idea, and it will undoubtedly do well at the auction. Who yet remains?"

"Two couples. Miss Madeley and Colonel Bedrell, as well as your brother and Miss Adbaston."

Fenella considered this. "I heartily suspect, knowing my brother's nature, that he divulged the identity of his collection and if not he, certainly Miss Adbaston would have done so, which leads me to this—do you tell me that you failed with Miss Madeley?"

He sighed heavily. "I fear I did. Quite a disgrace, I think. The information was not to be had at any price."

"Indeed?" Fenella cried. "Are you saying nothing you could offer, no charming compliment or kiss of the fingers, was able to persuade Miss Madeley to open her budget?"

He chuckled. "What a baggage you are! As it happens, no. She was most adamant on that point. She intended to keep her secret and the colonel felt obliged, as a gentleman of honor, to obey her wishes."

"I vow my opinion of her has increased dramatically. I am quite impressed she could not be bowled over by your charm!"

"It is curious," he responded, stroking his chin.

"You were surprised as well," she countered. "So you did expect her to tell you without a moment's hesitation. Admit it is so!"

He nodded. "You are right, of course. I enjoy something of an easy rapport with her and had no doubt whatsoever she would tell me."

"And were you sorely disappointed?"

"No," he answered succinctly.

"Now you have astonished me."

"I find I am rather astonished myself." He considered Miss Madeley for a moment. If anything had truly surprised him about his encounter with her, it was that he did not understand why he was not more interested in her generally.

The flirtation he had conducted with her in an attempt to glean the information he sought had been rather exciting. Miss Madeley was not only beautiful to look upon, but there was a decided glitter in her blue eyes that had led him to believe she would not have refused a kiss. Unlike Miss Trentham, however, he had every reason to believe that afterward she would have considered herself betrothed to him. He ought to marry, if for no other reason than to secure an heir for Morchards, and Miss Madeley would make a quite elegant marchioness. The very thought of it, however, brought a yawn to his lips.

"I will now tell you what collection your brother and Miss Adbaston are creating, but first you owe me an answer to a final question."

Fenella regarded him for a moment and wondered what had brought such a solemn expression to his eye. "Very well, but I hope it is not a very serious one."

A slow smile overspread his lips. "I take the question most

seriously, but somehow I doubt you will. What I wish to know is whether or not you desire that I should kiss you again?"

"You are not mistaken. I find the question ridiculous in the extreme and wholly unacceptable."

He shrugged. "I require some manner of answer, or I shan't reveal what Miss Adbaston told me."

Fenella was entirely torn. She wanted to know so badly what they were collecting. She wondered if there might be some way of answering his question without revealing the truth of her heart and her worries. Finally, she decided that a rather blatant honesty would serve her best. "Of course I do. You must know as much by how I have responded the last—Good God!—five times!"

A faint frown crossed his brow. "Not five, surely," he murmured. "I can recall but four, if you are indeed counting last night's kiss as a kiss."

She laughed. "It was hardly anything else, but I believe you are mistaken. You have kissed me five times. Last night at Briars Lodge, the library at Morchards, the woods at Dunball, the garden at midnight at Whitmore, and the—" She turned away from him, only barely repressing a sharp intake of breath. She could not credit that she had almost disclosed the very thing she had promised herself never to reveal to him, that he had kissed her five years ago in the maze at Morchards. "Well! You were right after all. Four times it is."

"Your cheeks are grown quite pink. I hope you are not embarrassed, Fennel. You ought not to be, for you are wonderful to kiss."

She turned back to him, meeting his gaze. So many thoughts flooded her at once that she felt overwhelmed as she often did in his presence. "Thank you," she murmured. "So are you."

He caught her chin, thereby preventing her from turning away from him again. Fenella overlaid his wrist with her hand. "No, Perryn," she murmured, her chest tight with desire. Why must any encounter with him be so utterly devastating?

"You ought not to be so beautiful," he murmured. At the same time, he turned into her, caught her arms, and lifted her suddenly to her feet. She was drawn into his powerful embrace before she could utter the smallest protest.

"Faith, but I adore holding you in my arms," he whispered against her cheek.

Fenella felt her will slipping away. She drew back to look at him, meaning to demur, but her gaze unfortunately drifted to his lips.

He tilted his head. "You have but to speak the word," he murmured. "I kissed you last night quite without conscience. Tonight, you must choose."

How easy it would be to acquiesce, to simply give a little nod and place her lips on his. How much she wished to do so. She would kiss him. She would.

Laughter drifted to her from the hallway beyond, seizing her attention. The spell was immediately broken and she pulled easily from his arms. Abruptly the door burst open and Miss Keele, Mr. Silverdale, and Mr. Aston and his sister entered the chamber.

Fenella composed herself swiftly, greeting them as though nothing untoward had happened, or even had been about to happen.

"Were you squabbling with Perryn again?" Mr. Silverdale queried in an unusually booming voice. Clearly, he was half foxed.

"Actually, for once we were not," she responded. She glanced at Perryn, who moved to stand beside her. He met her gaze and an understanding passed between them.

"Although," she added, "I daresay had you arrived five minutes later we probably would have been. We cannot seem to be together for a quarter hour at a time without brangling over some trifle or other."

Eleven

"I saw Missy this morning," Perryn said, "in the company of your maid, both of whom were taking a much needed turn about the gardens. She looked quite well."

Fenella lifted her gaze to him, if but briefly. "As you may imagine, she is thriving in Betsy's care." She had been dreading this moment, when she would once more be closeted with him in his coach. Would this journey never end that fostered between them so comfortable a rapport? She rather thought these daily exchanges were the reason she had very nearly surrendered to his kisses again. Had Miss Keele and the others not suddenly arrived at the conservatory, she had little doubt a kiss would have ensued.

"How is your ankle?"

"I am so well recovered that I hardly notice even the smallest twinge when I walk, but I do thank you for inquiring."

When he had handed her up into the coach this morning, she had seen the expression in his eye, glittering, amused, purposeful. She had taken up her seat, plopped her bandbox on her lap, and begun rummaging enthusiastically among the ribbons and thread while he settled himself on the forward seat opposite her. She knew he had been thinking of the conservatory. Her object this morning, therefore, would be to keep these same thoughts as far from his mind as possible.

"And your embroidery?" he queried.

"I am only six or seven villages behind," she responded. "Betsy, of course, has been helping me."

Now, as she stared down at her needlework, she realized this would have to do. In hand was the ribbon from the village of Ilchester. This small strip of peach-colored silk must protect her from Perryn's advances. "So where do we travel today?"

Perryn drew forth the itinerary. "To the town of Wells and your race with Miss Adbaston," he announced. "Betwixt, among other hamlets, are the villages of Street and Glastonbury. Wells is slightly northwest." He then withdrew a second piece of paper from his coat pocket."

"What do you have there?"

"Almington recommended a particular route to Street. Leaving Queen Camel, west to West Camel and Podimore, north to Mackrett, Kingweston, Butleigh, and Street. That should give us ample opportunity to add to our collection."

"Did you solicit this information from Mr. Almington?" she asked, a little surprised.

"Of course. I know how important our collection is to you. We discussed various routes, one of them through Somerton again, but since we had already collected kisses there, he recommended Street by way of Mackrett."

Another kindness, she thought, looking at him and wondering. He did not even seem to think what he had done was singular. Mr. Hanford's words came back to her again, that she should judge him against a larger backdrop and not just the narrow view of the drawing room . . . or the conservatory.

"Why do you smile?" he asked.

She shook her head. "Nothing to signify."

As the miles wore on and hamlet succeeded village, as the collection of ribbons grew, Fenella found herself grateful to Perryn in one particular respect—the confirmed rogue made no attempt to flirt, embrace, kiss, or otherwise seduce her while they were traveling and working on their collection. As it was, she had but to look at him, and all her hapless sentiments of longing and wishing would rise in her like a great mountain. Did Mrs. Almington have even the faintest notion the torturous situation in which she had placed her when she assigned Perryn to be her partner? One day she would tell her hostess just how angry she was at having been tricked into traveling with a man who had come to resemble a rather glorious sunrise in all his attraction to her. Wretched woman!

The day unfolded without incident, much to Fenella's relief. By the time the coach lumbered from the town of Glastonbury, she was feeling so very much at ease that she decided to bring forward a subject which had been plaguing her since the prior London Season.

"There is something I would say to you," she said.

Perryn, who had enjoyed a tankard at the last inn, blinked as he shifted his gaze to her. There was a sleepiness in his eyes that only a warm day, a gently rocking coach, and a large mug of beer could occasion. She could not help but chuckle.

"Yes?" he queried, barely restraining a yawn.

"I hope I do not provoke a terribly unhappy memory, but I wished you to know how very much I appreciated the missive you sent me over a year ago now, after we quarreled at Lady Astwick's ball."

"Good God," he murmured. "That was a very long time ago, indeed."

"Little more than a twelvemonth."

"I wondered if we would ever discuss that particularly stinging encounter."

"Perryn, there is something you should know, something I am loath to tell you, but I suppose in saying as much I am hoping to help you understand my difficulty with you."

"Is there a difficulty?" he queried teasingly. He sat up a little straighter, his attention clearly caught.

She chuckled. "When you approached me at Lady Ast-wick's ball . . . good God, how can I say this?" She strug-gled for a moment. "Very well, I suppose I must just speak the words. At any rate, at Lady Astwick's ball, I did not know you were so very near. When I lifted my gaze and you were standing before me, I vow I nearly fainted just looking at you. Do you have any notion whatsoever how handsome you are, particularly when you are dressed in a fine-tailored black tailcoat, which somehow suits your black hair and gray eyes as no color could? When you addressed me in that moment, I actually began to tremble. You are like this wave that I must continually find a way to glide over, else I shall be completely overpowered if you break on me and tumble me about in the surf. How would I ever rise again? Oh, never mind. It is hopeless to explain this without pandering to your vanity or your pride, and I fear you will mistake my intention entirely."

"You find me dashing, eh?"

"Do not be a sapskull!" she cried indignantly. "And do not think that these feelings are in any way special. Why do you think Mrs. Sugnell casts herself before your feet so readily—or Lady Elizabeth or Mrs. Millmeece?"

He grew a little more serious. "I am trying to understand your purpose in saying these things to me. However, I fear I do not."

"It is the cause of my frequently sharp tongue in your presence, besides the fact that you set up my back so often as you do by what you say to me. And you certainly sent me into the boughs that night."

"Yes, I recall I asked you where the champagne was you meant to throw on me in reference to the Season prior."

She smiled. "I attempted to ignore you."

Fenella watched him nod. The entire exchange returned to her as though it had happened but a few minutes earlier. She had remained silent in the face of his sarcastic query about champagne, but he had pressed her. She could hear the precise tone to his voice as he asked, "Do you not intend to greet an old friend?"

She had tried to ignore him further still, trembling lest he see through her restraint to the longing in the deep breaths she was taking. Had she at least seen him earlier that evening, she might have been better prepared to converse with him. As it was, he had taken her completely by surprise. She still marveled that any gentleman could rob her of breath, as Perryn did, and cause the usefulness of her knees to disappear entirely.

She had turned away from him, but he would not be ignored. He had reached for her arm, but he did not take it in hand. Instead, in a gentle glide, he had slid his gloved fingers down the exposed portion of her arm just above the elbow. Gooseflesh and shiverings assaulted her.

The longing she had been feeling turned to a desire so reminiscent of her experiences with him in the maze at Morchards that she nearly swooned. At the same time, the fear of being so completely within a man's power whom she so despised brought forth a rage that gave some strength to her failing legs. "How dare you touch me in that horrid manner!" she had cried.

"So, the Ice Maiden has a tongue," he retorted, his voice sultry, his meaning doubled. "Is no one allowed to approach you?"

"You do not *approach!* You insult and call it a compliment. I despise you!"

"How pretty you are with your cheeks flushed."

"And you, sir, are a rogue!"

"Of course I am. But what are you, I wonder? Does even a mite of passion reside beneath all that frost?"

She gasped, fearing he would discover the truth. Instinctively, she lifted a hand to strike him, regardless of the dozen guests scattered in groups nearby.

He caught her hand and clucked his tongue. "Come, come, Miss Trentham, surely your mother taught you better manners than to strike a gentleman in a ballroom. Is the lady present? I should have a word with her about your conduct."

"I beg you will never speak of my mother again, Lord Perryn. Her name does not deserve to rest for even a moment on your lips."

Fenella sighed at the memory. Her words had given him pause, and the next day he had sent her an apologetic missive.

> *Miss Trentham,*
> *Though I cannot pretend you and I enjoy more than the most contentious of acquaintances, my conduct and my words to you last night were unpardonable. I beg you will accept my deepest apologies.*
>
> *Perryn*

She addressed the marquess now. "You had insulted me and brought forward my mother's name, but in truth I was equally at fault. You may have behaved badly, but I never should have spoken so sharply to you or tried to hit you. I cannot think of my conduct without abhorrence. However—and this pertains to what I was attempting so lamentably to say to you earlier—I was afraid if I did not contest you in some manner, I would fall into your arms—as I am wont to do." Tears filled her eyes suddenly, and she found she could not look at him. She felt she had erred horribly in speaking of her most intimate feelings with a man she had always felt was devoid of comprehending or respecting such sentiments.

He frowned. "Are you saying you were merely attempting to be rid of me in that dreadful exchange?"

"Yes," she responded, nodding. "I wished you to go away, to never look at me again, to never appear in the same ballroom where I might be tempted by my inexplicable *tendre* for you. Yes, *tendre*. I can only imagine what you thought of me then, or of my temper."

"That you despised me."

"I do," she responded hotly, "which makes it all the worse."

"And which I resent, for you despise what is merely an impression, a bit of gossip—"

"You forget, my lord, that I have watched you torment Mrs. Sugnell night after night during this very caravan about Somerset—or do you truly not know what it is you accomplish in your odious seductions?"

He seemed stunned by her words. "She pursues me doggedly."

"And you are so powerless that you cannot merely nod politely and move on?" she returned sardonically.

He fell silent, his jaw working strongly.

She resumed her embroidery. She had not meant for the conversation to turn to Mrs. Sugnell, which it seemed to so frequently. "Now I regret speaking to you of this."

"As well you should!" he responded angrily. "You seem to take great delight in damning my character at every turn, even at the same moment you are telling me that you have formed something—of a bizarre attachment to me. Yes, Miss Trentham, you should regret very much having brought such a subject forward!"

The remainder of the journey to Wells passed in strained silence. Fenella did not think she had ever been so relieved as when the coach finally passed through the gates of Sewards Manor. Mr. and Mrs. Morden greeted them warmly, but only when she had been established in her bedchamber did she finally release a deep breath.

Mrs. Morden, before departing her room, said she had been informed by Miss Adbaston that a race was to be held at four o'clock in the lane to the south of the manor, if that would be suitable, and she had taken the opportunity to inform all the guests of it as well. "Mr. Almington has arranged for the horses to be harnessed and the curricles polished for the occasion."

"How kind of you to take so much trouble over our little race. I hope it is no inconvenience, for that was not my brother's nor my intention."

"If you must know," she added solemnly, "I was grateful to hear of the race, for I have been given to understand that the Marquess of Perryn delights in just such little amusements. To own the truth, I was not certain in the least how to go about ensuring his entertainment."

Fenella assured her hostess she need not be so concerned about Perryn's opinion, but Mrs. Morden disclaimed, "You have mistaken me. It is not his consequence which has caused my distress, though his rank does inspire a little awe, but rather my sense of obligation to him. Many years ago, he performed a very great service for Mr. Morden, for which kindness neither my husband nor I have known how to repay him."

"Indeed?" Fenella returned, her curiosity heightened. She knew it would be a great impertinence to inquire further and could only hope that in her attentive silence Mrs. Morden would take up her hint and tell her just what had transpired.

Mrs. Morden, fortunately, was of a confiding nature. "I know Lord Perryn does not like his generosities to be bandied about, but Mrs. Almington has assured me you are on quite an intimate footing with him. Four years past, several of Mr. Morden's investments all failed over the course of a six-month period. At the same time, a fire devastated the home of our most reliable tenant farmer. The situation was quite desperate unless we could secure a loan of some five thousand pounds, by which Mr. Morden knew he could salvage and even reverse our fortunes. There was not a banker in England who would listen to his requests or his plan. He would not have considered applying to any of our friends, but good Colonel Bedrell, whom my husband has known forever, spoke of our troubles to Lord Perryn, who came to Mr. Morden.

"At first, my husband absolutely refused, but then his lordship said something quite odd, that Mr. Morden would be doing him no small favor were he to accept his help at this juncture in his life—that he had been given to quite selfish and useless conduct and believed his redemption might be found in offering the assistance to Mr. Morden which was so completely within his power to render."

"And so he made your husband the loan of five thousand pounds?" she cried, astonished.

"An incredible sum, as well you know, and that to a mere acquaintance. Of course, Mr. Morden has a great many friends and is well trusted and beloved among them all. The entire estate was saved due to Perryn's extraordinary kindness. You can see now why I am anxious he might be happy here at Sewards Manor."

"Most certainly I can," Fenella responded.

Her hostess then excused herself, saying there were at least three coaches not yet arrived at Sewards and she was certain she would be needed downstairs shortly. Fenella was left to herself to wonder yet again about the Marquess of Perryn.

An hour later, at the far end of a makeshift race course, Fenella steadied her wildly beating heart as she gathered the reins of Mr. Morden's curricle into her hands, arranging them carefully. Aubrey had checked the harness quite thoroughly for both carriages and pronounced the race ready to commence.

The team before her was mettlesome, as was the team hitched to Miss Adbaston's vehicle. She glanced at her opponent. Miss Adbaston, her eyes glittering with excitement, inclined her head in response. Before them was a wide lane marked off in a half-mile length by the presence

of the entire party, who had gathered at the southern
boundary of Sewards Manor to witness the race. The fine
stone house presided in some dignity over the lane, situated
as the mansion was on a gentle incline to the north. The
ladies waved their kerchiefs in support.

Aubrey moved to the starting position and, holding his
arm aloft, called to the ladies. "Ready?"

Fenella nodded to him, as did Miss Adbaston.

With a quick swipe of his arm, he called out a hearty,
"Go!"

Fenella slapped the reins hard and called to her team.
Miss Adbaston was not far behind. The curricle jerked but
once as the horses were set in motion, and the sudden increasing speed of the well-matched beasts quickly took the
harnessed vehicle in tow. Just as she had hoped, the curricle
was soon flying down the lane. She cried out to her team,
again and again, her own voice mingling with Miss Adbaston's, who drove exceedingly well and who was keeping
pace with her. Ahead of her, the figures of the party, now
shouting encouragements to one or the other of them, were
fluttering kerchiefs and waving hats wildly. Fenella was in
little doubt any number of wagers had been staked on
either herself or Miss Adbaston.

Nearing the finish line, Fenella felt something in the
reins give way a trifle, one of them going completely slack.
Miss Adbaston moved ahead swiftly while Fenella attempted to draw on the remaining reins. She drew more
firmly still and the horses began to slow unevenly. Fear
tightened her chest. She could not comprehend what was
happening. She pulled harder still, and the horses began
to respond as she called out, "Whoa! Easy! Easy! Gently!"

Suddenly a cracking sound split the air, and a moment
later she was simply flying as if with wings, a surprised
sensation flooding her. She knew she was in trouble, but
the oddest thought rippled through her mind that the head

gardener ought to prune back the hedge a trifle. Then everything turned black.

Perryn had known the curricle was in trouble the moment Miss Trentham glanced down at her hands. He was running before he had formed the thought that she would very soon need his assistance. He heard her calling to the team to slow. He heard the crack as well.

One of the wheels broke, tipping the body of the carriage sideways so abruptly and with such force that Miss Trentham had been sent off her seat and to the left. The screams of the ladies of the party accompanied the unreal sight. Miss Trentham had landed at the base of a hedgerow in a patch of soft, slightly damp grass and earth.

In scarcely a minute, Perryn was beside her, turning her limp body over as gently as he was able. Her eyes fluttered, but she did not awaken. He wanted nothing more than to lift her into his arms, but common sense dictated he determine how seriously she was injured. He felt every limb. Much to his intense relief, he found each bone was wonderfully straight, strong, and unbroken. Mrs. Almington hurried forward and held a bottle beneath Fenella's nose.

She immediately began squirming to get away from the strong smell. Perryn slid an arm beneath her shoulders. "Fennel," he murmured, stroking her cheeks.

She blinked and looked into his eyes. She began to smile. "Oh, Perryn, I lost the race and you know how I hate to lose!"

The crowd now gathered about her chuckled nervously.

"Silly chit," he murmured. "Come, I mean to carry you into the house."

"I am certain I can walk."

He felt no responding movement in her limbs, however.

A sudden panic assailed him. "My dear, please move your foot and then perhaps you can stand."

He watched her half boot, his heart pounding in his chest. The crowd grew silent as apprehension filled the air.

A second passed, another and another.

Finally the boot moved.

A sigh of relief passed from person to person. Miss Keele began to weep as did several of the other ladies.

With his fears assuaged for the present, Perryn simply gathered her up in his arms and began carrying her to the house.

Mr. Morden called out that he would send at once for the doctor.

Fenella looked up at him. How odd she felt, as though the jolt she had received in being thrown from the curricle had pushed her into a different world entirely, where even though all the faces were the same, everything was somehow different. At the same time, particularly with Perryn holding her so tightly, she felt completely safe.

"Fenella!"

She heard her brother's voice, and Perryn paused for a moment so she could speak with him.

"Are you all right, dearest?" he cried, out of breath from running the entire distance from the starting point. "I never meant . . . I mean, the race was a stupid idea."

"Nonsense," she responded, her voice sounding far away. "I loved every moment of it. You should congratulate Miss Adbaston. I need to rest, though."

"Later, Trentham," Perryn said quietly.

"Of course, of course."

Fenella's ability to see and hear shifted about, like bits of dreams floating to her and moving away as swiftly. Perryn was mounting the stairs, she touched the whiskers on his cheek, the door of her bedchamber was suddenly before her, Betsy, her bed.

"Pray do not leave me, Perryn," she heard herself say.

"I shan't, I promise you."

She drifted in that manner for some time until what proved to be midnight, when she awakened to find she could see the clock perfectly and that the hour was twelve.

Every other item in the bedchamber was equally distinct. She shifted her head to look in the direction of the candle-light and saw Perryn was seated beside her, his elbows on his knees, his hands clasped together, his gaze fixed at some point beyond the bed. His thoughts appeared to be drawn inward.

"What are you thinking?" she asked.

He glanced sharply at her, moving slightly in order to possess himself of her hand. "You are awake?"

She nodded.

"And how do you feel?"

"My head hurts a trifle. I am very thirsty."

"That is good news," he said. He lifted her up and helped her to drink from a glass of what proved to be cold, refreshing water.

She lay back down. "How horrible!" she cried. "For I have just remembered I lost the race!"

He began to laugh and for a long moment could not seem to stop.

She smiled at him until finally he was reduced to a mere chuckle now and again. "Do not tell me you feared I was about to stick my spoon in the wall?"

"Yes, Fennel, that was precisely what I had begun to think."

"Gudgeon," she responded softly.

He drew his chair closer still, so that while sitting he might lean over her and pet her face. "I would not be happy in a world which you had already departed, my dear. You seem to have grown remarkably important to my happiness."

She nodded, thinking very much the same thing. "Is not this quite odd?" she queried, looking deeply into his eyes.

"Exceedingly odd."

She sighed. "I beg you will kiss me, Perryn."

He looked into her eyes and stroked her hair. "If you truly wish for it."

"More than anything in the world."

He leaned close and settled his lips on hers in a tender kiss. She slid her arm about his neck and fondled the hair at the nape of his neck.

After a time, Perryn drew back that he might look down at her, at the lovely shape of her mouth, at the straight beautiful nose, the sculpted cheeks, arched brows, and emerald eyes. How dear she had grown to him in but a few days, yet it seemed as though years had transpired since they first embarked on the collecting caravan. He recalled the first time she had ever looked at him, that cold, appraising glance, so different from every other lady of his acquaintance.

Something nagged at him, a memory forgotten perhaps. An image came to him of Fenella leaning over him and placing a kiss on his lips long before this moment. When could that have been? Not in the garden at Mrs. Almington's home, nor the woods at Dunball, and certainly not while in the library at Morchards. He gave himself a shake. He must have dreamed it. God knew he had had a score of dreams in which she had been a principal player.

He kissed her again, the pleasure of the softness of her lips against his beyond description. Her lips parted and he tasted of the depths of her, taking possession of her mouth. Desire rose in him, strong and demanding. He kissed her more deeply still and felt her arm tighten about his shoulders. He should not be kissing her. She was injured and he might injure her further.

He drew back, petting her face a little more, smiling into her eyes, delighting in her. What was this powerful feeling that had possession of him? Was it love? He had loved before, but this seemed like something greater, yet more mysterious. "Do I hurt you?"

She shook her head and sighed. "No, my lord," she whispered, a smile resting lightly on her lips. "Kiss me again."

He obliged her. He obliged her for the next quarter hour.

He did not want to leave her, but he knew he should. She must rest, and Betsy was waiting to take charge of her. "I must go," he whispered at last.

She nodded. "Until tomorrow?"

"It is already tomorrow."

She smiled again. "Until later, then."

"We have much to discuss you and I," he said solemnly.

"Indeed, I believe we do."

Fenella watched him go, her heart full to overflowing. She understood now what she had refused to comprehend before, what she had not wanted to admit to herself, that what she felt for him was not a mere *tendre,* but rather love. She loved him so dearly, so completely. She loved him and she would always love him, no matter what the next hour, or the hour after that, would bring. She had belonged to him from the moment some five years past when he had found her in the middle of his maze, talked with her and kissed her and afterward forgotten all that had been said between them. Dear, dear Lord Perryn!

She fell into a peaceful sleep, so deeply that when she awoke in the morning, she felt as though she had never been injured. Except for a slight stiffness in her neck and back, she was perfectly well. She was certainly eager to see Perryn and more eager still to make certain she was dressed in the finest manner possible. Today, she was convinced, would be the happiest day of her life. Whatever her concerns about his general character, his kind ministrations into the early hours of the morning had proven much to her.

"Oh, Betsy," she whispered, as that good lady combed out her long brown tresses. "I do believe I love him."

"Of course you do, miss," Betsy responded, grinning. "Even a ninnyhammer could see as much."

Fenella felt as light as air, as though nothing on earth could possibly affect the dizzy exhilaration which had enveloped her. She knew to a certainty that today Perryn would speak of marriage to her, and she knew to an equal certainty she would accept of his offer.

Lord Perryn whistled between each stroke of his razor. He had never known such happiness as this, not in his entire existence. His valet eyed him between chuckles and laid out his corbeau coat, embroidered buff waistcoat, buckskin breeches, and glossy top boots.

Perryn could hardly wait to see Fenella and wished her bedchamber was next to his. Had it been, he would have gone to her an hour past and kissed her again, for that was all he could think of doing, kissing the woman again whom he loved and whom he intended to make his wife. Yes, his wife.

He loved Fenella Trentham. He supposed he had loved her that first Season, when she had challenged him so ferociously with that cold, assessing gaze of hers. He had loved her because she had demanded the best of him. Never had she settled for less which, damme, was what most the ladies of his acquaintance did. He loved her because he could make her laugh.

A scratching sounded on the door and he knew at once she had come to him, surely as eager as he was to begin the day's glorious adventure, now that an understanding had been reached. He waved his valet to depart, nodding for him to permit Fenella to enter his bedchamber. He wiped the remaining soap from his face and turned to greet her.

But instead of Fenella, Mrs. Sugnell entered his room.

"What the deuce?" he cried.

She pouted. "This was not precisely the greeting for which I had been hoping," she said.

He looked her up and down. "You are in your nightdress, madame! I beg you will return to your bedchamber at once! This is most unseemly." All of Fenella's words of warning returned to him. *Do you have any notion how you affect the ladies with whom you flirt?*

"Perryn," she began, weeping, "pray do not send me away just yet. You cannot know what I suffer. Mr. Sugnell—"

Good God, this is a nightmare, he thought.

"Sit down then," he responded, agitated.

He gestured toward the chair by the window. However, she moved in the other direction and to his horror took up residence on his bed.

He remained where he was, near his shaving stand, unable to do anything except watch as her weeping became more vigorous and wonder just how he was to be rid of her. She dabbed at her eyes and cheeks with her kerchief. "What do you want of me, Mrs. Sugnell?"

"Your compassion," she said, lifting her gaze to him. "And . . . and a little comfort."

"Perhaps I should summon Lady Elizabeth. She is a particular friend of yours."

"She cannot give me what I desire most."

"What is that?" he asked as though he were the greatest simpleton in the world.

"You, of course. Perryn, please listen to me. I . . . I am in love with you, desperately. I would become your mistress, if you would have me. I know you have not taken a lady beneath your protection in a very long time, but I promise you, you would not be disappointed. I would not cling to you as some are wont to do, but I can no longer restrain the passion that has taken such powerful possession of my heart!"

She slid from the bed and fairly raced to him, wrapping her arms about his neck before he could prevent her. He tried to disengage her embrace but she pressed herself against him. "Tell me you like me, even if but a little, though I know you must when you have singled me out as you have."

"Mrs. Sugnell, I beg you will take control of yourself!

I do not mean to take a mistress. I do not love you. I do not even . . . that is, I beg of you, please desist!"

These words, spoken sharply, had a proper effect. Mrs. Sugnell moved away from him, more tears welling up in her eyes. "You do not love me? Even a little?"

Guilt shattered his mind. Fenella's remonstrations once more returned to him. He had behaved abominably, and now the primary object of his flirtations was before him, appearing hurt and bewildered. He did not know what to say to her. "A little, yes, of course," he said lamely. "Who could not love you?" The words seemed ridiculous to his own ears.

She smiled falteringly. "But not enough." Her shoulders fell and she buried her face in her kerchief, weeping softly.

Understanding penetrated his heart. He finally comprehended the extent of his own guilt. "Pray do not cry, my dear," he said, moving to stand in front of her. He put his arms about her and surrounded her in a warm embrace. "You will have to forgive me. I have behaved very badly toward you. You deserve far better." He meant to console her, to soften the harshness of his rejection.

"Oh, Perryn." Before he knew what had happened, she had slid her arms about his neck yet again, only this time, she found his mouth and began kissing him wildly. His attempt to console her had become something worse.

Fenella reached the door of Perryn's bedchamber, anxious to see him and prove she had recovered very well, when she heard the sound of another woman's voice speaking his name repeatedly and in a manner that seemed passionate in the extreme! Though in any other circumstance she would have returned to her bedchamber, at this moment she felt obligated to discover just what was transpiring in the room of the man she loved. She reached for the door

handle, gave a twist and a push, and let the door swing
wide.

In front of her, not ten feet away, she saw Perryn entan-
gled in an embrace with Mrs. Sugnell, who in turn was
wearing only her nightdress. Her gaze fell to Mrs. Sugnell's
bare feet. She had to stand on her tiptoes in order to kiss
Perryn.

"Oh, dear." Mrs. Almington's voice drifted over her
shoulder from behind her.

"Indeed," Fenella glanced at her. "And to think I . . ."
She did not finish her thought. The rest was something of
a blur. She ran to her bedchamber, moving so quickly that
she was standing within, having turned the key without an
awareness of what she had done. She heard Perryn calling
to her and pounding on her door, demanding admittance.
A variety of voices called to one another, members of their
caravan, from up and down the hall. Doors opened and
closed with great rapidity. Footsteps scurried here and
there and all the while, Perryn shouted, "Fennel, open the
door at once! At once!"

"Go away!" she called back. "Vile man!"

"Fennel, please open the door! You are mistaken! I beg
you!"

"How I despise you! Go away!"

Betsy called to her. "Miss, what has happened?"

Fenella felt her eyes burn with tears she refused to shed.
She heard Mrs. Almington's calm voice addressing Perryn, though she could not precisely understand what she
was saying to him. A few minutes later, the hallway was
once more quiet.

Fenella stumbled backward to her bed and sat down,
numb to her toes. What had she been thinking? She had
kissed him again, that was all. And merely because he had
shown her a mite of compassion in caring for her after the
accident, she had allowed herself to be tricked into believing love existed between herself and Perryn. What a fool

she was. He had not been able to wait but a scant few hours before kissing another woman!

Mrs. Almington knocked softly and asked to be admitted into her bedchamber. Fenella allowed her to come in, but only after ascertaining that Perryn was no longer insistent on entering her room as well.

Fenella then excused her maid who was standing nearby, her expression distressed.

Mrs. Almington appeared as serious as a judge. "I know it looked very bad, but he explained the whole of it to me. The blame must lay at Mrs. Sugnell's feet."

Fenella recalled Mrs. Sugnell's bare feet and a feeling of revulsion passed through her. "Mrs. Sugnell is to blame? And was this why Perryn was holding her and kissing her? Are you telling me that somehow Mrs. Sugnell was forcing him to enjoy her attentions?"

Mrs. Almington sighed heavily. "Very well. I will not attempt to justify either his or her conduct. I only ask you to not be hasty. I believe there must be some explanation."

"The explanation is quite simple—Perryn has flirted so outrageously with Mrs. Sugnell for the past sennight and aroused her passions so completely that of course she would go to him and kiss him. What man, then, could refuse such a lady's advances? Only a saint, I am sure of it, and my lord Perryn is no saint!"

Mrs. Almington sighed anew and shook her head in some bemusement. "Is there nothing I can say in his defense?"

Fenella pursed her lips together. Anger had now taken possession of her. "No," she responded succinctly.

"Very well, then let us proceed to other matters. Tell me how you feel this morning. Are you in any discomfort from your tumble yesterday?"

"Only a very little."

"And do you feel well enough to travel?"

She nodded. "Not with Perryn, however. Not today."

Mrs. Almington nodded. "I have already thought of that. Of course you cannot. For that reason, and the fact that I fear Mrs. Millmeece will do Mr. Aston a serious injury today if she spends another consecutive morning in his company, I mean to switch everyone about. Several other of the partners are squabbling badly as well. It would seem we need a respite from the caravan. I am thinking you might like to travel with Mr. Almington. Would that suit you?"

Fenella nearly collapsed with relief. "Nothing would suit me better, ma'am, I promise you."

"Consider it done. I shall have a tray sent up, and Mr. Almington will call for you when all the others have left."

"Thank you. That is precisely what I would have wished for."

"And do not fret about Perryn. He has agreed to let matters rest for the present, though I have never seen him so distraught, so desperate. He must love you a very great deal to have threatened to take an ax to your door."

"He never did!"

"Oh, yes! I was only able to dissuade him with great effort. He seemed as mad as bedlam! Well, I shall leave you to complete your packing for the next portion of our journey."

Fenella nodded. Her throat grew very tight once more and she was grateful her hostess chose at that moment to quit her bedchamber, for she was no longer able to keep a veritable flood of tears from pouring down her cheeks.

Twelve

Perryn regarded Miss Madeley, wondering if her constant chatter was in any manner enticing to other gentlemen. For himself, he was bored beyond belief.

Mrs. Almington's decision to change all the partners around for the day had resulted in his traveling with The Incomparable, a design which at first had pleased him. After the ridiculous and aggravating experience of having Fenella actually see him holding and kissing Mrs. Sugnell and then not allowing him an opportunity to explain either his conduct or what precisely had passed between them had been beyond bearing. He had never been so furious in his entire life. Yet this was precisely what he had come to expect of Miss Trentham. It would seem she was determined to believe the worst of him at every turn.

Yet now, after so many hours in Miss Madeley's company, all his relief at the new traveling arrangement was gone.

"Do you like the mode in which my abigail has arranged my hair today, Lord Perryn?"

He glanced at the blond ringlets surrounding her face, at the bonnet which held the coiffure forward so she appeared to be fairly engulfed in curls, at her confidence in her beauty. He could barely repress a sigh. "Quite lovely, Miss Madeley."

"I am glad it pleases you. I cannot tell you how greatly

my fears have been allayed, for when I learned you were to be my companion today I was completely alarmed and gave my abigail a fit of the nerves with all my concerns about which gown must I wear with which bonnet, whether to wear a spencer, a pelisse, or perhaps a shawl, would the sapphire ear bobs suffice or the simple gold pearls? She nearly quit my employ. In short, I was completely bowled over. You can have no notion!"

The latter part of this speech he did not believe by half. Miss Madeley was never bowled over—by anything. She was supremely convinced of her ability to attach any gentleman to her side, though he had to admit that for the past several villages, including Dinder, Croscombe, Shepton Mallet, Doulting, and West Cranmore, she had been making an expansive effort. He had never known her to be so charming, so eager in her praise, so willing to agree with whatever opinion he brought forth. Indeed, now that he watched her smiling and laughing, he thought he must have been something of a nodcock not to have been charmed.

However, he simply was not. He kept longing to have the lady opposite him lift her chin at his attempts at flirtation, to come the crab when he spouted his determination to do thus and so, or to contradict his opinions. Miss Madeley, however, or so it would seem, was entirely incapable of disappointing him in anything.

He thought he must be something of a sad wretch that this was what he had come to depend upon for his happiness—Miss Trentham's unwillingness to think well of him until he had proven his worth.

When Perryn finally handed Miss Madeley down at Leighton to enjoy a cup of tea before completing the remainder of the morning's journey to Frome, she held tightly to his arm. He realized then that he must tell her the truth.

"I am in love with Miss Trentham," he stated, without the smallest attempt at a preamble.

The lady could not proceed. She stopped before the door of the inn and turned to look up at him. "I beg your pardon?"

"There is nothing for it, Miss Madeley, but to speak in perfect honesty. Whatever hopes you might have had of attaching me to your side will not fadge. I am hopelessly in love with Miss Trentham."

The lady's face grew nearly as red as a beet. "How dare you," she cried, "when your addresses have been most particular? You have singled me out nearly every evening, flattering me with your compliments, and in a dozen other ways making your intentions known to me. Can you deny you have done so?"

Once more, Perryn recalled Fenella's admonishment that he did not know his effect upon the ladies of his acquaintance. And yet he could not quite credit that Miss Madeley's opinions of his conduct were entirely based on what had actually transpired. "I have engaged quite enthusiastically in a flirtation with several ladies of our party."

"The *married* ladies!" she retorted. "I was the only one of the unmarried ladies to whom you paid even the smallest deference, though occasionally you ceased quarreling with Miss Trentham long enough to cart her up the stairs when you had trod on her ankle. Otherwise your conduct was very pointed. What say you, my lord, to all the attentions you paid me? What was your meaning, for instance, at having requested me most especially to play for you at Tewins Court?"

Good God. She was right, though he could hardly tell her he had used her vanity to provoke Miss Trentham into taking up her own place at the pianoforte. It would seem he would have been wise to have taken his dear Fennel's reproaches to heart. He had been utterly heedless in his conduct with her in not allowing that any young lady, let alone one so convinced of her worth and full of so much ambition as Miss Madeley, would have had the right to think herself pursued in earnest.

"I never meant to mislead you. If I have, I most humbly beg your pardon. Although I cannot believe you to have tumbled in love with me." He watched her carefully and did not mistake the cold light which entered her eye. Coupled with her presently ruddy complexion, she was not precisely the vision of an angel. "Just as I thought. I expect you will manage your disappointment."

"You have quite said enough, my lord," she responded haughtily. She lifted her chin and passed through the portals of the inn.

Fenella found Mr. Almington's company that morning to be the very best balm for her troubled heart she could have hoped for. He was an easy gentleman to converse and to travel with. By the time his coach reached Buntings Court, where the next evening would be spent, she felt rested and peaceful of spirit. An alfresco nuncheon, served beside a charming lake to the south of Lord and Lady Knebworth's property, was an unexpected delight which further soothed her harried sensibilities, for there was nothing so fine as being out-of-doors on a lovely August day.

Throughout the morning, no matter which of their party chanced upon them as they made their way to Frome, Mr. Almington had remained by her side in the most considerate support. Even now he strolled beside her in the direction of a path which traveled around the perimeter of the lake. When Perryn approached them with his quick, commanding stride, she felt ready to bolt in the opposite direction. Mr. Almington must have sensed as much, for he patted her arm gently.

"Courage, my dear," he murmured. "Your refusal to speak with Perryn will only incite the worst gossip, since the entire party knows of Mrs. Sugnell's mischief."

Fenella glanced about the expansive lawn where an excellent meal was being served *alfresco* to the caravan guests. She doubted there was a single eye not cast in her direction.

She glanced at her host and smiled, if ruefully. "Oh, very well, but I cannot promise I will be in the least civil to him."

"At least permit the man to explain," he countered somewhat fervently. "Even a dog deserves the benefit of the doubt!"

"I beg your pardon, but usually the feathers in his mouth give him away entirely."

Mr. Almington could only laugh, but after greeting Perryn in his calm, gentlemanly manner, he relinquished her arm to him.

"Fennel," he murmured harshly, "walk with me."

"Do you mean to begin issuing orders now?" she asked coldly.

"No," he responded softly. "I did not mean to come the crab. Will you take a stroll about the lake with me?"

"Very well," she murmured in response. As they began to make the circuit, she remained silent, intending for him to bear the weight of their conversation.

After a time, he cleared his throat. "What did you say just now that caused Mr. Almington to laugh?" he began.

Fenella glanced at him. "We were speaking of poultry and dogs."

He smiled perfunctorily, but offered no further query on the subject. She could see he was much occupied with his thoughts and perhaps what it was he wished to say to her. "We must speak of Mrs. Sugnell," he said at last.

"I had rather not."

"You blame me," he stated, scowling.

"The day is so lovely. Must we quarrel?"

"There would be no need for quarreling at all would you but trust me a little."

At that she turned to stare at him. "My lord, you were holding the lady in your arms and kissing her. My eyes could not have deceived me in that! Wherein do you suppose my trust should lie?"

"You do not intend to ask me the particulars?"

"I do not believe I need to know them."

"I shall tell you anyway. The truth of the matter is that when I heard a rapping at my door early this morning, I thought you had come to me as you did several mornings earlier. Do you remember your having done so?"

"Of course. At Burnhill."

"I had just excused my valet because I wished for a private conversation with you. The next moment, Mrs. Sugnell was before me in her nightdress, which I can tell you shocked me greatly."

Fenella rolled her eyes in disbelief.

"I was shocked," he reiterated firmly. They were by now halfway round the lake. "And entirely dismayed, for your prophecies had come true. And worse, she was weeping. I meant only to comfort her as I was turning her from my room."

"By kissing her?" she asked, astonished at just how low even a rogue could sink.

"No!" he cried. "No, you misunderstand the situation."

"I do not think so."

"You are being most stubborn, but I intend to have my say anyway. I actually begged Mrs. Sugnell's pardon for having injured her. She professed her love for me, you see, and even begged to become . . . well, I suppose that is neither here nor there."

"Your mistress?" she suggested.

"Yes. In truth, I did not know how to be rid of her. In softening my demeanor, by asking her to forgive me, she thrust herself upon me, embracing me, clinging to me, kissing me. That was when you opened the door to my bedchamber."

"Oh, I see then," she responded facetiously. "You were merely expressing your remorse—and may I say how ardent it was?"

"You refuse to understand what actually happened, then?"

"You are wrong, Perryn. I believe I have taken a full and accurate measure of the situation."

"You are being cruel."

They had progressed a little further when she drew to a halt and released his arm. "Perryn, do you truly think the whole matter is so simple that you have but to feel a trifling remorse and in experiencing such a sentiment the whole of the situation is redeemed?"

He was silent, a furrow between his brows.

"With all the encouragement you have given that lady, I vow had I been in her shoes I would have felt outraged by such a spurning." She became quite agitated. "You are the sort of man who cannot even remember half of the important things you do or say or how such acts affect others. If I have a quarrel with you, it is in this."

Perryn watched her uneasily. Memories stirred within him, oddly, strangely. He struggled to bring them to the forefront of his mind. A memory floated to him of his angel, a light behind her. She was bent over him, whispering words that changed his life. *Will you remember me once I am gone?* she had whispered.

Why could he not remember? Yet the effect had been with him for so many years. He had changed in a dozen different ways, but not sufficiently, it would seem, to win the respect of the lady before him.

"You are choosing to believe ill of me exclusively, but will you not credit that the lady was engaged in the flirtation with an equal fervor?"

"Still you refuse to see where you are responsible."

"And I see you are not to be moved."

"No, Perryn, I am not, even though last night . . ." She could not finish her thought.

"Yes, last night," he murmured angrily. "I begin to think it was a very good thing Mrs. Sugnell came to my bedchamber this morning after all."

"As you say."

The stroll was completed in silence, even if the entire party was gaping at them. In the end he returned her to Mr. Almington.

When Perryn moved off briskly in the direction of the stables, her host queried, "And did he still have all those feathers in his mouth?"

She chuckled if painfully. "A great deal too many, I fear. But come, will you escort me into the house? I wish to retire for a time, and if I leave by myself it will give rise to even more speculation than what you have just witnessed."

"Of course."

Mr. Almington released her at the bottom of the stairs. She thanked him for his many kindnesses to her throughout the morning. After watching him disappear through the hall leading to the terrace and the lake, she began her ascent. She had not taken five steps when Aubrey called her name. She turned and saw his countenance was quite flushed. She could only suppose he had been running.

"Whatever is the matter?" she inquired, frowning.

"I must speak with you. It is a matter of some import."

She retraced her steps, for he seemed greatly overset.

"Come," he said, taking her arm. "The library is just beyond the next antechamber. Once there, we might speak privately."

Fenella could not quite discern just what was troubling him and wondered if Miss Adbaston's growing attachment to him had become more than he could manage.

Before she had barely crossed the threshold of the library, however, he made his troubles known to her in the plainest of terms. "I lost a great deal at vingt-un last night, four hundred pounds. You must send an express at once to Mr. Morden at Sewards Manor, to whom I am beholden."

Fenella felt herself pale. Even her fingers grew suddenly icy. "Four hundred pounds!" she cried. "Aubrey, how is that possible?"

"I was winning, you see. I had nearly won seven hundred, and I saw a chance to increase my fortune. Then perhaps I could be worthy of . . . well, that can hardly be of any significance now. Suffice it to say that I began to lose. You know how it is. You think your luck will turn at any moment. But the cards . . . I nearly accused Mr. Morden of cheating, but I saw it was no such thing. Fenella, you must help me! I promise this will be the very last time!"

Fenella felt sick at heart. Her brother's name and to some extent her own respectability were being threatened by a debt of honor which must be paid, particularly in view of the fact that the entire caravan through Somerset was being conducted under the auspices of Mr. and Mrs. Almington's patronage. Not to pay the debt was a thought not to be borne, yet she could not continue to relieve Aubrey every time he erred so wretchedly.

"Aubrey, you know I cannot," she murmured, shaking her head, the horror of the situation causing her heart to constrict painfully. "You must bear this as best you can, my dear brother, but I cannot continue to pay your debts."

An alteration in his countenance upon the utterance of these words caused her to take a step backward. His cheeks flamed. His brown eyes, which could be so full of sweetness on occasion, grew dark and stormy.

"You must see I have no other recourse," she said, opening her hands wide.

"I see how it is," he responded through gritted teeth. "But I tell you now, Fenella, this is the last chance you will have to do what is right by your brother. I should have had Toseland, not you!"

"Are we at that again?" she cried, her spirit rising. "Aubrey, that I am to inherit is not my fault, but it certainly is my responsibility, and I take it seriously—which has caused me to wonder, given your predilection for gaming, just what would have happened had Toseland been yours. Would you have gambled it away? Would you have run up a mountain of debts against the expectation?"

His jaw worked strongly. "How dare you accuse me of such conduct? I have done nothing on this caravan so very different from any other gentleman here. Even Almington lost two hundred last night."

"You would compare your conduct to his? Aubrey, he has seven thousand a year and is well able to sustain such a loss now and again. However, I am also given to understand that he gambles but rarely."

"I knew you would justify his losses, or anyone else's, but not mine!"

She knew there was no purpose in trying to argue with him, and she was certainly in no temper to continue quarreling. Her head had begun to ache severely as much from her earlier encounter with Perryn as from the sight of her brother's indignant countenance. "I take my leave of you, Aubrey. We can have nothing further to say to one another on this subject."

As she moved past him, he took strong hold of her arm. "Your very last chance to do what is right, sister!"

Her own anger rose at that. "I am done with you!" she retorted hotly, and because she was so distressed she added, "And you may go to the devil for all I care!"

He seemed a little taken aback, but he released her. With that, Fenella hurried to her bedchamber.

On the following morning, Fenella awoke in such a depression of spirits that she wondered if she would ever recover. She had this one last day to endure in Perryn's company before being freed at last from the trials of what had become a most painful journey about Somerset. She therefore straightened her shoulders and adjured Betsy to make her hair up as prettily as possible. She knew she would need a sprightly appearance to sustain her throughout the day, given the depths of her sadness where Perryn was concerned and the frustration she was experiencing with Aubrey's inability to master his appetite for gaming.

As she entered the drawing room, where the first half of the travelers were preparing to depart, she found she was able to greet Perryn with a degree of equanimity which surprised her. She felt her confidence increase that the morning at least would not be so intolerable as she had thought. When he had settled her in his coach and begun to beg her pardon yet again, she was able to smile. With a lift of her hand she assured him he need not apologize and that her only desire of the moment was to collect as many kisses as possible, since this was to be their last opportunity to add to their collection.

With a flurry of movement, she withdrew her embroidery hoop and nothing more was said on the subject. He was about to give the coachman the office to start when Fenella noticed Miss Adbaston had just emerged from the manor, weeping. Mrs. Almington was with her, appearing greatly vexed.

"Hold one moment, Perryn. Something is amiss." She recalled her brother's agitated and threatening manner of the night before.

Mrs. Almington came forward, although Miss Adbaston remained on the steps. "Miss Trentham," she began quietly, "I have just been informed that your brother quit Buntings Court early this morning without a word to anyone. Did you know of it? What excuse can he possibly have for using Miss Adbaston so very ill?"

Fenella sighed heavily. "I know nothing of his departure,

though I think I can guess at his purpose. He was unable to discharge his gaming debts to Mr. Morden of the previous night. I understand he lost a great deal and has not the smallest means of being able to redeem his vowels."

"I feared as much," Mrs. Almington said, glancing back at Miss Adbaston. "This is very bad. It has escaped no one's notice that a certain attachment has formed over the past several days, and for a moment I had entertained every hope that something useful might come of it."

"Is she very unhappy?" Fenella inquired, shifting her head to better see the poor young lady. Nothing could have been more woeful, however, or more indicative of Miss Adbaston's feelings than her sad countenance.

"I do not think anyone could be more so."

"Shall we take her up in our coach? There is ample room, and I have little doubt Perryn would be agreeable to the notion." She turned to regard him hopefully.

"Of course she may come with us," he murmured, quite sincerely.

"You are both very kind," Mrs. Almington said. "But I believe it would be best for her to travel with me today. Well, you should be going. I can see we are detaining the entire procession."

As she drew away from the coach, Fenella once more glanced at the sad young lady and felt miserable about her brother's general character. Though she had spoken harshly to him last night, she did not think their quarrel an excuse for such incivility on his part toward his partner.

She knew however that there was nothing to be done. Aubrey . . . was Aubrey.

"You must be grieved," Perryn said as the coach began gathering speed down the long, yew-lined avenue.

"You cannot imagine my feelings. We argued last night again about his gaming debts."

"And he was unmoved by your strictures?"

"For the past twelvemonth, he has been making a concerted effort not to let his enjoyment of gaming exceed his income. However, during this journey, his former appetites seemed to have returned, and that so powerfully. I felt at a complete loss as to what I could say to him. He is after all a man of five and twenty, not a little boy. Yet he seemed wholly unaware of the danger he was in. When he asked for my help in discharging the debt he acquired at Sewards Manor and I refused, he became enraged."

"Though I fear giving you pain, I believe your brother is a fool."

"He could never forgive me for inheriting."

"What did you say to him?"

"I . . . I told him to go to the devil which was very bad of me, but I was sick to death of hearing his complaints on the subject. He does not comprehend all that has been given to him. He can see only what he has lost in the unusual arrangement of the line of inheritance. Oh, but I can see I have given you a shock! I suppose I should not have spoken to my brother in such a manner, and I certainly should not have revealed as much to you, but I was so completely out of patience with him."

Lord Perryn laughed outright. "You never cease to amaze me in all that you do and all that you are. Miss Trentham . . . Fenella . . . I know you are quite disposed to think ill of me, but do you think you could set aside your opinions long enough to become my wife?"

Fenella blinked several times. She knew her mouth had fallen most unattractively agape, but there was nothing for it. "Have I heard you correctly?" she managed after a time. "Have you . . . have you actually made me an offer of marriage?"

"I have. Most sincerely." There was a crooked smile on his lips.

She did not think anything could have dumbfounded her more completely than such an offer from a confirmed bachelor, from whom she had longed to hear such words and yet without the smallest possibility she could ever accept his hand. Odd tears started to her eyes. "You know very well I cannot marry you."

"But you love me almost as much as I love you. Admit it is true."

"I will admit nothing of the kind." Had he said he *loved* her? How her heart fluttered at such words and yet . . . and yet, there was nothing to be done.

"Is this your answer, then?"

"I believe it must be."

Only briefly did her gaze flit to his, afterward dropping back swiftly to the purple embroidery thread held in her presently trembling fingers. She was attempting to fit it through what had previously been an easily navigated needle, but which now seemed to possess an eye that had shrunk to half its size.

"Very well."

Perryn had seen the hurt in her eyes as well as the determined set of her chin. He understood clearly then the mountain he must climb in order to win her, yet he was not dismayed. Something wonderful had transformed within his heart the moment he had asked her to become his wife. Any uncertainties he might have felt about his sentiments for his dear Fennel had been removed entirely in that instant and within his heart had been born a powerful determination to somehow persuade her to become the next Marchioness of Perryn. In a brilliant flash of comprehension he realized how deeply he loved her. He had known as much when he had cared for her through the night after the racing accident, but something now, in this moment, in asking for her hand in marriage, had revealed the absolute depths of his regard for her. She had become as necessary to his happiness as the air he breathed.

Only how to go about winning a lady who did not have confidence in his integrity? Somehow, in the next few days . . . weeks . . . years, if necessary, he meant to prove himself to her.

Early that afternoon, Fenella entered Mrs. Almington's home with a profound sense of relief. She could be at ease now, for the collecting and the traveling with Perryn, all in the privacy of his coach and in his sole company, was now at an end. She could begin to rebuild her heart, which was still in a state of chaos where he was concerned. That he had actually offered for her only added to her misery.

As she made her way to her bedchamber, however, she could not help but reflect that from the moment he had declared himself, something in his demeanor toward her had altered substantially. He seemed resolved in a manner which she had never before observed.

Though he had been a considerate partner during their travels, his attentions after having made his offer of marriage had become increasingly solicitous. The moment he detected her fatigue, he begged to know if she desired to break their journey. As they worked to collect the last of the kisses, he remained close by her side, and when a curricle flew up the high street at Norton St. Philip, nearly running her down, he protected her with an arm swung quickly about her waist, drawing her out of harm's way.

She removed her bonnet and sat down on the edge of the bed. The caravan most certainly had taken a toll on both her heart and her mind. She drew in a deep breath and released it slowly. She would do well, she decided, to remain closeted within her bedchamber the remainder of the afternoon. She certainly had an excellent excuse, for there was still much work to be done on the collection to make it ready for the auction.

Summoning her maid, she began laying the kissing-ribbons out quite carefully on the bed and could not help but smile. So many lip prints staring back at her could make even the most stoic of creatures laugh. In this, at least, she could be well satisfied. Whatever her troubles with Perryn, their adventure together in the collecting of so many kisses had been as amusing as it had been utterly delightful.

She thought for a moment about all the people she had met in the short space of a fortnight and tucked the favorites of these recollections deeply into her mind for future reverie. She found herself grateful for having had the experience.

When Betsy arrived, she discussed with her at length just how the maypole might be assembled. "If only we could devise some manner," Fenella said, "in which the maypole could be made to spin."

"Aye, what an excellent notion, for the ribbons would fan out and present a lovely sight. I believe I know what might be done. The head gardener is a remarkably clever fellow, and I suspect he could contrive just the thing for us."

"Excellent," Fenella said. "Are you sufficiently well acquainted with him to place such a request before him?"

"Aye, miss."

"Very well. Then while you are gone, I shall continue embroidering the remainder of the ribbons."

"Have you many left?"

"No. I believe I shall be finished before dinner."

Betsy returned an hour later with the gardener in tow. He proved to be an exceedingly handsome young man by the name of Mr. Cowling. He carried a pole which he thought might suit their needs and said that since the auction was not for two days, he felt certain he could contrive just the right anchor for the maypole that would allow it to spin without falling over. Fenella thanked him warmly and gave him liberty to do whatever he felt was required to accomplish the task.

The rest of the afternoon was spent quietly with Missy at her feet and her fingers plying her needle as she completed the embroidery work. Though her thoughts frequently drifted toward Perryn and the extraordinary events of the past twelve days in his company, she also could not help but think of her brother. She wondered just where he had gone this time and whether or not she should inform their father of his latest disgrace. She decided to delay any correspondence with their parent in hopes that Aubrey would arrive at Whitmore desirous of making amends. She wished more than anything that there was something she could do to help a sibling apparently set on a path of ruin.

Upon descending the stairs for dinner that evening, Fenella found herself addressed by Miss Keele and Miss Madeley.

"Tell me it is not true!" Miss Keele cried in some astonishment. "Did you actually refuse the Marquess of Perryn?"

"I beg your pardon?" she queried. How was it possible any of their party had learned of his proposal of marriage? "Where did you hear such tidings as these?" She glanced from one lady to the next. Miss Keele shook her head in disbelief while Miss Madeley's pale complexion gave her the impression the news had shocked her quite severely.

Miss Keele enlightened her. "From Mr. Silverdale, who had it from Mr. Millmeece, who learned of it by way of Mr. Almington who had just been informed by Colonel Bedrell that Perryn had asked for your hand in marriage earlier this morning but had been refused."

"Good God," she murmured, feeling faint. She had not expected this of Perryn, to expose her to all manner of mischief by revealing so private a matter. That Colonel Bedrell felt at liberty to speak of it was the greater wonder, for nothing short of Perryn's permission would have allowed the information to have been bandied about as it had. What could Perryn have meant by making his proposals, and her subsequent rejection of them, known so generally?

"Then it is true?" Miss Madeley asked in a quiet voice.

"Yes."

"I cannot credit you have refused him!" Miss Keele cried. "Am I to believe that the sensible Miss Trentham is as big a goosecap as the rest of us? Impossible!"

Miss Keele's mode of expressing herself could not help but make Fenella smile. However, for Perryn's sake she felt she had to respond with some degree of seriousness and civility.

"Lord Perryn did, indeed, honor me with his proposals, but I am convinced we would not suit, so of course I felt obliged to refuse him."

Miss Madeley shook her head, her expression disbelieving. "You would reject the opportunity of becoming the Marchioness of Perryn for such a reason? I begin to think you are addled, Miss Trentham. If for no other reason, you ought to have accepted him just to please your family. Such connections would be a blessing to all."

"My father would not give a fig for such things. He has always desired my happiness above everything."

The Incomparable rolled her eyes and turned away. Miss Keele remained a little longer, but even she did not seem satisfied. "I know you are in love with him," she whispered. "You cannot deny it. I have seen the way you look at him, as though your happiness rests in his eyes."

Fenella met Miss Keele's earnest gaze. She could see there would be no use in trying to deny what her friend had apprehended so completely. "I have never believed that love is an entirely reliable reason for doing anything."

"Then I believe I am sorry for you," she said, her expression compassionate. "For I believe you to be greatly mistaken on this score. But come, the entire party is assembled and I believe waiting to look at the young woman who refused the only offer of marriage Perryn has ever made."

The other single young ladies were equally as bewildered and disparaging about her refusal. By the time dinner had been concluded and she had endured even Miss Adbaston's reproofs, she felt obliged to take Perryn to task for having exposed her to so much amazed interest and censure.

She waited for him at the entrance to the drawing room, and as soon as the gentlemen returned from the dining hall after having enjoyed their port together in seclusion from the ladies, she drew him apart. "How could you?" she whispered quite without ceremony.

He leaned close. "I can see you mean to quarrel with me. Will you not, then, join me in the long gallery, where we might brangle in private?"

"An excellent notion," she responded hotly.

She remained silent until she was staring up at one of Mr. Almington's ancestors who wore a long curling black wig and a very thin mustache. "You have given me a shock," she began. "What ever possessed you to tell anyone of your proposals and my refusal? Do you have any notion what I have endured these past three hours since descending the stairs to dinner?"

He smiled. "For that I apologize. It was not my intention. I merely wanted the world to know that I was in love with you, that I have behaved ridiculously and foolishly in my flirtations on our journey, that I regret infinitely having not thrown a weeping Mrs. Sugnell from my bedchamber when she first burst into my room, and that I mean to have you if I possibly can."

She turned to stare at him, stunned by this extraordinary speech. She did not quite know which absurdity to address first, but chose the latter. "I have already made my sentiments known, Perryn. I shall never wed you. I do not believe you can make me happy when I cannot trust you."

"I know. It is most lowering."

"You are not being serious." She turned more fully to face him directly. "I can never wed you, my lord. You must see that."

"I see nothing, only the woman I love so deeply and dearly. You have been one of the strongest reasons I began altering my course so many years ago, only I never realized it until recently. Your strictures over the years have helped to set my feet on a proper path. I could only wish that I had ceased these ridiculous flirtations before we began our journey. Only tell me, you do believe what I have told you concerning Mrs. Sugnell, do you not?"

Though she knew it was hardly to the point, Fenella could not help but exclaim, "She had her arms slung about your neck, her feet were bare, she was in but her nightdress, and you were kissing her!"

"This much is true," he answered as a simpleton might. "But I had only one intent in that ridiculous moment—to be rid of her as quickly as possible."

"How did you hope to be rid of her by kissing her?"

"Actually," he said, "she was kissing me, but I believe that would be considered splitting hairs at the moment. Besides, your believing me in this instance is not necessary."

"And why is that?" she asked, confounded.

"Because I am persuaded that, far from your protests, you do trust me—only you will not allow it. That is the real wonder. However, I do not mean to relinquish my desire for you because of it. Indeed, I will wait as long as it takes for you to discover that my word is good and that when you marry me you will have no cause for disquiet on any score."

"You presume far too much, my lord!" she cried. "I will never marry you."

"Well, if that is the case, then I shall remain a bachelor the rest of my days. However, I will not relinquish hope.

And so, Miss Trentham, I warn you to prepare yourself for a siege." With that, he suddenly and quite violently took her in his arms and kissed her, so wickedly, so rakishly that her knees buckled, as they always seemed to do when he accosted her.

"My lord!" she cried, as he supported her strongly about her waist. "I beg you will desist!" She could not catch her breath. Not one whit!

"Never, for I find I delight in nothing more than how you fairly swoon each time I trespass your lips."

Once more he kissed her. She tried to be indifferent, to resist the passion that always seemed to envelop her when he embraced her and kissed her, but she could not. Her thoughts would be drawn back to the center of the maze where it had all begun so many years past, and she could do little more than submit to his tender assault. She even let him possess her mouth as he had that first night, the night he could not remember.

"I do love you, my dearest Fenella."

She drew in a deep, faltering breath. "I beg you will release me, Perryn. You cannot know the pain you inflict."

His smile was so warm and beckoning. "As you wish." Quite gently, she felt his arms relax.

She hesitated, longing to stay with him, wishing she could always be wrapped up so wonderfully in his arms.

She recalled, however, Mrs. Sugnell in her nightdress and she began moving, if unsteadily, away from him.

Thirteen

On the following morning, Mrs. Almington asked Fenella to take a turn about the gardens with her. "The day is exquisite, and I must confess I long to be out-of-doors. I have a most exceptional housekeeper, but between the number of guests presently ensconced in my home and the ball tomorrow night, she has more concerns to lay before me than I can at present bear."

"I should be happy to accompany you. I myself am working steadfastly to complete the display of our collection and descended in hope of a little exercise."

"Come, then. We shall both enjoy a little relief from our employment."

They had not walked long among the shrubbery when Mrs. Almington queried, "You do know that I made certain you were Perryn's partner?"

"Of course. I must have sprained my eye winking at you that first day, hoping you would not do what I had determined you were already determined to do."

Mrs. Almington hooked her arm about Fenella's. "You have not the smallest notion how perfect you are for him. I have been on the look-out for just such a lady as you these ten years and more. The closest I came was the Duchess of Cannock, but there was a problem."

Fenella could only laugh. "The duke, I would suppose?"

Mrs. Almington chuckled. "Yes, the duke. Nevertheless,

Perryn fell madly in love with her, and she with him, not long after the introductions were made."

"Indeed?" Fenella queried. Perryn had told her he had loved once. She wondered if he had been referring to the duchess.

"They became lovers within weeks of the acquaintance."

Fenella felt herself blush, though she tried not to. She had never spoken so openly of such things with anyone. "I see," she murmured, her eyes cast to the path before them.

"I hope you do not mean to be missish—or is it possible you know nothing of the Duke of Cannock?"

"You are right. I know very little of him."

"Lord Cannock was sixty if he was a day when he purchased his bride. Olivia Russell was but nineteen at the time and a very great heiress. The engagement was made on her behalf by a very selfish father who never once informed her of his intentions until she was led unexpectedly to the altar."

"Good God," Fenella murmured.

"She, however, did not evince the smallest bitterness once the event had taken place. The duke had chosen his bride well. I met her early in their marriage at his county seat in Oxfordshire. She conducted herself as one born to the station.

"She did not breed, however, much to the duke's exceeding dissatisfaction. He was intolerant and cruel. This I know, for I once saw her after a particularly brutal chastisement. Shortly thereafter, I made certain she became acquainted with Perryn. I had never seen either of them happier and the duke—well, his wife now had a protector, and believe me, the last man he desired to meet on a green some cold morning at dawn was the Marquess of Perryn."

Fenella sensed more than she wished to. "What became of her?"

"She was soon with child and gave birth to a stillborn son, but she did not survive above three weeks. She was sick with fever, common enough and so very tragic. I never saw a man strive so diligently to keep her with him in this life. He never left her side, poor man. He was not seen in society for some time. Your father, I believe, called on him during his darkest hour."

"When was this?" she asked. She felt dizzy, as though she already knew the answer.

"Four—no, five years ago this past June."

"Oh, dear God. I was there, at Morchards, with Papa. Perryn was completely foxed. But how could I have known of his misfortune? And of course Papa never would have breathed a word of the affair to me. And it would be so like my father to offer his support and condolence at such a time. I wish I had known." She remembered how Perryn had clung to her and kissed her. Sudden tears stung her eyes.

"Did he . . . that is, was his behavior toward you civil?" Mrs. Almington asked.

"When would his conduct ever be civil should he find a lady alone in a maze with the sun fully set and the moon alone providing a very weak protection?"

Mrs. Almington chuckled.

"I had thought him debauched—I had heard such tales," Fenella added.

"I suspected as much, and he is given to flirting with enthusiasm. You still do not hold him responsible for Mrs. Sugnell's absurd conduct, do you?"

"Of course I do," she responded.

Mrs. Almington paused in her steps. "There will always be silly women attempting to fill the vanity and boredom of their lives with the attentions of men. You must not put too much weight on Mrs. Sugnell's or Lady Elizabeth's or Mrs. Millmeece's conduct. Believe me, Perryn does not."

"But he has made such a cake of himself this past fortnight. I cannot tell you how many fingers he has kissed in the course of these two weeks."

"All to keep his own heart safe, I believe."

"Whatever do you mean?"

"I observed him countless times. He would be staring at you in such a way and then immediately seek out one of his favorites. It seemed clear to me you were rarely from his thoughts. Surely you knew as much?"

She shook her head. "I do not think I was ever entirely certain just what he was thinking from one moment to the next. How could I when I was so busily engaged myself in protecting my own heart?"

"Yet he offered for you."

"I believe that came as much of a surprise to himself as to me."

"Perhaps, for he did tell me he rather burst out with the notion instead of being wise and attempting to gentle your heart toward him beforehand. However, I long suspected the truth of his sentiments well before his arrival in Somerset."

"You cannot be referring to this past Season?" she asked incredulously.

When Miss Adbaston and Miss Keele were seen entering the garden at the far end, Mrs. Almington guided Fenella along another path that led into a nearby wood. "As it happens, I am, but then I had made it my object to observe him. Yes, yes, I know it was quite impertinent of me, but I have so wanted him to be as happy in love again as he was with Olivia. But I digress. Since I had been so purposeful in my spying on Perryn, you had not been in London much above a sennight before I noticed he was rarely far from your side."

"Even if that is true, he scarcely spoke above a dozen sentences to me the entire Season. How then can you account for his having fallen in love with me?"

"Though he may not have conversed with you, he attended to your conversations with others time and time again. I do not know precisely his purpose, but it was evident to me that he took great delight in doing so."

"He was undoubtedly laughing at me."

She shook her head. "In that I believe you to be mistaken. Ah, here we are," she said, gesturing to the path ahead. "Is that not a pretty copse? I do so love this portion of the wood. The stream is not far. Do you mind walking on?"

"Not a bit." Fenella took a deep breath. The conversation had stunned her in so many respects that it was pleasant to be diverted a little as she lifted her head and peered through the thick canopy of leaves to the blue sky beyond. The sweet, pungent redolence of ferns drifted up from about her feet as they strolled on.

When they reached the stream, Mrs. Almington sat on a large boulder nearby and, much to Fenella's surprise, began removing her shoes and stockings. "Will you not join me?" she asked, a challenging smile on her lips.

Fenella could not help but laugh. She had always enjoyed her hostess's company, but somehow this simple, girlish act of putting her bare feet in the cool stream fixed forever in her mind the belief she would always be on excellent terms with her. Mrs. Almington was of an age with Perryn and therefore not so far removed in age from her as she might have been, even though her daughter was nineteen. Mrs. Almington had been so fortunate as to have made a love match her first Season in London some twenty years past.

Fenella did not hesitate, but also took up a seat on a boulder and stripped her shoes and stockings off in brisk movements. Was there ever anything so pleasant as hot bare feet in a cooling stream?

Thus settled and quite content, Fenella regarded her hostess. "So Perryn attended to my conversations and by this you determined he had tumbled in love with me?"

She nodded. "The waltz you shared with him at my town house on the very evening I was dreading hearing you announce you had become betrothed to Mr. Clavering fixed my opinion completely that Perryn was in love with you—but not only that, that you were not so indifferent to him as you always seemed. So tell me, were you disinterested?"

Fenella sighed. "Not by half, I fear. I will confess something to you that no one knows. I fell quite violently in love with Perryn that night at Morchards some five years past, but I have never trusted that love. I still do not. I cannot explain it even in light of your revelations about the Duchess of Cannock."

"Well, Perryn certainly seems intent on having you," she said, smiling. "I daresay he will wear you down and we shall enjoy a wedding before Michaelmas."

"It is not so simple, I fear."

"I know," she responded. "Only, I would offer this simple word to you: judge him by all that he is, not just these silly flirtations."

"Mr. Hanford said something quite similar to me just a few days past."

"Mr. Hanford is a man of great sense."

Fenella watched Mrs. Almington wiggle her toes in the water. She was an exceedingly content lady and Fenella felt certain she ought to heed her hostess's advice. Yet, however was she to do so when images of Mrs. Sugnell wrapped up in Perryn's arms kept intruding into her thoughts?

"Mr. Cowling!" Fenella exclaimed, staring at the creation the head gardener had brought for her inspection. "I have never seen anything so clever in my life. And you say with but a touch of the foot pedal, the entire pole spins?"

Mr. Cowling beamed with pride. "Aye, miss. Try it and ye'll see!"

Betsy smiled and nodded her encouragement as well.

Fenella approached the maypole, which stood some six

feet in height. The pedal was attached to a curious and rather large box in which the pole was fixed. Lifting her skirts slightly, she pressed firmly on the pedal with her foot and the pole began to spin. By pressing the pedal again and again, the pole could be kept in a constant whir of motion.

She jumped back, clapping her hands. "It is perfect! Perfect! When I have all the ribbons attached, it will be even more wonderful than I could ever have imagined! Thank you so very much."

" 'T'were nothing, miss." A touch of red colored each cheek.

Though he might have been embarrassed by her fulsome praise, she was indeed enchanted by the inventive mechanism that so greatly improved her original idea.

For the duration of the afternoon, Fenella worked to assemble the maypole so that within a few hours a plume of ribbons layered over the upper ten inches of the pole upon increasingly larger rings of fabric, appeared to have fairly exploded from the top of the pole. She crested the pole with a jaunty bouquet of pink silk flowers. Once set to spinning, the kissing maypole made a remarkable, amusing, and fascinating spectacle. The kisses at a distance appeared to be heart shapes imprinted the length of each ribbon. When the pole was spun by the foot pedal, the varied short and long strips of silk fanned out into a whirling mass that made a sound like the soughing of the wind through well-leafed trees.

"Oh, miss," Betsy cried. "You shall surely win the prize, for it is quite the most beautiful thing I have ever before seen."

"Thank you. I could not be happier with how it looks. Your efforts alone made the completion of the embroidery possible, although I begin to think the gardener is half in love with you to have done as much for me. He must have had another motivation entirely."

Betsy blushed quite deeply. "Oh, miss, how can you speak so when he is twenty years my junior if a day!"

"Not twenty, surely! Although he might be fifteen. But he is ever so handsome!"

"No man should be so easy to look upon," Betsy responded, sighing. Mr. Cowling was the scourge of the undermaids and every lady's maid he encountered.

Fenella thought of Perryn, in particular just how many times she had had the same notion about him, that it was quite cruel of nature to have put so much beauty in one face and figure. How was she to continue resisting the strenuous efforts of such a roguish creature when he was so deucedly handsome! She recalled with a renewed dizziness the kiss he had forced so wretchedly yet so delightfully upon her last night. How brazen he had been! How determined! Was it possible he would, as Mrs. Almington had predicted, simply wear her down? This she could not permit to happen, not if she was to know a jot of peace.

"Is that the hour?" Betsy cried.

Fenella's attention was drawn immediately toward the mantel, where a clock chimed the half hour. "I fear I have been so much engaged in completing the maypole that I have quite forgot the hour. There is scarcely time to dress for dinner!"

The next few minutes were spent scampering out of one gown and into another and urging Betsy to arrange her curls more quickly.

As soon as the last of the three small white roses gathered from the garden had been tucked among her brown locks, Fenella intended to race from her bedchamber. At the last moment, she recalled that Perryn had not yet seen their collection. She said as much to Betsy.

"Why do you not fetch him?" her maid suggested. "If he has not left his bedchamber, you will be but a few minutes late to the drawing room, which will hardly signify."

Fenella nodded. "And I should so like him to see the

maypole before we go downstairs. He has a right to see the results of all our collecting, for he gathered far more kisses than I did. I shall be right back."

She opened the door to leave, excited by the prospect of showing her afternoon's labors to him. However, when the door swung wide, Miss Madeley was standing before her, one hand raised in preparation of knocking. Her gaze immediately flew past Fenella's shoulder to the maypole which of the moment was in its full glory, since Betsy was once again operating the foot pedal.

"Oh!" she cried. "I had not meant to intrude but, my dear Miss Trentham, is that your collection? I find I am utterly astonished." Betsy released the pedal and the silk ribbons floated back into place. "Only, whatever is it?"

Short of thrusting Miss Madeley back into the hallway, there seemed to be no way of preventing her from entering her bedchamber. How unlucky! "A maypole, Miss Madeley, made up of silk ribbons. I . . . I hope you will tell no one." She had no confidence whatsoever that Miss Madeley would remain silent on the subject.

The young woman moved toward the maypole as one completely stunned. Fenella closed the door, releasing a disappointed sigh.

"Why, there are kisses on all these ribbons!" The Incomparable cried. "You sly thing! No wonder there were so many red-lipped ladies—and not a few gentlemen—in all the villages we passed through. You were collecting kisses all this time, as was Perryn, if I do not much mistake the matter."

"You have the right of it," Fenella agreed. She found herself caught between pride in their achievement and frustration that the lady whom she considered her strongest rival for the Pavilion prize had discovered the nature of their collection.

"Oh, come, Miss Trentham, do not be cast down. I promise you I would tell you even now what it was Colonel

Bedrell and I collected, but I fear he would have my head."
She stepped forward and extended her foot to the pedal.
"May I?"

"Of course," Fenella murmured, exasperated.

She worked the pedal and the ribbons began to fly once
more. "I have never seen anything to equal what you and
Perryn have accomplished here."

"Thank you. You are very kind."

Miss Madeley smiled, but Fenella thought her expression rather stiff and unhappy. "I suppose I should go. Mrs.
Almington will wonder where we are should we tarry much
longer."

"You are right, of course."

As she turned to take her leave, Fenella inquired, "Miss
Madeley, why did you wish to see me?"

"Oh, as to that," she responded, casting her hand in the
direction of the maypole, "I believe all my questions have
been answered!"

She swept from the bedchamber just as Perryn arrived.
He bowed to her as she moved swiftly over the threshold
and began a quick progress down the hall. He scarcely
glanced in that lady's direction, but rather moved briskly
into the room. "I came to find out if you had finished . . .
good God, is that it?"

"Yes, it is," she responded. When she could see that the
sight of the maypole had rendered him speechless, she addressed her maid, "Betsy, will you depress the pedal?"

Her maid obliged her.

Perryn exclaimed. "And it moves! How incredible! I
vow I am all amazement! You are greatly to be congratulated!"

Fenella closed the door, her sense of exhilaration dulled
perceptibly by Miss Madeley's unexpected and most unwelcome visit.

He turned back to her, his expression rather stunned.
"Truly, it is marvelous . . . only tell me why you are frown-

ing. I would think you would be *aux anges* of the moment. Oh, I see what it is—Miss Madeley has learned the nature of our collection."

"Precisely. And I am certain she will just happen to mention it to Miss Keele, Miss Adbaston, Miss Almington, and anyone else who will listen to her crowing. I had so wanted it to be a great surprise—a triumph!—and now *she* has triumphed over me."

"I suppose there is nothing that can be done about it now," he said, smiling sympathetically. He reverted his attention to the maypole and shook his head. "I am utterly, utterly astonished. You can have no notion. How does it spin?" He glanced down at the box and moved toward it for closer inspection. Betsy released the foot pedal so that he might examine the contraption at will.

Fenella's temper softened beneath so much sincere praise. "Mrs. Almington's head gardener is a man of some quickness of mind. He fashioned this for us by his own design."

"Indeed? How very singular."

"I could not agree more, which leads me to believe it will fetch a goodly sum at the auction—which of course is what one wishes for the most."

"What a rapper!" he cried, laughing. "You wish for the prize and to have your efforts proclaimed the very best. Admit it is so!"

"Oh, very well," she returned, chuckling guiltily. "I suppose there is no use dissembling with you. I know I ought to desire only that we might be able to earn a vast deal for Mrs. Almington's charity, but I do so want to win."

"I for one have every confidence that your kissing-ribbon maypole shall prevail tomorrow night."

Fenella might have protested any such thing, but she could not help but notice a quite knowing light in his eye. "There is something you are not telling me!" she cried.

His expression was so complacent that she opened her eyes wide.

"You must tell me! At once! What do you know?"

"Only that Colonel Bedrell made a trip to Bath this morning in his coach and returned with several very flat packages, each wrapped in brown paper and string, and of an equal size."

"Their collection?"

Perryn nodded.

"I believe that could be anything that was framed."

"Precisely, but over the past fortnight I have heard reports of the pair of them visiting churches in every village."

Fenella pondered what this might mean. "Brass rubbings?" she queried. "Do you think that is it? They made rubbings and had them framed?"

"I believe so."

Fenella began to smile. "Such a collection would of course have its charms," she said.

"I thought you might take to preening once you knew."

"Oh, but Perryn! Rubbings? I cannot help but think we shall win!"

He chuckled and said, "Well, if you are done gloating in this manner, permit me to escort you to the drawing room, where Mrs. Almington has hired a troupe of actors to entertain us this evening."

"Thank you," she responded.

Once quitting her bedchamber, he proffered his arm, which she accepted.

He glanced at her gown. "And may I say how beautifully that particular shade of green suits you?"

"Polite? Issuing compliments quite grandly? Pandering to my vanity by assuring me we shall win the prize? I begin to believe you are flattering me to a purpose."

He smiled. "Of course. I have no other object at the moment, or for the next several years if necessary. If compliments, civility, and flattery will prompt your heart toward mine, then I shall make any or all of these the order of the day."

Fenella felt in danger all over again, not this time because of anything he was saying but rather because there was an ease between them that pleased her so very much. This she would hardly say to him, however. He might be holding a weapon in his hands, but she did not have to prime it with gunpowder and pistol ball.

Once arrived at the drawing room, however, a little of Fenella's contentment dimmed, for she was besieged immediately with inquiries as to what precisely the maypole looked like and just how it was that she and Perryn had come upon the notion of collecting kisses in the first place. For her part, Miss Madeley stood near the fireplace beaming her triumph. Fenella had never liked her less.

On the following afternoon, the day of the auction ball, Fenella had just finished her nuncheon when Perryn offered to escort her back to her bedchamber to retrieve the ribbon maypole. The hour had come for all the participants to present their collections exclusively to the members of the caravan party.

Perryn said, "I do not give a fig whether Miss Madeley feels she has trumped you or not in having made known the nature of your collection."

"Our collection," she countered strongly just as she reached the door of her bedchamber. "Had you not had so much charm, there would have been but half the amount of kisses present on our ribbons." She turned the handle.

"Very well, *our* collection. However, you should be content that Miss Madeley's collection could never equal— good God, what is it, Fennel?"

"I—I do not believe it," she murmured, her heart constricting with horror. She then pushed the door wide for Perryn to see.

"Hell and damnation!" he cried. "Who would have done such a thing!"

"Who do you think?" Fenella countered. Only with the strongest effort did she keep a veritable flood of tears from streaming down her cheeks at the sight of all the ribbons, now cut to pieces, scattered like autumn leaves at the base of the maypole. The clean edges of the ribbons indicated that a fine pair of scissors had been the offending instrument by which the deed had been accomplished. Not a single ribbon remained attached to the maypole. "All our work," she murmured. She stooped to pick up several of the pieces, fingering them gently. "All for nothing. I feel as though something beautiful has been destroyed."

"I am so very sorry, Fennel. I know what this means to you." He reached down and took her hand, giving it a squeeze.

"Am I being ridiculous?" she asked, her voice breaking as she looked up at him. Tears finally slipped from her eyes.

He lifted her to her feet and slid an arm comfortingly about her shoulders. At the same time, he pressed his kerchief into her hand. "To be completely overset? No, not a bit. Anyone who knows with what fervor you applied yourself to this collection would easily comprehend your distress."

After weeping a little more and wiping her eyes with his kerchief, she was able at last to collect herself. She moved to sit on the bed, all the while staring at the bits of ribbon on the floor. For a very long while she was unable to speak, since there did not seem to be precisely the right words with which to give expression to the sadness she felt.

"It was so beautiful," she murmured at last, shaking her head.

Perryn remained politely by, his gaze, as well, fixed in an assessing manner on the debris. "Fennel," he began quietly, his voice solemn. "Never destroyed."

She turned to meet his gaze. "Whatever do you mean?"

He joined her by the bed and once more possessed himself of her hand. "I wish you to know that I shall hold dear the memory of every generous soul who contributed so enthusiastically to our collection. I do not think I could have enjoyed myself half so much without meeting such a variety of people and allowing them to participate in our project. For that I have you to thank. So our efforts have been spoiled. Never destroyed." He smiled.

"Why must you speak so kindly, so rationally when what I wish to do of the moment is to break something?"

He laughed. "I know you are terribly competitive but what does it matter after all?"

"Again you wound me with your philosophizing. I beg you will rant and rave and allow me the pleasure of . . . of . . . throwing at least one piece of furniture out the window. That little bedside table, perhaps, or—" She stormed toward a very fine mahogany chair and picked it up. "Or this!"

Though he laughed heartily at her antics, he also took the precaution of crossing the room swiftly and taking the chair out of her hands.

She smiled in return, but sudden tears filled her eyes. "How could she have done this?" she asked, dropping into the very chair she had meant to toss from the window. "Surely she could not have desired to win Mrs. Almington's prize so very much that she felt she had to ruin our collection?" She wiped her cheeks again with his kerchief.

He was thoughtful for a moment. "Perhaps to spite me. I fear I erred when I told her I loved you. I have never seen a lady fly so quickly into the boughs before."

"When was this?" she inquired.

"The day we switched partners. The day you found Mrs. Sugnell in my arms. Miss Madeley traveled with me that morning and attempted to engage my interest. After a time, I had grown so fatigued with her exertions to obtain my good opinion by agreeing with me at every turn that I felt it necessary to make certain she understood my heart was not free."

"Indeed?" So he had proclaimed his love for her to poor Miss Madeley. She felt oddly pleased, as though somehow his declaration gave a greater weight to his feelings. "You told her of your love for me that very day?"

"Yes." He smiled if crookedly. "But come, I intend to take care of our collection right now."

"What do you mean to do?" She glanced down at the bits of ribbon once more.

"I do not know precisely, but will you permit me to attend to the business myself?"

"I should help you pick up all these pieces, at the very least."

He shook his head. "No, I should like to do it myself, for it can only increase your pain to be handling these ribbons in such a condition."

"Perryn, I do believe you take too much upon yourself, though the offer is very kind."

"Nonsense," he retorted, turning her in the direction of the door. "You have borne the larger portion of the responsibility for our collection for the past fortnight. Now it is my turn." She attempted to argue further, but he would have none of it. "I shall take it most unkindly in you if you will not permit me to do this—although there is something else of an equally difficult nature which must be performed. Would you be so good as to tell Mrs. Almington that our collection has been damaged?"

"Of course. I shall go to her at once. Do you intend to simply dispose of all these pieces?"

"No, of course not, merely to gather them together. We

can discuss what is to be done with them at a later hour. Tomorrow will be soon enough."

"Very well," she murmured. "And you are right. Should I remain much longer, I daresay I should begin weeping anew and be unable to stop for an entire sennight."

"Go, then. I shall join you forthwith." She had walked but a few feet down the hall when he called to her from the doorway. "Miss Trentham, would you do me a favor?"

"Of course, anything."

"As it happens, I have just recalled I have a very important engagement in Bath. I must leave as soon as I have cared for matters here. Would you be so good as to make my apologies to Mrs. Almington?"

She frowned at him. "Of course, but does this mean you will miss the ball?"

"I shall be returned by then. Will you save me a waltz?"

Fenella felt a most familiar and quite painful squeezing of her heart. "Of course," she responded, knowing full well it would not be wise in the least to dance with him. How could she refuse him, though, when he was being so very kind?

Fourteen

Later that evening, Fenella descended the staircase to enjoy the auction ball. The guests were arriving, and the entrance hall was a veritable cacophony of excitement and noise.

Miss Keele espied her and ran up three steps to take her arm for her remaining descent. "Miss Almington and I believe we know what happened to your collection," she whispered.

"Indeed, we do," Miss Almington agreed, joining them.

The two ladies then drew her down the hall in the direction of the ballroom. Miss Keele continued, "We both heard Miss Madeley boasting that though she was sorry that something untoward had happened to your collection and that it would not be auctioned after all, she believed it had not been all that wonderful to behold in the first place. In fact, she said she had thought the entire thing to be rather silly in both nature and execution. What do you think of that?"

Fenella had little desire to become involved in an intrigue that would serve no one well, least of all herself, since there could never be the smallest proof of Miss Madeley's guilt. "I hope you do not mean to accuse her of causing mischief merely because she saw my collection and somehow disapproved of it."

"Of course not," Miss Almington said. "Miss Keele and

I acted upon our suspicions by inquiring of every one of the party whether or not they had seen your collection. No one had, except Miss Madeley, and she of course has a motive for wishing you harm."

"Do you think so, truly?" she inquired innocently, even though she was of the same opinion.

"Yes, for she has been pining for a handle to her name and she was convinced she would be betrothed to the Marquess of Perryn by the end of our journey about Somerset. You cannot imagine how furious she was to learn he had actually offered for you instead."

Fenella did not know what to say. "Even if she was somehow involved, of what use can it be to expose her?"

By that time, they had arrived at the entrance to the ballroom. Miss Madeley even now was surrounded by no less than seven gentlemen.

"It would at least bring her down a peg or two!" Miss Keele complained. "I vow it becomes tiresome to have her always petted and fawned over wherever she goes."

At that moment, Beau Silverdale and Sir John approached their small party and the subject of Miss Madeley was let drop. The gentlemen begged for dances from all three ladies and were accepted graciously by all three in turn. Fenella was about to excuse herself to find out if Perryn had yet returned from Bath when he suddenly appeared at the far end of the chamber with Colonel Bedrell and Mrs. Millmeece.

How her heart fluttered at the sight of him, a response which made her stamp her right foot. If only he was not so deuced handsome!

"Oh, my," Miss Keele murmured. "Lord Perryn is returned from Bath. Miss Trentham, how ever did you find the strength to refuse such a man? I vow I would fall into his arms the moment he but smiled in my direction."

Miss Almington, a degree younger than Miss Keele, was properly shocked, but Fenella could only laugh. Even Mr.

Silverdale lifted a brow as he studied Perryn's coat. "I am half in love with him myself, or at least with his tailor. Must be Weston—but, by God, no man should be allowed such excellent shoulders. Quite puts the rest of us to shame!"

The ladies abused him quite thoroughly for his self-deprecating comments, after which the first of the dances commenced.

Later, after Fenella had gone down an elegant cotillion with Mr. Millmeece, Perryn caught her arm and begged her to come with him. "I have something I would show you, Miss Trentham."

"Indeed?" she queried, looking up at him and attempting quite hard to keep her heart from jumping about so wildly. "And what would that be?"

"It is a very great secret. Will you attend me? I fear we must walk some distance—or are you committed to the next dance?"

"I am not engaged." With that, he offered his arm to her and she took it.

When they had passed through the great press of crowds, she asked after his business in Bath. "Was it concluded successfully?"

"Quite, as you will soon see."

"You are being very mysterious."

He merely smiled in response, refusing to give her even the smallest hint.

He marched her down two hallways, through a beautiful antechamber of rose hues, and into the large receiving room where the auction collections were gathered.

"Why did you bring me here?" she asked quietly, her heart sinking at the memory of the ribbons scattered about her bedchamber floor. Earlier, after she had told Mrs. Almington what had happened to their collection, she had taken a few minutes to look at the remainder of the collections herself. She had felt a certain degree of pride in how beautifully most of the collections had been arranged and displayed, except for perhaps Mr. Aston's and Mrs. Millmeece's rather paltry two butterflies. She had laughed at the sight of them sitting on a square of linen, one of the wings shredded. However, the next collection had brought a great sadness to her. Colonel Bedrell and Miss Madeley's framed rubbings were exquisite. There could be no doubt, regardless of her guilt, that The Incomparable's collection would win the Pavilion prize.

The auction was to be held later in the evening so that at present the chamber was quite empty. There was not even a servant in sight. He escorted her to a large, indistinguishable object covered in a swathe of pink silk. With a careful jerk he removed the fabric and beneath, though slightly altered in shape, was her original maypole, upon which were attached all the kissing-ribbons.

She stared at it for the longest moment. "Our maypole!" she cried. She could not credit what she was seeing. How was it possible—so many pieces of silk all stitched together? "I cannot believe it! However did you accomplish so impossible a feat?"

"I watched you employ your needle and decided to take up the art myself." He lifted a hand and pretended to inspect his fingers. "Although I must say I have quite worn myself to the bone. Hard work, embroidery, would you not agree?"

Fenella glanced at his gloved hand and shook her head. "Do be serious! How were you able to have every bit of ribbon reattached? I must insist on knowing!"

He chuckled. "Very well. If you must know, my sister sends to Bath each year for her gowns to be made up by a particular dressmaker whose skill apparently is unequaled in all of England. I applied to her, making use of my sister's annual patronage as a trump card, and she more than willingly obliged me. She set her seamstresses to work at once, and this is the result." He operated the foot pedal and set the ribbons to spinning.

"I am completely and utterly dumbfounded," she cried, letting her fingers ripple over the ends of the flying ribbons. "Do let it stop for a moment, Perryn." When he obliged her, she began examining the stitchwork which had served to repair all the horrid scissor cuts. "Very elegant work."

"Yes, I believe it is. I was most impressed."

She released the ribbons and turned toward him. "And you did this for me?" she asked, her heart feeling in greater danger than ever before.

"Of course."

"It was a very great kindness and I thank you from the bottom of my heart." Without thinking, she slipped her hand behind his neck and placed a kiss of gratitude on his lips. She released him just as swiftly. "Oh, Perryn, pray forgive me!" she cried, feeling a warm blush steal up her cheeks. "I should not have done that."

He caught her about the waist and shook his head. "I have told you before, my dear Fennel. Never, *never,* apologize to a rogue for kissing him." He then completely devastated her by dragging her once more into his arms and kissing her recklessly. She submitted, quite nonsensically, for the longest time, then finally drew back.

"Perryn, you should not."

"You are so easy to love, Fenella. You can have no notion."

She smiled, feeling quite vulnerable. "I hope you do not think that I, that we . . ."

"Oh, no," he assured her in mock sincerity. "Of course not. You are completely set against wedding me. That I comprehend utterly."

She saw at once that he did not believe what he was saying. "Perryn, I meant my kiss only to be an expression of gratitude. Nothing has changed."

"I have changed," he stated firmly, holding her arms in a tight grip. "You have been working that miracle in me for the past four years."

Fenella did not know what to say, though hope did seem of the moment to be soaring in her breast. She searched his gaze, wondering if what he had said was true. Since a servant entered the chamber at that moment, he released her and afterward escorted her back to the ballroom.

For the next two hours, Fenella danced every dance, at the same time avoiding Perryn as much as possible. She could feel his charms working on her poor heart again, but she strove to remind herself of all that she knew of him.

This was an unfortunate consideration, however, since a great deal of what she now knew of him involved many finer aspects of his character than she had previously known existed. She recalled just how tenderly he had conducted himself with the children at Huntspill, how kindly he had spoken to them, how he had drawn the youngest onto his lap, then helped each of them place a rouged kiss on one of the ribbons. She remembered how he had been of such paramount assistance to Mr. Morden in saving his entire estate. She was still incredulous each time she thought of his having loaned that good man five thousand pounds.

However, in all her recollections, the one that seemed to affect her most deeply was the manner in which he had loved and cared for the unfortunate Duchess of Cannock. Knowing now that she had first met him while he had been in the grip of a powerful grief plucked at her reserve fiercely. Was this not a quality she could embrace wholly?

And yet what was she to think of Mrs. Sugnell, Lady Elizabeth, and Mrs. Millmeece, particularly since they were not singular in themselves, but represented the unhappiest parts of his character? She was deeply troubled, for she simply did not know what to think of Perryn.

Near the ten o'clock hour, Fenella was standing in the

rose drawing room awaiting the announcement that the
auction would begin when Miss Almington approached
her.

"Miss Keele and I just saw your collection," she said,
smiling softly. "It was beautifully repaired. Indeed, the
stitchery is so fine that unless one had known it had been
cut to bits as it had, one would think a lovely design had
been added merely for the effect. We both believe yours
will take the prize." She then smiled wickedly. "When we
told Miss Madeley your collection had been repaired, she
positively turned the color of chalk. I vow it was so. There
can be no doubt she was the culprit."

"That may be the case, Miss Almington, but I beg you
will say nothing of it. Perryn was so kind as to restore the
collection, and that is enough for me."

"If that is truly what you desire, of course I shall abide
by your wishes." She shook her head, appearing quite perplexed. "Although I still cannot credit she would be so bad
as to do harm to anyone's collection."

"Sometimes there is simply no accounting for another's
conduct."

Miss Almington was silent, then said, "Your idea and its
execution was so striking, so unusual, Miss Trentham. I
cannot tell you how greatly I admire the whole of it, even
if it was in its way rather scandalous."

"Many of the kisses were from children," Fenella offered.

"What fun you must have had! And did the children
enjoy offering their kisses? I should imagine there was a
great deal of giggling involved."

"Most certainly there was, but I think generally it was
a happy experience for everyone."

"Whyever did you decide on such a daring collection?"

Fenella thought for a moment. "I had come to believe
that, however altruistic the nature of the caravan, the whole
notion of putting collections together for auction was un-

likely to appeal to the gentlemen involved in general. For that reason, I felt obligated to make the collecting process as agreeable as possible. Knowing Perryn's inclinations and that he would take no small degree of pleasure in charming kisses out of the village maidens, I somehow managed to conceive of the kissing-ribbons. I am persuaded he enjoyed himself immensely, which was my primary object."

Miss Almington blushed. "And how well you succeeded, for it prompted him to make you an offer of marriage!"

"What a sly thing to say!" Fenella cried.

Miss Almington laughed and moved away. Fenella could not help but note that the young woman had benefitted greatly from the experience and trials of the journey. She seemed to have grown in stature over the past fortnight. Certainly her confidence had blossomed. She began to think her hostess a rather wise woman.

Fenella was about to return to the ballroom when Miss Adbaston approached her. Her light blue eyes seemed paler than usual against the dark circles beneath her eyes. "Miss Trentham, I could not help but overhear Miss Almington speak of your collection and I, too, wanted to compliment you on how beautiful it is."

"Thank you." She felt uneasy in her presence, given her brother's inconstancy. At the same time, she wondered if there was something she might be able to say to her to ease her distress.

The lady, however, was before her. "Have you, perchance, spoken with your brother this evening?"

Fenella frowned slightly. "I do not take your meaning. I have not seen him since he quit Buntings Court so precipitously."

"Oh, then you do not know."

"Know what, Miss Adbaston?"

"He is here. Mr. Trentham is here, at Whitmore."

"You have seen him?" Fenella asked, astonished.

"No, not as yet. However, my maid exchanged a greeting with him not an hour past when he entered the house by way of the terrace."

Fenella shook her head. "I was wondering if he would return. I mean I was hoping he would, but I have not heard from him these many days."

"It is all so very strange," she confided. "I cannot imagine where he has been or why he would leave Buntings Court as he did. Although I have thought—" She paused, and Fenella could see that she was struggling to say something. Finally, she lifted her gaze and blurted, "Am I the reason he disappeared as he did? Has he been trying to avoid me?"

Fenella shook her head. "Not by half. Did Mrs. Almington not tell you why he absented himself so abruptly from our caravan?"

"No, she did not, and to own the truth I was afraid to ask her. I did not want to hear that he had grown to think ill of me. However, now I must know. Am I to blame for his odd behavior?"

Fenella shook her head. "No, Miss Adbaston, you most certainly are not. I have it in my power to give you certain relief on that score. There is only one cause for Aubrey's unhandsome conduct. He lost four hundred pounds at Sewards Manor without the smallest capability of repaying even a farthing of it."

She watched Miss Adbaston's fair complexion grow so very pale that she thought she might swoon. "Pray sit down!" she cried, taking her arm abruptly and guiding her to a nearby chair of rose silk.

Miss Adbaston dropped into it, leaning forward and struggling to draw breath. "Four . . . hundred . . . pounds! I cannot imagine! How could he do such a thing! I cannot credit it is true. Miss Trentham, are you saying—I mean, is it possible that your brother is a . . . a gamester?" There was so much repugnance in her expression that Fenella began to feel hopeful. With such information now in hand, she trusted Miss Adbaston would soon begin to believe herself well out of such a match.

Fenella did not mince words. "I am afraid he is."

"Good God. And I thought . . . I believed . . ."

Fenella saw the young woman's eyes well up with tears. She immediately took up a seat beside her and possessed herself of one of her hands. "Whatever Aubrey's faults," she said quietly, ignoring the many interested stares from those standing about nearest them, "and regardless of his intentions in singling you out as he did, I vow I never saw him happier than when he was in your company. For a time, I even cherished the hope that your society would have a beneficial effect upon him. But let me impress upon you that my brother, whom I love so very much, has been struggling with his love of gaming for many years now. I only wish he had met you before all of this began. How different his life might have been."

Miss Adbaston looked at her, her eyes shimmering with tears. A smile trembled on her lips. "How very generous of you to say as much to me. I shall never forget this kindness, Miss Trentham, and I thank you so very much." She shifted her gaze slightly to the doorway. "And here is Mrs. Almington. I would imagine she has come to announce that the hour of the auction has arrived."

Miss Adbaston, her countenance quite woeful, thanked her again. Then, after rising to her feet, she moved away.

Fenella watched her go, feeling deeply frustrated by her brother's unreliable conduct. There could be no doubt Miss Adbaston's heart had been very much engaged. Had Aubrey been in possession of a little more restraint, she rather believed the match would have been an excellent one on many counts.

She was happy, however, to learn he had returned to Whitmore, for she was certain he meant to begin making amends for his wretched conduct—although she thought it rather ignoble that he would steal into the house by way of the terrace rather than the front door. Regardless, she hoped he meant to commit himself once more to avoiding the gaming table.

When Mrs. Almington announced that the auction was ready to commence, the many guests chatting in the rose drawing room moved into the hall to join a host of fellow guests who were making their way to the grand salon as well, but from the direction of the ballroom. After some few minutes, Fenella arrived at last at the grand salon and immediately found herself congratulated again and again on the unusual and extraordinary maypole which was to be seen in a constant state of flutter, since a great many people wished to work the foot pedal. She thanked everyone in turn, her stomach leaping excitedly that the auction was about to begin.

She glanced about the crowd and caught sight of Perryn, who began making his way toward her. Once beside her, and in the press of the crowd, he took secret hold of her hand. "Good luck," he whispered against her cheek.

"And to you," she returned with a smile.

When the guests were finally assembled, Mrs. Almington quieted everyone and began the presentation of the Pavilion prize. "First, I would like to thank the participants of our charity caravan. There is little doubt in my mind that everyone involved deserves an award merely for having endured the difficulties attendant in such a journey as we have just completed. The only wonder is that any of us have remained friends." A general laughter rippled through the crowd. "As it is, only one pair of collectors can be granted the prize of a trip to the Royal Pavilion at Prinny's express invitation."

Fenella regarded the maypole, which had been once more set to spinning. She could not help but smile as the ribbons fluttered through the air. Perryn gave her fingers a squeeze. She looked up at him and he winked. Her heart began racing. Here was the moment for which she had been waiting for an entire fortnight!

Mrs. Almington continued to speak for a few minutes more of the general quality of effort which had been made in all the collections. "Although," she added, "one or two more butterflies might have improved at least one of them."

Fenella glanced at Mrs. Millmeece, who turned to scowl at Mr. Aston. His return smile was quite lopsided, the result, no doubt, of his having fortified himself with a great deal of champagne over the past two hours. "Deuced hard creatures to catch!" he cried out. When a hiccough followed, the entire crowd roared with laughter. Mrs. Millmeece glared at him anew.

Mrs. Almington continued, speaking at length about the great need for aiding the poor of Bath and how much the proceeds of the auction would be of benefit in easing their sufferings.

At last, however, she smiled broadly and began the presentation. "Though several of the fortnight's efforts were of a superior quality, in particular the framed brass rubbings of Colonel Bedrell and Miss Madeley, the collection to which the highest award goes tonight truly reflects the nature of our auction because of its involvement of scores of villagers and townsfolk throughout Somerset. I hereby award the prize of a visit to the Royal Pavilion to Miss Fenella Trentham and the Marquess of Perryn for the kissing-ribbon maypole."

A round of huzzas and applause thundered through the assembled guests as Fenella, her heart overflowing with exhilaration and triumph, took Perryn's proffered arm and began moving to the makeshift stage upon which Mrs. Almington stood awaiting them. The applause continued for a long time. As she passed through the crowd, her fellow travelers as well as any number of guests offered their congratulations.

Fenella suddenly felt overwhelmed as she received a small roll of parchment from Mrs. Almington upon which the invitation to the Pavilion was printed. When Perryn had received his, Mrs. Almington once more quieted the crowd. "I believe we should hear from our winners!" she cried. "What do you think?"

A new burst of applause brought panic to Fenella's heart. She had not thought she would be called upon to make a speech. She was hardly prepared to say anything.

Perryn leaned close. "You may go first," he said.

"I do not know what to say," she whispered.

"Just speak of what the experience meant to you."

Fenella drew a deep breath. Her heart raced at the very thought of addressing so large an audience. She looked down at the roll of parchment in her hands. She thought for a moment as the crowd grew quieter still. Anticipation hung in the air. Finally, she said. "I did not know what to expect when we began our journey about Somerset. At first, I had but one object, to keep my partner from perishing of boredom."

A faint laughter ensued as she glanced at Perryn.

"However, once we had settled on kissing-ribbons—an odd notion, I know—not only did it soon appear we would both be able to tolerate collecting a great quantity of so unusual an object, but I soon realized a great many people of all ages, and perhaps especially the children, were eager to support us along the way. I was put forcibly in mind of the fact that we, none of us, travel through life alone. Because of our comings and goings in one another's lives, we learn and grow and find our greatest pleasures and triumphs. That I was, indeed, blessed with a most exceptional partner made the whole of the experience not just tolerable but a delight." She turned to Perryn at the conclusion of her speech, and curtsied in acknowledgment of his effort.

Fenella saw the great affection which had overtaken his features and felt her heart swell in response. He bowed to her in turn, but afterward wrapped his arm snugly about hers, unwilling to let her move into the shadows. "I was in good hands from the first," he said in his strong voice. "Whatever our collection is, I owe the entire success of it to Miss Trentham, whose unflagging enthusiasm carried us from Bath to Milverton and back, with at least two score of hamlets betwixt, in the most productive manner possible. I, too, was gratified by the support we received along the way and have but one request to make of you"—here he gestured to the hundreds of guests before him—"that you find it in your hearts to honor the efforts of Mrs. Almington's charity caravan tonight by bidding generously."

A warm applause followed this speech, after which Mr. Almington stepped forward to begin the auction.

The bidding on each collection was swift and filled with excitement, for as soon as the spirit of the event was engaged, scarcely a one did not offer a bid, even if merely an increase of a few pounds, just to be part of the excellent event.

When at last the maypole was brought forward, Mrs. Almington asked Fenella to come forward and demonstrate the movement of the lever at the base of the pole. With delight, she hurried to the dais upon which the maypole had been elevated and with a smile began working the foot pedal. The ribbons once more flared, fluttered, and made the sounds of leaves in the wind. The guests expressed their delight in scattered applause and laughter. To her great pleasure, the bidding began at an enormous one hundred pounds.

From there over a space of fifteen minutes, the bids rose higher and higher, until the five hundred mark was reached, at which time a quiet fell over the crowd. Five hundred it would be.

"One thousand," a strong, masculine voice called out from the back of the crowded chamber.

"Perryn," Fenella murmured, stunned. A murmuring

passed through the crowd along with a ripping of applause. "He is in love with Miss Trentham," greeted her ears more than once.

"A thousand pounds from the Marquess of Perryn," Mrs. Almington announced, nodding and smiling. "What generosity. Do I hear another bid?"

Fenella sought out his face and saw that he was watching her and smiling, a secret knowing smile, and then she understood. He wanted their collection with him forever. The very thought of his intent so affected her heart that she felt for a moment as though she might faint.

It quickly became clear his offer would stand. No one, it would seem, desired to bid against love.

"A thousand pounds it is!" Mrs. Almington called out triumphantly.

A rousing cheer accompanied her pronouncement. In turn, Fenella once more set the maypole to whirling briskly. Her heart felt very much like the ribbons flying around and around. He could not have made his sentiments more clearly known had he shouted his love for her across the grand salon. She was moved, more than he would ever know.

Oh, dear. This was so much worse, so much more difficult to withstand than just his flirtations or his agreeable company. Perryn declaring his love in every manner possible was proving a formidable force to resist.

She glanced back at him, however, and some of her mounting vulnerability toward him dimmed. He had become besieged quite suddenly by several Bath beauties, all fawning over him. She felt a familiar sinking sensation in the very pit of her stomach as she waited for him to begin lifting waiting fingers to his ready lips. How soon would it be before he began smiling in that way of his and in turn the objects of his flirtation would begin their simperings and blushings?

As though he knew she had been watching him, he

glanced at her and winked. *What a rogue,* she thought. She shook her head before descending the dais and observed him for a moment more, waiting painfully for his wretched attentions to begin.

He most certainly had reverted his attention to the ladies flocked about him, but his demeanor was so very different. She moved slowly toward the end of the dais, her gaze fixed the entire time to where he was situated. Five ladies were grouped about him. Still, he drew no trembling fingers to his waiting lips.

He would do this for me? she wondered.

But what meaning could she ascribe to what she thought was probably a momentary restraint? Were she to wed him, would he grow bored in the society of just one lady? Would he seek the delights of flirtation and more elsewhere? She had never been one to believe that romantic love was powerful enough to rout an entrenched defect of character, so what was she to truly think of this gesture? Given all that she now knew of Perryn, she simply did not know.

When she descended the dais, a servant approached her with a missive. She opened it and quickly scanned the signature. It would seem Aubrey was, indeed, at Whitmore. His message was succinct.

> *My dear sister,*
>   *I beg you will meet me in the garden as soon as you receive this, by the gate nearest the rose arbor.*
> *Aubrey*

Fenella wished he had been more courageous in his return to Mrs. Almington's home. The nature of his arrival and now a request to meet with her in relative secrecy spoke both of his guilt and the weak nature of his character. She could only suppose he meant to beg her yet again to discharge his debt.

For a brief moment, she almost refused to go to him.

Let him make himself known to his hostess and behave the gentleman first. Let him own up not to just his gaming debts but his social obligations as well. She tapped the missive with her finger, debating just what she ought to do. After a time, however, she relented. She had much she wanted to say to him. Should he disappear again, she might not have another opportunity for several weeks or months until she once more returned to Toseland.

She desired foremost to remind him just how much she loved him and that whatever was amiss she was willing to help, but that they should go together to speak with their father. Perhaps their good parent could find a solution to the troubling dilemma that would be satisfactory and thereby persuade Aubrey down a more honorable, worthy path. She could only hope he would be reasonable, for she did not in the least relish the notion of quarreling with him again.

Glancing once more at the missive, she smiled, thinking that Aubrey's choice of location for their meeting was quite odd. That was the very place where she had kissed Perryn two weeks earlier. Well, she had deliberated long enough. Time to confront her dear brother. Her determination fixed, she quit the grand salon.

From the moment Perryn watched Fenella descend the dais and secrete the missive into the pocket of her gown, he began making a quick progress across the room in her direction. He found it somewhat difficult to make his way through a crowd so determined to congratulate and tease him on his auction bid, but the moment she disappeared from view he risked offending those well-wishers he encountered by pressing quite strongly in her direction.

He had seen her reaction to the missive. Being so well acquainted with her now, after having been so often in her company over the past fortnight, he knew she was distressed, however placid her countenance might appear.

Once in the hallway, he found no sign of her and wondered which way she might have gone. He could only suppose the message she had received somehow involved her brother, particularly since rumors had been circulating for the past two hours that he had returned to Whitmore, albeit rather surreptitiously, in his opinion. He waited, wondering what he should do, if anything. Surely she would wish for a little private conversation with her brother, except . . . except he did not trust Aubrey Trentham.

An uneasiness worked in him. The day of the race at Sewards Manor, Mr. Trentham had taken great pains to ascertain the safety of both Miss Adbaston's and his sister's carriages. He would have thought nothing of it had the accident not ensued. Even then he was loath to ascribe such villainy to anyone so nearly connected to Fenella.

However, Mr. Trentham's conduct in so many respects was not of an honorable mode. Very soon a prescience of dread filled him, which he could not dispel by any rational means. When one of Mrs. Almington's upper maids appeared at the end of the hallway, he hurried toward her.

"Have you seen Miss Trentham, perchance?"

The maid's expression brightened. "Aye, m'lord, but a minute or so past, passing through the music room."

"Thank you." The music room was one of several chambers that looked out onto the gardens at the back of the house. He did not wait, but moved briskly in the direction of the gardens.

The night air chilled Fenella as she passed beneath the rose arbor. The sweet, heavy fragrance of the flowers drifted all about her.

"Aubrey?" she called out, opening the gate and moving into the rose garden. An eerie silence returned to her, something cold and unfeeling.

"Brother, are you here?" she queried again.

The movement from her left was so swift she did not

know what had happened until she felt a terrible tightness about her throat. She could no longer breathe. She could make no sound, utter no cry for help. She could only drag at the fabric strangling her. She caught a hand in her frantic movements and turned hard in order to see her assailant. She looked up to find herself staring into the face of her brother, her dear Aubrey, the little boy who had toddled behind her in all her child's play!

His name came to her lips, but there was no air with which to push the sound through.

Her lungs began to ache. Panic flooded her. She grasped at her throat and flailed about wildly. Suddenly, she fell hard to the brick path, the fabric loosening from about her throat. She pulled at the thick length of silk, at the same time dragging air into her grateful lungs.

"Fenella, Fenella, what have I done?" Aubrey dropped to his knees beside her and began to unwind what proved to be a white silk shawl.

Fenella wept, struggling to breathe still. Horror worked within her. How could Aubrey have done this?

"I am so sorry, my dearest Fenella. I do not know what is wrong with me. I beg you will—"

He got no further. He was dragged away from her by Perryn, who clearly believed her to still be in some danger.

"No," she croaked. But her protest was indistinguishable as Perryn pulled Aubrey to his feet and with incredible swiftness struck him a blow to his chin of such force that he flew backward, landing at the base of a thorny rose bush.

Perryn stood over him, his fists clenched, his body taut, waiting. Aubrey, though breathing raggedly, did not move. One blow had rendered him unconscious.

Fenella sat holding the shawl on her lap, tears flowing down her cheeks. She wanted to rise, but she could feel within her limbs so severe a trembling that she did not trust herself to stand.

"My darling, are you all right?" Perryn cried, dropping down beside her. He took the shawl from her hands and wrapped it about her shoulders.

She nodded. "Yes. Indeed, yes. Shaken badly, but I am well. He . . . he regretted it at the end. But . . . oh, Perryn, he meant . . . he meant . . ."

"I know, dearest," he murmured, drawing her into his arms. She turned her face into his coat and began to cry in earnest.

"He's my brother," she whispered, between sobs.

"I know," Perryn murmured against her cheek. "I know."

After a few minutes, she drew in a faltering breath and pulled away from Perryn. She searched about in the pocket of her gown and withdrew a kerchief, with which she blew her nose quite soundly. "We quarreled at Buntings Court," she explained. "Over his debts. He threatened me, but I never thought—oh, my brother, my poor brother. Whatever is to become of him?"

"Do not think of that just now," he said.

Fenella glanced at Aubrey, who was still lying prone, unmoving. "Is he all right? You struck him with such force I thought you might have killed him."

Perryn turned around and looked at Mr. Trentham. "He is still breathing, though I might have broken his jaw. Small enough punishment for so vile an act."

He felt her hand on his arm. "Thank you, Perryn, for being here just now."

Turning back to her, he meant to say that he wished to be with her always. Instead his voice caught on the words. He was stunned by what he saw.

Light from the house beyond her flooded the grounds and tumbled over her hair. The vision before him was so familiar that he could not keep from murmuring, "Good God, is it you?" Her face was entirely in shadow and her brown curls appeared lit with a golden glow.

He was looking at . . . his angel.

But that was impossible. He blinked and shook his head. He stared at her, at the way the curls formed a halo about her face. But it was not just the light on her hair. There was something more—the set of her countenance, a feeling.

"What is it, Perryn?" she queried.

Even her voice in this moment was entirely familiar.

Suddenly, he was flooded with the memory of that night, five years past, as though through mysteries he would never comprehend he was meant just at this moment to regain every recollection of that evening—with Fenella! All this time, Fenella Trentham had been his angel, and yet he had been such a rogue, following her to the maze with a bottle of champagne in his hands, stumbling as he made his way drunkenly to the center in search of her.

"You spoke to me that night. You said to me, 'Where is your heart that you are letting your life drift through your fingers?' I remember all of it now. You were there. I had brought champagne to the maze, having seen you enter earlier. I caught you and kissed you. No wonder you have thought me such a libertine. But later, you kissed me in return, so sweetly. Fenella, you do not know the changes wrought in me that night. I was so very lost, but your compassion and your words brought me out of my despair."

She caressed his cheek. "You grieved your lady," she said simply.

"You know of the duchess, of Olivia?"

She nodded. "I learned of her yesterday morning. Mrs. Almington related the whole story. Five years ago, when father and I called at Morchards that day, I did not know you had lost someone you had loved so very dearly."

"You were wearing a white muslin gown and a white shawl, much like this one." He slid his hands over her shoulders. "You appeared as an angel that night. You touched my face, you spoke such words to me, and then you kissed me." He smiled suddenly. "I am now recollecting how, just a few days past, you said we had kissed five times and I argued there had been only four occasions. You had inadvertently given me a clue as to the truth, but I still did not remember until now, now when I felt in such danger of losing you. Oh, my darling Fenella."

"Perryn, had I known about the Duchess of Cannock, I believe I might not have been so cruel to you the Season following, or the Season after. I . . . I . . . Perryn, I believe I have misjudged you."

He looked at her and quickly gathered her up in his arms. "Say that again," he commanded. At the same time, he turned her more directly into the path of the light so that he might see into her eyes. He was not certain if she understood the import of what she had just said. He felt, he knew, the battle would be won or lost here. "Is that what you think?" he asked. "That you misjudged me? I must know."

Fenella stared into his eyes, now lit with a fervor that quite stunned her. Had she misjudged him? She felt a trembling so deep within her that she could not think. Fear rose about her like a great lion. Was she about to be devoured?

"Fenella, do not fail me now. Tell me you have not been so long in my company these past two weeks without having come to comprehend me a little, without knowing that I am more than all these silly flirtations I conducted beneath your nose merely to torment you. I beg you to see past them for what they were. I was afraid of loving you. Every time we were alone together in that deuced coach, you charmed me a little more with your teasing and your laughter and your complete unwillingness to foster my conceit."

"You were afraid of loving me?" she asked, her voice sounding distant and strange.

"So very much. After I lost Olivia, I did not ever want to entrust my heart to another again. I avoided you during the London Seasons for that very reason as well, though I would listen to your conversations with others quite covertly. You never ceased to delight me in the outrageous things you would say. But you cannot know how very much I dreaded this fortnight."

"Not nearly so much as I did," she said, tears once more seeping from her eyes.

He gave her the smallest little shake. "Fennel, tell me you trust me. Tell me you know enough of my character to trust me."

A wind blew over her in that moment, of change, of rebirth, of the world, her world, being made new. She even thought she heard the heavens singing the words she was about to speak. "Oh, Perryn, I do trust you, even more than life itself!"

He did not hesitate, not one whit, as he caught her against him in a crushing embrace. The kiss which followed pierced every thought, shattering her doubts to pieces and allowing her for the first time to feel without restraint the fullness of her love for him. In the sweet savor of his lips, she realized that all the previous kisses they had shared were but symbols of the love awaiting them both, now confessed, acknowledged, and understood.

"Marry me?" he asked softly against her lips.

She whispered her assent against his mouth and kissed him anew. Mrs. Almington, it would seem, was right after all. There would be a wedding before Michaelmas.

Fenella regarded Perryn and her father, her heart aching. Five days had passed since Aubrey's aborted attempt to do her harm. He had been utterly subdued since the incident and so remorseful that Fenella's inclination had been to forgive him entirely and begin anew. The gentlemen, however, had a different notion entirely.

Her father, his aging features lined with worry, shook

his head. "Indeed, my dear, neither Perryn nor I will be at ease if he remains in England. If the inclination was there once. 'Twill be there again, no doubt." Aubrey had since confessed to having left the books on the stairs at Morchards in hope that she might suffer a fatal injury and even to having loosened the reins on her curricle when she and Miss Adbaston had raced at Sewards Manor. The wheel having broken as it did had been a mere matter of chance. "No, he must leave. Perhaps a new climate and scenery will bring about those changes which all my strictures, and yours, have failed to effect."

She was reclining on a chaise longue in Mrs. Almington's morning room, where the August sun beamed warmly through the southerly windows. She shifted her gaze to Perryn, who sat nearby. "And are you in agreement?" she asked, her throat constricting.

He nodded, his expression also quite solemn. "I think I should go mad with worry otherwise."

Fenella sighed heavily. She knew both gentlemen were right. Aubrey had acted more than once in quite a malicious manner. Should he once more find himself desperate in his gaming propensities, surely he would attempt to do her injury again. At the same time, he would always be her younger brother who had followed her about Toseland as though she had been the sun, moon, and stars all in one. "Then, Papa, there is something I wish you would do for him, for my sake."

Mr. Almington nodded solemnly. "Anything short of his staying on this island."

A tear escaped her eye. "I beg you will settle a sum of three thousand pounds on him. That will give him a very great opportunity of making his way well in the Americas."

Mr. Trentham frowned severely. "You know his debts, which we have both settled over the years, have amounted to at least that sum, if not more."

"I know, Papa. And perhaps it is imprudent, but that is

my wish." She turned to look him fully in the eye. "I am most determined."

"Very well," he said, nodding. "It shall be done."

On the following morning, Fenella held her brother in a tight embrace, though at the same time protecting his still bruised jaw from even the smallest pressure. Today he was traveling to Bristol, where he would board a ship to the Americas. However, even with the horses restless in harness, she was having difficulty in releasing him. She had the strongest prescience she would never see him again. "You must write to me, Aubrey."

She felt him shudder. "I cannot believe you would forgive me so readily," he said.

"You are my brother," she said simply. "Nothing will ever change that."

He sighed deeply. "Thank you again for . . . well, for everything."

"Of course." She knew he was referring to money.

He disengaged himself at last and climbed aboard the coach to take a seat beside their father.

Fenella glanced at him. "We will expect you back this evening, Papa."

He nodded, his expression still quite sober as it had been for the past few days.

The footman was about to close the door when Aubrey stayed him with a hand. "I nearly forgot," he said, searching in his pocket. Withdrawing a sealed missive, he handed it to her. "Will you please give this to Miss Adbaston? It contains, along with a note, the ten pounds she loaned me."

Fenella smiled faintly. Here was reason to hope, if a very small one. Aubrey had never been known to repay anything in his life unless forced to do so. "Most certainly I shall," she responded.

"She would have made me a good wife," he said sadly.

"She would have, and she was so very fond of you. I am glad you took the trouble of writing to her."

"The very least I could do."

With that, the door closed. As the coach pulled away, she waved a final farewell to her brother.

Perryn moved next to her and offered his arm, which she took gratefully. "I am so sad, Perryn. You can have no notion."

He patted her arm. "I believe the journey he is about to embark on will be the making of him."

"I hope so. How dearly I hope so." She waved one last time as the coach reached the end of the long lane and turned west toward Bristol and Aubrey's waiting ship.

"Come. We do not need to stand here watching the dust settle. Why do we not take a turn about the rose garden?"

At that, she could not help but smile. "Do you mean to get up a flirtation with me, my lord?"

"A very serious one," he responded. "Particularly since I have not held you in my arms once this morning and it is nearly eleven o'clock."

"Scandalous!" she returned. "Very well, the rose garden it is."

He guided her there, smiling all the while. Love, confessed and accepted, flowed between them so that very soon the ache in her heart subsided. Her thoughts were turned now entirely toward the man beside her, dear Lord Perryn, whom she had tormented for four Seasons and who had teased her mercilessly in return, but who, in just another fortnight, would become a most beloved husband.

Once arrived at the garden gate, he drew her into his arms. "Happy?" he queried, smiling down into her eyes.

"Immensely so. You can have no notion."

"Oh, I think I do," he murmured, afterward settling his lips on hers in what soon became an infinitely sweet and familiar assault.

She responded as she always did, with a sharp weakening

of her knees forcing him to hold her more tightly still in order to keep her from crumpling to the brick walk below. She slid her arm about his neck, returning kiss for kiss, aware with every tender pressure on her lips that what had been given to her was so very dear.

Fenella drew back after a time, and though still held tightly in his arms, she gazed into his eyes. "Do you think we will still be brangling when we are in our dotage?"

He chuckled. "What a romantic subject to be pondering, to be sure, and that while I am kissing you so prettily."

"You always kiss prettily, my lord," she returned, smiling. "But I was looking very deeply into the future. I believe I saw us old and withered. We were arguing about how many kisses we had shared before the auction ball."

"There is only one answer to that," he announced strongly. "So we will settle it now—*not nearly enough!*"

Fenella laughed outright and then embraced him fully. "How you make me laugh," she whispered, her cheek pressed to his. "I believe I love that most about you."

"Do you know what I love most about you?"

"Indeed, I do not."

He hugged her. "The way you feel in my arms. That will never change."

The notion was so very sweet, though wholly unlikely. She decided, however, not to warn him that he might feel very differently after she had born him several children and her figure was no longer so youthful in feel and appearance.

"Yes, yes," he said, as though having read her thoughts. "But all of that is best left unsaid."

She drew back fully. "Whatever do you mean?" she queried. "You cannot possibly know what I was thinking."

He chuckled and once more wrapped her arm about his and began guiding her down the central path of the garden. "That is true. Unfortunately, I know how you think. You once described yourself as a *very practical girl.* However, in defense of my position, I will only add that regardless of how the very nature of life may take its toll on either of us, I will always love you as I do now, so very, very dearly. Nothing will ever change that, not even your most rational argument."

She looked up at him and gave his arm a squeeze. "My darling," she said, her heart swelling as it always seemed to do in his presence, "on this particular subject, I give you leave to always be right, to always have the upper hand, and to win every future argument."

"Generous to the last," he responded, facetiously.

"I flatter myself, I am," she returned, chuckling anew.